WOMEN IN GERMAN YEARBOOK

9

EDITORIAL BOARD

Leslie A. Adelson	Ohio State University	1992–94
Angelika Bammer	Emory University	1992–94
Barbara Becker-Cantarino	Ohio State University	1992–94
Jeannine Blackwell	University of Kentucky	1992–97
Gisela Brinker-Gabler	State University of New York, Binghamton	1992–97
Helen L. Cafferty	Bowdoin College	1992–97
Susan L. Cocalis	University of Massachusetts, Amherst	1992–97
Gisela Ecker	Universität-Gesamthochschule-Paderborn	1992–97
Elke Frederiksen	University of Maryland, College Park	1992–94
Katherine R. Goodman	Brown University	1992–94
Patricia Herminghouse	University of Rochester	1992–97
Ruth-Ellen B. Joeres	University of Minnesota, Minneapolis	1992–97
Anna K. Kuhn	University of California, Davis	1992–97
Sara Lennox	University of Massachusetts, Amherst	1992–94
Ricarda Schmidt	University of Sheffield, England	1992–94
Edith Waldstein	Wartburg College	1992–94

WOMEN IN

Feminist Studies in German Literature & Culture

GERMAN

Edited by Jeanette Clausen & Sara Friedrichsmeyer

YEARBOOK

9

University of Nebraska Press, Lincoln and London

© 1994 by the University of
Nebraska Press. All rights
reserved. Manufactured in
the United States of America.
Published by arrangement
with the Coalition of
Women in German.
The paper in this book meets
the minimum requirements of
American National
Standard for Information
Sciences – Permanence of
Paper for Printed Library
Materials, ANSI Z39.48-1984.
ISBN 0-8032-4770-2 (cloth)
ISBN 0-8032-9754-8 (paper)
ISSN 1058-7446

TABLE OF CONTENTS

Acknowledgments		vii
Preface		ix
Ann Taylor Allen	Women's Studies as Cultural Movement and Academic Discipline in the United States and West Germany: The Early Phase, 1966–1982	1
Susan Signe Morrison	Women Writers and Women Rulers: Rhetorical and Political Empowerment in the Fifteenth Century	25
Christl Griesshaber-Weninger	Harsdörffers *Frauenzimmer Gesprächspiele* als geschlechts-spezifische Verhaltensfibel: Ein Vergleich mit heutigen Kommunikationsstrukturen	49
Gertrud Bauer Pickar	The Battering and Meta-Battering of Droste's Margreth: Covert Misogyny in *Die Judenbuche*'s Critical Reception	71
Kirsten Belgum	Domesticating the Reader: Women and *Die Gartenlaube*	91
Katrin Sieg	Equality Decreed: Dramatizing Gender in East Germany	113
Katharina von Ankum	Political Bodies: Women and Re/Production in the GDR	127
Friederike Eigler	At the Margins of East Berlin's "Counter-Culture": Elke Erb's *Winkelzüge* and Gabriele Kachold's *zügel los*	145

Karin Eysel	Christa Wolf's *Kassandra*: Refashioning National Imagination Beyond the Nation	163
Petra Waschescio	Auseinandersetzung mit dem Abendlanddenken: Gisela von Wysockis *Abendlandleben*	183
Dagmar C.G. Lorenz	Memory and Criticism: Ruth Klüger's *weiter leben*	207

Focus: Antiracist Feminism

Sara Lennox	Antiracist Feminism in Germany: Introduction to Dagmar Schultz and Ika Hügel	225
Ika Hügel	Wir kämpfen seit es uns gibt	231
Dagmar Schultz	Racism in the New Germany and the Reaction of White Women	241

Sara Friedrichsmeyer and Jeanette Clausen	What's Missing in New Historicism or the "Poetics" of Feminist Literary Criticism	253
About the Authors		259
Notice to Contributors		263
Contents of Previous Volumes		265

ACKNOWLEDGMENTS

In addition to members of the Editorial Board, the following individuals reviewed manuscripts received during the preparation of volume 9. We gratefully acknowledge their assistance.

Judith Aikin	University of Iowa
Evelyn Beck	University of Maryland, College Park
Beth Bjorklund	University of Virginia
Ute Brandes	Amherst College
Thomas Fox	Concordia College, Bemidji
Miriam Frank	New York University
Marjorie Gelus	California State University, Sacramento
Valerie Greenberg	Tulane University
Karen Jankowsky	University of Wisconsin, Madison
Nancy Kaiser	University of Wisconsin, Madison
Susanne Kord	Georgetown University
Jill Anne Kowalik	University of California, Los Angeles
Myra Love	Boston, Massachusetts
Linda S. Pickle	Westminster College
Carol Poore	Brown University
Karen Remmler	Mount Holyoke College
Ferrel Rose	Grinnell College
Monika Shafi	University of Delaware
Marc Silberman	University of Wisconsin, Madison
Heidrun Suhr	Deutscher Akademischer Austauschdienst
Elaine Tennant	University of California, Berkeley
Arlene A. Teraoka	University of Minnesota, Minneapolis
Margaret Ward	Wellesley College
Sarah Westphal-Wihl	McGill University
Gerhild Scholz Williams	Washington University
Linda Kraus Worley	University of Kentucky
Susanne Zantop	Dartmouth College

Special thanks to Victoria M. Kingsbury for manuscript preparation.

PREFACE

We complete our editing of *Women in German Yearbook 9* with a sigh of relief and satisfaction. The present collection, like last year's again spans German literary history from the middle ages to the present. And again, perusal of the finished volume reveals even more recurring themes and overlapping concerns than we had anticipated during the process of article selection. Among the issues addressed by more than one author are the construction of gender differences in literature, popular culture, and public policy; theories of the construction of a national identity; racism and antisemitism in German literature and society; and the persistence of gender bias in literary criticism. Several contributions highlight the interdisciplinary nature and activist roots of feminist scholarship and teaching. And in different ways, the articles illustrate the interrelatedness of literature, scholarship, and politics.

The volume begins with historian Ann Taylor Allen's comparison of the Women's Studies movements in West Germany and the USA. Her analysis of the different patterns of institutionalization in the two countries will interest everyone who has grappled with the need for both feminist autonomy and institutional support for Women's Studies teaching and research. Allen's historical perspective also invites reconsideration of strategies for achieving the utopian goal of transforming knowledge with which the Women's Studies movements began.

The next four articles offer fresh approaches to texts from the fifteenth to the nineteenth centuries. Susan Signe Morrison reexamines the Early New High German prose novels of Elisabeth von Nassau-Saarbrücken and Eleonore von Österreich, arguing that their adaptations of French sources were inspired by the desire to represent women rulers as models for emulation. Morrison's analysis expands our understanding of the role that noblewomen in the late middle ages played in the development of German-language literature as well as of women's role in the political arena. Gender-specific models of communication in Harsdörffer's *Frauenzimmer Gesprächspiele* are examined by Christl Griesshaber-Weninger. Drawing on recent research by sociolinguists such as Fishman, Tannen, and Trömel-Plötz, she finds evidence for a centuries-old tradition of gendered speech. Gertrud Bauer Pickar offers a close reading of *Die Judenbuche* that is informed by a subtle understanding of Droste-Hülshoff's sympathy for the lot of married women in Westphalian villages. Pickar argues that Droste's depiction of the battered wife Margreth is more positive than critics echoing the misogyny of the novelle's narrator have acknowledged. Kirsten Belgum discusses strategies used in the popular nineteenth-century magazine *Die Gartenlaube* to construct a cohesive national identity predicated on the ideal of a bourgeois family in which women bridged the space between home and nation. She argues that the domestication of women, both as they appeared in the magazine and as readers, was a crucial element in the concept of the nation as an "imagined community."

German unification and the subsequent opening of archives previously inaccessible to Western researchers paved the way for the new perspectives in GDR Studies provided in the next two articles. Turning to hitherto neglected women dramatists of the 1950s and early 60s, Katrin Sieg examines the tensions in their works between officially proclaimed gender equality and the authors' recognition of the "double burden" increasingly imposed upon women. Complementing Sieg's article is Katharina von Ankum's survey of abortion legislation in the GDR from the early years to legalization in 1972. Threading her way through a maze of documents, von Ankum analyzes the GDR's ultimately unsuccessful efforts to recruit women for both production and reproduction through an aggressively pronatalist policy. These articles will be useful for anyone seeking to understand the conflicting messages about motherhood, pregnancy, and abortion in many works by GDR authors.

The next two articles offer post-unification perspectives on the study of GDR literature. Examining the writings of Elke Erb and Gabriele Stötzer Kachold, both associated with the Prenzlauer Berg circle, Friederike Eigler argues that the formal and linguistic experiments of these two writers are an integral part of issues such as gender and power relations. Her article challenges the work of those scholars who have read GDR literature with more attention to cultural politics than aesthetic form. Karin Eysel discusses Christa Wolf's *Kassandra* in the context of recent theoretical work on nationalism. She argues that Wolf not only succeeds in laying bare the politics of nationalism but also in imagining a transnational community beyond gender, class, and race. Both contributions underscore the ongoing need for critical rereadings of GDR writers.

A contemporary West German writer, Gisela von Wysocki, is introduced by Petra Waschescio, who provides an analysis of her complex and innovative first drama *Abendlandleben*. To establish a basis for further scholarly discussion of this work, Waschescio outlines Wysocki's radical critique of masculinist Enlightenment discourse. We think readers will agree that this "Gesamtkunstwerk" has much to interest feminist critics and theorists. An even more recent book, WIG member Ruth Klüger's 1992 memoir *weiter leben*, is discussed by Dagmar C.G. Lorenz. She presents Klüger's book as a feminist challenge to commonly held views on Holocaust literature as well as to other works by Holocaust survivors.

The focus section, introduced by Sara Lennox, contains contributions by the publishers of Orlanda Frauenverlag in Berlin, who have played a central role in German antiracist feminism. Ika Hügel provides a personal account of her experiences as an Afro-German growing up among white Germans. Dagmar Schultz analyzes the white women's movement in Germany and emphasizes the need for committed antiracist work at all levels of German society. The volume concludes with the editors' challenge to new historicism; we argue that new historicism has nothing "new" to offer feminist critics, and that some of its practices are in fact directly opposed to the theories and practices of feminist *Germanistik*.

Jeanette Clausen
Sara Friedrichsmeyer
September 1993

Women's Studies as Cultural Movement and Academic Discipline in the United States and West Germany: The Early Phase, 1966–1982

Ann Taylor Allen

The article compares the origins and early development of Women's Studies in West Germany and in the United States, focusing on differing patterns of institutionalization. While most American Women's Studies offerings were from the beginning located in academic institutions, many of the first German courses were taught outside of universities. The article outlines the discussions that were held in each country about the appropriate institutional setting for Women's Studies. It shows how the resulting processes of institutionalization were related to the administrative structures, purposes, and student constituencies of systems of higher education in the two countries. (ATA)

The creation of Women's Studies, including the critique of existing academic disciplines for their androcentric bias and the discovery of new approaches to learning and knowing, must be counted among the most innovative and lasting achievements of the feminist movements of our own era. Among the most striking features of Women's Studies, as academic discipline and as cultural movement, has been its international scope. From its beginnings in the United States in the mid-1960s, Women's Studies spread to many Western countries in the 1970s. A comparative study of Women's Studies in its initial phase in the United States and West Germany shows the importance of political, cultural, and institutional context in shaping the development of the field. One of the most important questions facing early advocates of Women's Studies concerned the appropriate institutional setting for this new form of education. Controversies over institutionalization highlighted many of the central intellectual, political, and educational issues raised by the new field. The article will therefore focus on the period during which institutional patterns first became established, from the mid-1960s to the early 1980s, when Women's Studies was first integrated into American college and university curricula and the first West German research institutes were founded. Developments from the early 1980s to the present, briefly alluded to here, will be discussed in greater detail in a subsequent article.

The greatest change in the composition of university student bodies in the postwar period—and one of the greatest changes in higher education systems as a whole—was the massive increase in the number of women students. In the United States, women students enrolled in higher education made up about 30% of the total in 1949, about 40% in 1969, and about 50% by 1979 (*Digest* 166). In West Germany, the percentage of women enrolled in academic universities (excluding colleges of education, in which they were a majority) rose from 18% in 1955 to 22% in 1960 and to 30% in 1969; by 1980 their share in total enrollments was about 38% (Max Planck Institute 282). This increase in itself substantially fulfilled the demands of the first feminist movements, which had campaigned chiefly for the admission of women to higher education on the same terms as men. By the 1960s, however, a few American feminist educators began to assert that this appearance of equality in the coeducational universities in fact concealed the reality of continued inequality between the sexes. The Women's Studies movement, starting as an attempt to remedy this inequality, developed into a critique of the structure, content, and function of higher education. The movement soon became international; German educators, partially inspired by the American example, created a Women's Studies movement within and outside the university starting in the 1970s.

The earlier integration of Women's Studies curricula into American universities sometimes reinforced conventional assumptions about the greater advancement of American feminist movements in general (Altbach 3). In fact, such judgments are oversimplified. The American form of Women's Studies arose out of highly specific aspects of American history, culture, and educational systems. Feminist educators in West Germany had somewhat different aims and faced a different set of problems arising from their own national history, culture, and political structure. Their attitude toward the American model showed a keen awareness of its weaknesses as well as its advantages.

In the United States, Women's Studies was produced by a unique combination of liberal and radical feminist ideologies that developed during the years 1964–1969. Both of these forms of feminist ideology were decisively influenced by the Civil Rights movement of this same era. Liberal feminists responded to this movement's emphasis on legal equality and its choice of educational institutions as a locus of struggle. New approaches to knowledge and pedagogy developed by Freedom Schools, in which many future feminist activists worked, influenced radical feminists' emerging vision of the power of education to transform society (Echols 23–31; Howe 1975, 48; Evans 83–102). The passage of the Civil Rights Amendment of 1964, which prohibited discrimination in employment against both Blacks and women, showed the linkage between early phases of the Civil Rights and feminist movements. Another factor of great importance in formulating the first American feminist agendas was the contact between the earlier generation of feminists who had sponsored the first Equal Rights Amendment, many of whom were still politically active, and younger feminists (Davis 29-43). Major national feminist organizations such as NOW (National Organization for Women) and WEAL (Women's Equity Action League) made equal opportunity for women in higher education into a central goal.

The liberal feminist organizations of the 1960s were initially highly integrationist; their ideology and practice emphasized equal rights within existing structures. This approach was effective because it was particularly appropriate to American higher education in the 1960s. Partly because the American system included many types of public and private institutions without uniform standards or regulations, various forms of legal and overt discrimination against women faculty and students—in admissions, access to educational programs, financial aid, faculty hiring policies and pay scales, and many other aspects of college or university life—were ubiquitous. Such overt forms of discrimination could be combated through the courts. Starting in 1970, female students and faculty initiated many lawsuits, often supported by national feminist organizations. Although at first basing their claims only on an obscure executive order forbidding sex discrimination in the awarding of federal contracts, feminist organizations soon successfully advocated two federal laws specifically banning sex discrimination in higher education: Title IX of the Education Amendments (passed in 1972) and the Women's Educational Equity Act (passed in 1973). The Equal Employment Opportunity Act, which mandated affirmative action to compensate for past racial or gender discrimination, also reinforced women's struggle (Astin and Beyer 333-59; Davis 205-27). The sense of solidarity among women faculty was expressed by the formation of women's organizations and caucuses within disciplines, starting in the late 1960s. To be sure, the percentage of women among all faculty members rose very slowly, from about 19% in 1960 to about 22% in 1977; their representation among junior faculty ranks rose somewhat more rapidly, from 27% in 1974 to 30% in 1977 (Wandersee 103-55). But the new generation of women faculty members had an impact disproportionate to its numbers.

The first feminist intellectual agendas were shaped by the radical feminist movement which, starting with the secession of feminist groups from the student movement in 1968-1969, formed autonomous feminist groups. Rejecting the integrationist agenda of the liberal groups, radical women insisted that the goal was not participation in, but transformation of higher education (Davis 220-29; Echols 103-39). They developed the critique of androcentric bias and the vision of an alternative feminist education that became the bases of research and teaching in Women's Studies (Howe and Ahlum 1973, 393-99). Despite their contempt for liberal feminism, however, the academic radicals often owed their academic positions and the cultural authority that these conferred to liberal campaigns for equality. The mid-1970s also saw the emergence of another feminist ideology, cultural feminism, which advocated the creation of separate women's cultures outside of mainstream structures (Echols 243-86). In the United States, this ideological shift did not discourage the establishment of university-based Women's Studies programs; rather, it justified the actual situation of such programs as sometimes isolated enclaves of female culture within male-dominated universities. Thus the American form of Women's Studies was the product of a unique historical moment in which liberal, radical, and cultural trends in feminist ideology and practice converged.

In West Germany, the development of Women's Studies was shaped by the very different chronological development and political and cultural context of feminist movements. To be sure, the event that is generally considered to have initiated the feminist movement—the secession of women's groups from the male-dominated student movement—was parallel to American developments of the same period, 1968-1969 (Schwarzer 13-21; Schenk 83-103). But because liberal feminism had not developed in West Germany to nearly the same extent as in the United States, the radical feminists could not establish the same dialectical relationship to a mainstream movement. One reason for the absence of mainstream liberal feminism was lack of contact with the older generation of feminists, many of whom had been driven into exile under National Socialism (Frevert 288). Another was that formal and legal equality for West German women was already guaranteed by the constitution; thus the American struggle that culminated in the failed campaign for the Equal Rights Amendment could have no counterpart in West Germany (Frevert 281). Moreover, many forms of formal and legal discrimination against women faculty and students in university systems, administered by state education ministries and subject to uniform regulations, had been abolished (at least in theory) by the 1960s. Partly for this reason, the German student movement for the democratization of the universities in the 1960s did not make gender equality a major issue. This did not mean that gender discrimination did not exist or was not recognized. On the contrary, several works of the early 1970s described cultural biases against female students, such as pressures to enter female-identified fields, the misogyny of an overwhelmingly male professoriate, and the effect of an anonymous and impersonal atmosphere on young women who had not been trained to assertiveness (Herve 56-66). The biases of search committees ensured that very few women received senior faculty appointments. But in the absence of liberal feminist movements, the integration of women into institutions, including those of higher education, received far less emphasis in the beginning phases of the German than of the American movement; in fact, systematic programs to combat discrimination against women in universities were not established in German universities until the 1980s (Reiss-Jung 17–29). Although a few women were appointed to professorships in the 1970s, no new generation of women professors emerged. Most women employed as university teaching personnel were in lower level and short-term positions and had little influence on university policies.

An important difference between American and West German feminist movements was in social composition. Unlike the American movement, which though predominantly middle-class and white included women of many occupations, almost all the early West German feminists were students or junior university faculty members. The Germans' emphasis from the beginning was strongly theoretical. This theoretical orientation was at first an obstacle to the development of a feminist critique of higher education. Among students and progressive faculty members, the works of Marx provided the most fashionable basis for critical theory. Male Marxists universally decried gender inequality as a mere "secondary contradiction" and scornfully rejected feminism as a diversion from the "main contradiction," class struggle (Schwarzer 21; Schenk 135–48; Frevert 296–97). Unlike American radical feminists, who in addition to Marxism drew on concepts derived from American feminist movements or from contemporary Black Power movements, German feminists (who were only beginning to discover the history of their own movement) had no such readily available theoretical alternatives. Moreover, some dismissed the writings of their American counterparts as theoretically naive. But Marxism provided an unsatisfactory basis for the understanding of female experience. "The difficulty was," stated a historical account of the Frankfurt Women's Council founded in 1970, "that we had to deal with texts in which the problems that we had as women simply were not mentioned. So, the longer we read Marxist theory, the less we emphasized the oppression of women" (*Frauenjahrbuch* 21).

The first West German university courses on issues concerning women struggled to interpret these issues within the dominant Marxist framework. Carol Hagemann-White, at that time a junior faculty member at the Free University of Berlin, recalls the University's first feminist seminar, entitled "Marxism and Feminism," held in 1975. Among the topics discussed were the working conditions of female students and faculty. Many German feminists finally made the break from Marxism in the mid-1970s, proclaiming themselves "autonomous." This conception of feminist autonomy was based not only on a radical critique of patriarchal institutions, but also on the "cultural feminist" theory and practice of separatism. As in the United States, ideology was adapted to fit the real-life situation of its creators. Because most of the early German Women's Studies advocates did not hold regular or long-term university positions, they used separatist arguments to justify the development of Women's Studies outside of academic structures, which they denounced as bastions of male dominance and intellectual elitism (Schwarzer 80-100).

These different historical conditions contributed to different patterns of development in the field of Women's Studies. In the United States, Women's Studies, though also developed by community-based groups, was from the first located chiefly in higher education. The first Women's Studies courses were taught in 1966 and the trend spread rapidly; by 1970 there were over 1000, and by 1973 over 2000 Women's Studies courses at colleges and universities in the United States, most of them taught by faculty members in existing departments, such as English, History or Sociology; separate Women's Studies departments were rare (Boxer 1982, 661-74). At some institutions, these courses were combined to form undergraduate major and minor programs; the first such program was approved at San Diego State College in 1970, and by 1977, 276 programs had been founded (Howe 1977, 15-28, 393-99). Like the American feminist movement as a whole, the Women's Studies movement formed a national organization, the National Women's Studies Association, in 1977. International conferences such as the Berkshire Conference on the History of Women (first held in 1974) and the Women in German Conference (first held in 1976), and journals such as *Feminist Studies* (founded 1972) and *Signs* (founded 1975) marked the emergence of the new academic field.

In West Germany, by contrast, the first Women's Studies courses developed in institutions of adult education outside of universities. Unlike American adult education, which is often conducted through university extension courses, German adult education is usually located in an extensive network of public, continuing-education schools (*Volkshochschulen*). The first of the West German courses was a Woman's Forum held in Berlin in 1972 and attended chiefly by housewives. The course, which stressed consciousness-raising, was so successful that many others were initiated and continue to be offered in adult-education programs (Schmidt-Harzbach). Such courses were often led by university-trained feminist scholars who had no opportunities for employment within universities.

In 1973, a group of junior university faculty met in the newly founded Berlin Women's Center to discuss women's issues, including the possibility of academic Women's Studies courses. The first major attempt at interdisciplinary cooperation, the Summer University programs for women were organized for the most part by these same women faculty members but outside of formal curricular structures (Tröger). "Like the women's movement in the U.S.A. with its 'Women's Studies,'" read the announcement of the first Summer University in 1976, "we, too, demand opportunities to work on and investigate themes relevant to women" ("Frauen und Wissenschaft" 1976). Although the first Summer University, a week-long program of seminars, workshops, lectures, and cultural events, was intended chiefly for academic women, the second was expanded to include women working in other occupations. The organizers applied to local governments for recognition of this event as a continuing-education program, for which employees were legally entitled to a paid leave of absence. "We don't want merely to add the so-called 'women's perspective' to academic knowledge," declared the opening statement. "We want more than to become objects and subjects of science; we want to change it and society. Radically" (*Frauen als Bezahlte und Unbezahlte Arbeitskräfte* 12).

The theoretical basis of Women's Studies in the two countries was in many ways similar. The perception of the absence of women as subjects and objects of disciplinary research and teaching became the basis for a far-reaching critique of these disciplines themselves. Knowledge purporting to be objective and universal was unmasked as the product of the self-serving biases and limitations of the men who created it. Although this perception, based on leftist critiques of scientific objectivity, was not new, feminist scholars developed it by insisting on a new practice of research and teaching (DuBois 18-36). Knowledge about women, unavailable through the academic disciplines, could be gained only through the examination of female experience, beginning with the individual woman and developing toward a collective consciousness and sense of identity. One of the best-known statements of this position was the model for feminist research constructed by West German sociologist Maria Mies. Mies described the process through which women social scientists founded a center for battered women in Cologne, first compiling data on the need for such an institution, then engaging in the political process of gaining support and funding from the city government, and finally conducting interviews with clients that served both as personal counseling and social research. Such research, Mies and other feminist scholars asserted, challenged conventional academic norms requiring non-partisan "objectivity." Like many early feminist scholars in both countries, Mies assumed that the common experience of women could transcend class and other differences. Faced with the attempts of contemporaries in the socialist movements to discredit feminism as a mere "secondary contradiction," many feminists asserted the primacy and universality of gender oppression.

However, the different political and cultural contexts of the two feminist movements also resulted in important differences of emphasis. The West German feminists, though ultimately rejecting Marxism, retained their emphasis on the critique of capitalism and on economic theories of oppression. The best example of such a theory was the analysis of housework and reproduction. Women of all classes, both heterosexual and lesbian, asserted many West German feminists of the 1970s, shared common working conditions requiring unpaid service and maintenance work for men. This public/private division, they argued, had been created in the early phases of capitalism and had been revealed in its full oppressive implications by the recent influx of women into paid work and the resulting double burden. "At the basis of all power relationships in our society," wrote Gisela Bock, "is a central power relationship—between paid and unpaid work, between men and women (and children); this implies a double morality—work for money, work for love" (209). By demanding state-supported pay for domestic work as well as equal opportunity in the public labor market, many German feminists sought to overthrow the public/private dichotomy (*Frauen als Bezahlte und Unbezahlte Arbeitskräfte* 494–505).

American feminist scholars started from models based not only on Marxism but also on ethnic studies, especially Black Studies. Like their West German counterparts, they were drawn to universal theories of gender oppression, but in the racially and ethnically diverse American feminist movement, the authority of predominantly white and middle-class academics to define universal "female experience" was much more widely challenged. From the mid-seventies on, Black women and women of other minority groups asserted that gender identity existed only in relation to other identities, such as those of race and class. The influential manifesto of a Black feminist organization, the Combahee River Collective, stated in 1977 that "the major systems of oppression"—class, racial, sexual, and heterosexual—were always "interlocking" (362). Moreover, again influenced by theoretical models derived from ethnic studies, the focus of many American feminist scholars had shifted by the mid-1970s from women's oppression to their strategies of resistance, including the formation of a "women's culture" analogous to the culture of other oppressed groups (DuBois 48–59). "Women were not only oppressed," wrote historian Gerda Lerner in 1972. "Women's collective past constitutes actually a different culture, in the sense that the culture of black people and white people living in the same country is a joint culture, insofar as they have a separate and different experience in life. So it is with men and women" (34). American Women's Studies derived much of its intellectual legitimation from its position in a wider campaign (which had no direct counterpart in Germany) led by ethnic and racial as well as feminist groups to challenge traditional intellectual paradigms and to create their own perspectives on knowledge. Its linkage to ethnic studies had both advantages and disadvantages: as one minority position among many, academic feminism was both tolerated and trivialized. "In the

USA," remarked German sociologist Sigrid Metz-Göckel in 1979, the concept of feminism "has been freed from theoretical controversies and accepted as the 'feminist perspective.' In West German discussions...it is still regarded as marginal" (Metz-Göckel 33-34).

New feminist approaches to teaching, though fundamentally similar, also differed according to the intellectual and cultural contexts of the West German and American movements. Feminist instructors in both countries sought to overcome hierarchical relationships between teacher and student through non-authoritarian approaches to pedagogy. In both countries, teaching methods also challenged the conventional separation between objective and subjective and between rational and emotional ways of knowing.[1] The major theoretical difference was in attitudes toward separatism. American Women's Studies courses in coeducational universities admitted men, although only a small number of men usually enrolled. This policy reflected the integrationist basis of much American feminist ideology as well as university rules against discrimination.

By contrast, many German Women's Studies instructors and students insisted, even against opposition, on separate, all-female seminars to which men were not admitted. Their arguments on a theoretical level stressed the grounding of Women's Studies in specifically female experience, and on a practical level the constraints imposed on female students by male incomprehension or hostility. Instructors Carol Hagemann-White and Inge Schmidt-Harzbach scornfully rejected accusations of discrimination. "For how many years have our male colleagues...guaranteed male dominance in their research projects through the discreet formula, 'admission by personal interview only....' But when women wish to restrict participation in their projects to those who have already reflected on their experiences as women, this is seen as minority terrorism" (179).

In both countries, the proponents of this iconoclastic approach to education at first debated the question: autonomy or institution? That is, in what kind of environment should feminist education be located—in or outside existing structures of higher education? This conflict first came to a head in the United States. Women's Studies faculty and university administrations often disagreed on the academic and administrative structure of the new programs, and the requirements of the private foundations that supported some of the earliest programs added to this conflict. The first Women's Studies program in the United States, founded at San Diego State College in 1970, provides an example. Believing that academic Women's Studies programs should have close ties to the community, the program's faculty members planned a community outreach center to be administered by a board representing faculty, students, and community. The College sought funding for the program from the Ford Foundation and therefore requested that the board select a leader (preferably a professor) to engage in negotiations with Foundation representatives. The program's members, who had hitherto made decisions collectively, perceived this as a move to isolate the academic leaders from their community-based constituency in order to make the program more academically and politically respectable to the private foundations. In response, the original faculty resigned and left the campus to found a Women's Center in downtown San Diego (Boxer 1978, 20-23; 1982, 687-92). Had the Women's Studies Program "come under the control of the Ford Foundation," wrote one faculty member, Roberta Salper, "the Program would be devoid of any study of the political, economic and social aspects of the American power structure...and of any interaction between movements for social change around the school and those outside it" (176).

In the United States, however, actions such as that of the San Diego faculty were few and the role of higher education as the primary sponsor of Women's Studies gained ever more support—in fact, the San Diego program was reconstituted with a new faculty in 1974. The reasons for this development may be found in many aspects of the structure of American higher education, the most important of which was the position of women faculty members. The total percentage of female faculty at all ranks in the United States in 1974 was about 22% (Robinson 202-03); in West Germany, women made up 11% of all teaching personnel in 1977 (Mohr 210). This difference, it is important to note, was not due to any inherently feminist or democratic tendencies within American higher education, but chiefly to its diversified structure. In the American universities that were most similar to their German counterparts—major, state-funded, and research-oriented institutions—the status of women faculty in the 1970s was much the same as in Germany. In 1970 only 2% of tenured professors at the University of California at Berkeley were women, compared to 6% at the Free University of Berlin. But other institutions, such as community colleges where 25%, and private women's colleges where 23-58% of the faculty was female, offered a more hospitable environment for Women's Studies (Robinson 202-03). Because teaching and scholarship on women sometimes justified and advanced their careers, these faculty members had a strong personal interest in supporting the development of Women's Studies in their institutions.

Certainly the leadership of these women faculty was contested. In the 1970s some students and community activists expressed considerable resentment of the professors for their supposed elitism and remoteness from the movement (Siporin ix). But this position was rarely supported by the professors themselves, who declared that their professional and activist roles did not conflict. Catherine B. Stimpson, a pioneer of the early Women's Studies movement who taught at Barnard College, denounced these "sour, internecine quarrels," and accused her critics of masking personal insecurity and resentment behind their aggressive rhetoric.

Not only the status of women faculty, but the larger educational structure in which they worked, shaped the development of Women's Studies as a peculiarly American phenomenon. Developing historically from the British college, American institutions of higher education have from the beginning professed responsibility for the moral as well as the academic and professional education of their students. This moral and social mission has been constantly expanded to include the integration of new groups—immigrants, minority racial and ethnic groups, and women—into the mainstream of American society. The undergraduate program, which as a combination of general and specialized education has no counterpart in continental Europe, has often been entrusted with this educational mission. Justifications for Women's Studies at the university level emphasized higher education's moral and social responsibilities. Women's Studies, wrote literary scholar Marcia Landy, was concerned with "the way research becomes responsive to human problems, mirroring profound needs for altering the social system of which the university is a part" (58). Since the turn of the twentieth century, the method of integrating these new agendas has been the modular course system, which awards degrees for combinations of courses, each a self-contained unit, rather than (as in Europe) for a comprehensive examination set by the university or the state. This system allows for the satisfaction of demands for new content without greatly displacing or modifying existing curricula (Rothblatt 48–49).

The introduction of new material such as Women's Studies courses or programs was further facilitated by the diversity and decentralization of American higher education. Unlike state-run European systems, American universities, especially private ones, have substantial autonomy in setting curriculum. Public universities, though more subject to state regulation, can also differ greatly in curriculum and administrative structure. American universities have been driven by market forces rather than by state bureaucracies. From the beginning, they have competed for students through the prestige and attractiveness of their offerings. In the 1970s, especially for women's colleges, which were often under-enrolled, a Women's Studies program could make a campus more attractive. Universities and colleges also established research institutes, usually supported by private foundations, of which the Wellesley and Stanford Centers for Research on Women were the best known.

But the very aspects of American higher education that facilitated the introduction of Women's Studies curricula in the 1970s—its diversity, decentralization, modularity, professed moral mission, and receptivity to market forces—also often led to their marginalization. As historian Sheldon Rothblatt remarks, "what emerged in twentieth-century America was not a liberal education canon but a liberal education sampler" (49). This approach to curriculum made it easy for universities and colleges to respond to social or market pressure by introducing new content without major structural or philosophical change. And in the absence of such change, the new programs often found themselves in an isolated and precarious situation. Women's Studies programs that were not supported by private foundations, such as the Ford Foundation, often received minimal financial support from universities. Struggling against marginalization, some Women's Studies faculty at first opposed the creation of separate Women's Studies departments, preferring interdisciplinary programs in which most faculty members and courses were firmly anchored in traditional disciplines (Boxer 1982, 688-89). But such interdisciplinary programs were also at a disadvantage in institutions where power over budget, curriculum, and faculty hiring is centered chiefly in departments.

In West Germany, both the situation of women faculty and the structures of higher education initially raised barriers even to this level of integration. Like other European higher-education systems, the German system places power over professorial appointments, and thus over curriculum, in the hands of state education ministries. Responsibilities for moral character formation, for general education, and for the integration of disadvantaged groups are all assigned to schools rather than to universities, which are devoted to research and to professional training. The sense of institutional mission that had encouraged the acceptance, however superficial, of Women's Studies in the American higher education was thus completely lacking in German universities. In the 1970s, German women instructors, like their American counterparts, offered many courses (usually seminars) on women's issues in various disciplinary units. Individual instructors often had almost unlimited freedom to define the content of these courses. The newsletter of the women students at the Free University of Berlin advertised seminars on "Sexuality and Authority," "Oral History," "Women under Fascism," and "Women in Film," among many others (*Nebenwiderspruch* 1977, Nr. 6). But the progress of German students toward the first degree, which resembles an American M.A. more than a B.A., depends not (as in American undergraduate programs) on a series of self-contained courses but on a comprehensive examination in a field and usually on a thesis. Although some universities allowed junior women faculty to advise examination candidates and even to conduct oral examinations, control over these requirements rested with full professors, among whom there were very few women. Moreover, junior faculty members, most of whom had short-term appointments, were seldom in a position to bring about enduring curricular change. In general, the appointment of a tenured professor, who has considerable power over funding, curriculum, and research priorities, is necessary to the establishment of a new field in any discipline (Mohr 210; Dorhofer and Steppke, 65-66). And access to professorships was much more difficult in the German than in the American system. Not simply the highest rung on a career ladder, as in most American universities, German full professorships usually require a special appointment that must be approved by the state education ministry as well as faculty recruitment committees. Appointments to such positions, which carry prestige, high pay, and power, often involve heated political controversies in which women, as a minority group with little influence, were (and still are) seldom in a position to prevail (Rauschenbach 119-36).

The composition of German student bodies also affected German feminists' attitude toward the institutionalization of Women's Studies in universities. Although German universities charge no tuition, in the 1970s their student bodies represented a smaller segment of young people than those of their American counterparts. Various structural factors, such as the more advanced level of study and the older average age of student bodies chiefly accounted for this difference. In 1980 only about 12% of males from 21 to 24 years of age (the most numerous age-group in universities) and about 6-9% of females attended academic universities, the only institutions of higher education where Women's Studies was offered. The figure for all American institutions of higher education (many of which, whether junior colleges, four-year colleges, or universities, offered some Women's Studies) was about 25% of the age-group from 18 to 22 (*Digest* 181). Thus the composition of student bodies raised the issue of elitism more sharply for German Women's Studies educators than for their American colleagues. Activist scholars who had challenged conventional notions of scientific objectivity and impartiality were disturbed at the possibility that university-based Women's Studies might actually increase the separation between elite women scholars and the women who became the objects of their research but could not make use of the results.

For these practical and ideological reasons, the issue of institutionalization in higher education was very much more controversial in Germany than in the United States. This controversy came to a head in 1978 over the founding of the first German university-based Women's Studies institute. Since 1975, a group of Women's Studies scholars, almost all of whom held temporary junior university appointments, had discussed various possibilities for the institutionalization of Women's Studies without deciding whether such an institution should be within or outside university structures (Hagemann-White 1992; Nienhaus 1992; FFBIZ). An immediate issue faced by this group was the search for a new location for a valuable library of early feminist works belonging to the Helene Lange Stiftung. In 1978, Hanna-Beate Schöpp-Schilling, a prominent member of the Social Democratic Party who at that time was on the faculty of the Kennedy Institute of the Free University, visited several American Women's Studies centers. On her return to Berlin, Schöpp-Schilling proposed to Berlin's Senator for Science and Research, Peter Glotz, a fellow Social Democrat, that a similar center be founded at the Free University of Berlin. Schöpp-Schilling's conception of the center's function included coordination of research, provision of a library and information service, sponsorship of special programs, and other measures designed to encourage research in Women's Studies in the various faculties (Schöpp-Schilling 1978, 158–73; 1979, 28–29). Senator Glotz, under pressure to fulfill a recent campaign promise to do something for women in Berlin, allocated funding for a two-year planning process and for a planning conference to which representatives of Women's Studies programs in Germany and in six foreign countries were invited.

Only after these negotiations had been initiated was the project announced to other organizations and individuals concerned with Women's Studies. Predictably, these groups and individuals objected, not only to the lack of democratic process but also to the concept itself. The founding of a single, probably under-funded center, they argued, would perpetuate the marginal status of Women's Studies by diverting funding and attention from the more important task of integrating teaching and research on women's issues into all of the Free University's faculties. While Schöpp-Schilling praised the success of the American Women's Studies programs, her opponents pointed to their limitations. "The American examples on which the proposal is based," wrote a group composed of academic Women's Studies scholars, "confirm in many cases the danger of ghettoization." Moreover, claimed this and other groups, the location of Women's Studies in the university would work against the aim stated by the Summer Universities of including women "from all classes of the population."[2] A group of women who opposed the University Center developed an alternative proposal for an autonomous community-based Women's Research, Education and Information Center (*Frauenforschungs-, -bildungs- und -informationszentrum* or FFBIZ), which would provide a library and an archive and would sponsor educational programs available to all women regardless of academic status or occupation (FFBIZ 37–44).

One of the first events of the planning conference, convened in 1980, was a highly publicized walk-out by approximately fifty women who represented about fifteen German feminist organizations, most of which supported the alternative proposal for the community-based center. In addition to the concerns noted above, representatives of these groups took a mistrustful view of the political implications of state support for the institutionalization of Women's Studies in the university rather than in the community (*Ziele* 28–35). Since the mid-1970s, police and legislative measures against leftist terrorism had created a very hostile political atmosphere for progressive or radical activities (Jacobs 165-74). "Why should Women's Studies be institutionalized by state power at this particular point?" asked sociologist Irene Stoehr, speculating that the consignment of the field to the university would defuse its radical political message and subject it to governmental supervision. Stoehr adduced Senator Glotz's admiration for American feminist movements, which he had praised for their pragmatic and moderate spirit, as evidence of this sinister design (175). Other speakers echoed Stoehr's opinion of American Women's Studies programs as not only marginal and ineffective but as politically compromised through their financial dependence on universities (*Ziele* 29, 31, 110). Only through autonomy, these speakers implied, could the political purity of Women's Studies be preserved.

Peggy McIntosh, Director of the Wellesley Center for Research on Women, admitted that her Center took money from whomever offered it and urged a pluralistic and pragmatic approach, endorsing both community and university-based Women's Studies (McIntosh 24-26). And many German speakers, such as sociologist Lerke Gravenhorst, argued that their colleagues' definition of feminist autonomy also had its limitations. While criticizing American programs for taking money from private foundations, they themselves proposed applying for support from the state government of Berlin for their project (*Ziele* 105-08). In fact, Gravenhorst and others ruefully concluded, women who command few financial resources must either depend to some extent on male-dominated private or state agencies or must engage in the unpaid work that has always been the lot of women.

The result of the debate was that both institutions—the Women's Research, Education and Information Center and the Central Institute for Women's Studies and Research on Women—were founded and now work cooperatively. The FFBIZ, which maintains an archive and a library and conducts educational programs, is supported by a combination of private and state funding. Founder Ursula Nienhaus sees no contradiction between feminist autonomy and state funding; women too, she declares, are taxpayers and deserve some services for their money. The original plan for the Central Institute was considerably modified, partly in response to fears that the creation of a separate teaching and research program would discourage the development of Women's Studies in the faculties. The Central Institute was therefore founded as a service organization, which distributes information and coordinates special events; until the recent establishment of an office specifically for this purpose, its staff also monitored and reported on the status of women students, faculty, and staff in the University. It has no research or teaching mission. The controversy over "autonomy or institution," wrote the Central Institute's leaders recently, has "taken a pragmatic turn. Most women have abandoned an 'either-or' for a 'both-and' position." But the same report alluded ruefully to the very limited gains made by women faculty and by Women's Studies programs during the ten years of the Central Institute's existence. "Theoretical skepticism about the possibilities of modifying institutions, however, has not been dispelled" (*Zehn Jahre* 4).

During the same time period, controversies surrounding the establishment of other university-based Women's Studies institutes also centered on actual or potential conflicts between feminist autonomy and institutional structures. In 1980, the application of a group of women faculty and students to found a Women's Studies center at the University of Bielefeld was approved by the University Senate and by the Ministry of Education and Research of the State of Nordrhein-Westphalen.[3] In 1981, in the midst of the planning process, the Center hosted the national Conference of Women Historians. When four men—all assistants or junior teaching faculty—attended a plenary session, the women present, resorting to the practice of separatism developed in the early Women's Studies seminars, asked them to leave because "their presence disturbed some of the women" ("Dokumentation" 119). One of the men appealed to two very powerful senior professors of his faculty, Jürgen Kocka and Hans-Ulrich Wehler, both of whom sent letters of complaint to the head of the Women's Studies center (with copies to the University's Central Administration). Hinting that they might oppose the founding of the new Center, the professors protested this discrimination against their colleagues. Kocka alluded to "other occasions" when scholars had been excluded from German universities "on account of their heritage, race, or religion" (Rpt. in Landweer 317). This comparison of feminist separatism to genocidal Nazi racism moved the women to an outburst of bitter fury and rhetorical overkill. It was incredible, they declared, that prominent representatives of a university system that had excluded women for many centuries, and of a discipline in which women were still invisible, should accuse women themselves of discrimination. As to the history of discrimination in Germany, had women been responsible for it? "Who sent the Jews, gypsies and others to the gas chambers? Who rapes a woman in the Federal Republic every 15 minutes? Who starts one war after another?" Before men criticized women's sexist and discriminatory practices, the statement concluded, they should deal with their own ("Dokumentation" 119–20). The Bielefeld center was founded in 1982 as the Interdisciplinary Group for Research on Women. Unlike the Berlin center, it sponsors research projects (usually financed by outside grants) as well as providing information on, and coordinating, research in the faculties. As Women's Studies has become better established, the desirability of such a separate research program has been called into question.

A major difference between the development of Women's Studies in the United States and in West Germany was the German feminists' insistence on the need for research centers outside of universities. The problems of maintaining feminist autonomy within institutional structures, however, often beset these non-university centers as much as their university counterparts. One of the most important is the Institute on Women and Society, founded in Hannover in 1982. This institute owes its existence to the initiative of several women leaders of the conservative Christian Democratic Union, and especially Rita Süssmuth, a professor of education who became its first director, though resigning the position after three years to hold political office in Bonn. Major financial support for the Institute was provided by the state government of Niedersachsen and by the federal government (Hagemann-White 1992; "Von harten Helden"). Many feminist educators immediately suspected that the new Institute's purpose was to create and impose a new, conservative orthodoxy on Women's Studies research; "there are already visible tendencies to present the Institute as a governmentally authorized and respectable agency of 'solid' research," protested the professional organization of women sociologists (Determann 291). Indeed, during its first years, the Institute, though not subjected to direct political intervention, was strongly influenced by Süssmuth's brand of conservative, family-oriented feminism. But more recently, its leadership has attempted to develop a non-partisan, independent profile. The major themes of its research program—women in the family, the work place, and public life—emphasize equal rights, career opportunities, education, and marital and familial problems (Institut Frau; Hagemann-White 1992). The Institute's emphasis on such themes as equal opportunity and affirmative action in the workplace suggest that in Germany the development of a liberal feminist agenda has followed rather than (as in the United States) preceded the emergence of radical and cultural feminism.

The present director of the Institute, Carol Hagemann-White, a professor of Educational Theory and Women's Studies at the University of Osnabrück, strongly supports university-based Women's Studies. But she emphasizes the continuing necessity for non-university research centers. The university, she notes, is still an inhospitable environment for research on women, not only because of continued discrimination against women students and faculty but also because of administrative structures that make interdisciplinary research very cumbersome and difficult (Hagemann-White 1992).

Because later developments, from 1982 to the present, will be covered in a second article, I shall add only a brief conclusion. Most Women's Studies educators in both countries now agree that the dilemma of "autonomy or institution" was always oversimplified. Both academic and political independence and institutional structure are necessary conditions for the development of the field. "Mainstreaming"—that is, the integration of Women's Studies theory and content research and teaching in all the disciplines—has become a dominant trend among university Women's

Studies educators in both countries. As of 1989, eleven West German universities (out of a total of about 100 institutions of higher learning in West Germany) had research institutes or other programs supporting Women's Studies, which are sometimes linked to broader efforts to improve the status of women faculty, students, and staff ("Stand"; Schlüter). A similar center, the *Zentralinstitut für interdisziplinäre Frauenforschung* was founded at Humboldt University in the former East Berlin; its development has been disrupted by the reorganization of the university. Increasing support of the field by state Education Ministries and university administrations has also been expressed by the founding of several new professorships in various faculties ("Stand"). This support in part reflects a new awareness of market pressures by once overcrowded, but now underenrolled, faculties of humanities, social science, and education. These new professors, though they play a vital role in the legitimation of the study of women in mainstream curricula and research programs, have been characterized by some feminists as a small elite of "queen bees," more than ever separated from activism and from the rank and file of the movement (Meyer-Renschhausen 51–53). West German universities offer few opportunities for interdisciplinary teaching, and Women's Studies faculty show far more interest in working within their faculties than in establishing interdisciplinary programs that they fear would be relegated to marginal status. There are also fourteen community-based Women's Studies centers of various types, most of which are dependent on local government funding and therefore lead a precarious existence (Förder-Hoff 28–38). In the United States in 1991 there were 621 Women's Studies programs, of which 187 included a major and 425 a minor program; 68% of all universities, 48% of all four-year colleges, and 26% of all two-year colleges offer some course-work in Women's Studies (National Women's Studies Association 71).

Total autonomy has in general proved an impractical option for a group with little political power and few financial resources, and institutionalization—whether within or outside universities—has involved compromise and adaptation. The more utopian hopes cherished by academic feminists of the 1970s have not been realized. Women's Studies programs in both countries have not transformed, but rather adapted to, university structures that allot power over budget, hiring, and faculty to departments, require hierarchical governance structures, and usually relegate interdisciplinary programs to the margins. Feminists outside the academy often regard professors of Women's Studies as more concerned with the academic legitimation of their field than with feminist activism. Some feminist scholars in the academy also voice this concern. The editors of the prominent feminist journal *Signs* recently complained of the specialized vocabulary of recent articles, and admitted that "the institutionalizing process has not always been beneficial or benign for us. There is, indeed, a sense of loss that accompanies that process" (Joeres 702). The concentration of Women's Studies scholars in the humanities and social sciences makes them vulnerable to the financial measures that have cut back the development of these fields in both the United States and Germany.

Under these circumstances, the high visibility of Women's Studies as a center of intellectual vitality and creativity in both countries is all the more notable. The transformation of knowledge envisaged by the first feminist scholars is still in its early stages—who knows what the future may bring?

Notes

I would like to thank Ursula Nienhaus and the staff of the *Frauenforschungs-, -bildungs- und -informationszentrum,* Berlin, Helgard Kramer and the staff of the *Interdisziplinäre Forschungsgruppe Frauenforschung* at the University of Bielefeld, Ulla Bock and the staff of the *Zentraleinrichtung zur Förderung von Frauenstudien und Frauenforschung an der Freien Universität Berlin,* and Carol Hagemann-White and the staff of the *Institut Frau und Gesellschaft* in Hannover for their help with my research. I am also grateful to the *Deutscher Akademischer Austauschdienst* for a grant that made this research possible. Juliane Jacobi of the University of Bielefeld and Sara Lennox of the University of Massachusetts gave me valuable comments and suggestions on a preliminary version of this article. All translations are mine.

[1] For extensive examples of syllabi and program descriptions see Howe and Ahlum, eds, *Female Studies IV* and Siporin, ed, *Proceedings of the Conference V.*

[2] Letter from the *Initiativgruppe für ein Frauenforschungs-, -bildungs- und -informationszentrum* to Senator Peter Glotz, 26 Feb. 1978. I am obliged to Carol Hagemann-White for showing me this letter.

[3] On the founding of the *Interdisziplinäre Forschungsgruppe Frauenforschung,* see Hilge Landweer, vol. 1.

Works Cited

Altbach, Edith Hoshino. "The New German Women's Movement." *German Feminism: Readings in Politics and Literature.* Ed. Edith Hoshino Altbach, Jeanette Clausen, Dagmar Schultz, and Naomi Stephen. Albany, NY: State U of New York P, 1984. 3-26.

Astin, Helen S. and Alan F. Beyer. "Sex Discrimination in Academe." *Academic Women on the Move.* Ed. Alice Rossi and Ann Calderwood. New York: Sage, 1973. 333-59.

Bock, Gisela. "Lohn für Hausarbeit—Frauenkämpfe und feministische Strategie." *Frauen als Bezahlte und Unbezahlte Arbeitskräfte.* 206–14.
Boxer, Marilyn J. "Closeup: Women's Studies Programs at San Diego." *Women's Studies Newsletter* 6 (Spring 1978): 20–23.
———. "For and About Women: The Theory and Practice of Women's Studies in the United States." *Signs* 7 (Spring 1982): 661–95.
"Combahee River Collective, A Black Feminist Statement." *Capitalist Patriarchy and the Case for Socialist Feminism.* Ed. Zillah R. Eisenstein. New York: Monthly Review, 1979. 362–72.
Davis, Flora. *Moving the Mountain: The Women's Movement in America since 1960.* New York: Simon, 1991.
Determann, Barbara, Harriet Hoffmann, and Ursula Nienhaus. "Institutionalisierung von Frauenforschung am Beispiel des CDU-Instituts in Hannover." *Wollen wir immer noch alles?: Frauenpolitik zwischen Traum und Trauma.* Berlin: Dokumentationsgruppe der Sommeruniversität für Frauen e.V., 1980. 289–97.
Digest of Education Statistics. Washington: National Center of Education Statistics, 1990.
"Dokumentation des 3. Historikerinnentreffens in Bielefeld, April, 1981." *Beiträge zur feministischen Theorie und Praxis* 23 (1981): 119–28.
Dorhofer, Kristin, and Gisela Steppke. "Von Oben nach Unten? Von Unten nach Oben?" *Autonomie oder Institution: Über die Leidenschaft und Macht von Frauen.* Berlin: Dokumentationsgruppe der Sommeruniversität der Frauen e.V., 1981. 60–73.
DuBois, Ellen Carol, Gail Paradise Kelly, Elizabeth Lapovsky Kennedy, Carolyn W. Korsmeyer, and Lillian S. Robinson. *Feminist Scholarship: Kindling in the Groves of Academe.* Urbana: U of Illinois P, 1987.
Echols, Alice. *Daring to be Bad: Radical Feminism in America, 1967–1975.* Minneapolis: U of Minnesota P, 1989.
Evans, Sara. *Personal Politics: The Roots of Women's Liberation in the Civil Rights Movement and the New Left.* New York: Vintage, 1989.
Das FFBIZ. Frauenforschungs-, -bildungs- und -informationszentrum (bound collection of typescripts held in the library of the FFBIZ). Berlin, 1980.
Förder-Hoff, Gaby, and Heidi Hilzinger. *Was hilft der Frauenforschung: Vorschläge für die mittelfristige Förderung von Frauenforschung in Berlin.* Berlin: Sigma, 1987.
Frauen als Bezahlte und Unbezahlte Arbeitskräfte: Beiträge zur Berliner Sommeruniversität für Frauen, Oktober 1977. Berlin: Dokumentationsgruppe der Sommeruniversität der Frauen e.V., 1977.
Frauen und Wissenschaft: Beiträge zur Berliner Sommeruniversität für Frauen. Ed. Gruppe Berliner Dozentinnen. Berlin: Dokumentationsgruppe der Sommeruniversität der Frauen e.V., 1977.
"Frauen und Wissenschaft: Sommeruniversität für Frauen." 6–10 Juli 1976 (brochure).

Frauenjahrbuch '75. Ed. Frankfurter Frauen. Frankfurt: Roterstein, 1975.

Frevert, Ute. *Women in German History: From Bourgeois Emancipation to Sexual Liberation.* Trans. Stuart McKinnon-Evans. Oxford, UK: Berg, 1988.

Hagemann-White, Carol. Interview. 11 July 1992.

Hagemann-White, Carol, and Ingrid Schmidt-Harzbach, "Warum Frauenstudien?" Schwarzer. 178-80.

Herve, Florence. *Studentinnen in der BRD: Eine soziologische Untersuchung.* Köln: Pahl-Rugenstein, 1983.

Howe, Florence. *Seven Years Later: Women's Studies Programs in 1976.* Old Westbury, NY: Feminist Press, 1977.

——, ed. *Women and the Power to Change.* New York: McGraw, 1975.

Howe, Florence, and Carol Ahlum, eds.. *Female Studies IV.* Collected by the Commission on the Status of Women of the Modern Language Association. Pittsburgh: Know, 1971.

——. "Women's Studies and Social Change." *Academic Women on the Move.* Ed. Alice Rossi and Ann Calderwood. New York: Sage, 1973. 393-99.

Initiativgruppe für ein Frauenforschungs-, -bildungs- und -informationszentrum. Letter to Senator Peter Glotz, 26 February 1978. Ms. in papers of Carol Hagemann-White.

Institut Frau und Gesellschaft. *2 Forschungsberichte: Januar 1989 bis April 1992.* Hannover: Kleine, 1992.

Jacobs, Monica. "Civil Rights and Women's Rights in the Federal Republic of Germany Today." *New German Critique* 13 (Winter 1978): 165-74.

Joeres, Ruth-Ellen Boetcher. "On Writing Feminist Academic Prose." *Signs* 17 (Summer 1992): 701-04.

Landweer, Hilge. "Interne Dokumentation der IFF: Die Konflikte um die Institutionalisierung der Geschäftsstelle Frauenforschung an der Universität Bielefeld: Von den Anfängen bis zum 1 August, 1983." Unpub. typescript, n.d., Archive, Interdisziplinäre Forschungsgruppe Frauenforschung, Universität Bielefeld.

Landy, Marcia. "Women, Education, and Social Power." *Female Studies V: Women and Education: Proceedings of the Conference.* Ed. Rae Lee Siporin. Pittsburgh: Know, 1971. 53-63.

Lerner, Gerda. "On the Teaching and Organization of Feminist Studies." *Female Studies V: Proceedings of the Conference: Women and Education, A Feminist Perspective.* Ed. Rae Lee Siporin. Pittsburgh: Know, 1972. 34-38.

Max Planck Institute for Human Development and Education, Berlin. *Between Elite and Mass Education: Education in the Federal Republic of Germany.* Albany, NY: State U of New York P, 1983.

McIntosh, Peggy. "The Women's Studies Conference in Berlin: Another Chapter in the Controversy." *Women's Studies Newsletter* 8 (1980): 24-26.

Metz-Göckel, Sigrid, ed. *Frauenstudium: Zur alternativen Wissenschaftsaneignung von Frauen.* Hamburg: Arbeitskreis Hochschuldidaktik, 1979.

Meyer-Renschhausen, Elisabeth. "Die Universität als Bastion zünftiger Männlichkeit." *Kommune* 7 (1989).

Mies, Maria. "Methodische Postulate zur Frauenforschung, dargestellt am Beispiel der Gewalt gegen Frauen." *Beiträge zur feministischen Theorie und Praxis* (1978): 41-63.

Mohr, Wilma. *Frauen in der Wissenschaft: Ein Bericht zur sozialen Lage von Studentinnen und Wissenschaftlerinnen im Hochschulbereich.* Freiburg: Dreisam, 1987.

National Women's Studies Association. *Liberal Learning and the Women's Studies Major.* College Park, MD: NWSA, 1991.

Nebenwiderspruch. Mimeographed Student Newsletter, Freie Universität Berlin, 1974-1977.

Nienhaus, Ursula. "Wir fördern Beides: Autonomie und Geld." *Autonomie oder Institution: Uber die Leidenschaft und Macht von Frauen, Dokumentation der Sommeruniversität der Frauen.* Berlin: Dokumentationsgruppe der Sommeruniversität der Frauen e.V., 1981. 118-24.

———. Interview. 13 July 1992.

Rauschenbach, Brigitte. "Bei ungleicher Qualifikation." *6 Jahre Danach: Dialektik eines Fortschritts.* Berlin: Zentraleinrichtung zur Förderung von Frauenstudien und Frauenforschung an der Freien Universität Berlin, 1986. 119-36.

Reiss-Jung, Vera. *Frauenförderung an den Hochschulen: Analyse und Dokumentation.* Marburg: Mauersberger, 1988.

Robinson, Lora H. "Institutional Variation in the Status of Academic Women." *Academic Women on the Move.* Ed. Alice Rossi and Ann Calderwood. New York: Sage, 1973. 199-238.

Rothblatt, Sheldon. "The Limbs of Osiris: Liberal Education in the English-Speaking World." *The European and American University since 1800: Historical and Sociological Essays.* Ed. Sheldon Rothblatt and Björn Wittrock. Cambridge: Cambridge UP, 1993. 19-73.

Salper, Roberta. "Women's Studies." *Female Studies V.* Ed. Rae Lee Siporin. Pittsburgh: Know, 1971.

Schenk, Herrad. *Die feministische Herausförderung: 150 Jahre Frauenbewegung in Deutschland.* München: Beck, 1983.

Schlüter, Anne. "Zur Situation der Frauenforschung an den Hochschulen." *Zeit und Geld für Frauenforschung: Dokumentation zur Tagung vom 15-16 Dezember, 1988, in Berlin.* Ed. Ellen Hilf and Eva Madje. Berlin: Rotation, 1989. 39-50.

Schmidt-Harzbach, Ingrid. "Women's Discussion Groups at Adult Education Institutions in Berlin." *German Feminism: Readings in Politics and Literature.* Ed. Edith Hoshino Altbach, Jeanette Clausen, Dagmar Schultz, and Naomi Stephan. Albany, NY: State U of New York P, 1984. 342-48.

Schöpp-Schilling, Hanna-Beate. "Frauenstudien, Frauenforschung, und Frauenforschungszentren in den USA: Neuere Entwicklungen." *Neue Sammlung* (1978): 158-73.

———. "Women's Studies Research Centers: Report from West Germany." *Women's Studies Newsletter* 8 (1979): 28-29.

Schwarzer, Alice. *10 Jahre Frauenbewegung: So fing es an*! Köln: Emma Frauenverlag, 1981.

Siporin, Rae Lee. "The Conference as Catalyst." *Proceedings of the Conference Women and Education: A Feminist Perspective.* Ed. Rae Lee Siporin. Pittsburgh: Know, 1971. iii-xiv.

———, ed. *Female Studies V.* Pittsburgh: Know, 1971.

"Stand und Perspektive der Frauenforschung." Deutscher Bundestag, 11. Wahlperiode, Drucksache 11/8144 (18. Oktober 1990): 10-33.

Stimpson, Catherine R. "What Matter Mind: A Theory about the Practice of Women's Studies." *Women's Studies* 1 (1973): 293-314.

Stoehr, Irene. "Auf dem Weg in den Staatsfeminismus: Zum Verhältnis von Frauenbewegung und Staat anläßlich der Auseinandersetzung um die Institutionalisierung von Frauenforschung an der FU Berlin." *alternative* 120 (1978): 174-80.

Tröger, Annemarie. "Summer Universities for Women: The Beginning of Women's Studies in Germany?" *New German Critique* 13 (Winter 1978): 175-80.

"Von harten Helden und Ehekrisen." *Hannoversche Zeitung* 30 April 1991.

Wandersee, Winifred. *On the Move: Academic Women in the 1970s.* Boston: Twayne, 1988.

Zehn Jahre Später: Zentraleinrichtung zur Förderung von Frauenstudien und Frauenforschung and der Freien Universität Berlin, 1981-1991. Berlin: Druckerei der Freien Universität Berlin, 1991.

Ziele, Inhalte und Institutionalisierung von Frauenstudien und Frauenforschung: Dokumentation der Internationalen Konferenz vom 16. bis 18. April 1980 in Berlin (West). Berlin: Planungsgruppe für einen Frauenstudien- und -forschungsbereich, 1980.

Women Writers and Women Rulers: Rhetorical and Political Empowerment in the Fifteenth Century

Susan Signe Morrison

The first prose novels in the German language have been attributed to two writers of the late Middle Ages, Elisabeth von Nassau-Saarbrücken (c. 1393-1456) and Eleonore von Österreich (1433-1480). These Early New High German texts have been typed by scholars as *Trivialliteratur,* a classification this essay questions. Eleonore and Elisabeth transform their source texts, *chansons de geste,* to increase the political role for women. I argue that the authors' own international political skill and marital experience affected their revisions. Rhetorically, women are depicted as speaking honestly, unlike the characterization of women's speech so prevalent in medieval misogynistic texts. Finally, this essay suggests future theoretical approaches for analyzing these works. (SSM)

Christine de Pizan takes issue with misogynistic literature in her early fifteenth-century work *The Book of the City of Ladies,* going further than her major source, Boccaccio's *De mulieribus claris,* to figure illustrious women in a positive light.[1] She projects herself as questioning Rectitude, writing:

> I am surprised that so many valiant ladies, who were both extremely wise and literate and who could compose and dictate their beautiful books in such a fair style, suffered so long without protesting against the horrors charged by different men when they knew that these men were greatly mistaken (184-85).

Did medieval female authors—with the self-proclaimed exception of Christine—passively accept negative depictions of women in literary texts? Certainly not all of them, as I will show in discussing three Early New High German prose novels and the authors' strategies of revision.

My essay is situated in current theoretical discussions calling for a heightened awareness of the interrelationship between language, gender, and power in medieval literature (see esp. Lomperis). In order to move away from the tendency towards binary thinking—women with no power versus women with (limited) authority—scholars can analyze how fictional female figures are constructed in discourse. Constructions of female or male identity may draw on similar literary conventions yet evolve in highly diverse ways. Tracing this development exposes a more complex figuring of represented women in literary fictions than previously determined. In terms of Elaine Showalter's division of feminist literary theory, this essay performs a "gynocritical" reading, that is, an analysis of texts written by women authors that have been generally disregarded or little read (Showalter 125–43).

In the Middle Ages great German and Latin religious texts were written by such Germanic women as Hrotsvit von Gandersheim, the canoness and dramatist of the 10th century; Hildegard von Bingen, who wrote numerous mystical works, nature treatises, medical books, and spiritual songs; and Mechthild von Magdeburg, author of *Das fließende Licht der Gottheit*. But few medieval German women have been identified as authors of secular fictional works. No German counterpart to Marie de France, the twelfth-century author of fables and *lais*, exists. Yet the noblewoman in German-speaking regions was crucial in her role as patroness for the medieval blooming of lyrical poetry, *Minnesang*, knightly tales and epics as well as Christian texts (Bell). The scene in Hartmann von Aue's *Iwein* in which the daughter of the house reads a French book aloud to her parents has been cited as an indication of how literature may have been received and spread at both French and German courts (cf. J. Müller 1985; Scholz). Vernacular literature was dedicated to and created for women, and with the coming of the fifteenth century women play leading roles in the vernacular literary culture in German-language areas.[2] The first prose novels in the German language have been attributed to two writers of the late Middle Ages, Elisabeth von Nassau-Saarbrücken (c. 1393–1456) and Eleonore von Österreich (1433–1480).[3] Their works are translations and rewritings of French verse epics from the tradition of the *chanson de geste* (Liepe 1920, 133). Elisabeth revised four works that function as a cycle since each text is concerned with some member of Charlemagne's family and line of rule. Eleonore reworked *Ponthus et la belle Sidoyne*, an anonymous French prose version of the Anglo-Norman *Horn et Rimenhild*. These artists are revolutionary in that they introduced a new genre to German literature (Roloff 9).

Earlier scholars focused on the generic characteristics of these texts that exemplify the *Volksbuch*,[4] especially focusing on issues of audience and content.[5] Much commentary emphasizes the bloody and almost disgusting war scenes, citing them as examples of a "dying chivalry."[6] Typed by literary scholars as a kind of "Unterhaltungsliteratur" or "Trivialliteratur,"[7] these works have been misrepresented as the decadent swan songs of medieval literature or as the forerunners of highly popular printed tales of the sixteenth century. Such generic classifications are questionable at best. For example, to assess Elisabeth's manuscript as a product intended for a mass popular readership is anachronistic since the original audience for her work was undoubtedly limited to the court (Linn 116; J. Müller 1985). Not until over fifty years after it was written did *Huge Scheppel* become popular, being reprinted numerous times in the sixteenth century as *Hug Schapler*.

Walter Haug has argued for a more sophisticated approach, recommending that we develop an "alternative aesthetic" for understanding such texts (200, 204).[8] I would view an "alternative aesthetic" as one that takes into account revisions from source texts, works stemming from socio-political literary sites different from Elisabeth's and Eleonore's own. As I will show, the revisions made by Elisabeth and Eleonore increase and glorify the political role for women. Rhetorical analysis reveals how the discursive dimensions of truth-telling and lying affect the way women are perceived and treated at court. Finally I would suggest that we speculate as to how the authors' own *real* international political skill and marital experience may have influenced their revisions.

Elisabeth's *Huge Scheppel*

In Elisabeth von Nassau-Saarbrücken's *Huge Scheppel*, the hero, son of a noble knight and butcher's daughter, succeeds in his rise to power and becomes king of France.[9] Hugh Capet appears as a butcher's son in the twentieth Canto of Dante's *Purgatorio*. *Hugues Capet*, the French *chanson de geste* that served as Elisabeth's source, was most likely written shortly after 1312.[10] The story reflects the popular legend of how the throne changed from the Carolingian to the Capetian dynasties.[11] Of interest to commentators have been the connections and revisions between the true historical events and those in the text concerning the change of royal power (Kindermann xxvi–vii). Huge's success is made possible only through the support of the citizens of Paris who endorse the legitimate ruler, the queen Wyßblüme, named Blanchefleur in the French source, and her daughter Marie. Crucial to the fight against their enemies is the collaboration of the people. The enemies threaten again and again[12] to destroy Paris, which functions metonymically—to destroy Paris means to subvert the ruling power. Huge ultimately wins Marie, the daughter of Wyßblüme and Ludwig, son of Charlemagne, for his wife.

The plot turns upon laws of inheritance—the daughter of the dead king inherits sovereign control of the country. This motivates the evil Count Savari, who seeks to marry Marie and plots with other evildoers to disinherit the queen so that her daughter can usurp all power and wealth. The violence caused by power-hungry men gives rise to a new law instituted with Huge and Marie's marriage. If Huge and Marie have no male issue, twelve male members of the royalty will elect a new king after Huge's death. If they do have a son, then he may become king. A daughter would inherit nothing save what is settled on her (41v7f).

The text concerns itself with the question of the line of rulership and what constitutes proper leadership. Although women are finally disempowered by the new inheritance law, female governance in Elisabeth's text actually functions as an exemplary guide for Huge in his education in becoming a leader. The representation of female rule suggests that women are in fact eminently suited to rulership. A comparison of the reigns of Wyßblüme and Huge and their behavior as leaders shows Wyßblüme to be an ideal ruler and Huge learning to rule properly by her example. For example, Wyßblüme first appears in her public role as queen after her husband Ludwig dies. The enemies, the Counts Savari and Friderich, come to the court and demand Marie's hand in marriage. The queen is surprised, afraid, and "antwerte yme gar syttenclich" (6rb28). We are also informed that, after the king's death, "die künigynne vndyre [sic] dochter DaJnne die sere betrübet warent vmb des künigs dot willen" (6ra10f). This is an attenuation of the outwardly expressed grief in the French version: "La royne et se fille en geterent maint cris" (21). This change in the German version underscores the self-control of Wyßblüme, at least in her public and official capacity as ruler.

Rather than acting autonomously, the queen consistently hears the viewpoints of others. Realizing that a ruler receives praise only through public sanction, she carries out the people's request that Huge be rewarded by knighting him. Wyßblüme tries to ease the potentially disastrous tension by saying that she will accept on behalf of her daughter a spouse of whom the free citizens of Paris approve. Not only does she consult the common people, but her courtly advisors as well, who suggest asking the citizens of Paris for aid against her enemies. She follows their advice and also writes to all her loyal lords for assistance. Wyßblüme creates a safety net of supporters by weaving them into her actions.

A number of men violently compete for the princess Marie in order to gain power. But a perilous situation develops between Wyßblüme and Marie: both mother and daughter love Huge. This situation, though, does not result in bloody antagonism as male rivalry does in the text—it is instead peacefully resolved through diplomacy. The queen thinks Huge to be the best-looking man she has ever seen and offers him a broiled peacock as a present for his brave deeds. He refuses to accept it until he has killed more enemies. When the two women hear this vow "Alle yre blüt begonde yn zu gryselen" (14ra14f). Generally there are more references in the German than in the French tale to the queen's love for Huge, frequently expressed in the phrase "ir blüt begonde ir zu gryselen" (15va41f). The insistent reminder in the German text of the queen's personal emotions and inner agitation makes her public decorum and self-possession all the more admirable and foregrounds the very question of how one should properly rule. In the French text the reader is less frequently presented with public demands and private desires. Blanchefleur's emotional upset is physically apparent: "Là gete maint soupir et souvent tresalli" (92). In the German version, Wyßblüme's thoughts and feelings are contrasted with what she expresses publicly. She does not allow emotional upset to affect her public actions, but internalizes her emotions and thinks of how she loves Huge, "Dye konigynne gedochte manchen wilden gedanck" (21va39).

The daughter Marie falls in love with Huge at first sight and secretly wants to marry him. When her mother confesses her own love for Huge, Marie claims that she herself needs a man who can defend the country well and requests that her mother choose someone else. For the fifteenth-century reader and clearly for Elisabeth this is a public event, or at least a situation with public consequences. Elisabeth's revision increases in the reader's consciousness the conflict of public versus private duties and desires. In the French version Blanchefleur blushes: "Quant le dame l'entent, tout ly frons ly rougi" (93). Just as she minimized the queen's confusion earlier in this scene, Elisabeth again emphasizes the inward and not the outward changes taking place in the queen: "Do die künigynne Das gehorte / Da gieng es ir gar tieff zü hertzen / vnd betrugte sij eyn gude wijle / was / das sy nit ein wort gesprechen möchte ye doch so hub sij an / vnd sprach glich Sittenclich..." (21vb33). Wyßblüme always answers decorously even if she suffers emotional turmoil.

Wyßblüme calls for Huge and gives him the lands of her deceased brother in Orléans and the title Duke of Orléans. Then the queen asks Huge to decide from whom he will receive a kiss, from her or her daughter (22rb35f). Huge's choice of Marie resolves the whole conflict. Rather than becoming violent, the women allow the man to choose his mate for himself.[13] This scene in particular shows the importance of stable public and private behavior for a sovereign. The queen's love for Huge is never again publicly uttered, although the reader knows that she still loves him (34rb27f). While she has already privately agreed to the marriage of her daughter to Huge, Wyßblüme creates a public ceremony in which Huge receives the permission of the court (41r18f). The loyal advisor Drogne then publicly suggests that Huge should marry Marie. Again, the queen does not act spontaneously on her own private desires but for the general good of the kingdom, consulting with advisors rather than acting alone.

The love of the queen for Huge is alluded to more frequently in the German than the French text. The insistent contrast between her inner dislocation and her outward control as ruler highlights her gift of leadership. The transference from outward signs in the French to inward evidence in the German could be read as a deepening of female psychology through avoiding stereotypical female appearance or behavior. This psychologizing makes the queen seem more "reasonable" and in control and thus more capable of ruling an entire nation than her French model. Further, this heightened tension between public and private behavior and spheres, which for the queen coincide and blur, foregrounds the entire issue of proper leadership. The German text explicitly shows the necessity for rulers to act *hierarchically* rather than *charismatically*. The hierarchical system of rulership, where the leader relies on external advice from loyal courtiers, minimizes the danger of poor—spontaneous and emotion-inspired—leadership.

Penny Schine Gold in *The Lady & the Virgin* compares the epic, *chanson de geste*, and romance of a period several hundred years prior to the works of Elisabeth. Her conclusions concerning the social and political response inherent in each genre can help us to view fifteenth-century texts. Gold points out the dichotomy highlighted between private and public spheres in the romance, where the hero's identity is created through the attainment of the heroine. In contrast, the epic or *chanson de geste* fuses the realms of public and private. Female characters

> themselves devoted to the epic values of family and community, can, through their nurture and advice, enhance (or try to enhance) the hero's achievement of these social concerns.... In the *chanson de geste*, the private (home) sphere of women is integrated with the public (battle) sphere of men through the common base structure of the family.... Because of this integration, through the family, of public and private spheres, women, though still on the periphery of power, can sometimes be influential (37, 40, 42).

This power of the female in the *chanson de geste* is apparent in *Huge Scheppel*. Huge has to learn reflective and hierarchical rulership during his adventures.[14] Immediately after he becomes king, Huge forces his enemies to swear fidelity to him (42rb13f). He believes that as king he will be obeyed, never doubting his own power. His hubris is diminished when he later realizes that his enemies, ignoring their pledge of loyalty, have betrayed him.

Huge does learn not to act independently. When his enemies believe that Huge is dead, and he is unable to return to court, he meets a hermit who offers him black bread, little expecting that Huge will accept such simple fare. However, Huge is happy to eat this humble meal and thankfully borrows a simple set of clothes. Huge is beginning to depend upon other people for help and no longer behaves autocratically as he did towards his enemies. Recognizing their betrayal, he confesses his unhappiness to the loyal Count of Dampmartin (51va4f). After this confession, something new occurs: "Nu bidden ich uch vmb gottes willen / mir üwer getruwen Rait her Jnne zu geben wie ich mich an dem verretern gerechen..." (51va32f). Huge has learned to ask his social inferiors for advice and, with it, carries the day.

As the work closes, King Huge must convict his two enemies, Friderich and Asselin. Again he seeks advice. The Count of Dampmartin suggests that the enemies be condemned to death, because otherwise they will simply stir up trouble again. All agree, including Huge, who comments: "Er hatt sehr wol gerathen" (56v18). The French version contains no explicit statement that the request for advice will bring praise, whereas the German text underscores this lesson of rulership (56v10f). Likewise, in the French version Huge responds to Drogne's advice with "C'est voirs" (235), while Elisabeth has him underscore her point with "Er hatt sehr wol gerathen." Huge has learned how to behave like Wyßblüme: not as an independent authority, but as a ruler who accepts useful advice.

Elisabeth's *Huge Scheppel* provides rich material for theoretical analysis and comparisons to generically different works. For example, Huge's low point, when he laments his fate and before he is reintegrated into society by the hermit, could be compared to Iwein's loss of identity in Hartmann von Aue's Arthurian romance. A psychoanlytic interpretation might also be undertaken, reading Huge's induction into proper and successful rule by his mother-in-law—or symbolic mother figure—as a result of the loss of his father. We could also read Huge's development in terms of a feminized male ruler. The queen cannot rule without taking advice, and Huge learns that his strength lies in taking this seemingly weak stance. Those who are dependent, by definition women, must take advice and are the stronger for it.[15] Carolyn Dinshaw's work on Chaucer would be suggestive here. She defines "reading like a man" as interpreting texts with the intention and result of closure, whereas "reading like a woman" allows for alternative scenarios, focuses on contradictions, and resists closure.[16] Perhaps "ruling like a man" is ruling autocratically, while "ruling like a woman" is ruling hierarchically, taking the advice of loyal courtiers into consideration. Only through his "feminization" of conduct does Huge learn to "rule like a woman," that is, well.

The presupposition of the text—war is caused when women inherit—is foregrounded by Elisabeth's revision[17] of the French *chanson de geste*. Elisabeth shows that the correlation between male violence and female rulership is not natural, inevitable, or desirable. She also highlights how men engender violence *despite* the proper leadership of women. Elisabeth could easily have had a personal stake in demonstrating the capability of women to rule. It is believed that she wrote *Huge Scheppel* around 1437, roughly eight years after the death of her husband, Count Philipp the First, at which time she took over the leadership of Nassau-Saarbrücken. When her eldest son Philipp came of age in 1438, one year later, Elisabeth made a contract with him and his brother, promising to give up the lands in her widow's jointure if she were to marry and, presumably, give birth to potentially rival heirs. If she remained unmarried, she would maintain half of the revenue of the county of Saarbrücken. She never married again and died in 1456. During her rulership she also took part in a struggle for sovereignty. Her uncle, Charles of Lorraine, died without a male heir. Charles's son-in-law, René of Anjou, Duke of Bar, wanted to inherit, but Antoine de Vaudémont, Elisabeth's brother, declared himself ruler. Elisabeth took the side of her brother and tried to bring peace to the land (Burger 86-87; J. Müller 1989).

From this sketchy description of her life we can see that the questions of inheritance and of rulership were certainly high in Elisabeth's thoughts. She herself is said to have ruled admirably,[18] but had to give up her power under the law when her eldest son came of age (Burger 86-87). Perhaps we can see a reflection of Elisabeth in her depiction of Wyßblüme. Both widowed, Wyßblüme and Elisabeth ruled to general praise. Wyßblüme shows how women can renounce their own interests in favor of those of their children. Elisabeth herself showed that women can rule well and her protagonist Wyßblüme teaches the energetic Huge through her example how one should rule—with the help of loyal advisors. This text certainly offers much to entertain (*Unterhaltung*), but is far from being "trivial."

Elisabeth's *Die Königin Sibille*

Die Königin Sibille[19] tells the tale of a queen falsely accused of adultery. Although she protests her innocence and the king's loyal advisors tend to side with her, the king refuses to believe her. She nevertheless remains true to her husband and her splendid innocence is finally rewarded by his acceptance after she has patiently suffered for years. In *Die Königin Sibille,* variations on the word *verreder* are used repeatedly to define and describe the betrayers of the king Karl and his wife.[20] The subversion of honest speech permits the—albeit temporary—exercise of power over a truthful discourse of protest and denial.

The queen tells the king what we readers know to be true: that she knew nothing about the dwarf lying in her bed and that she would rather die than sleep with such a creature. Although she pleads for mercy, the king reprimands her as follows, "Ffrouwe sprach der konnig jr kunent viel klaffens / Aber jr enkünent des dinges nit geleucken" (124.7-8). Claiming that she can manipulate language well but cannot deny the events and circumstances in evidence before him, he dismisses her honest tale as a lie. Since the king's word is law, his definition of her discourse becomes actualized. Simply through his utterance, her honest speech is transformed into lies.

The innocent queen subsequently is to undergo the punishment a truly guilty perpetrator would have had to suffer, proclaiming before she is to be burned at the stake that she has been falsely accused. We then encounter the first use of the word *verreder*.[21] The evil men who had recommended to the king that she burn go to the dwarf and bribe him to encourage that the queen be burned: "Die *verreder* die geraden hatten / das man die konnigynne verbornen solde / die gingen zu dem getwerg vnd sprachen zü yme" (126.7-9). The dwarf then lies to the king, claiming that the queen coerced him to come to her. The dwarf is burned to death for sleeping with the queen and Karl exiles his wife.

At this point Markair, who plans to rape and behead the queen, heads off for the forest following the exiled and shamed woman. He comes from a whole family of lying louts: "Konnig Karle ginge zü dische myt siner ritterschafft / vnd hait in syme hoffe eynen bösen schalck / vnd *verreder* / der was geheyssen Mayrkar / vnd was geborn von den *verredern* / die hertzog Herpin *verrieden*..." (128.8-11). When he catches up with the couple, he lies (128.20). The *verreder* becomes the metonymous signification for Markair who kills the loyal escort Abrye but fails to capture the queen. When the queen tells her faithful rescuer and companion, the farmer Warakir, of her unhappy fate, she says, "Aber Markair der *verreder* ylt mir nach..." (130.37). Warakir escorts her to a nearby shelter and relates the truth to their host (132.12-13). Already evil is associated with lying and goodness with truthtelling.

The subversion of truthful speech is underscored by many characters through numerous references to *verreder*. For example, Karl's loyal courtier and advisor, Nymo, whom we readers trust since he suspects the truth as we know it, has misgivings and mistrusts Markair. He tells Karl: "Nv duncket vns jr habent in uwerm hoiffe *verreder* die uber hant nement / Nü wollen wir gerne den dag leben/ das ir der *verreder* enttragen würden / vnd wir sagen üch hüdent uch wan es dut üch noit" (135.1-3). Only with the evidence of Abrye's corpse does Karl recognize the truth of Markair's activities: "Jch versorgen hie sye mit *verrederye* vmbgangen..." (136.3-4). After Markair's confession of his treachery, the king laments: "Horent zu sprach konnig Karl widder Nymo von Beyern was vns der *verreder* sage / Ach edele konnig [ynn] e [sic] sprach konnig Karl / jch besorgen sere jr sint *verrederij* halb verdrieben worden" (142.32-143.2). *Verreder* is the signifier for those men who slander the queen and attempt to overthrow the legitimate rulership.[22]

During the queen's exile, twelve murderers in the woods plan to rape her and kill Warakir and her son Prince Ludwig. A battle ensues and Warakir kills the head murderer, proclaiming: "Jr falschen bosen *verreder* jr müssent alle hie sterben" (147.20). When they meet up with the queen's uncle, a hermit in the forest, they tell of the events leading up to their sorry condition (149.25-36). The word *verreder* is repeatedly used to designate those men who bring about hardships for the queen. Her feeble defense of the truth against the muscular vigor of duplicitous lies does not provide a sufficient defense of her innocence.

Towards the conclusion of the text, a great deal of confusion concerning the label *verreder* takes place. The honest Warakir is mislabeled and not believed when he accurately accuses the evil men of being *verreder*. Nymo wants to give his king the good advice to accept his wife (160.5), whereas Maucion, "eyn *verreder*" (160.13), suggests Karl not take back his wife and slanders Warakir. The king repeatedly calls Warakir a "*verreder*" and commands his men to follow him (162.22, 162.32). Since readers know the king to have faulty judgement, his wrongful designation of Warakir as a *verreder* stands out. After the ensuing battle between the men of father Karl and son Ludwig, Karl finally distinguishes the true *verreder* from those falsely accused when he commands that the true reprobates be hanged: "Nement die *verreder* die es mit mir gemacht hant vnd bindent iglichen an eins phertz zagel vnd sleyffent sye an den galgen vnd henckent sye alle daran" (173.3–5). The queen pleads with the king to have mercy on her at the end, proclaiming that she had been unjustly treated (172.17–18). The king at last believes her.

The text also presents two instances that vary the above pattern. Markair returns to court and tells Karl that Abrye had his way with the queen (133.10–14). This is untrue, but Markair then tells the truth deceptively, saying that Karl will never see Abrye again at court. This is true of course, since he has killed him, but he intends that Karl should interpret it differently. The king does so, believing his wife to have run off with Abrye.

In one sense the moral of the tale is that the truth will out if one (i.e., woman) suffers long enough.[23] The *verreder* finally get their just rewards and punishments. Violence against language parallels physical violence against women. Truth and the telling of things "the way they are" proves to be a weak defense against the strength of deceptive rhetoric. The *verreder* instigate civil war and insurrection, threatening to overthrow the stability of the kingdom. Karl ignores his good advisors and instead follows his own erratic inclinations, accepting false advice from *verreder*. Faulty leadership is exacerbated not by the existence of *verreder*, but by a king's belief in them. Karl finally acknowledges his errors with humility. Deference is the appropriate mode in a kingship based on a hierarchy of advisors. The king's most loyal advisors are clearly on the side of the queen. Not only, of course, is this kind of advisor crucial to a true, honest, and moral leadership, but belief in one's wife is essential for fair and reasonable judgments.

Elisabeth depicts the ruling queen here as helpless and totally within the power of her consort's whims and orders, but also as exemplary, brave, and honest. The discourse of *verrederei* is in direct opposition to that which women use. This is only one of many medieval texts that illustrate that medieval women's speech was not universally represented as deceptive. R. Howard Bloch has recently written about the topos of "woman as riot," most especially in Old French where *riote* means "chaos" or "upset."[24] In Elisabeth's work, chaos ensues indeed from perverted speech, but that speech is given voice by men exclusively. Elisabeth could, like Christine de Pizan, be responding to the strong cultural climate that endorsed a view of women as cheats, liars, and deceivers. We should in fact read Sibille's spouse as ruling weakly *because* he "buys" the misogynist view that a woman is "always already a deceiver, trickster, jongleur" (Bloch 1987, 5).

The only help for a woman in a threatening political situation, one that favors male hegemony, is reliance on the good advice of loyal counsellors. But if the advisors are *verreder*, the role of the queen is precarious. One source of power and support for women is hierarchical rulership with trusty advisors. This is the political structure Elisabeth advocates in these works for rulers of both sexes.

Eleonore's *Pontus and Sidonia*

Like Elisabeth's works, Eleonore von Österreich's *Pontus und Sidonia* gives prominence to good advisors. Her source is the English ballad *King Horn*, later transformed into a *chanson de geste*, *Horn et Rimenhild*. This version was adapted as a French romance, *Ponthus et la belle Sidoine*, perhaps written by Geoffrey de la Tour Landry at the end of the fourteenth century (*King Horn* xv-xvi; Ruh 472). Eleonore's version of *Pontus und Sidonia* dates from between 1449 and 1465 (Liepe 1920, 26). It was printed numerous times in the sixteenth and seventeenth centuries, attesting to its great popularity (Ruh 472-73). Differences from the original English text are many as far as names and places are concerned, but the story is essentially unchanged.[25] The plot is based on the repeated partings of a young pair of lovers and the eventual defeat of their heathen adversaries. Among her revisions, Eleonore foregrounds the role of queen at court.

As in the other German texts examined here, the exchange of advice is of vital importance for the maintenance of a stable government. For example, King Argill asks for advice when the Sultan's son invades Brittany (136.22-23) and Pontus suggests writing to other Christians for help (136.28-29). His advice is well received (137.14-16). Later Argill asks his court to suggest who should succeed him. All but the evil Gendelet recommend Pontus. When Pontus has captured the Irish king, the English king listens to the advice of his courtiers, but Pontus, in disguise as Sordit, has the last word. When he recommends that the captured king marry the youngest English princess, the Scottish king voices everyone's approval of such advice. Pontus functions as the loyal and well-respected advisor.

But the smooth rule of a kingdom depends on courtly skills as well as good advice. In Eleonore's text a good leader must also be capable of wielding clever rhetoric and, ideally, should also be skilled in *list* or craftiness as Pontus proves to be. For example, Pontus circulates a rumor that he is fighting in Hungary, while in fact he challenges knights weekly in disguise as the Black Knight to show his devotion and spirit to Sidonia. Later at the English court, he shows himself to be a consummate master of all the courtly arts. When Pontus goes back to the court of Brittany on the day of the bridal feast between the bad duke and Sidonia, he disguises himself as a poor pilgrim and manages to meet with Sidonia, subtly exposing his identity to her before saving the day. Clever speech and disguises are a necessary part of Pontus's bag of tricks as he struggles to win back his own kingdom and win his true love.

Eleonore distinguishes between her hero's "good lies" and the villain's evil ones. Our hero uses *list* for good purposes and the reader admires him for it. Clearly we are meant to disapprove of the evil Gendelet, one of the original noble boys saved with Pontus and now consumed with envy, who continuously plots Pontus's destruction. His stratagem to gain power is facilitated by guileful speech and wicked lies. "Gendelet...der gar ein neidiger Mensch was; vnd kund auch *wol reden vnnd falsche Wort fürpringen* vnd waz dem Pontus gar hessig" (168.17f). Taking advantage of the king's senility, Gendelet recommends that he force Pontus to swear an oath, knowing Pontus will refuse. Like Sibille, Pontus is a dependent whose status hinges on the king's taking good advice. When the king suspects the innocent Pontus of insurrection, Pontus leaves the court in disgrace for seven years and flees to England disguised as Sordit. The court at Brittany is genuinely unhappy, while Gendelet feigns distress at Pontus's departure.

With Pontus out of the way, Gendelet does not hesitate to act on his own plans. He manages to obtain the position of seneschal from Herland by means of his clever speech (187.36-188.1). He then persuades the king to promote the marriage of Sidonia to the bad Duke of Bumgoczne. Luckily Pontus comes back in time to save Sidonia from her evil fate. Gendelet again feigns sympathy (199.32-33). After he marries Sidonia, Pontus must go to Galicia to conquer the heathens, while Gendelet, ever the snake in the grass, remains behind: "Durch *falsche Wort* bleib bej dem Künig Gendelet vnnd bey Sydonia..." (205.14f). Gendelet sends forged letters, supposedly by Pontus, which state that he has lost his battle and direct that Gendelet should marry Sidonia and receive all the treasure Pontus had brought back from England. Sidonia and the court believe Pontus has died and Gendelet persuades the king to talk his daughter into marrying him: "Der Künig was alt vnd Gendelet thet als vil mit seinen *gescheiden Worten*, das der Künig seinen Willen darzu gab" (217.40-218.1). When Sidonia protests she wants to become a Beguine,[26] Gendelet goes to talk with her: "Darnach do gieng er zu ir vnd wolt sy mit *hübschen Worten* plenden" (218.19-20). When she continues to resist he turns from persuasion to threats: "Vnd *droet ir*, do er mit *hübschen*

Worten nichtz an ir gehaben mochte..." (218.37-38). His manipulative language is described as "false," "clever," and "pretty."

Eleonore too uses the word *Verrätterey* which, as we have seen, Elisabeth in *Die Königin Sibille* repeatedly uses to signify the male evildoers. After Pontus leaves to conquer heathens, Gendelet plans an evil scheme, intending "*Verrätterey* ze thun" (216.33). Like the evil slanderers of Sibille, Gendelet is repeatedly referred to as the speaker of treacherous canards (e.g., 227.7; 225.12-14). As in *Die Königin Sibille*, the betrayer or *Verreder* is one who uses language cleverly by perverting it.

In Eleonore's work, as in Elisabeth's, the importance of good advice is crucial to smooth rulership. Eleonore, however, highlights the troubles a bad advisor can brew as potentially the most devastating when the king becomes senile and childish. The court at Brittany represents a worst-case scenario of the destabilizing consequences of bad advice. This is a new element to the story added by Eleonore. In *King Horn*, the king of Westernesse (Brittany), named Almair, is not senile, but in fact quite strong.[27] With this alteration Eleonore highlights the delicate balance between ruler and advisor. She confronts the reader as well with a lesson in rulership. In the concluding pages of *Pontus und Sidonia*, Pontus gives Polidas, the future king of England, advice on how to rule properly, including the suggestion to be cautious about believing words one hears and not always to believe one's civil servants (233.24-26; 234.7-9). The good leader should be able to distinguish between good and bad advisors and, while it is crucial to listen to advice, one should not believe every rumor. Also, while the use of *list* is permissible for good purposes and when manipulated by noble characters, it is only to be condemned when evil characters master it.

While the text points out how an evil advisor is to be guarded against, it also highlights the positive role of advice given by women. Sidonia has the proper attributes of a good advisor. She is wise enough to assess the connection between her father's senility and Gendelet's increasing power (189.14-18). When she urges that those loyal to her lock themselves into a tower, they approve of her advice (219.17). She cleverly employs a Penelope-style postponement of her marriages to both the duke and Gendelet in hopes that Pontus will return in time to save her—which of course he does.

Pontus realizes that women are to be respected and dealt with carefully. When he is still very young he points out that one should not believe all bad rumors one hears about women, directly refuting the misogynist discourse of the Middle Ages: "Vnnd wenn man von Frauen, Junckfrauen, Edelleuten, Priestern oder andern Dingen ubel redett, das was im gar ein groß Mißfallen; vnnd sprach, man solte nit alle Ding gelauben vnnd sagen, was man höret" (126.14-17). When Polidas is to marry the princess Genefe and become the acting head of England,

Pontus gives advice about rulership and suggests that he listen to the complaints of women:

> Auch, lieber Vetter, darzu ist zuuersteen, das ir das pillicher gegen eurem Gemahel thut, dann gen yemant anders durch vil Vrsach wegen. Wan durch Gütikeit vnd durch Ere mugt ir jr Lieb genczlich zu euch bringen vnd solt ir nit grob sein, anders sy mocht sich sunst verkeren. Vnd die Lieb, die sy zu euch solt haben, die mochtz anderswo anlegen, dadurch sy ir solchen Vnmut mocht nemen, daz ir in großen Vnwillen geneinander möcht kummen, daz irs nit wider möcht bringen, wen ir woltt. Auch, lieber Vetter, schauett, daz ir ir treu seyt; als Got redt jm Ewangelio, das ir sy für kein andere verkert. Das ist zuuersteen, daz ir mit keiner andern Geselschafft habt.... Vnnd hort alle Freitag besunder den Ruffe von den Armen vnd von den Frauen, die Wittib feind vnnd last in gute Gerechtikeit nit verzeihen (233.32–234.7).

A ruler is urged to listen to women, but what is to be their specific role at court? As in the case of Marie in *Huge Scheppel,* Genefe inherits the line of rulership but her husband rules. Eleonore envisions an active queen at court while accepting the woman's admittedly more limited power. Only in Eleonore's version of the tale does the English court function as a model of correct rule. Interestingly, it is the only one to have an active queen. The model court aspect of the English court is *not* present in *King Horn* with its Irish court and absent queen. In Eleonore's text the queen of the English court is always mentioned with the king. The king is also shown to consult not only with his advisors but with the queen as well (174.19–22). Although clearly not as important as the king, she is always included in discussions, is respected and active at court. She is mentioned so frequently along with the king that one senses she is crucial to the balance and well-being of the nation.[28]

After Gendelet has been conquered, Pontus goes to England to plan a marriage between his cousin, Polidas, and Genefe, the English princess. When the English court hears of this, the king and queen discuss it and the king agrees to the queen's sensible suggestion that the king of England should live in England to prevent possible insurrection and civil war (227.37–40). The English king makes an effort to avoid the worst-case scenario of Brittany, where the childish king becomes the prey of an evil advisor. Both the king and queen wish to ensure the stability of the realm by marrying their daughters to strong knights and kings who can maintain the security of the realm and tighten relations with other nations through peacekeeping marriages. The proper role of a queen is that of advisor. The king's proper duty is to seek out this advice.

The position of the queen mother is also highlighted in Eleonore's revision. Pontus's mother, who hid for fourteen years in a hermitage while the heathen hordes overtook her land of Spain, is at last reunited with her son.[29] She advises well, as a queen properly should (214.16-17). When Pontus meets her he immediately crowns her queen (213.39-40).[30] Sidonia also pays her mother-in-law much respect (235.8-9).

Unlike her source texts, Eleonore emphasizes that peaceweaving marriages should unite only willing couples. After the war with Ireland, Pontus suggests that the youngest princess marry the Irish king as part of the truce only after he has obtained her assurance that the Irish king pleases her (180.17f). Then Pontus asks the Irish king his opinion (182.15-21). Only after everyone agrees does the wedding take place. The thought of uniting Pontus to Genefe, the English king's daughter, is dropped once the court realizes Pontus opposes it. When Pontus suggests wedding Polidas, his cousin, to Genefe, the king will support the marriage only if the young man pleases his daughter: "Sicher, sprach der Künig, so gefellt er mir gar wol, gefiel er allein meiner Tochter" (227.33-34). The importance of desire is underscored by the failed effort to force Sidonia into marriage with the duke and Gendelet. Further, the alliances that are assented to willingly are, we are told, successful reigns with the queens governing alongside their husbands. Pontus and Sidonia have a happy reign: "Der Künig Pontus vnnd die Künigin Sydonia regnierten eyn gut vnd gar ein lange Zeit nach irer Landtschafft Gefallen" (236.9-11).

Eleonore accepts the limited political role available to queens, but underscores the importance of advisors for queens and kings. In *Pontus und Sidonia* only the courts with effective female advisors successfully retain their stability. I would not hesitate to suggest that Eleonore's own biography played a part in her version of the *Pontus and Sidonia* legend. Eleonore herself had vast experience with the exercise of official political power. The sixth child of James I of Scotland, she lived at Charles VII's court in France starting in 1445. Then in 1448 she married Duke Siegmund of Tirol from whom she twice took over the leadership of the realm during his absence, from 1455 to 1458 and again in 1467 (Liepe 1920, 26). Her text teaches the reader how a court can function smoothly and advantageously with the help of a respected queen. Furthermore, since her marriage was reputed to have been an unhappy one (Ruh 470), it is more than likely that her emphasis on the importance of mutual desire in aristocratic marriages came from her own experience.

Conclusions: Future Possibilities for these Texts

The works examined in this essay are concerned with political stability and the proper role of women rulers. The authors emphasize the importance of listening to women. The queen mother in *Huge Scheppel* functions didactically by her example as an ideal leader and thereby trains the young, charismatic Huge in the proper way of hierarchical leadership. *Pontus und Sidonia* envisions an ideal court where the king is certainly in charge but the queen is sought out publicly for advice, which is then followed and respected. In these texts, the dominant role figured for women is that of political diplomat. A related issue is the discourse of truth-telling to indict deceptive language and expose illegitimate male authority. Truthtelling can be disempowering, that is, the woman telling the truth can be ignored as in the case of Sibille. Yet the deceptive discourse of *list* is generally politically effective for male figures only for a short time. The discourse of women is revealed to be true and the women—or their offspring—ultimately become empowered politically. While Eleonore and Elisabeth do not *radically* subvert the secular material they translated and reworked, their representation of women as truthtellers and men as users of deceptive speech confers on the queens a powerful role at court.

Gold's arguments about twelfth-century generic differences between the *chanson de geste* and the romance may help us to understand why Elisabeth and Eleonore worked within a genre that has usually been seen as a debased form of the *chanson de geste*.

> ...In *chanson de geste*, a genre that embraced and idealized the past, women were accepted into the values and the world of action that were dominated by men. In romance, a genre that created a fantasy world, women were separated from the world of men and became a goal to be attained by men through love (42).[31]

The *chanson de geste*, unlike the romance, allowed for the possibility of female political power or influence. Elisabeth and Eleonore were not trapped by their source texts and could manipulate them to emphasize the importance of female role models for male rule.

Worthy of further analysis is the "feminization" of male activity and speech. The proper male ruler learns to rule well and successfully by following female role models or taking female advice into consideration. While female speech in the medieval period was often allied with lies and deception, in both Elisabeth's and Eleonore's works liars are exclusively male. Even the hero of *Pontus und Sidonia* is "crafty" in his speech. Perhaps these works would profit from comparison with Christian or hagiographical works in which truthtelling is endorsed as the "proper" rhetorical mode and often exposes illegitimate male authority.[32] *Die Königin Sibille*, for example, would profit from comparison with the "patient Griselda" tale or Chaucer's *Man-of-Law's Tale*.[33]

Also worthy of further investigation is the fact that Elisabeth and Eleonore were not native to German-language areas, but married into foreign cultures. Susan Groag Bell has shown the important literary fertilization that took place due to cross-cultural marriages (135, 136). While Bell mainly deals with religious texts, her conclusions are suggestive for secular material as well. One aspect of particular importance is the intellectual legacy passed on from mother to child. Elisabeth, coming from a French family famous for its literary connections (Liepe 1920, 8-9, 18-19), was especially influenced by her mother, Margarete de Vaudémont. She is to be thanked for Elisabeth's knowledge of the texts she translated; indeed, Margarete had the source *chansons de geste* copied in 1405. Elisabeth's brother Antoine produced courtly lyric poetry and belonged to a literary circle centered around Charles d'Orléans. The court of her uncle Charles de Lorraine was famous as well for its theatrical spectacles and patronage of the visual arts. Although immersed in French traditions, Elisabeth existed politically between two nations.

Likewise Eleonore von Österreich's background is international. She was the daughter of James the First of Scotland, himself the author of *The Kingis Quair*, and Joan Beaufort, niece of the Bishop of Winchester and the Chancellor of England (Mackenzie). As an adolescent she lived at the court of Charles the Seventh in France and then at the age of fifteen married Siegmund von Tirol. Both Elisabeth and Eleonore, writing in German, appropriated literary conventions that crossed national boundaries. This process of cultural "translation" was also important in earlier eras, such as when Arthurian romances were adapted by Hartmann von Aue and Wolfram von Eschenbach, presumably through international patronage. In the cases of Elisabeth and Eleonore, international marriages spawned these translations and rewritings, an aspect of these works that should prove fruitful for future scholarly research.

One crucial aspect of feminist projects is to uncover or rediscover forgotten voices. Only by their retrieval can we properly hear the sounds of the fifteenth and other centuries. Recent scholarship[34] has investigated the coincidences and differences between historical political options available to real women and the literary offerings allotted them. The texts by Elisabeth and Eleonore offer much potential for scholars who wish to recover both fictional and real women's experiences. Not only could works like these by Elisabeth and Eleonore potentially "enter the canon," but they can help us to understand better the canon as it has traditionally been understood and taught.

Notes

I would like to thank the following people for their advice, comments and encouragement for this essay: Michel-André Bossy, William Crossgrove, Maria Müller-Breuer, Erika Kartschoke, and the editors and reviewers of the *Women in German Yearbook*.

[1] For a discussion of Christine's reception of Boccaccio, see Earl Jeffrey Richards's Foreword to his translation of her *The Book of the City of Ladies* (xxxv ff.).

[2] For a discussion of how feminist medieval scholarship could revitalize German studies in the United States as well as the teaching of the Middle Ages in general, see Classen, "Women in Medieval Literature and Life."

[3] For a discussion of the disputed authorship of *Pontus und Sidonia*, see Classen, who concludes that we cannot dismiss Eleonore as the author of the text due to the feminine perspective evident in the text (1993). Also see Günther Müller and Liepe. Jan-Dirk Müller takes issue with Liepe and problematizes the question of prose novels in Germany (1980, 395). He alludes to the prose Lanzelet, among other works, which complicates any attempt to simplify the question as to when prose novels arose and what constitutes them as a genre.

[4] In his definitive 1985 essay, Jan-Dirk Müller discusses the problem for literary scholars in distinguishing the *Volksbuch* from the *Prosaroman*. He suggests that "Volksbücher" are defined more through their audience and reception whereas the "Prosaroman" is more typically used for long fictional stories of the fifteenth and sixteenth centuries. See also pages 38 ff. for an analysis of the printings of such texts and how such printings might be brought to bear on this question of genre designation.

[5] Marie-Luise Linn asks if a *Volksbuch* is distinguished by its content or its audience (112-13). Winifred Frey writes that the works of Eleonore and Elisabeth are "Literatur des Adels für den Adel." Further, it is literature meant to be read. The introduction of *Hug Schapler* "*Ein lieplichs Lesen*" articulates a shift in reception of the text. Reading becomes personal and individual as opposed to the traditionally public, and more easily regulated, performance and reception (70-71, 73).

[6] J. Müller also points out that this prose functions as a "Zeichen des Kulturzerfalls" (1985, 15). Frequently the designation of "Verbürgerlichung" stems from the critic's own idealization of the nobility (53).

[7] J. Müller calls the authors "fürstlichen Dilettantinnen"! (1985, 30). Heinz Otto Burger writes, "Gräfin Elisabeth übersetzte einige bereits depravierte Rechenepen Frankreichs: ein Versuch, der den deutschen Roman vorbereitete" (125). Linn warns the reader from following this school of thought (138). J. Müller describes the usual model that scholars have used to type a work as "trivial": "insgesamt eine Entdifferenzierung der poetischen Organisation, die als 'Trivialisierung' gedeutet wurde und ihren Grund in der 'Verbürgerlichung' des

literarischen Publikums haben sollte, das eben nicht mehr über die ästhetischen und sozialen Standards der adelig-höfischen Hörerschaft verfügte, deren kulturelle Überlieferung aber als Statussymbol für sich beanspruchte" (1980, 396).

[8] While I disagree with some of Haug's conclusions about what constitutes this "alternative aesthetic," I do agree that the work is surprisingly modern in its endorsement of women's speech.

[9] I cite Urtel's edition of Elisabeth's *Huge Scheppel*. "Da unsere Handschrift zweifellos in einem sehr nahen Verhältnisse zum Originalmanuskripte der Übersetzerin steht und überdies die einzige bekannte Handschrift des Romanes ist, so schien es am angemessensten sie buchstaben-, zeilen- und seitengetreu wiederzugeben" (7).

[10] All parenthetical references to the French version cite the De La Grange edition.

[11] See J. Müller for a discussion of the historiographical aspects of the work (1985, 65 ff.).

[12] The enemies mastermind three main intrigues in both the original French and Elisabeth's revision, which Huge succeeds in foiling. First they poison King Ludwig, whose daughter the evil Count Savari wants to marry. Then Count Friderich wants to avenge the death of his brother, Savari, and asks for the hand of Marie as compensation. When this is denied, war breaks out. After Huge marries Marie, Count Friderich and the son of the murdered Duke of Burgundy, Asselin, undertake a third intrigue. While Huge is away the two queens are kidnapped and locked up. An assassination attempt on Huge's life takes place and it is believed Huge is dead. When the enemies bring Marie to the church to wed her off to Count Friderich, Huge and his companions arrive to destroy them at last. The reader is consoled with a happy ending.

[13] In the French version the feudal overtones and implications of such a bestowal are more in evidence, unclouded by the eroticization of this embrace between Huge and Marie with which Elisabeth fills out the scene (De La Grange 95): "vff myne trüwe sprach marie Juncher ir sollent ein heisen von mir han / Sij nam yn gütlichen in yre armen In grosser liebe Vnd fruntschafft Jn solicher fugen qwam huge Jn Staedt vnd in wesen / vnd wart also zu hohem adel vnd grossen eren erkorren" (22rb44f).

[14] J. Müller types Huge as an example of Georges Duby's "jeunes/juvenis" (1980, 412). One could also interpret Huge's initiation process within the guidelines of rulership Müller discusses in "Sîvrit: künec-man-eigenholt" (85-124).

[15] I thank the anonymous reviewer, known to me only as "reviewer #1," for her excellent and provocative suggestions throughout, but especially concerning this point and my discussion of misogyny below.

[16] Dinshaw is careful to point out that "reading like a man" is not an activity restricted to readers gendered male or that "reading like a woman" is restricted to real women. Rather it is a type of reading (70, 72, 89).

[17] Sixteenth-century printed versions of Elisabeth's *Huge Scheppel* emphasize the claim that women should have no rights of inheritance. In the 1500 printing it is explicitly stated two times, additionally appearing at the end of the first address to the reader, which contains a summary of *Loher und Maller*, another text translated by Elisabeth that contains historical background to *Huge Scheppel*.

[18] Ursula Liebertz-Grün comments: "Bei allen Unterschieden ist den beiden Autorinnen [Elisabeth und Eleonore] eines gemeinsam: In Abwesenheit bzw. nach dem Tod ihrer Ehegatten haben sie zwar ihre Territorien jahrelang selbständig regiert, aber ihre Frauengestalten sind männerfixiert, unselbständig und etwas dümmlich. Man tut beiden Autorinnen gewiß kein Unrecht, wenn man ihr Frauenbild als wenig aufgeklärt—oder im heutigen Sprachgebrauch schlichtweg als repressiv bezeichnet" (32-33). I of course disagree with Liebertz-Grün's interpretation of the female figures, but I do wish to emphasize the real experience the two authors had in government.

[19] I uses Tiemann's edition, since it is the most readily accessible.

[20] According to the Grimm Dictionary, *verreden* means "falsch reden" and *verraten* "falschen rat geben, falsche unterstützung geben, irre leiten."

[21] I will italicize the variations of the word *verreder* to underscore how prominent a concept it is in the text.

[22] Writing about *Pontus und Sidonia*, Classen comments on the evil character who resembles Markair in his nasty plans. "Gendolet repräsentiert schlichthin den Hofneider, also die Gruppe derjenigen Leute um den König oder Fürsten, die sich darum bemühen, die Karriere erfolgreicher Ritter zu bremsen oder gar zu unterbinden und damit letztlich auch die Herrschaft der Königsfamilie an sich untergraben..." (1993, 10-11).

[23] Classen discusses women in this genre as passive sufferers we are meant to sympathize with (1993, 15-16). While I agree Sidonia suffers, I read the women as more active. I am mainly interested in how violence to rhetoric enacts physical violence.

[24] See "Medieval Misogyny" and *Medieval Misogyny and the Invention of Western Romantic Love*. Also crucial to Bloch's argument is the response to his *Representations* article, which appeared in the *Medieval Feminist Newsletter* 6 (1988): 2-11 and his subsequent response in *MFN* 7 (1989): 6-10. To read more medieval misogynist texts, see Alcuin Blamires.

[25] "It would, however, be wrong to imply that a direct line of continuity links Rymenhild with her queenly forebears in Old English poetry—or indeed with the women of the pre-Conquest historic records, who clearly had a powerful say in the direction of their own lives. Too much time and history lie between. The text of *King Horn* as we have it belongs to the thirteenth century, and although we do not know its ultimate origins there is no doubt that its immediate source was not English at all but a poem written perhaps as much as a century before in Anglo-French" (Fell 175).

[26] Sidonia's desire to become a Beguine fits in with Power's comment that it "has indeed been argued that the prominent part which women played in

heretical or near-heretical movements, such as catharism, or the Order of the Béguines, was a manifestation of women's discontent with their lot in the world" (30). Sidonia certainly would find the life appealing since it was designed for women who either could not find husbands or preferred to live in chastity, thus she could avoid marrying Gendelet. Choosing to become a Beguine rather than a nun offers Sidonia the option of returning to secular life and marrying. See also Uitz (177 ff.).

[27] For example, he suggests to Herland to raise the fourteen boys in the courtly arts rather than vice-versa. Also Almair orders Horn (Pontus) to go when the court betrayer has lied. This is in stark contrast to *Pontus und Sidonia* where Pontus suggests going whereupon the king expresses his dismay since he needs Pontus.

[28] Classen also points this out (1993, 13).

[29] In *King Horn* Godhild, mother of Horn, escapes from the Saracens and prays for Horn; she also follows a Christian way of life (77–86).

[30] In *King Horn* when Horn meets Godhild again there is no crowning but he does throw a party.

[31] Gold also writes that when "in reality, the public sphere began to be more defined, and public functions previously exercised privately by the male nobility were taken over by royalty, the epics express directly the anxiety and anger of the nobility, while retaining as the valued world to be portrayed one in which the noblity itself is, or should be, in control. The epics are in this sense a kind of escape to an imagined world of past time in which traditional values were maintained" (40).

[32] In numerous saints' lives, female saints resist "bad" pagan male rulers who wish to marry and/or convert them. The saints invariably uphold God's truth and expose the frailty of earthly rule and power.

[33] My dissertation has begun this comparison.

[34] Petra Kellermann-Haaf summarizes the political activities of women in about sixty German medieval epics and romances and then analyzes the interface of *Realpolitik* and these fictional representations of female political activity.

Works Cited

Alighieri, Dante. *The Divine Comedy: Il Purgatorio*. Trans. and ed. John D. Sinclair. New York: Oxford UP, 1977.

Bell, Susan Groag. "Medieval Women Book Owners: Arbiters of Lay Piety and Ambassadors of Culture." *Sisters and Workers in the Middle Ages*. Ed. Judith M. Bennett, et al. 135–61.

Bennett, Helen T., Clare A. Lees and Gillian R. Overing. "Anglo-Saxon Studies: Gender and Power: Feminism and Old English Studies." *Medieval Feminist Newsletter* 10 (1990): 15–20.

Bennett, Judith M., Elizabeth A. Clark, Jean F. O'Barr, B. Anne Vilen, and Sarah Westphal-Wihl, eds. *Sisters and Workers in the Middle Ages*. Chicago: U of Chicago P, 1989.

Blamires, Alcuin, ed. *Woman Defamed and Woman Defended: An Anthology of Medieval Texts*. Oxford: Clarendon, 1992.

Bloch, R. Howard. "Medieval Misogyny." *Representations* 20 (1987): 1-24.

———. *Medieval Misogyny and the Invention of Western Romantic Love*. Chicago: U of Chicago P, 1991.

———. Response to *Medieval Feminist Newsletter* 6 (1988): 2-11. *Medieval Feminist Newsletter* 7 (1989): 6-10.

Burger, Heinz Otto. *Renaissance, Humanismus, Reformation: Deutsche Literatur im Europäischen Kontext*. Bad Homburg: Gehlen, 1969.

Chaucer, Geoffrey. *The Riverside Chaucer*. 3rd ed. Ed. Larry D. Benson. Boston: Houghton, 1987.

Christine de Pizan. *The Book of the City of Ladies*. Trans. Earl Jeffrey Richards. New York: Persea, 1982.

Classen, Albrecht. "Die leidende und unterdrückte Frau im Roman des 15. Jahrhunderts: Zur Verfasserschaft des frühneuhochdeutschen Romans *Pontus und Sidonia*." *Seminar* 29 (1993): 1-27.

———. "Women in Medieval Literature and Life: Their Role and Appearance—Pedagogical Perspectives in Medieval Studies." *Michigan Germanic Studies* 14 (1988): 1-15.

De La Grange. *Hugues Capet: Anciens Poetes de la France VIII*. Paris: Franck, 1864 (Neudruck: Nendeln, 1966).

Dinshaw, Carolyn. *Chaucer's Sexual Poetics*. Madison: U of Wisconsin P, 1989.

Eleonore von Österreich. *Pontus und Sidonia. Volksbücher vom sterbenden Rittertum*. Ed. Heinz Kindermann. Weimar: Böhlaus Nachf., 1928. [1500 printing]. 115-236.

Elisabeth von Nassau-Saarbrücken. *Huge Scheppel. Der Huge Scheppel der Gräfin Elisabeth von Nassau-Saarbrücken nach der Handschrift der Hamburger Stadtbibliothek: Veröffentlichungen aus der Hamburger Stadtbibliothek 1*. Ed. and Foreword Hermann Urtel. Hamburg: Gräfe, 1905.

———. *Die Königin Sibille. Der Roman von der Königin Sibille in drei Prosafassungen des 14. und 15. Jahrhunderts*. Ed. Hermann Tiemann. Hamburg: Hauswedell, 1977.

Fell, Christine with Cecily Clark and Elizabeth Williams. *Women in Anglo-Saxon England and the Impact of 1066*. Oxford: Blackwell, 1984.

Fenster, Thelma, ed. Reactions to R. Howard Bloch's work on "Medieval Misogyny." *Medieval Feminist Newsletter* 6 (1988): 2-11.

Frey, Winifred, ed. *Einführung in die deutsche Literatur des 12. bis 16. Jahrhunderts. Band 3: Bürgertum und Fürstenstaat: 15./16. Jahrhundert*. Opladen: Westdeutscher Verlag, 1981.

Gold, Penny Schine. *The Lady & the Virgin: Image, Attitude, and Experience in Twelfth-Century France*. Chicago: U of Chicago P, 1985.

Haug, Walter. "Huge Scheppel: Der Sexbesessene Metzger auf dem Lilienthron." *Wolfram-Studien XI: Chansons de Geste in Deutschland*. Ed. Joachim L. Heinzle, Peter Johnson, and Gisela Vollmann-Profe. Berlin: Schmidt, 1989. 185-205.

Kellermann-Haaf, Petra. *Frau und Politik im Mittelalter: Untersuchungen zur politischen Rolle der Frau in den höfischen Romanen des 12., 13. und 14. Jahrhunderts*. Göppingen: Kümmerle, 1986.

King Horn, Floriz and Blauncheflur, the Assumption of Our Lady. Ed. (1866) J. Rawson Lumby. Ed. (1962) George H. McKnight. Early English Text Society 58. London: Oxford UP, 1962.

Liebertz-Grün, Ursula. "Autorinnen im Umkreis der Höfe." In *Frauen—Literatur—Geschichte: Schreibende Frauen vom Mittelalter bis zur Gegenwart*. Ed. Hiltrud Gnüg und Renate Möhrmann. Stuttgart: Suhrkamp, 1989. 16-34.

Liepe, Wolfgang. *Beiträge zur Literatur- und Geistesgeschichte*. Neumünster: Wachholtz, 1963. [Reprinted from *Zeitschrift für Deutschkunde* 36, 1922: 145-61].

———. *Elisabeth von Nassau-Saarbrücken: Entstehung und Anfänge des Prosaromans in Deutschland*. Halle a.S.: Niemeyer, 1920.

Linn, Marie-Luise. Afterword to *Hug Schapler: ein lieplichs lesen und ein warhafftige Hystorij*. Deutsche Volksbücher in Faksimiledrucken. Vol. 5. Ed. Ludwig Erich Schmitt and Renate Noll-Wiemann. Hildesheim: Olms, 1974.

Lomperis, Linda. "Collaborative Work in Literature and History: What Literary Scholars Want from Historians." *Medieval Feminist Newsletter* 9 (1990): 2-5.

Mackenzie, W. Mackay. Introduction. *The Kingis Quair*. London: Faber, 1939.

Morrison, Susan Signe. *Discursive Violence: Women with Authority in Old English, Middle English, Middle High German and Early New High German Texts*. Diss. Brown U, 1991.

Müller, Günther. *Deutsche Dichtung der Renaissance und des Barocks*. Wildpark-Potsdam: Akademische Verlagsgesellschaft und Athenaion, 1927.

Müller, Jan-Dirk. "Held und Gemeinschaftserfahrung: Aspekte der Gattungstransformation im frühen deutschen Prosaroman am Beispiel des 'Huge Schapler.'" *Daphnis: Zeitschrift für Mittlere Deutsche Literatur* 9 (1980): 393-426.

———. "Rezeption." *Wolfram-Studien XI: Chansons de Geste in Deutschland*. Ed. Joachim L. Heinzle, Peter Johnson, and Gisela Vollmann-Profe. Berlin: Schmidt, 1989. 211-12.

———. "Sivrit: künec-man-eigenholt: Zur sozialen Problematik des Nibelungenliedes." *Amsterdamer Beiträge zur Älteren Germanistik* 7 (1974): 85-124.

———. "Volksbuch/Prosaroman im 15./16. Jahrhundert: Perspektiven der Forschung." *Internationales Archiv für Sozialgeschichte der deutschen Literatur*.

Ed. Wolfgang Frühwald, Georg Jäger, and Alberto Martino. Tübingen: Niemeyer, 1985.

Power, Eileen. *Medieval Women*. Ed. M. M. Postan. Cambridge: Cambridge UP, 1975.

Roloff, Hans-Gert. *Stilstudien zur Prosa des 15. Jahrunderts: Die Melusine des Thüring von Ringoltingen*. Köln: Böhlau, 1970.

Ruh, Kurt, ed. *Die deutsche Literatur des Mittelalters: Verfasserlexikon*. 2nd ed. Berlin: de Gruyter, 1977.

Scholz, Manfred Günter. *Hören und Lesen: Studien zur primären Rezeption der Literatur im 12. und 13. Jh*. Wiesbaden: Steiner, 1980.

Showalter, Elaine, ed. *The New Feminist Criticism*. New York: Pantheon, 1985.

Strayer, Joseph R. and Dana C. Munro. *The Middle Ages: 395-1500*. New York: Appleton, 1970.

Uitz, Erika. *Die Frau in der Mittelalterlichen Stadt*. Leipzig: Edition Leipzig, 1988.

Harsdörffers *Frauenzimmer Gesprächspiele* als geschlechtsspezifische Verhaltensfibel: Ein Vergleich mit heutigen Kommunikationsstrukturen

Christl Griesshaber-Weninger

This article analyzes the construction and legitimization of a gender-specific hierarchy of communication in Georg Philipp Harsdörffer's *Frauenzimmer Gesprächspiele* (1641-1649) that shows striking similarities to patterns observable today. Both the historical dimension and the durability of this construction are highlighted by correlating Harsdörffer's responses to the Baroque "querelle des femmes" with recent findings in the field of sociolinguistics. The comparison of specific examples taken from Baroque and contemporary discourse identifies some communication patterns "discovered" by linguists as diverse as Fishman, Tannen, and Trömel-Plötz as belonging to a centuries-old social organization of sexual difference. (CG-W)

Wer die zeitgenössische Diskussion um den sogenannten "Gendergap" im Sprachverhalten verfolgt hat, weiß, daß alle Bemühungen, ein für alle Mal zu definieren, was daran "essentiell" feminin und was "essentiell" maskulin ist, bisher gescheitert sind; zu sehr ist unser Blickwinkel von unserem eigenen kulturellen Standort geprägt, zu sehr sind wir ständige Opfer gängiger Stereotypen und überlieferter Konventionen. In diesem Sinne hat Karin Petersen noch vor einiger Zeit festgehalten, wie "das 'Weibliche' [immer noch] ein Stereotyp [ist], Abgrenzung und Einengung zugleich, auch in den Köpfen der Frauen. Die Unterschiede männlich-weiblich sind die, 'die durch einen bestimmten Typ von Gesellschaft so streng aufgezwungen werden, daß es uns unmöglich ist, zu wissen, welches die natürlichen Unterschiede sind'" (71). Aber gibt es "natürliche Unterschiede"? Und was bedeutet hier "so streng aufgezwungen"? Über welche Zeiträume erstrecken sich solche "Zwangsprozesse"? Und wie wirken sie sich auf unser Sprachverhalten aus? Auf diese letzte Frage versuchen seit einigen Jahren vor allem feministisch orientierte soziolinguistische Untersuchungen eine Antwort zu geben. Was ihnen bei aller Aktualität fehlt ist jedoch die historische Tiefendimension. So gelingt es ihnen zwar bis zu einem gewissen Grad, *heutige* geschlechtsspezifische Differenzen zu analysieren und zu kategorisieren, doch bleibt damit ungeklärt, wie es zu solchen Unterschieden gekommen ist und auf welche Weise sie sich in unserem Sprachverhalten festsetzen und perpetuieren konnten. In diesem Sinne versteht sich die folgende Abhandlung als Beitrag dazu, an historischem, genauer gesagt: literarhistorischem Material probehalber nachzuweisen, wie heutiges geschlechtsspezifisches Kommunikationsverhalten Produkt einer Frauenbelehrungstradition sein mag, die sich Jahrhunderte weit in die Geschichte unserer Sprache und Kultur zurückerstreckt.

Um eine solche historisch kontrastive Folie herzustellen, wende ich mich dreieinhalb Jahrhunderte zurück in die erste Hälfte des 17. Jahrhunderts. Zu dieser Zeit wird nicht nur in der damals in Europa führenden Kulturnation Frankreich, sondern bereits auch schon in Deutschland heftig über die "Frauenfrage" diskutiert; es erscheinen mehrere wissenschaftliche Abhandlungen, die sich mit der gesellschaftlichen Rolle der Frau und ihrer Erziehung befassen. Auch literarische oder religiöse Werke, die mit Ratschlägen für die Geschlechter, insbesondere natürlich für Frauen angefüllt sind, oder die sich mit zwischengeschlechtlichen Beziehungen im allgemeinen auseinandersetzen, kursieren und werden allenthalben kommentiert. Zwar wären einige dieser Schriften aus heutiger Sicht eher als frauenfeindlich denn als frauenfreundlich einzustufen, doch bieten sie gerade dadurch ein einprägsames Bild der Zeit. Innerhalb dieser Diskussion bewegt sich auch der Nürnberger Georg Philipp Harsdörffer mit seinen Schriften zur "Frauenfrage", den (Frauenzimmer) *Gesprächspielen* von 1641–1649.[1]

Der aus einem Patriziergeschlecht stammende Harsdörffer (1607–1658) lebte, abgesehen von einer längeren Bildungsreise in die Schweiz, nach Frankreich, Belgien, England und Italien, hauptsächlich in Nürnberg. Dort sammelte er auch eine literarische Gruppe, die sogenannten Pegnitz-Hirten, um sich, die nach italienischem Vorbild den Pegnesischen Blumenorden gründete. Im Gegensatz zu anderen deutschen Sprach- und Literaturgesellschaften des 17. Jahrhunderts gehört der sich vor allem an der Schäferdichtung orientierende Pegnesische Blumenorden "zur Avantgarde in der deutschsprachigen Literatur ihrer Zeit" (Böttcher 289). Ziel des Ordens, der ausdrücklich beiden Geschlechtern offenstand, war es, daß er

> seinen Landsleuten Anlaß geben möchte, als gebohrne Teutsche, sich der Reinigkeit der deutschen Sprach, so wol im Reden, als Schreiben, zu befleissigen, und, wann ja dieser Endzweck, wie er wohl voraus gesehen, bey dem gemeinen Volk nicht könnte erhalten werden, doch zum wenigsten diejenige, die durch gute Künste und Wissenschafften sich von dem Pöbel zu

unterscheiden pflegen, mit ihm, ihre Mutter=Sprach zu verbessern, sich möchten angelegen seyn lassen (Herdegen 3-4).

Bei diesem Konzept fällt sofort ins Auge, daß zwar das Geschlecht bei der Aufnahme in den Orden kein Hindernis bedeuten soll, was für die damalige Zeit in Deutschland allein schon ungewöhnlich ist, doch hat die aufzunehmende Person über die nötigen Sprachkenntnisse zu verfügen. Handelt es sich zudem um eine Frau, so muß diese zusätzlich noch edel, keusch und gelehrt sein (vgl. 255). Durch diese Einschränkung, die die Angehörigkeit zu den gehobenen Ständen des Adels und des Bürgertums voraussetzt, wird somit der Frauenzugang auf einen engen Personenkreis limitiert.[2]

In diesem Kontext sind auch die zwischen 1641 und 1649 im jährlichen Abstand veröffentlichten acht Bände der *Frauenzimmer Gesprächspiele* anzusiedeln. Hervorzuheben ist vorweg, daß Harsdörffer nur den beiden ersten Teilen—die in der folgenden Analyse als Textbasis dienen werden—diesen Titel gibt, während er sich ab dem dritten Band mit dem Titel *Gesprächspiele* begnügt. Die Bände fanden große Resonanz, die soweit ging, daß sich die darin dargestellte Art der geselligen höfischen Gesprächspiele bald vielerorts etabliert hat, wie Harsdörffer im sechsten Band (105) selbst feststellt. Die Herzogin Sophie Elisabeth von Wolfenbüttel bietet vielleicht das anschaulichste Beispiel (vgl. Brandes, "Baroque Women Writers"). Zu Gast in Nürnberg lernen sie und ihr Gemahl Herzog August die dortigen intellektuellen literarischen Gepflogenheiten kennen, woraufhin Sophie Elisabeth in Wolfenbüttel ihren eigenen literarischen Zirkel gründet, der am Muster der *Frauenzimmer Gesprächspiele* orientiert ist.

Daß gebildete Frauen wie diese Adlige von Büchern wie Harsdörffers *Frauenzimmer Gesprächspielen* besonders beeinflußt wurden, liegt natürlich an der besonderen pädagogischen Orientierung dieses Werkes, in dem es programmatisch heißt: "Das Frauenzimmer ist bey diesen Gesprächspielen eingeführet / zu Folg / der offt angezogenen Italiänischen Scribenten / welcher Erfindungen sonderlich dahinzielen / wie in dergleichen Zusammenkunfften die Zeit mit nützlicher Kurtzweil zugebracht werden möge" (III, 15). Der Autor verweist hier auf seine Vorbilder und betont den erzieherischen Gehalt seines Vorhabens, indem er den speziell für Frauen "nützlichen" Inhalt hervorhebt. Im gleichen Zusammenhang hinterfragt er das bisherige System und sucht nach den Ursachen, warum Frauen aus Gesprächen ausgeschlossen wurden und noch immer ausgeschlossen werden, und woran es liegen mochte, daß sie ihr Wissen und ihren Verstand nicht äußern konnten, durften oder sollten.

Das Beispiel der bürgerlichen Anna Maria von Schurmann (1607-1678) ist ihm schließlich Beleg dafür, daß Frauen "den Weg des Verstands zu gehen nicht verbotten [ist] / man wolle sie dann von der Gemeinschaft anderer Menschen absondern / und sie für Sinn- und

Redlose Bilder halten / Wie der Ruhm Weibliches Geschlechts Anna Maria Schurmanns in einem besonderlichen Büchlein kunstrichtig erwiesen" (III, 16). Anna Maria von Schurmann, "das Wunder des Jahrhunderts" (Bovenschen 84), ist durch ihre für damalige Verhältnisse ungewöhnliche und außerordentliche Bildung bekannt. Die Gelehrte befaßt sich in ihrer 1641 erschienenen Dissertatio *Num foeminae christianae conveniat studium litterarum?* mit dem Thema des Frauenstudiums; wie Harsdörffer bezieht sie sich dabei nur auf adlige Frauen und wohlhabende Bürgerinnen, die allein ihres Erachtens die für ein Studium nötige Muße besitzen. Für Schurmann ist die prinzipielle Begabungsgleichheit der Geschlechter die argumentative Ausgangsbasis, was natürlich eine zu diesem Zeitpunkt nicht nur heftig diskutierte, sondern auch sehr umstrittene These ist.[3] Begabungsgleichheit der Geschlechter gilt ja im 17. Jahrhundert im allgemeinen für eine mit dem religiösen Weltbild inkompatible Ansicht. Schließlich dominiert noch die im christlichen Glauben festgeschriebene Vorstellung von der Gottesebenbildlichkeit des Mannes, woraus man die gottgewollte oder auch "naturgegebene" Inferiorität der Frau ableiten zu können glaubte, eines Wesens, das Thomas Aquin einst als "animal imperfectum" (Blinn 13) kategorisiert hatte.

Schurmann jedoch bestreitet dies. In ihrer inhaltlich anspruchsvollen Dissertatio hält sie sich formal strikt an die wissenschaftlichen Bräuche der Zeit.[4] Sie tritt darin mit der These an, daß "der christlichen Frau...das Studium der Wissenschaften zu[kommt]" (Gössmann, *Frauenzimmer* 48) und stellt dies auch noch ausführlichst unter Beweis.[5] Während Schurmann von Harsdörffer noch als positives Modell vorgeführt wird und sie ihm sogar als Beleg dafür gilt, daß Frauen mit Erfolg gelehrt sein können, berufen sich andere Autoritäten in der Folgezeit wiederholt gerade auf ihren Fall, um sie als "Kronzeugin des Antifeminismus" (47) zu diffamieren. Verantwortlich dafür ist nicht zuletzt ihre spätere Zusammenarbeit mit dem Frühpietisten Jean de Labadie. Von der herrschenden Kirche wird sie nunmehr aufgrund ihrer religiösen Orientierung als "Abtrünnige" (Hanstein 31) gebrandmarkt; andere nehmen ihren Lebensweg zum Anlaß festzuhalten, wie sehr sich doch "das Studium der Wissenschaft [auch] verwirrend" (31) auf gebildete Frauen auswirken könne.

Daß sich Harsdörffer auf eine schon zu ihren Lebzeiten weitbekannte bürgerliche Gelehrte beruft, zeichnet ihn als Mann aus, der sich der Frauenfrage gegenüber zum wenigsten nicht von vornherein als voreingenommen zeigt. Das wird besonders deutlich, wenn man sein Werk im Kontext seiner Epoche betrachtet, wo in gelehrten Kreisen das Für und Wider bezüglich des Frauenstudiums mit zunehmender Intensität diskutiert wird, eine Diskussion, die in den folgenden Jahrhunderten nie mehr abbrechen sollte.[6] Johann Michael Moscherosch zum Beispiel weist in seinem mit Harsdörffers *Gesprächspielen* zeitgleichem Werk *Insomnis*.

Cura. Parentum. Christliches Vermächnuß oder, Schuldige Vorsorg eines Trewen Vatters bey jetzigen Hochbetrübtsten gefährlichsten Zeitten von 1643 darauf hin, daß "eine Jungfraw...weder fluchen noch schwehren [soll], Nimmer reden, sie werde dann gefragt: und doch so kurtz antworten, als sie immer kan" (67). In ihre Hand gehören "diese zwey Stücke: Ein Bettbuch, und Eine Spindel" (63). Mit dieser Erwartung an die Frau ist Moscherosch natürlich dem Weltbild Luthers verpflichtet, der in seiner Predigt vom Ehestand (1525) betont hatte, daß "des Weibes Wille, wie Gott saget, dem Manne unterworfen sein [soll]" (70). Soweit würde sich Harsdörffer nicht versteigen. Seine Frauen werden weder an die Spindel gesetzt, noch hält er sie zur ausschließlich religiösen Lektüre an. Johannes Henricus Mylius, ein Jurist, der sich in seiner Disputatio *De praejudiciis* (1675) ebenfalls über Frauen ausgelassen hat, schreibt schon als Sechzehnjähriger folgendes:

> Es kann allerdings nicht bestritten werden, daß ein kälteres Temperament, wie es den Frauen eignet, die Erfindungs- und Urteilskraft (ingenium et iudicium) gewissermaßen abstumpft. Zudem fehlt bei denjenigen gewöhnlich die Pflege und Ausbildung der Begabung, die meistens durch häusliche Sorge, Spinnkörbchen, Spinnrocken (Faden) und Töpfe okkupiert und selten zu schönen Künsten und Wissenschaften bestimmt sind.
> Daher verrät dieses Geschlecht häufig durch die Dreistigkeit einer zügellosen Zunge den Mangel an Urteilskraft, da es schnell und voreilig, vom Wort und Urteil anderer abhängend, unbeständig und seinen Affekten ergeben ist (Gössmann, *Frauenzimmer* 118-19).

Seine durchaus zeittypische Äußerung bezüglich der Frauenbildung bescheinigt der Frau nur negative Züge. Daß die Frau nicht für die Wissenschaften bestimmt sei, ist im übrigen der Topos der Frauenbeschreibung, gegen den sich auch Anna Maria von Schurmann zur Wehr setzen mußte. Schließlich läßt sich bei Georg Schultze (*De blanda mulierum rhetorica* 1678) nachlesen, wie sich eine "rechte" Frau zu verhalten hat: "Dazu ist eine Haußfraue erschaffen / daß sie ihren Mann erfreuen und erquicken / sich freundlich zu ihn halten (wie das hebräische Wort vermag Gen. am 2. Capitel) ihm Rede angewinnen / freundlich zusprechen / ihm den Unmuth und betrübniß außreden / mit Wahrheit und von Hertzen gegen ihren Haußwirth sich erzeigen / ihre Mannes Lust und einige Freudenmacherin seyn" (Gössmann, *Frauenzimmer* 122). Hier sehen wir die Frau auf die Rolle der Haushälterin und des Sexualobjekts reduziert.

Moscherosch, Mylius und Schultze stehen beispielhaft für die zeitgenössische frauenfeindliche Gegenposition, von der sich Harsdörffers *Gesprächspiele* deutlich absetzen. Auch Wilhelm Ignatius Schütz hält ihnen in seiner 1663 erschienenen Schrift *Ehren=Preiß Deß Hochlöblichen Frauen=Zimmers* entgegen, daß "das WeibsVolck von Natur eben so wol als der Mannsstamm zu Ubung der Tugenden und Verrichtung löblicher Thaten qualificirt sey" (Gössmann, *Frauenzimmer* 56), und er spricht sich ausdrücklich für das Frauenstudium aus.[7] Doch wird dieser Ansicht 1666 in der unter dem Pseudonym Poliandin erschienenen Schrift des Johannes Gorgias *Gestürzter Ehren=Preiß des hochlöblichen Frauen=Zimmers* widersprochen, der sich wie folgt über Frauen äußert: "Sie sind leicht vergeßlich / leicht parteyisch / leichtlich beredlich / u.s.f. So bald das Weib gebohren / hält man es gar recht zur Nadel / Spinnrad: denn weil sie sonst was zu erlernen untüchtig ist; als muß man sie ihrem Beruf gemässe Sachen lehren. Wenn mans wolte zum Studieren halten / wäre nicht zu hoffen / das sie ihrer Vergeßligkeit wegen zu was könne gebracht werden" (Gössmann, *Frauenzimmer* 82). Johannes Gorgias arbeitet mit dem misogynen Stereotyp der geschwätzigen Frau, die für das Studium zu vergeßlich und in der Konsequenz dazu unfähig ist. Seine Ansicht ist in etwa mit der von Moscherosch vergleichbar. Beide bescheinigen der Frau wenig intellektuellen Sprachraum, geschweige denn die Möglichkeit zur sinnvollen (zwischengeschlechtlichen) Kommunikation.

1629 entstand ferner die *Disputatio philosophica de mulieribus* von Godofredus Cundisius / Johannes Bergmann, und 1671/1676 erschien *Diatribe academica de foeminarum eruditione* zwei unter einem Titel veröffentlichte Abhandlungen von Jacob Thomasius, Johannes Sauerbrei und Jacob Smalcius. Bergmann beruft sich in seinem Werk auf die Frauen von Natur aus übertragenen häuslichen Pflichten, zu denen das Studium der schönen Literatur *nicht* zu rechnen sei. Im Gegenteil, gebildete Frauen neigen—wie "weise Männer" kundgetan haben (Gössmann, *Frauenzimmer* 37)—zur Begierde und zur ausschweifenden, der männlichen Kontrolle sich entziehenden Lebensart. *Diatribe academica de foeminarum eruditione* gestattet demgegenüber der Frau zwar zu studieren, läßt sie aber "von Natur der Macht (imperium) des Mannes unterworfen [sein]. Die Vernunft, die dem Schöpfer ohne Zweifel als Gesetz diente," heißt es dem Rationalismus gemäß mit bemerkenswerter Logik weiter, "fordert nämlich das Übergewicht an Begabung bei dem, der befiehlt" (Gössmann, *Frauenzimmer* 101). Beide Ansätze zielen auf Dominanz des einen und Unterwerfung des anderen Geschlechts. Diese explizite Art der Frauenfeindlichkeit läßt das Werk Harsdörffers vermissen.

* * *

Harsdörffer hat als vielbelesener und vergleichsweise gut gereister Literat vornehmlich weitergegeben, "was er in Geschichte und Gegenwart eingesammelt hatte," meint Böttcher (292), und man kann davon ausgehen, daß es sich bei seinen Spielen nicht um einen rein imaginierten Diskurs handelt, sondern daß diese Art des Gesprächs und der Dialogform (wie sie teilweise auch im *Pegnesischen Schäfergedicht* anzutreffen ist) "die Schüler schon auf den Lateinschulen lernten, und gewiß haben sich auch die Schäfer während ihrer Zusammenkünfte mit solchen Spielen unterhalten" (*Pegnesisches Schäfergedicht*. Nachwort 22). In dem Grad wie nun auch Frauen zu diesen Spielen zugelassen werden, ist man bestrebt, ihnen entsprechende Instruktionen zur "munteren geselligen Plauderei" (Hanstein 50) zu erteilen. Daß sie dieser Lehre bedürfen, läßt jedoch gleichzeitig darauf schließen, daß es sich bei dem Spiel- und Dialogsdiskurs der *Frauenzimmer Gesprächspiele* in erster Linie um eine erlernte Kunstsprache handelt. Entsprechend ihrem geschlechtsspezifisch unterschiedlichen Erziehungshintergrund steht diese Sprache den Frauen des gehobenen Bürgerstandes und des Adels, die ja die Lateinschule nicht besuchen durften und zumeist von Hauslehrern unterrichtet wurden, nicht so ausgeprägt zur Verfügung.

In diesem Sinne liefern uns Harsdörffers *Frauenzimmer Gesprächspiele* Auskünfte unterschiedlichster Art, denn sie illustrieren nicht nur das damalige Wissen und Denken, sondern eben auch die Umgangs-, Verhaltens- und Sprachformen bestimmter gesellschaftlicher Kreise und Schichten. Sie widerspiegeln somit ein als nachahmenswert ausgegebenes geschlechtsspezifisches Verhalten. Die *Frauenzimmer Gesprächspiele* wollen ein "unvermercktes" (II, 61), meint Harsdörffer selbst, also ein unbewußtes Modell für die Lesenden darstellen, die auf subtile, subliminale Weise beeinflußt werden sollen.

Harsdörffers Figuren in den *Gesprächspielen* stammen alle aus dem Adel und den obersten Bürgerschichten. Sie werden wie folgt vorgestellt: "Angelica von Keuschewitz / eine Adeliche Jungfrau. Reymund Discretin / ein gereist-und belesener Student. Julia von Freudenstein / ein kluge Matron. Vespasian von Lustgau / ein alter Hofmann. Cassandra Schönlebin / eine Adeliche Jungfrau. Degenwert von Ruhmeck / ein verständiger und gelehrter Soldat" (I, 22). Diese Typen führen natürlich "sprechende Namen" (Böttcher 302). Hess geht im übrigen davon aus, daß sich Harsdörffer am stärksten mit Reymund Discretin identifiziert, der als vielgereister und belesener Student am ehesten den Typus des an deutschen Höfen zugelassenen bürgerlichen Gelehrten repräsentiert. Nicht zuletzt ist er es auch, der sich—außer den Frauen—innerhalb der *Frauenzimmer Gesprächspiele* wiederholt für die Integration und Bildung der Frau ausspricht.

Innerhalb der *Frauenzimmer Gesprächspiele* geht es darum, Kurzweil auf höfische Art zu vertreiben. Es sitzen sich dabei drei Frauen und drei Männer gegenüber. Die Männer werden aufgrund ihres Berufes und ihrer Beschäftigung klassifiziert, während die Frauen anhand ihres (Familien-)Standes definiert sind. Es fällt sofort auf, daß die Sprechbeteiligung sehr ungleich verteilt ist, denn die Männer sprechen weitaus häufiger und ausführlicher als die Frauen. Auch innerhalb der Geschlechter ist die Rangordnung ungleich: den älteren Menschen wird mehr Sprachraum zugestanden als den jüngeren; bei den Männern sticht Vespasian mit Abstand heraus, und die Matrone Julia redet um einiges mehr als die Jungfrauen. Daß der erste Teil von Vespasian und der zweite Teil von Julia begonnen wird, unterstreicht diese Beobachtung. Diese Darstellungsart der Konversationsform illustriert deutlich die zur Barockzeit übliche Konvention des Diskurses, in dem die Umgangs- und Verhaltensweisen sowie die Sprachformen stets von der sozialen Klasse, dem Geschlecht und dem Alter dirigiert werden. Die daraus resultierenden unterschiedlichen Verhaltensweisen und Kommunikationsformen der Geschlechter wollen wir im folgenden näher beleuchten.

Als erste Verhaltenskonstante fällt sofort die Konzentration der Frauen auf ihren engeren Lebensbereich auf.[8] Dazu gehören Äußerungen über die Mode im In- und Ausland (I, 119 f.), das Schminken sowie über die Zubereitung von Speisen. In einer Bemerkung Cassandras erscheinen die beiden letzten Bereiche sogar gedanklich verknüpft: "Ich wolte abbringen," meint sie, "die böse Gewonheit sich zu schminken / und das Angesicht mit fremden Farben zu bemahlen: und aufbringen / daß man wie vor etlich hundert Jahren / an stat des Zuckers und der Gewürtze nur Honig / Saltz gebrauchet" (28-29). Der von Männern besprochene Erfahrungsbereich handelt stattdessen vom Trinken (26) und von Macht (92). Die von ihnen aufgegriffenen Themen sind eher abstrakter Natur wie die Dolmetscherkunst (290), Rang- und Klassenunterschiede (58) oder die Sinnbildkunst (72).

Daß auch die Beteiligten selbst durchaus zwischen den Geschlechtern große Unterschiede zu machen wissen, zeigt sich z.B. daran, wenn Vespasian vom "geschwinden Verstand" (30) von Frauenzimmern spricht, eine Geliebte mit Luzifer verglichen wird (46) oder das Weib primär in Verbindung mit Gebären gesehen wird (57). Angelica sagt schließlich: "Kundbar ist / daß die Weibspersonen von Jugendauf zu den Künsten und Wissenschaften nicht angehalten / auch wegen ihrer Blödigkeit deroselben fast unfähig geachtet werden" (281). Aus solchen Betrachtungen geht deutlich hervor, daß die geschlechtsspezifischen Andersartigkeiten von den Figuren keineswegs nur beobachtend neutral festgestellt, sondern eindeutig wertend aufgefaßt und vermittelt werden. Dabei wird die Frau—etwas überspitzt formuliert—reduziert auf "unwissend und gebärend".

Für unsere Zwecke wichtiger sind jedoch die geschlechtsspezifischen Unterschiede, die sich aus dem Sprachverhalten der benutzten Figurengruppe ergeben. Bemerkenswert ist zunächst, wie Frauen häufig auf die Aussagen und Äußerungen der Männer dadurch reagieren, daß sie Bitten äußern (281) oder Fragen stellen. Schon im ersten Gespräch, als das Spiel eingeführt wird, wird der Redefluß Vespasians immer wieder durch Julias knappe, aber präzise Zwischenfragen unterbrochen: "Warum wird solche Kurtzweil von den Herren mit dem Namen der Gesprechspiel bemerket?"

(24), "So können unter den Gesprechspielen allerley Fragen begriffen werden?" (25), "Welcher Gestalt müssen dann solche Fragen vorgetragen werden?" (25). Die Männer fragen zwar gelegentlich auch, aber mit Abstand seltener. Innerhalb dieses Frageverhaltens lassen sich wiederum verschiedene Kategorien ausdifferenzieren:

- Frauen fragen, um mehr Information zu erhalten (24, 25, 69, 75, 104, 113, 124, 237, 242)
- oder sie wollen einen Rat (96, 113, 164, 170, 216). Angelica fragt: "Wie aber / wenn jemand in der Gesellschaft nichts weiß darzu zu sagen?" (92).
- Beides erhalten sie in der Regel, indem sie eine kurze Zwischenfrage stellen (95, 96,105,167, 178 , 237, 242, Teil 2: 29, 68, 240).
- Darüber hinaus stellen sie lebensbezogene, praktische Fragen. "Wie aber?" (68), erkundigt sich Cassandra, als darüber diskutiert wird, ob man Gedächtnisgebrechen beeinflussen kann. Angelica äußert an anderer Stelle: "Wann man die Sachen von aussen ansihet / möchte ich wol wissen / wie man sich doch kleiden müste / daß es jederman gefiele" (117). Cassandra möchte dagegen wissen, "ob die Jungfrauen jedesmals sollen vorgehen?" (298).

Weiter ist zu beobachten, wie sich Frauen in den *Frauenzimmer Gesprächspielen* gegenseitig solidarisch unterstützen, wenn sie von einem Mann kritisiert werden. In einer Szene (27) korrigiert Vespasian eine Aussage der Frau Julia, in der sie sich mit dem Thema des Trinkens befaßt. Julia bedankt sich für den "wolgemeinten Unterricht," kontert aber umgehend, daß doch jeder die Macht haben soll, "seine Meinung ungescheut zu eröffnen." Diese Ansicht wird von Angelica sofort bekräftigt. Statt sich mundtot machen zu lassen, weil sie als Frauen eine andere Einstellung zum Trinken haben, ist ihrem Argument durch diese Art der weiblichen Solidarität eine größere Wirkung beschieden.

Neben solchen bestärkenden Verhaltensweisen fällt auf, daß Frauen ihr Wissen vielfach auch herunterspielen, etwa um zu betonen, wie sie etwas nicht oder nur unzureichend wissen oder verstehen (27, 40, 42, 51, 52, 69, 86, 94, 128, 148, 191, 206, 300, 305), woraufhin ihnen von den Männern umgehend die Antwort erteilt wird. Im Gegensatz zu den Frauen tun die Männer ihr Wissen im Diskurs häufig demonstrativ kund, bedienen sich dabei einer komplizierten Sprache und streuen trotz des Protests seitens der Frauen unzählige Fremdwörter in ihre Gespräche ein (74). Nicht selten belehren die Männer die Frauen (53, 75, 84, 92, 94) oder berichtigen sie sogar (146). Der Mann redet stets bestimmt und mit einer unbedingten Überzeugung; Frauen neigen eher dazu, diplomatische Wendungen einzusetzen wie "wann so zu reden verlaubet ist" (56, 110). Nur in der Sprache der Frau zeigt sich eine Konstruktion, die den generischen maskulinen Artikel zu umgehen erlaubt, insofern als sie gleichzeitig die maskuline und feminine Form erfaßt ("daß der / oder die" 57). Durch die Einführung dieser frauenspezifischen Redeformel wird von Harsdörffer unterschwellig der Sachverhalt thematisiert, daß es innerhalb der Sprache Strukturen gibt, die Frauen ausschließen und ihre Präsenz im Diskurs spürbar herabsetzen.

Was Harsdörffers im Ansatz "frauenfreundliche" Sprachdarstellung zum mindesten belegt, ist die Tatsache, wie semantisch nuanciert das geschlechtsspezifische Sprachbewußtsein bereits zur Zeit des Barock sein kann. Wenn dieser Sprachgebrauch dann nicht konsequent durchgehalten ist, so ist das eben nicht anders als wie bei der Rechtschreibung. Im übrigen verwenden Frauen und Männer vergleichbare syntaktische Strukturen, nur daß die Frauen eben bedeutend weniger reden, auffallend viele Fragen stellen und sich an die barocke Bescheidenheitsetikette halten, indem sie ihre Unwissenheit (und somit ihre Inferiorität) unterstreichen. Auch verhalten sich die Frauen darüber hinaus kritisch gegenüber Lob (31), indem sie Information der männlichen Höflichkeit vorziehen (106), was wie eine subtile Kritik am höfisch höflichen "small talk" wirkt. Hier bedient sich der Gelehrte Harsdörffer der Stimme einer Frau, um höfische Gesprächsformen anzuprangern, hinter denen der eigentliche Inhalt verloren geht.

Während die Frauen stets bereit sind, Kritik zu empfangen, sind die Männer umgekehrt bereit, Anweisungen zu verteilen und zu belehren (53, 54, 75, 84, 92, 94, 146). Doch auch die Frau kann in Ausnahmefällen Wissen demonstrieren (69, 131); als sich Julia z.B. hinsichtlich der Sinnbildkunst und dem Zeichnen des Ölbaumes auf den biblischen Zusammenhang beruft, wird sie von Reymund eines Besseren belehrt (88). Andernorts finden wir die Frau als die Schweigsame typologisiert (96, 175). Tendiert die Frau dazu, Sachverhalte zu vereinfachen oder nur vage anzudeuten (109, 130), so betonen die Männer die Komplexität der Dinge (100). Die Männer berufen sich auf eine Autorität; Frauen wissen dagegen nicht immer eine Quelle anzugeben (168) oder zeigen sich eher dazu bereit, ihre Beispiele aus der eigenen Privatsphäre zu schöpfen. Sie betonen ihr Defizit, indem sie sagen, daß sie lernen wollen, und geben den Anschein, als dürsteten sie nach Bildung. Am Ende des ersten Teils steht für die Frauen daher fest, daß sie dieses Spiel gerne weiterführen möchten, weil es ihnen "Unterricht" (322) bietet.

Genau das wird ihnen dann im zweiten Teil geboten. Zwar beginnt in diesem Teil eine Frau mit dem Spiel, doch setzt sich die ungleiche Sprechlänge zwischen den Geschlechtern auch hier zugunsten des Mannes fort; es läßt sich daher dieselbe "weibliche" Fragestrategie wie im ersten Teil beobachten. Selbst als es um das Thema Jungfrau geht und Julia vorbringt: "So kan ich doch den HErrn versichern / daß viel vermeinen / es ärgern sich die jungen Leut / aus offt besagtem Büchlein der Gesprächspiel / vorgebend / es sey den Jungf. viel nohtwendiger mit der

Nadel und Spindel zuspielen / als sich mit müssigen Gesprächen zu belustigen" (51), reagieren die Männer darauf mit langen ausführlichen Erklärungen. Während die Frauen nicht mehr zu Wort kommen, wird den Männern eine Sprache in den Mund gelegt, die die folgende Reaktion seitens der Frauen provoziert: "Wollen die Herrn haben daß wir ihnen sollen zuhören / so geruhen sie zu reden / daß wirs allerseits verstehen können" (55). Daraus geht nicht allein hervor, daß die Jungfrauen zu diesem Thema, das ja eigentlich "ihr" Thema ist, keine eigene Meinung haben (sollen) und deshalb folglich keine äußern können, sondern auch, daß ihre Redefreiheit de facto von den gesellschaftlichen Verhaltensmaßregeln beschnitten wird. Wir finden das in den *Gesprächspielen* in den verschiedensten Kontexten bestätigt. "Was haben aber die Jungfrauen bey solchen neuen und unbekanten Spielen zu thun?" fragt einmal Angelica," worauf die Antwort lautet: "Sie sollen ihnen gefallen lassen zuzuhören / und ihre Meinung darvon sagen / welcher unter vorwesenden Vorschlägen ihres Erachtens der Beste seye" (320). Zuhören also, um danach ihr Urteil abzugeben, nicht mitdiskutieren, das ist die an die Frau gestellte soziale Erwartungshaltung. Als bei der Diskussion der Sinnbildkunst die Frauen nicht viel zu sagen wissen, kommentiert Vespasian, daß sich das Spiel auch so führen läßt, daß "das Frauenzimmer außer Gutheißung / oder Widersprechen / nichts darzu zu sagen schuldig" (I, 96) ist. Umgekehrt kommen spezielle Frauenthemen, die die Männer sprachlos lassen, gar nicht erst vor. Unterordnung und Zuhören ist die männliche Erwartung an die Frau, selbst im Gesprächspiel, wo es um den Dialog zwischen den Geschlechtern geht.

Daß Harsdörffer seine Frauen mit dieser Erwartungshaltung konform gehen läßt, entspricht natürlich nur den Konventionen der Zeit. Daß er aber eine Frau als Vermittlerin dieser Verhaltenserwartung einsetzt, macht umso deutlicher, mit welch subtiler Didaktik er die Unterordnung der Frau unter das Wort des Mannes für sein lesendes Publikum zu steuern weiß. Karin A. Wurst kommt bezüglich der Leserin, der ein ständiges Schweigen vorgehalten wird, zu der Beobachtung, daß dies Einfluß auf ihr tatsächliches Handeln haben könne (vgl. 633). So werden es Frauen nach der Lektüre der *Gesprächspiele* als ihre "natürliche" Aufgabe ansehen, zuzuhören; Männern hingegen wird suggeriert, daß sie "das Sagen haben". Der thematische Sprachraum und das formale Sprachverhalten sowohl von Männern als auch von Frauen werden auf diese Weise von Harsdörffer zwecks Bekräftigung der patriarchalen Gliederung der zwischenmenschlichen Kommunikationsstrukturen präzisiert und legitimiert.

Verhält sich nun eine Person nicht diesen in den *Gesprächspielen* entworfenen Richtlinien gemäß, so kann ihr vom jeweiligen Spielleitenden (in der Regel die Person, die ein Thema eingeführt und somit eine neue Spielrunde eingeläutet hat) eine Strafe abverlangt werden. Während die

Frauen im allgemeinen zu ihrer Strafe stehen, sie also nicht hinterfragen oder gar abwenden wollen, debattieren die Männer, sobald ihnen das zugeteilte Strafmaß nicht behagt (60). Gelegentlich steuern sie die Strafverteilung, beispielsweise eine Pfandgabe, solange, bis sie im Grunde keine wirkliche Strafe mehr erdulden müssen. Diese Beredtheit der Männer begegnet uns auch in Situationen, da eine Frau keine Geschichte zu erzählen weiß (106, 189, 246); in diesen Fällen führt der Mann das Spiel weiter, während die Frau bloße Zuhörende bleibt. In diesem Zusammenhang wird auch der Umstand unterstrichen, daß es Bereiche wie den kaufmännischen gibt (240), die den Männern vorbehalten sind und wo sich Frauen nicht auskennen, sie sich daher auch nicht darüber äußern können.

Die Rolle der Frau bei den *Frauenzimmer Gesprächspielen* kann zusammenfassend als recht eng und auf das Zuhören und Bewerten des Gehörten eingeschränkt beschrieben werden. Auch werden Initiativen, Ideen oder gar neue Spiele von den Frauen nicht erwartet. Ihre Bestimmung beschränkt sich in aller Regel darauf, passiv zu sein und sich den männlichen Gesprächspartnern unterzuordnen. Dennoch darf nicht übersehen werden, daß die Frauen der *Frauenzimmer Gesprächspiele* für die damalige Zeit durchaus häufig zu Wort kommen, und vor allem, daß sie in den Spielen als Teilnehmende völlig integriert sind. Insofern sind sie für den Gesprächsverlauf unerläßlich. Harsdörffers Dialogverteilung illustriert deshalb sowohl, wie sorgfältig und vorwärtsweisend er eine Rolle konzipiert, die der Frau einen erweiterten diskursiven Aktionsradius einräumt, als auch wie er bei seiner Geschlechterdarstellung trotz allem einem festgefügten Weltbild gehorcht, das der Rolle der Frauen nach wie vor recht enge Grenzen setzt.

Wenn in den *Frauenzimmer Gesprächspielen* Frauen im Spiel und im Dialog integriert werden, so entspricht dies im Kontext des Barock durchaus einer frauenfreundlichen Darstellungsabsicht. Die Frauen der *Gesprächspiele* stellen hier keine bloßen Randfiguren mehr dar, die völlig stimmlos dem Mann untergeordnet wären. Selbst wenn ihnen keine gleichberechtigte Rolle beim Gespräch zufällt, sind sie doch innerhalb der Gesprächsrunde unerläßlich, schließlich sind sie es, die von den Männern belehrt werden. Daß es sich dabei natürlich nur um adlige und gelehrte bürgerliche Frauen handelt, die zu jener Zeit Zugang zu dieser Art der Kommunikationsgemeinschaft hatten, versteht sich von selbst.

Harsdörffers psychologisch durchaus subtile Darstellung einer sechsköpfigen Gesprächsrunde beim Spiel läßt auf ein detailliertes Aufnahmevermögen, präzise Beobachtungsgabe und wohlwollende Einfühlungsfähigkeit seitens des Autors schließen. Seine Figuren erfüllen nicht nur spielerisch, sondern auch didaktisch ihren Zweck, denn sie dienen den Lesenden als Modell, an dem sie sich orientieren können. Seine GesprächsteilnehmerInnen haben folglich in erster Linie exemplarischen

Charakter, sie sind nicht als wirklichkeitsgetreue Wiedergabe damaliger Umgangsformen zu verstehen, sondern stehen als pädagogisch stilisierte Figuren in engem Zusammenhang mit Harsdörffers utopischer Weltsicht. So sollen jene Frauen und Männer, die die *Frauenzimmer Gesprächspiele* lesen, durch ihre Lektüre dazu angeregt werden, ihr Gesprächs- und Sozialverhalten zu modifizieren, so daß auf beiden Seiten sensiblere Erwartungen voneinander entstehen oder schon bestehende Erwartungen verstärkt werden und sich vertiefen. Nicht zu übersehen ist dabei allerdings aus heutiger Warte, wie alle dargestellten kommunikativen Verhaltensregeln nach wie vor in eindeutig limitierender Weise am Geschlecht festgemacht werden.

* * *

Wie aber steht es um unsere heutigen kommunikativen Verhaltensregeln? Innerhalb der letzten zwanzig Jahre sind im Bereich der Soziolinguistik vermehrt Untersuchungen angestellt worden, die sich mit möglicherweise geschlechtsspezifischem Sprachverhalten von Frauen und Männern befassen. Sprachformen und Sprechstil der Geschlechter werden hierbei auf der Basis heutiger kommunikativer Kontexte beobachtet und analysiert. Dabei wird unter anderem immer wieder bemerkt, wie Männer beim Gespräch dominieren und wie sich Frauen alternativer rhetorischer Strategien bedienen müssen, um "zu Wort" zu kommen. D.h., es treten Kommunikationsdifferenzen auf, wie wir sie schon in Harsdörffers *Frauenzimmer Gesprächspielen* entdecken konnten. Wenn ich im folgenden näher auf solche Parallelen eingehe, geschieht das in der Absicht, der zeitgenössischen linguistischen Debatte anhand der *Frauenzimmer Gesprächspiele* probeweise jene bislang meist fehlende literarhistorische Tiefendimension hinzuzufügen. Das aber erlaubt wiederum konkrete Rückschlüsse im Hinblick auf die Frage nach den Entstehungsgründen und der möglichen Geltungsdauer solches geschlechtsspezifischen Sprachverhaltens.

Angesichts der Jahrhunderte lang von Männern propagierten und aufrechterhaltenen Vorstellung und Norm, daß sich der Wirkungskreis der Frau auf Familie und Glaubensgemeinde zu beschränken hat, ihr in anderen Dingen aber kein Urteil zusteht—was bekanntlich von Luthers Lehre bekräftigt und perpetuiert wurde—und angesichts der bis in die Antike zurückreichenden Maßregel, daß die beste Frau diejenige sei, von der man am wenigsten spricht, gelangt Senta Trömel-Plötz in ihrem Buch *Frauensprache: Sprache der Veränderung* zu dem Schluß: "Gebote und Verbote überall und von alters her, was unser [weibliches] Sprechen betrifft" (28). "Gebote und Verbote"—die Formulierung deutet schon an, daß Frauen zu allen Zeiten damit fertig werden mußten, von der Teilnahme an bestimmten Bereichen des offiziellen Diskures ausgeschlossen zu sein. Gleichzeitig verlangt jede solche Ausklammerung Strategien der versteckten Beteiligung. Trömel-Plötz selbst weist z.b. darauf hin, wie "Frauen...sehr viel mehr Fragen als Männer [stellen]—auch bei gleichem Wissensstand" (98), eine Beobachtung, die sie bei allen Klassen macht, die von ihr untersucht wurden. Frauen leiten demzufolge ihre Fragen kaum ein und neigen in der Regel eher dazu, Einzelfragen zu stellen statt ausführliche Fragenkomplexe zu entwickeln. Diesem knappen Frageverhalten steht das elaborierte Sprachverhalten der Männer gegenüber, die ihr Wissen oft zuerst weitschweifig unter Beweis stellen, ehe sie zur Ausformulierung ihrer eigentlichen Frage kommen. Es wurde beobachtet, daß über 71% der Männer Fragen mit solchen Einleitungen versehen, während dasselbe Verhalten seitens der Frau lediglich 19% beträgt (155).

Wie wir gesehen haben, sind es auch in Harsdörffers *Frauenzimmer Gesprächspielen* stets die Frauen, die die meisten Fragen stellen; desgleichen sind ihre Fragen in aller Regel kurz und bündig, zugleich aber prägnant. Robin Lakoff, die ebenfalls diese Art "femininen" Verhaltens am Beispiel moderner Gesprächssituationen untersucht hat und sie als Zeichen weiblicher Unsicherheit auslegt, wird jedoch von Pamela Fishman widersprochen, die in Fragen stattdessen "powerful utterances" (94) zu entdecken vermeint. Fishman erkennt, daß eine Frage immer eine zweiteilige Sequenz eröffnet; indem Frauen Fragen stellen, werden sie aktiv und beteiligen sich an der Gestaltung des Gesprächsablaufs. Sie leisten dadurch ebensoviel—wenn nicht sogar mehr—wie Männer, um eine Konversation nicht nur zuerst in Gang zu bringen, sondern sie dann auch noch am Leben zu erhalten. "The failure of the women's attempts at interaction," kommentiert deshalb Fishman,

> is not due to anything inherent in their talk, but to the failure of the men to respond, to do interactional work. The success of the men's attempts is due to the women doing interactional work in response to remarks by the men. Thus, the definition of what is appropriate or inappropriate conversation becomes the man's choice (98).

Fishmans Deutung solcher Kommunikationsabläufe wird von Forschungsergebnissen von Deborah Tannen untermauert. Sie hat in ihrer teilweise umstrittenen Studie über zwischengeschlechtliche Kommunikationsprobleme *You Just Don't Understand* festgestellt, daß ein wesentlicher Teil der Kommunikationsabläufe gar nicht vom gesprochenen Wort getragen wird, wobei ihr Fazit lautet: "Much—even most—meaning in conversation does not reside in the words spoken at all, but is filled in by the person listening" (37). Das will besagen, daß dem bisher als passiv bewerteten Zuhören eine aktivere Rolle als bisher angenommen zugeschrieben werden muß. Tannen weist z.B. nach, wie der Mann durch kurze "weibliche" Zwischenfragen ermuntert wird weiterzureden, weil die Frau damit ihr Interesse bekundet und ihre Hörbereitschaft signalisiert.

Die kurze Zwischenfrage ist folglich nicht als Passivität mißzudeuten, sondern eher als ein signifikanter "Marker" innerhalb einer zwischenmenschlichen kommunikativen Sequenz zu begreifen. Daß diese Technik von Frauen eher bevorzugt wird als von Männern, hängt damit zusammen, daß "the men's style is more literally focused on the message level of talk, while the women's is focused on the relationship or metamessage level" (142). Für Männer bedeutet das Zuhören vorwiegend, sich dem Gegenüber unterzuordnen; das aber wird als Schwäche ausgelegt und widerspricht ihrer Vorstellung von Männlichkeit.[9]

Bezeichnenderweise paßt auch das Sprachverhalten von Harsdörffers Frauen- und Männergestalten in dieses Schema. Die Frauen zeigen sich hier in dem Sinne aktiv am Gespräch beteiligt, als sie durch ihre Art zu fragen in der Lage sind, die Männer zum Weiterreden zu animieren, was diese denn auch gerne tun. Wenn die Frauen nun Wendungen gebrauchen wie: "So viel ich mit meiner schwachen Vernunfft ergreiffen kan" (I, 40), "und wo es vieleicht vonnöthen / mich eines bessern zu berichten erbietig ist" (42), "ob ich wol in diesen Sachen wenig erfahren bin" (51), so könnte man diese Äußerungen, außer sie als zeitgemäße Formeln der Bescheidung und Höflichkeit einzustufen, oder wie Karin A. Wurst, als Zeugen der "Nicht-Wissenden" (632) auch wohl als Zeichen und Bestätigung des Minderwertigkeitsgefühls von Frauen ansehen. Es wäre jedoch zu einseitig, mit Trömel-Plötz anklagend festzustellen, wie ein solches Verhalten unterschiedslos eine bloße "negative Erwartung" perpetuiere, die "uns zum Verhängnis [wird], denn es hat einen Einfluß darauf, wie wir reden. Wir reden mit weniger Sicherheit, Selbstverständlichkeit, Selbstbehauptung und Autorität. Wir schränken ein, was wir sagen, wir drücken uns vorsichtig, unbestimmt, tentativ aus, wir entschuldigen uns und werten uns selber ab" (29). Der Mechanismus der Selbstabwertung wie der des Fragens erfüllt nämlich auch die gegenläufige Funktion, Frauen, die vom Diskurs oder von bestimmten thematischen Teildiskursen ausgeschlossen sind, mitsteuernd einzubeziehen. Dies ist für gebildete Frauen, wie man an Harsdörffers Frauenfiguren erkennt, seit alters her eine Taktik der Integration statt eine der Ausschließung: das erklärt zum Teil sicher auch die positive Resonanz seiner Schriften bei den höfisch gebildeten Frauen seiner Zeit. Selbstabwertung muß demnach auch als aktive Strategie im Kommunikationsgeschehen erkannt werden, zumal es "bis weit ins 19. Jahrhundert hinein" der Norm in höfischen und gelehrten Kreisen entspricht, daß Männer allein als "die offiziellen Vermittler von Wissen und Bildung" (Becker-Cantarino 171) gelten. Die Integration kann nur über den Umweg der vorgeschützten Unterordnung gelingen, d.h. nur dadurch, daß an der Rollenverteilung zumindest nach Außen hin nicht gerüttelt wird.

So hat die Tradition der progressiven Frauenbelehrung—in die sich ja Harsdörffers *Frauenzimmer Gesprächspiele* einordnen lassen—eine doppelte Stoßrichtung. Indem sie Frauen dazu anleitet, sich erfolgreich, d.h. auf von Männern sanktionierte Weise am Diskurs zu beteiligen, wird dazu beigetragen, ihnen einen größeren Wirkungsradius zu sichern; gleichzeitig erlaubt sie weibliche Verhaltensstrukturen und Sprachformen zu konstruieren und definieren, die männlicher Kontrolle unterstehen. Selbst wenn also Harsdörffers Utopie einer standesvermischten Kommunikation, wo er innerhalb einer absolutistischen Standesgesellschaft gebildetes Bürgertum und Adel gesellig miteinander kommunizieren läßt, sich kaum noch auf die heutige Gesellschaftsstruktur des industrialisierten Westens übertragen läßt, so ist nicht von der Hand zu weisen, daß "Rückstände" dieser historisch vorkommenden geschlechtsspezifischen Strukturen auch noch heute unsere zwischenmenschlichen Umgangsformen charakterisieren.

Selbst wenn hier festgestellt werden muß, daß viele der in Harsdörffers Werk nachweislichen weiblichen Verhaltensformen heute noch, d.h. drei Jahrhunderte später, in ähnlicher Form kurrent sind, so ist das kein Anzeichen dafür, daß wir es hier mit etwaigem geschlechtsspezifisch "natürlichem" Verhalten zu tun haben, ganz im Gegenteil; damit ist allenfalls gesagt, daß Sprachformen wie die Frageverteilung unter Männern und Frauen über solch lange Zeiträume hinweg "antrainierte" Eigenschaften geblieben sind, daß sie aber ohne die nötige historische Tiefendimension heute manchem als "natürlich" erscheinen mögen. Die Konstanz der Sprachregelung ist ein Hinweis auf die außerordentliche Wirkungsmächtigkeit nicht nur der allgemeinen gesellschaftlichen Sozialisationsformen und -formeln von Frauen (und Männern), sondern im engeren Sinne auch Beleg für die erhebliche didaktische Wirksamkeit solcher Diskursformen wie der Literatur, wozu unter anderem eben auch Harsdörffers *Frauenzimmer Gesprächspiele* gehören. Die Parallelen, die hier hervorgearbeitet werden konnten, sollen unterstreichen, daß jene Strukturen, weil sie über Jahrhunderte hinweg von Frauen und Männern gleichermaßen adaptiert, internalisiert und perpetuiert wurden, historische Strukturen sind und sich gerade nicht auf etwaige geschlechtsspezifisch biologische Differenzen zurückführen lassen. Gleichzeitig zeigt sich, daß viele ursprünglich modellhaft explizite Formen des geschlechtsspezifischen Verhaltens uns heute nur noch als implizite Verhaltensweisen begleiten und wir uns daher selten ihrer Geschichte und ihrer Geschichtlichkeit bewußt werden.

Daß wir bei unserem historischen Vergleich zwischen kommunikativen Strukturen heute und denjenigen von vor dreihundert Jahren auf Parallelen stießen, macht zum Schluß auch deutlich, wie festgefahren und vor allem—Ursache und Resultat dieser Festgefahrenheit zugleich—langfristig konditioniert menschliches Verhalten doch ist. Das, was wir heute geschlechtsspezifisch beobachten—auch wenn es dazu derzeit erst im Ansatz Untersuchungen gibt, und manche davon zu einseitig und kontextlos erhoben wurden (vgl. Barrie Thorne et al.)—resultiert aus der Langzeitwirkung von geschlechtsspezifischen diskursiven Modellen und aus dem Fortdauern von internalisierten Verhaltensweisen und Denkstrukturen bei beiden Geschlechtern. Die über Jahrhunderte zurückreichende, teilweise durchaus wohlmeinende patriarchale Literatur der Frauenbelehrung trug, so ließ sich zeigen, zur Bildung von internalisierten Sprach- und Verhaltensformen seitens beider Geschlechter bei. Es polarisierten sich Lehrende und zu Belehrende, während die Trennungslinie zwischen beiden Gruppen stets am Geschlecht gezogen wurde. Dieses Muster zu durchbrechen und folglich zu einem präskriptionslosen Konversationsmodell zu gelangen, in dem es keine Geschlechtsschranken gibt, also ein Konversationsmuster zu etablieren, das nicht von vornherein durch konventionelle Macht- und Rollenverteilung sowie traditionelle Normvorstellungen festgelegt ist, ist derzeit eine gewiß utopische Vorstellung. Denn Veränderungen von Kommunikationsstrukturen sind nun mal Prozesse, die sich nur über ausgedehnte Zeiträume hinweg vollziehen, und es bedarf der Mitwirkung aller an den Kommunikationsprozessen Beteiligten, um eine ausgewogenere Rollenverteilung herbeizuführen. Dabei spielen nicht nur unsere Erziehung, unsere Sozialisation, unsere Persönlichkeit, unsere Umgebung, unsere Umwelt und die herrschenden Machtverhältnisse eine Rolle, sondern es ist auch ein gezielter Wille zur politischen Erneuerung, zum gesellschaftlichen Umdenken und zum sozialen Ausgleich vonnöten, was ein Akzeptieren und Tolerieren des "anderen" Geschlechts voraussetzt, das nicht allein an engen patriarchalen (oder matriarchalen) Vorstellungen gemessen wird, so daß nach und nach ein gleichberechtigter zwischengeschlechtlicher Dialog zuwege gebracht werden kann: Ein Dialog mit Kommunikationsstrukturen, bei denen das Geschlecht nicht das ausschlaggebende Moment bildet. Nur so läßt sich die "conditio humana der Frauen" (Gössmann, *Eva* 17) sowohl für jede Frau ganz individuell, als auch für sie innerhalb der Gesellschaft in Deutschland (oder anderswo) herstellen.

Anmerkungen

Für Lynne Tatlocks konstruktive Kommentare und vor allem auch für ihre ermutigende Unterstützung möchte ich mich an dieser Stelle aufrichtig bedanken.

[1] Harsdörffer, ein "vielbelesene[r] Sammler" (Böttcher 300), ist außer für seine (Frauenzimmer) *Gesprächspiele* vor allem noch für den *Poetischen Trichter: Die Teutsche Dicht- und Reimkunst / ohne Behuf der Lateinischen Sprache / in VI. Stunden einzugiessen* und als Koautor des *Pegnesischen Schäfergedichts* bekannt.

² In seiner Arbeit über "Die Frauen der Sprachgesellschaften" betont Karl Otto, daß die Frauen des Pegnesischen Blumenordens als "Künstlerinnen" (500) tätig waren und daß mindestens die Hälfte unter ihnen "Gedichte oder andere Werke" (500) schrieben. Darüber hinaus stellt er fest, daß im Gegensatz zu anderen deutschen Sprachgesellschaften gerade der Pegnesische Blumenorden nicht nur adeligen, sondern auch bürgerlichen Frauen den Beitritt ermöglichte.

³ Die romanistische Literaturwissenschaft spricht seit Ende des 19. Jahrhunderts von der "Querelle des Femmes". Man versteht darunter den seit der Renaissance in Europa geführten Streit um die Frau und um die Frauengelehrsamkeit (vgl. Gössmann, "Für und wider"; Schlumbohm).

⁴ Es wurde von Gössmann darauf hingewiesen, daß Anna Maria von Schurmann, im Gegensatz etwa zu der Venetianerin Lucretia Marinella (1571-1653), die in ihrer Schrift *Le Nobilità et Eccellenze delle Donne et i Diffetti e Mancamenti de gli Huomini* (1600/1608/1621) "ohne jede weibliche Bescheidenheitstopik" ("Für und wider" 190) auskommt, sich stets an die Bescheidenheitsetikette der Frauen hält. Durch diese Technik erreicht sie ihr Ziel, in Deutschland auch von den Männern beachtet zu werden. Auch von der Französin Marie de Jars de Gournay (1565-1645), mit der Schurmann korrespondiert, setzt sich die deutsche Gelehrte ab. Denn Gournay fordert eine "breit angelegte Frauenbildung" (193) und setzt sich für eine in politischen Bereichen integrierte Frau ein, während sich Schurmann nur für das allgemeine Frauenstudium aber nicht für dessen öffentliche Anwendung ausspricht. Die religiösen und sozialen Schranken, gegen die Anna Maria von Schurmann anzugehen hat, lassen sich an ihrem Briefwechsel mit dem Theologen André Rivet (vgl. Gössmann, *Frauenzimmer*, "Für und wider") ablesen. Gegenüber dem erweiterten europäischen Kontext sticht Anna Maria von Schurmann mit ihren Schriften nicht als sonderlich provokativ ab. Was sie jedoch im deutschen Kontext von ihren schreibenden—zumeist adligen—Zeitgenossinnen absetzt, ist die Tatsache, daß sie sich als Bürgerliche in ihrer Dissertatio wissenschaftlich mit der Frauenfrage auseinandersetzt, während adlige Frauen am Hof—den höfischen Erwartungen und Normen entspechend—sich eher in literarischen Genres betätigen (vgl. Gössmann, "Für und wider"; Brandes "Studierstube").

⁵ In ihren Argumentationen arbeitet Anna Maria von Schurmann heraus, daß Frauen genauso wie Männer unter die Kategorie Mensch fallen. Wenn also Menschen "von Natur die Prinzipien oder die Potenzen der Prinzipien aller Künste und Wissenschaften eingegeben [sind]" (Gössmann, *Frauenzimmer* 48), so gilt dies implizit auch für Frauen. Gott hat die Frauen so geschaffen, daß auch ihnen "die Kontemplation und Erkenntnis der sublimen und himmlischen Dinge zu[kommt]" (49). Denjenigen, die sich gegen ein Frauenstudium wenden, erwidert Anna Maria von Schurmann, daß sie Frauen mit Begabungsschwäche das Studium abgesprochen hat, denn sie fordert ein mittleres "Ingenium" (51). "Höchste Begabungen sind nicht unbedingt erforderlich, zumal wir sehen, daß auch die Zahl der gelehrten Männer sich durchweg aus mittleren Begabungen zusammensetzt" (51). Ferner betont sie, daß es unstatthaft sei, den Frauen prinzipiell den Geist zum Studium abzusprechen, nur weil es bisher wenige Frauen gab, die studieren konnten. Da aber Akademien und Kollegien für Frauen fehlen, haben die gebildeten Frauen den zum Studium nötigen Intellekt bewiesen. Sie widersetzt sich der Behauptung, daß Frauen, die im Privaten

lebten, keine darüberhinausreichende Bildung benötigten insofern, als sie daraus die Forderung ableitet, daß dies dann auch für Männer, "die als Privatiers leben" (52), zu gelten hätte. Daß sie den Frauen die ganze Breite der damaligen Wissenschaftsdisziplinen zum Studium empfiehlt, zeigt wie extrem sie—zumindest für deutsche Verhältnisse—zu argumentieren imstande war.

[6] Daß und wie sich die Frauenbelehrung fortsetzt, läßt sich unter anderem in der Schrift *Acta Philosopharum, das ist, Nachricht von der Philosophie des Frauenzimmers* (1721) (Gössmann, *Eva*) von Christoph August Heumann oder in Adolf Franz Ludwig von Knigges *Über den Umgang mit Menschen* (1788) nachlesen. Darüberhinaus liefert uns Hansjürgen Blinn mit seinem Buch *Emanzipation und Literatur* einen Ein- und Überblick zur Diskussion der Frauenfrage, in dem er eine große Auswahl an Texten zu diesem Thema zusammengetragen hat (z.B. Theodor Gottlieb von Hippel: *Über die bürgerliche Verbesserung der Weiber*—1792, Betty Gleim: *Erziehung und Unterricht des weiblichen Geschlechts*—1810, Anonymus: *Mahnwort eines Seelsorgers an junge Hausfrauen*—1882, Ernst Bloch: *Kampf ums neue Weib*—1946/1959, Martin Sperr: *Gedanken zur Emanzipation*—1972/1983).

[7] Sigismund von Birkens *Pegnesis: oder der Pegnitz Blumgenoß-Schäfere FeldGedichte in Neun Tagzeiten: meist verfasset / und hervorgegeben durch Floridan* (1673) enthält eine von ihm dargestellte Reaktion seines Blumenordens auf Schütz' *Ehren=Preiß*. Im Zusammenhang mit einer Diskussion der Frauenfrage werden der Schäferin Dorilis die folgenden Worte in den Mund gelegt: "Wie solten wir zur Vollkommenheit gelangen / da man unsere Fähigkeit in der blüte sterbet / uns zu haus gleichsam gefangen setzet / und / als wie in einem Zuchthause / zu schlechter Arbeit / zur Nadel und Spindel / angewöhnet? Man eilet mit uns zur Küche und Haushaltung / und wird manche gezwungen / eine Martha zu werden / die doch etwan lieber Maria seyn möchte. Ja so gar sind wir zur Barbarey und Unwissenheit verdammet / daß nicht allein die Mannspersonen / sondern auch die meisten von unserem Geschlecht selber / weil sie in der Eitelkeit und Unwissenheit verwildert sind / uns verachten und verlachen / wann eine und andere auf löbliche Wissenschaft sich befleißet / und nichts auf Gelehrte Weibspersonen halten. Man gibt uns den Titel / und will / daß wir Tugendsam seyen: wie können wir es aber werden / wann man uns das Lesen der Bücher verbietet / aus welches die Tugend muß erlernet werden? Soll uns dann dieselbe / wie die gebratene Tauben in Utopien / aus der Luft zufliegen?" (Gössmann, *Frauenzimmer* 95) So geschickt Birken seine Schäferin den wunden Punkt der Bildungsdiskussion bezeichnen läßt, so wenig darf uns dies verleiten, in ihm den großen Frauenfreund zu erkennen. Nicht nur besorgt er, daß das Gespräch sofort in das Gebiet der Frauenschönheit überlenkt, sondern er läßt auch seine Dorilis später "Eines Weibes Hoheit" bescheidener umschreiben als "edle Demut; und ihre einige Ehre / wann sie den Mann ehret / von dessen Sonne-strahlen sie / als Luna glänzet. Sie thut auch solches willig und gern / weil GOtt ihren Willen dem Mann unterworfen / und ihn zum Herrn vorgesetzet. Solcher Befehl wird / in der Göttlichen Schrift / zum öftern wiederholet" (Gössmann, *Frauenzimmer* 97). So endet eine Diskussion, die "galant und großzügig beginnt", laut Gössmann, "gar nicht galant, sondern streng an die alte Geschlechterordnung mahnend" (86).

[8] Dabei muß betont werden, daß am barocken Hof durchaus differenzierte Frauenbereiche mit unterschiedlichsten Aufgabenbereichen existieren. Harsdörffers Darstellung ist diesbezüglich nicht als Realitätsbeschreibung aufzufassen. So läßt sich z.B. bei Ute Brandes über die unterschiedlichsten Schreibräume adliger Frauen nachlesen. Auch die jeweils anders gearteten Pflichten der Frauen, je nachdem ob sie verheiratet oder ledig sind, oder aber an welcher Art von Hof sie leben, werden hier von Harsdörffer unberücksichtigt gelassen. Man sollte ihn im Konstruieren seiner Frauenrolle eher im Sinne der von Karin A. Wurst hervorgearbeiteten These lesen, daß es sich hier um "eine fiktive Spielsituation mit fiktiven" (616), meines Erachtens auch utopischen SpielerInnen handelt, denen Harsdörffer "durch die Ortszuweisung [der Frau] in der geselligen Freizeit sowie durch die Spezifik seiner Bildungskonzeption Schranken auferlegt" (616).

[9] Senta Trömel-Plötz wirft Deborah Tannen interessanterweise vor, den Status quo zu verkaufen (*Emma* 3/92 31). Während für Trömel-Plötz Sprach- und Kommunikationsstrukturen stets auf allgemeine politische Unterdrückungsmechanismen und Machtverhältnisse zurückzuführen sind, bewegt sich Tannens Analyse deskriptiv eher im Bereich der privaten Observation. Anstatt nun aber beide gegeneinander auszuspielen, halte ich es für sinnvoller und ergiebiger, beide Ansätze als sich ergänzend zu lesen.

Zitierte Werke

Becker-Cantarino, Barbara. *Der lange Weg zur Mündigkeit: Frauen und Literatur in Deutschland 1500–1800*. München: Deutscher Taschenbuch, 1989.

Blinn, Hansjürgen. *Emanzipation und Literatur: Texte zur Diskussion: Ein Frauen-Lesebuch*. Frankfurt a.M.: Fischer Taschenbuch, 1984.

Böttcher, Irmgard. "Der Nürnberger Georg Philipp Harsdörffer." *Deutsche Dichter des 17. Jahrhunderts: Ihr Leben und Werk*. Ed. Harald Steinhagen and Benno von Wiese. Berlin: Schmidt, 1984. 289–346.

Bovenschen, Silvia. *Die imaginierte Weiblichkeit: Exemplarische Untersuchungen zu kulturgeschichtlichen und literarischen Präsentationsformen des Weiblichen*. Frankfurt a.M.: Suhrkamp, 1980.

Brandes, Ute. "Baroque Women Writers and the Public Sphere." *Women in German Yearbook 7*. Ed. Jeanette Clausen and Sara Friedrichsmeyer. Lincoln and London: U of Nebraska P, 1991. 43–63.

———. "Studierstube, Dichterklub, Hofgesellschaft: Kreativität und kultureller Rahmen weiblicher Erzählkunst im Barock." *Deutsche Literatur von Frauen*. Ed. Gisela Brinker-Gabler. Bd. 1. München: Beck, 1988. 222–47.

Fishman, Pamela. "Interaction: The Work Women Do." *Language, Gender And Society*. Ed. Barrie Thorne et al. Rowley, MA: Newbury, 1983. 89–101.

Gössmann, Elisabeth, ed. *Eva Gottes Meisterwerk*. München: Iuducium, 1985.

———. "Für und wider die Frauengelehrsamkeit: Eine europäische Diskussion im 17. Jahrhundert." *Deutsche Literatur von Frauen*. Ed. Gisela Brinker-Gabler. Bd. 1. München: Beck, 1988. 185–97.

———, ed. *Das Wohlgelahrte Frauenzimmer*. München: Iudicium, 1984.
Hanstein, Adalbert von. *Die Frauen in der Geschichte des Deutschen Geisteslebens des 18. und 19. Jahrhunderts*. Bd. 1. Leipzig: Freund, 1899.
Harsdörffer, Georg Philipp. *Frauenzimmer Gesprächspiele*. Ed. Irmgard Böttcher. Tübingen: Niemeyer, 1968.
Harsdörffer, Georg Philipp, Sigmund von Birken, and Johann Klaj. *Pegnesisches Schäfergedicht*. Ed. Klaus Garber. Tübingen: Niemeyer, 1966.
Herdegen, Johannes. *Historische Nachricht von deß löblichen Hirten= und Blumen=Ordens an der Pegnitz Anfang und Fortgang: / bis auf das durch Göttl. Güte erreichte Hundertste Jahr / mit Kupfern geziert und verfasset von dem Mitglied dieser Gesellschaft Amarantes*. Nürnberg: Riegel, 1744.
Hess, Peter. "Harsdörffer's Frauenzimmer Gesprächspiele: A Male Education Program for Women?" Vortrag. AATG Convention, Nashville, 18 Nov. 1990.
Knigge, Adolf Franz Ludwig von. *Über den Umgang mit Menschen*. Hannover: Schmidt, 1788.
Lakoff, Robin. *Language and Woman's Place*. New York: Harper Colophon, 1975.
Luther, Martin. "Eine Predigt vom Ehestand (1525)." *Vom ehelichen Leben und andere Schriften über die Ehe*. Ed. Dagmar C.G. Lorenz. Stuttgart: Reclam, 1983. 63-74.
Moscherosch, Johann Michael. *Insomnis. Cura. Parentum. Christliches Vermächnuß oder, Schuldige Vorsorg Eines Trewen Vatters bey jetzigen Hochbetrübtsten gefährlichsten Zeitten*. Straßburg: Mülben, 1643.
Otto, Karl F. "Die Frauen der Sprachgesellschaften." *Europäische Hofkultur im 16. und 17. Jahrhundert*. Bd. III. Wolfenbütteler Arbeiten zur Barockforschung 10. Ed. August Buck, Georg Kauffmann, Blake Lee Spahr, and Conrad Wiedemann. Hamburg: Hauswedell, 1981. 497-503.
Petersen, Karin. "'Essen vom Baum der Erkenntnis'—Weibliche Kreativität?" *Die Überwindung der Sprachlosigkeit: Texte aus der Frauenbewegung*. Ed. Gabriele Dietze. Frankfurt a.M.: Luchterhand, 1979. 70-81.
Schlumbohm, Christa. "Die Glorifizierung der Barockfürstin als 'Femme forte.'" *Europäische Hofkultur im 16. und 17. Jahrhundert*. Bd. II. Wolfenbütteler Arbeiten zur Barockforschung 9. Ed. August Buck, Georg Kauffmann, Blake Lee Spahr, and Conrad Wiedemann. Hamburg: Hauswedell, 1981. 113-22.
Tannen, Deborah. *You Just Don't Understand: Women and Men in Conversation*. New York: Ballantine, 1990.
Thorne, Barrie, Cheris Kramarae, and Nancy Henley. *Language, Gender And Society*. Rowley, MA: Newbury, 1983.
Trömel-Plötz, Senta. "Du willst mich nicht verstehen." *Emma* 3 (1992): 30-31.
———. *Frauensprache: Sprache der Veränderung*. Frankfurt a.M.: Fischer Taschenbuch, 1982.

Wurst, Karin A. "Die Frau als Mitspielerin und Leserin in Georg Philipp Harsdörffers *Frauenzimmer Gesprächspielen*." *Daphnis* 4 (1992): 615–39.

The Battering and Meta-Battering of Droste's Margreth: Covert Misogyny in *Die Judenbuche*'s Critical Reception

Gertrud Bauer Pickar

Examination of Margreth Mergel's life as presented in *Die Judenbuche* not only clarifies the image of her as a victim of family and society, but by extension also raises questions about the negative treatment accorded her in secondary literature. Critics have tended to ignore the evidence presented within the text, accepting instead the societally generated stance of the work's fictive narrator at face value. They have consequently infused interpretations of *Die Judenbuche* with an insidious misogyny that maligns and marginalizes the figure of Margreth and also suggests the presence of a persistent bias in critical Germanistic scholarship. (GBP)

In Annette von Droste-Hülshoff's best known work *Die Judenbuche*, Margreth Mergel, neé Semmler, is clearly a victim—abused by her husband, bullied by her brother, neglected by her son, ignored and insulted by her neighbors, and ultimately allowed to waste away in poverty and isolation. More surprising than the conditions of her life, conditions that are not unusual in the world depicted in Droste's fiction, however, is the treatment Margreth is accorded in the critical literature devoted to *Die Judenbuche*. Examination of the scholarship on this subject reveals a covert and perhaps unconscious misogyny that has colored the discussion of Margreth as a fictional figure and has adversely affected the image of her projected by secondary literature.

The work itself needs to be examined not only for its depiction of Margreth and her life, but for the context Droste provides the reader. An important dimension here is the narrative mode in which the *Novelle* is cast. As in most of Droste's prose works, the stance assumed by the narrator, who throughout the work maintains a position of limited knowledge, is one of presumed "objectivity." Events are purportedly presented as they took place or as they have been transmitted by others;

the narrator espouses a position of reliability and abstains from direct expression of personal bias.[1] Only rarely does the narrator indicate a degree of distance from the events he is depicting, as for example in his introduction which places the setting into the past as "ein Fleck, wie es deren sonst so viele in Deutschland gab" (3), and in the inclusion of occasional moralizing comments. Significantly, however, Droste's narrator, here and elsewhere, speaks as an insider, one who not only accepts the societal values of the day but also has assimilated them. As a result, the narrative stance remains congruent with the dominant thinking of his society; indeed the narrator becomes the purveyor of its attitudes, attitudes which are not necessarily Droste's own.[2] The narrator, who consistently refrains from commentary that might be interpreted as critical of the established order and who indeed seems often oblivious to the ramification of the abuses he depicts, thus serves to provide the societal context for the events presented in the narrative.

The *Novelle* begins with a report of Mergel's first marriage, which takes place before the story proper and before the introduction of Margreth herself. Hermann Mergel, an eligible bachelor considered a good catch, had no difficulty winning the hand of a young village girl: "ein recht hübsches und wohlhabendes Mädchen." Less than a week after the wedding, the young woman was seen running "schreiend und blutrünstig durch's Dorf zu den Ihrigen." The narrator records the villager's immediate assessment—"ein großer Skandal und Aerger für Mergel"—and notes that Hermann, "der allerdings Trostes bedurfte," turned to alcohol. His bride remained at the home of her parents, "wo sie bald verkümmerte und starb." The narrator expends no further word on her and displays no sympathy toward her. Indeed her demise is presented as if a logical consequence of her deserting her husband, fleeing to her parental home, and abandoning her dowry. The phrase "alle ihre guten Kleider und neues Hausgeräth im Stich lassend" suggests that in the eyes of the community, the blame was hers.[3] In contrast the passage as a whole seems to indicate both sympathy for Hermann Mergel as the abandoned husband and understanding for his subsequent behavior: "er schien der Trostmittel immer bedürftiger und fing bald an, den gänzlich verkommenen Subjekten zugezählt zu werden."[4]

To the apparent surprise of the villagers, Mergel, "ein verlegener und zuletzt ziemlich armseliger Wittwer" (5) whose house and farm suffered from neglect, remarried. This time the bride was older—"Margareth Semmler war eine brave, anständige Person, so in den Vierzigen, in ihrer Jugend eine Dorfschönheit." Since Margreth was considered "noch jezt als sehr klug und wirthlich geachtet, dabei nicht unvermögend," the match was beyond the community's comprehension as the narrator affirms: "so *mußte* es Jedem unbegreiflich seyn, was sie zu diesem Schritte getrieben" (5, italics mine). The narrator records Margreth's pronouncement: "Eine Frau, die von ihrem Manne übel behandelt wird, ist dumm oder taugt nicht: wenn's mir schlecht geht, so sagt, es liege an mir" (6), and indicates that her words reveal an inappropriate arrogance. Her words—read without the narrator's evaluative cast—are less a statement of hybris or an indication of an assumption that she could control Hermann than evidence of the degree to which she, too, is imbued with prevailing attitudes. Ironically Margreth's words are themselves interpreted by the narrator as indicating a fatal flaw; speaking for the community, he notes: "*Wir* glauben den Grund eben in dieser ihrer selbstbewußten Vollkommenheit zu finden" (5, italics mine). Behind a feigned expression of sympathy, his subsequent comment—"Der Erfolg zeigte leider, daß sie ihre Kräfte überschätzt hatte" (6)—seems to register a sense of satisfaction with the course of events.

As if personally affronted by Margreth's self-assurance, the narrator—and literary critics following his lead—seems to attribute to her the subsequent problems in the Mergel household. Adopting as it were her comment suggesting that a woman can be held responsible for any ill that befalls her, the narrator hints that Margreth deserves the treatment she receives. Indeed he suggests that the abuse she suffers is a result of her own untoward efforts to control her husband and his alcoholism:

> Anfangs imponirte sie ihrem Manne; er kam nicht nach Haus oder kroch in die Scheune, wenn er sich übernommen hatte; aber das Joch war zu drückend, um lange getragen zu werden, und bald sah man ihn oft genug quer über die Gasse in's Haus taumeln, hörte drinnen sein wüstes Lärmen und sah Margreth eilends Thür und Fenster schließen (6).

The use of the essentially pejorative term "imponirte" in the description of Margreth's initial treatment of Hermann Mergel and the word "Joch" in the following sentence to describe the impact of her attitude toward his drinking clearly indicate the narrator's orientation. The situation subsequently worsens, for as the narrator reports:

> An einem solchen Tage—keinem Sonntage mehr—sah man sie Abends aus dem Hause stürzen, ohne Haube und Halstuch, das Haar wild um den Kopf hängend, sich im Garten neben ein Krautbeet niederwerfen und die Erde mit den Händen aufwühlen, dann ängstlich um sich schauen, rasch ein Bündel Kräuter brechen und damit langsam wieder dem Hause zugehen, aber nicht hinein, sondern in die Scheune (6).[5]

The vagueness of the phrase "[a]n einem solchen Tage" suggests the occurrence was not a solitary one, and the aside "keinem Sonntage mehr" indicates that Hermann was no longer "ein sogenannter ordentlicher Säufer, d.h. einer, der nur an Sonn- und Festtagen in der Rinne lag und die Woche hindurch so manierlich war wie ein Anderer" (5),[6] but was now recognized as a habitual and daily drinker. A significant change of position within the household is also recorded. Hermann now holds the dominant position in the house, even when drunk, and it is Margreth who seeks refuge in the shed. The remark with which the narrator concludes the incident—still without personal commentary—reveals the consequences for Margreth: "Es hieß, an diesem Tage habe Mergel *zuerst* Hand an sie gelegt, obwohl das Bekenntniß nie über ihre Lippen kam" (6, italics mine).

In this incident and throughout the *Novelle,* Margreth is shown to be defenseless against her husband's abuse and isolated in her suffering. Although the townspeople are aware of her plight, neither sympathy nor assistance is accorded her. Neither here nor later is there mention of compassion for her or indication of any attempt to provide even moral support; and nowhere is there any indication that Margreth is aided or comforted by her neighbors, who tolerate, even accept, such behavior. One reason for the lack of involvement by others in scenes of marital abuse may be its acceptance as a norm; indeed Droste—through her narrative voices and her literary figures—indicates such treatment as a regrettable, but common fate for a woman. Droste's description in *Westphälische Schilderungen* of the lot of married women in the villages of Paderborn suggests that experiences such as those of Mergel's wives were not unusual for the residents of that area, where

> kaum eine Barackenbewohnerin ihr Leben beschließt, ohne Bekanntschaft mit dem sogenannten "braunen Heinrich", dem Stocke nämlich, gemacht zu haben. Sie aber finden es ländlich, sittlich, und leben der Ueberzeugung, daß eine gute Ehe, wie ein gutes Gewebe, zuerst des *Einschlags* bedarf, um nachher ein tüchtiges Hausleinen zu liefern (V, 1: 56).

In the same paragraph Droste also comments: "Die Ehe wird in diesen dürftigen Hütten den Frauen zum wahren Fegfeuer, bis sie sich zurechtgefunden..." (V, 1: 57). Of special significance is the term *zurechtfinden,* which seems to indicate that the solution lay not in the cessation of the mistreatment, but in its acceptance by the women.

The text of *Die Judenbuche* indicates no interaction between Margreth and those who either witnessed her behavior or were aware from hearsay of the abuses she suffered. Instead Margreth is excluded from the community and even feels under surveillance by her neighbors, a situation that makes her isolation and helplessness all the more complete. However, Margreth, following the societal code of obedience for wives,[7] never complains of the physical abuse she suffers; indeed she neither admits its occurrence nor criticizes Hermann in public, although in the privacy of her home she does make disparaging remarks about her husband. Subsequent domestic violence is not recorded in the text, though a reader could question if Margreth's hearing loss might not be evidence of further physical abuse. When Hermann Mergel dies ten years later, his death brings not relief, but feelings of bereavement: "Zehn Jahre, zehn Kreuze. Wir haben sie doch zusammen getragen, und jetzt bin ich allein!" (8). Although the years were ones of suffering, Margreth nevertheless registers a sense of loss rather than release, and her own assessment of her married life cited here reflects thinking representative of her community.

A son Friedrich had been born in the second year of their union and, "obwohl unter einem Herzen voll Gram getragen," the boy proved to be "ein gesundes, hübsches Kind" (6). Margreth's fate as mother, however, is shown to be no better than that as wife. Her life reveals that for her, as well as for many other women figures in Droste's works, motherhood, like marriage, is less a guarantee of happiness, than a likely source of pain, disappointment, and anguish.[8] Margreth's reiteration of the saying common in Westphalia at the time and still in use today, "Ach Gott...wenn die Kinder klein sind, treten sie uns in den Schooß, und wenn sie groß sind, in's Herz!" (22), is justified by Friedrich's irresponsible behavior and lack of concern for his mother's plight after he enters his uncle's employ. Although she takes pleasure in his apparently improved status which his better clothing and physical appearance indicate, she is now alone, without the income or assistance in house or field which his presence in her home might have meant:

> Margreth hatte bisher ihren Sohn nur geliebt, jezt fing sie an, stolz auf ihn zu werden und sogar eine Art Hochachtung vor ihm zu fühlen, da sie den jungen Menschen so ganz ohne ihr Zuthun sich entwickeln sah, sogar ohne ihren Rath, den sie, wie die meisten Menschen, für unschätzbar hielt und deßhalb die Fähigkeiten nicht hoch genug anzuschlagen wußte, die eines so kostbaren Förderungsmittels entbehren konnten (16).

As a widow living in poverty, Margreth had little access to the community, which tended either to blame her or to ignore her plight. If anything, Margreth's increasing economic deprivation seems to elicit further scorn, and she is blamed for her husband's debauchery and her own subsequent poverty.[9] The prevalent attitude in the village toward Margreth is mirrored by the forester Brandis in the harshness of his words and the antagonistic tone that mark his altercation with Friedrich, for the incident with Friedrich itself, including the forester's annoyance with Friedrich's reluctance to answer his question, could hardly have elicited such a vitriolic attack:

> Ihr Lumpenpack, dem kein Ziegel auf dem Dach gehört! Bis zum Betteln habt ihr es, Gottlob, bald gebracht, und an meiner Thür soll deine Mutter, die alte Hexe, keine verschimmelte Brodrinde bekommen. Aber vorher sollt ihr mir noch Beide in's Hundeloch! (19).[10]

Even Simon seems to place the blame on his sister for her economic plight, as his reference to her eagerness to wed, unseemly in a woman of her age, indicates: "Ja, Mädchen, zu spät gefreit, hat immer gereut!... Jedes Ding hat seine Zeit. Aber wenn ein altes Haus brennt, dann hilft kein Löschen" (9-10).

The lack of concern for his mother and the apparent rejection of any filial obligations that mark Friedrich's treatment of Margreth during the period of his employment by Simon, particularly after the unresolved murder of Brandis, may have been predisposed by the earlier treatment Friedrich witnessed her receiving at the hands of his father, whom he liked; and it may well have been further encouraged by the disparaging attitude his uncle displayed toward his sister as it is revealed in the one conversation between them included in the *Novelle*. The narrator, however, focuses less on the impact of Friedrich's behavior on Margreth than on its implications for his character which he presents in moralistic terms:

> Und in Friedrich lagen Eigenschaften, die dieß nur zu sehr erleichterten: Leichtsinn, Erregbarkeit, und vor Allem ein grenzenloser Hochmuth, der nicht immer den Schein verschmähte, und dann Alles daran sezte, durch Wahrmachung des Usurpirten möglicher Beschämung zu entgehen. Seine Natur war nicht unedel, aber er gewöhnte sich, die innere Schande der äußern vorzuziehen (26).

The narrator though does draw a contrast between the new Friedrich and his mother: "Man darf nur sagen, er gewöhnte sich zu prunken, während seine Mutter darbte" and then notes the change in Margreth: "man bemerkte, daß Margreth immer stiller über ihren Sohn ward und allmählig in einen Zustand der Verkommenheit versank, den man früher bei ihr für unmöglich gehalten hätte." The hard years of marriage and widowhood, exacerbated by her treatment by son and villagers, take their toll on Margreth so that little trace of her former self remains: "Sie wurde scheu, saumselig, sogar unordentlich, und Manche meinten, ihr Kopf habe gelitten" (26).[11]

Friedrich's attitude toward Margreth is also in alignment with that of the townspeople whose treatment of her the narrator documents from the beginning of her marriage through her increasing economic deprivation as a widow and single mother to her ultimate near-abandonment. It is no wonder that she was not among the merrymakers at the later wedding which ends with the murder of Aaron and the disappearance of both Friedrich and Johannes. When in the course of the ensuing investigation, the *Gutsherr* visits her now ramshackle dwelling, he almost fails to recognize Margreth, "so blaß und steinern sah sie aus" (31). With the cursory inspection completed, the *Gutsherr* leaves "ohne daß Margreth ein anderes Lebenszeichen von sich gegeben hätte, als daß sie unaufhörlich die Lippen nagte und mit den Augen zwinkerte" (32). The pathetic picture of Margreth in a state of physical and emotional decline presented here for the reader records the impact upon her of poverty and neglect; it also marks her last appearance in the *Novelle.*

In the years following Friedrich's disappearance, the reader later learns, Margreth had deteriorated into a condition of "völliger Geistesdumpfheit." Her alienation from the villagers was complete, and again the narrator indicates only she was to blame for her abandonment: "Die Leute im Dorf waren es bald müde geworden, ihr beizustehen, *da sie alles verkommen ließ, was man ihr gab...*" (37, italics mine).[12] Only minimal support was provided by the *Gutsherr,* whose generosity critics seem wont to laud. Betty Weber alone notes that the *Gutsherr* 's treatment was not as generous as it might appear:

> At first glance, the treatment of Margreth seems exemplary: "Die Gutsherrschaft sorgte sehr für sie, schickte ihr täglich das Essen und ließ ihr auch ärztliche Behandlung zukommen...." One could hardly paint a more idyllic, beneficent picture of the aristocracy. But the remainder of this very sentence nullifies these apparently beneficient acts. Droste concludes the sentence with: "als ihr [Margreths] kümmerlicher Zustand in völlige Abzehrung übergegangen war."

Continuing, Weber notes: "After the woman has lost her means of livelihood, her home, her self-respect as a human being, the aristocracy provides only the subsistence with which to prolong her miserable existence" (210, note 27).[13] The treatment accorded Margreth and its consequences stand in marked contrast to the fate of Aaron's widow. Not only is she not neglected by the Jewish community, but unlike Margreth she is reintegrated into her group and later rejoins mainstream life: "die Judenfrau tröstete sich am Ende und nahm einen andern Mann. Nur die arme Margreth blieb ungetröstet" (34).[14]

Examination of Margreth's life thus lends credence to a reading of the *Novelle* that reveals that *Die Judenbuche* is yet another work manifesting Droste's private agenda: the realistic portrayal of the misery that so frequently dominates the course of women's lives. Her covert criticism of its tolerance and acceptance by society is to be found here[15] and in other works, in the quiet detailing and recording of the abuse of women—physical, verbal, economic, and social—whether in the state of marriage, in widowhood, or in motherhood.[16] Such a careful reading of *Die Judenbuche* not only clarifies the much maligned figure of Margreth Mergel as a protagonist within the *Novelle,* but also raises questions about the highly negative treatment of Margreth in the secondary literature. Ironically critics have tended to ignore the evidence presented within the text and have instead accepted at face value the societally generated stance of the work's fictive narrator. Furthermore, critics, by affirming the attitude of the narrator and the villagers, have infused interpretations of *Die Judenbuche* with an insidious misogyny that effectively maligns, or at least marginalizes, the figure of Margreth. The result is a highly skewed image of Margreth that also suggests the presence of a persistent bias in critical Germanistic scholarship.

Perhaps the most common treatment of Margreth is one in which she is minimized and reduced to the role of hapless and pathetic victim. By such casting she is stripped of any control over her life, and her character is reduced to a one-dimensional role. In addition, the act of aggression or exploitation itself becomes less reprehensible, for the responsibility has been shifted from the perpetrator, or from society in general, to the victim. Thus when Walter Silz, who calls Margreth "pious and upright" (1949, 691), insists that "[h]er example shows how little piety and good intentions avail in a wicked world" (1949, 680), he in effect reduces her to a function and consequently denies her uniqueness and ignores her as a viable participant within the action depicted in the *Novelle*. By dismissing Margreth simply as "prey to the inescapable duplicity of things" (1949, 691), he makes her into a one-dimensional figure that is not even gender-specific,[17] but when he substantiates his view by noting: "She is grievously deceived in the man she marries, in her own brother, and finally in her loved and admired son" (1949, 680), he concomitantly changes the emphasis from the men as perpetrators to her as duped victim and simultaneously shifts the blame for her lot from the men to Margreth herself. In the same vein is Frederic Coenen's comment that "Margaret's disillusionment had broken her spirit" (205). By attributing to her *a priori* the nature of victim, this view tends to ignore the responsibility of other individuals for her misery and obscures the destructive impact of forces at work in her community; it also preempts any examination of the work as a potential document of social criticism.

The use of vegetative comparisons, a frequent practice in literature as a mode of describing and perceiving women figures, is unfortunately also prevalent in scholarly criticism, where it leaves the poetic realm and impedes critical inquiry. The equating of women with plant life, and hence with unconscious and passive life, denies the efficacy of mind or will for women and invalidates their identity as rational, thinking individuals.[18] It is in this vein that Silz's comment "As Friedrich goes from bad to worse, Margret *wilts* " (1949, 680, italics mine) is to be condemned. Similarly suspect is Hermann Pongs's depiction of Margreth after the flight of her son—he describes her as dying "*wie eine Pflanze*, deren Keim tödlich getroffen ist" (210, italics mine). Such interpretations, which stress the plant-like nature of women, present their demise as a "natural" and hence acceptable phenomenon, as part of the natural order of things and therefore not a subject for outrage, or even concern. Mary Morgan combines this approach with a "moral" one and articulates a covert condemnation in her assessment that "Margreth...follows an entirely natural and tragical path through life, involved as she is in her son's crimes, culminating in near-idiocy" (164).

For other critics, Margreth is cast as the villain and the reverberation of the narrator's stance is evident in harsh indictments. Thus Ronald Schneider speaks of Margreth's "Hochmut und Eitelkeit" (87), qualities found in the text only in the narrator's subjective assessment. Similarly, Coenen calls her "[o]ver-confident" and "overbearing" (205), and Silz condemms her as "selfrighteous and selfconfident" (1956, 47). Even in the 1980s, Rudolf Kreis claims Margreth seeks to escape the fate of the first bride "dadurch...daß sie an ihrem prügelsüchtigen Mann zur Dompteuse werden will" (87), and Heinz Rölleke states: "Margret hatte *geprahlt*, sie werde dem nach der Heirat *steuern* können... und tatsächlich ging ihr zunächst nur noch sporadisch betrunkner Mann in solchem Zustand 'nicht nach Haus oder kroch in die Scheune'" (340, italics mine). Following Simon's lead, Silz also charges that Margreth was "over-old" when she married, suggesting that there, too, lay a character flaw (1956, 47). Kreis also speculates about the sexual drive behind Margreth's marriage to Mergel, hints at a "düstere sexuelle Verfehlung" (98), and attributes the shock of the *Gutsherr* at seeing the aged Margreth to his recognizing in her appearance "das Hexengesicht einer entmenschten Sexualität und ihrer 'versteinernden' Folgen" (103). Both Kreis (93) and James McGlathery (238) even proffer the possibility of an earlier, incestuous relationship between Margreth and her brother Simon, one not found in the text. Raleigh Whitinger in turn suggests that the presence of Friedrich's double, Simon's stable boy and illegitimate son Johannes, demonstrates "that moral frailties also abound on proud Margreth's side of the family" and reveal her preoccupation with outward appearances (279, note 46).[19]

Some critics have recognized the physical abuse Margreth suffers—Larry Wells, for example, explains Margreth's behavior in the garden as "furtively gathering herbs with which to ease the painful bruises from her drunken husband's blows" (1979, 479).[20] Though Rölleke, too, acknowledges the "Gewalttätigkeiten ihres betrunkenen Mannes," he focuses his attention more on Margreth's reactions to her "Niederlage" becoming public than on the abuse she suffers, and describes her behavior on that occasion as an "unordentlicher Aufzug" and an "unkontrollierter, hilfloser Wutausbruch" (340). The general tendency, however, has been to blame Margreth for her fate. Following the lead of the fictive [male] narrator, critics seem to endorse the view that a battered wife is deserving of the treatment she receives. For Coenen, Margreth is "an overbearing woman whose spirit breaks when she sees herself defeated" (205); for Emil Staiger she is a person "die sich getrauen wollte, den lasterhaften Mann zu meistern und unter dessen zäher Resistenz zusammenbrach" (53). Not surprisingly, Margreth is accorded little sympathy by critics for the misery of her later years. Representative is Coenen's simple comment: "After her son's disappearance she lives in a helpless stupor, depending constantly on the charity of others until her death" (205). Silz seems to find an elevating quality in her suffering when he states: "An average person, like her son, she becomes truly tragic in her collapse after his crime and flight: a deeply moving study in human deterioration" (1956, 39).

As a mother, Margreth is also found wanting. In some cases her shortcomings are linked to innate weakness and she is treated, on occasion, with a degree of sympathy. Thus Clemens Heselhaus sees Margreth as so demoralized, "daß sie nichts zur Rettung ihres Jungen Friedrich tun kann" (154); Edson Chick states: "She knows what she is doing but tries to rectify the wrong with useless words of piety" (153); Staiger speaks of her as "die fromme, aber hilflose Mutter" (50); and John Guthrie refers to her as "a pious woman" who is, "like many others in this community, superstitious and of limited intelligence" (79). Silz, who charges Margreth with unwittingly contributing to Friedrich's undoing, states: "In her very first attempt at moral counseling, when, after the death of his father, she has sole charge of the boy, she, ironically, instils [sic] prejudices instead of good precepts into his questioning young mind" (1949, 691–92). Staiger, too, blames Margreth for her son's later erring, claiming it was "sogar der gute Wille der Mutter, [der Friedrich] den Weg zur Hölle weis[t]." He places the seeds of his downfall "gleich im ersten erzieherischen Gespräch bei Förstern und Holzfrevel" (53), though he does acknowledge some effort on her part when he notes "wie sie als Witwe wieder ihre Kraft zusammennimmt, um wenigstens mit dem Kind ins Rechte zu kommen" (53). Joyce Hallamore similarly blames Margreth for her son's susceptibility to his uncle's influence, claiming she had "[u]nwittingly...pre-conditioned her son to become a pathetically easy prey to Simon's cunning" (70). Erik Wolf in turn indicts Margreth, noting: "Verbrechen wachsen aus unrichtiger und törichter Behandlung des Kindes" and suggesting that the prejudices she transmitted robbed her son "um Schärfe und Klarheit des Urteils" (248). As late as 1980, Karl Philipp Moritz notes: "Seine Mutter vermag ihm weder Halt noch Orientierungshilfe zu bieten; sie wird vielmehr mit ihren Vorurteilen...zum 'geheimen Seelendieb' und beginnt so unbeabsichtigt mit der Zerstörung seines intakten kindlichen Rechtsempfindens" (127–28). Morgan reiterates this position, noting that Margeth imbued her son "with the local standards of morality" with regard to wood theft and treatment of Jews and concluding these were "significant lessons in the light of what was to follow" (160). Morgan subsequently sharpens her indictment of Margreth, stating: "Her upbringing of the boy certainly helped to sow the seeds of these crimes, as we see when she informed the child of impressionable age that neither wood-stealing nor Jew-beating was wrong" (164). Doris Brett goes so far as to conclude: "The ultimate responsibility for Friedrich's corruption may be seen to rest with Margreth, his mother, rather than with his uncle" (158). Indeed Brett takes critics to task both for excusing Margreth for her adverse influence on Friedrich and for viewing her as a basically pious woman (162). For Brett, Droste's view of Margreth is quite different, and she insists that while Droste's "ironic portrait of Margreth contains just enough protestations of the woman's piety and pathetic simplicity to allow her disastrous effect to go largely unnoticed" (162), Droste nevertheless had intended to present a negative image of Margreth as mother.[21] In this context Brett postulates that Margreth's "doctrination" of her son "permanently distorted Friedrich's concept of right and wrong and damaged his moral reasoning beyond repair" (165). Ignored in the general critical condemnation of the lawlessness and the racial prejudice evidenced by Margreth's remarks is one important aspect: Margreth was not just reiterating the prevalent thinking of her community, she was also supporting the male hierarchy of her village society. It is in this vein that her oft-cited conversation with Friedrich is to be understood—Margreth supports the wood thieving activities of her area, criticizes those in the service of the authorities (Brandis), defends the integrity of the male figure of authority in the community (Hülsmeyer) against the accusations of the outsider (Aaron), and reflects in her words the anti-Semitism of her rural community (cf. Freund 247).

Although Margreth's remarks can be condemned for their promulgation of prejudice, it is surprising that critics have rated Margreth as inferior to Hermann Mergel and Simon Semmler in her execution of the parental role. Thus Silz, who calls Friedrich a "neglected child," notes: "His mother gives him affection, but no intelligent guidance" and as contrast emphasizes his father's "special tenderness for his little son" (1956, 48), a view still echoed in Morgan's 1984 biography of Droste (158). Jane Brown, too, extolls Hermann's virtue as father in contrast to that of Margreth as mother: "Hermann always brings him presents...but we never see Margreth say a single kind word to the child, nor are we ever told that Friedrich entertains (or should entertain) any warm feelings for Margreth as he does for his father" (841). Janet King also emphasizes Simon's role, noting he was "Friedrich's surrogate father" and that "the child was responsive to their relationship"; she even insists that "the older man's influence upon his ward is described in positive terms prior to the *Blaukittel* incident" (353).

Also at issue is Friedrich's adoption by Simon. Although Margreth allows Friedrich to enter his employ and household, the text not only indicates that the poverty-stricken widow worries about her son and has justifiable misgivings about her brother Simon, but also specifically mentions the sacrifice Margreth accepted—"Sie wußte am besten, was eine kränkliche Wittwe an der Hülfe eines zwölfjährigen Knaben entbehrt, den sie bereits gewöhnt hat, die Stelle einer Tochter zu ersetzen. Doch sie schwieg und gab sich in Alles" (11). Her acceptance of Simon's offer, however, has nevertheless been harshly judged by critics.[22] While Silz attributes good intentions to her—"She means to do the best for her child by giving him into her brother's keeping"—he nevertheless concludes: "yet this is the worst thing she could have done" (1949, 692). Silz also suggests that her religious naiveté may have been a contributing factor: "She deludes herself with the hope that daily prayer will counteract the contamination to which Friedrich is exposed" (1949, 692). Winfried Freund similarly cites Margreth's gullible nature as contributing to her error, but finds her no less guilty: "Margreth, jedoch, die nichts von seinen selbstischen Gründen ahnt, läßt sich von dieser scheinbar so liebevollen Anerkennung irreleiten und fühlt sich in ihrem mütterlichen Stolz bestätigt" (248).[23] Even here in the last phrase there seems to be an echo of the narrator's earlier charge of undue personal pride on Margreth's part. Most extreme in his criticism is Kreis. He both criticizes the "eagerness" with which which Margreth agrees to the arrangement after learning of her brother's interest in Friedrich and imputes a selfish economic motive to her act, when he charges: Margreth "ergibt...sich im Grunde sehr bereitwillig in den vorgeschlagenen 'Handel' und *verkauft praktisch den Sohn*" (93, italics mine). Not only does Kreis add that she does so "obwohl alles darauf hindeutet, daß Simon nur daran denkt, die kindliche Arbeitskraft ohne wirkliche Gegenleistung auszubeuten statt zu fördern" (93), but he also fails to note that Margreth neither received nor was promised any material benefit for surrendering her son; and that furthermore the only benefit accrued to Friedrich, who presumably would then become Semmler's heir; this, however, constituted in fact no gain, since Semmler's property at his death would in any case have been passed on to Friedrich as his only legal male heir.[24]

Margreth's personal treatment of Friedrich, as well, has been denounced as either too lenient or too harsh. Thus Silz notes that Margreth "brings him up over-tenderly, cherishing his golden curls and training him to play the part of a daughter to an ailing widow" (1956, 48); and Ernst Feise claims she spoils Friedrich "wie die Pflege seiner blonden Locken bei sonstiger Verlumpung ahnen läßt" (405). On the other hand, Clifford Bernd emphasizes Margreth's "bitter answers" to her son's questions, which he views as "typical of an impatient, almost desperate mother" (70); and Kreis calls the mother-child relationship in *Judenbuche* "eine erheblich gestörte Beziehung" (88). For Kreis, Margreth's language toward her child "ist deutlich von Haß geprägt" and "entspricht voll und ganz dem Zärtlichkeitstabu des feudalen Kindheitsschemas" (89).

Not surprisingly Margreth's treatment of Johannes has also come under negative scrutiny. Kreis, describing her as "[f]ast schon zur Furie werdend," condemns her behavior toward Johannes and cites it as yet further evidence of her aggressive and destructive treatment of Friedrich (100). A similar view is expressed by Irmgard Roebling, who extrapolates Margreth's confusion when she mistakes Johannes for Friedrich as representing not merely a failure to identify her son, but also a symbolical castration of him (1988, 63). For Wells, "[t]he confusion of identities suggests that the mother who cannot recognize her own son externally has little hope of grasping his inner being" and indicates her inability to detect both his "stunted spiritual growth" and "the incipient 'Ehrgeiz und Hang zum Großtun'" evidenced by "his patronizing demeanor" toward Johannes (1977, 112).[25]

There are, of course, yet other treatments of the *Novelle* in which Margreth is not mentioned once, perhaps the best example of her marginalization, but this brief review of critical stances toward Margreth may suffice to indicate, at least in small part, the misogyny in scholarship dealing with *Die Judenbuche*. Incidentally, Mergel's wives are not the only figures so maligned, for a similar case could be made for the treatment of Aaron's widow accorded her by the narrator and subsequently by literary critics. The narrator portrays her as overly emotional, even hysterical, and suggests an inappropriateness in appearance and behavior in the description he provides of the widow's sudden interruption of the *Gutsherr*'s family at evening prayer:

> Die Thüre ward aufgerissen und herein stürzte die Frau des Juden Aaron, bleich wie der Tod, das Haar wild um den Kopf, von Regen triefend. Sie warf sich vor dem Gutsherrn auf die Knie. "Gerechtigkeit!" rief sie, "Gerechtigkeit! mein Mann is erschlagen!" und sank ohnmächtig zusammen (30).

Her remarriage, as well, is presented in a manner that minimizes both her and her loss: "die Judenfrau tröstete sich am Ende und nahm einen andern Mann" (34). Following the narrator's lead, critics have tended to deprecate the widow and her plight, and references to the widow focus on her "hysterical" appearance after the discovery of her murdered husband and her perceived "quickness to remarry" (e.g., Franzos, Heitmann, Feise, and Chick). Though but a secondary figure, she too has suffered from the capriciousness of critical bias in the treatment of *Die Judenbuche* and its women figures.

The past few years have seen renewed interest in Droste, and recent scholarship has focused new light on Droste and her writings, resulting in a greater understanding of her as a woman and author and new recognition of the dimension of her literary stature. Attention has been directed to aspects of her writing and works long ignored by literary critics—witness the recent interest in her letters (Arend[26]; Gödden) and in her early works (Frederiksen and Shafi). Both individual works, as well as aspects of her life and literary production, have also benefited from recent feminist reexamination (Peucker; Roebling; Niethammer and Belemann[27]; and Friedrichsmeyer). As Monika Salmen stated a few years ago in a publication of the Thomas Morus Akademie:

> Von ihrem Schreib- und Leserbewußtsein her ist die Droste mehr, als herkömmliche Vorstellungen von der Dichterin tradieren: Sie ist nicht nur in erster Linie eine biedermeierliche, eine westfälische oder auch eine katholische Dichterin. Vielmehr ist sie eine schreibende Frau, die sich in der geistigen Auseinandersetzung mit den gesellschaftlichen wie religiösen Bedingungen ihrer Zeit, in der Rolle als unverheiratete Frau, auf die Suche nach ihrer Ich-Identität begibt und im Schreiben zu einem Befreiungsakt gelangt, der die äußeren Konventionen sprengt (6).[28]

As such work proceeds and Droste's writings become increasingly freed from the fetters of earlier, often intellectually limited and biased assessments, then, perhaps, Droste will receive the acclaim and the recognition she deserves—not as the first German woman to be included in 1961 in the series *German Men of Letters* (Schatzky), but as a significant author who articulated women's concerns with a woman's voice even while she maintained in her personal life an apparent acceptance of the status quo.

Notes

[1] I am treating the sexually-unidentified narrator in *Die Judenbuche* as male in accord with Droste's general practice of attributing a masculine identity to authorial and narrator figures in her prose works and ballads—a device she employed to grant greater credibility to the textual claim of authenticity.

[2] Within this narrative situation, and perhaps because of it, I contend that Droste was nevertheless able to incorporate her own views and to offer criticism of the status quo, albeit covertly. For her, the ostensible narrative stance—one that can be seen as reflecting the thinking Droste found in her own family and its circle of friends—was a protective ploy with which to cloak her own position, and one she on occasion used effectively in prose as well as poetry.

[3] A residue of such thinking can still be found in secondary literature. Note Guthrie's addendum to Hermann Mergel's two ruined marriages—"the second of which to a respectable girl, Margreth" (79)—with its implicit deprecation of the first bride.

[4] Mergel's deterioration is presented in specific and graphic detail: "So war denn auch am Nachmittage keine Scheibe an seinem Hause mehr ganz, und man sah ihn noch bis spät in die Nacht vor der Thürschwelle liegen, einen abgebrochenen Flaschenhals von Zeit zu Zeit zum Munde führend und sich Gesicht und Hände jämmerlich zerschneidend" (5). Droste's *Westphälische*

Schilderungen also indicates her awareness of serious alcohol abuse in rural areas of Paderborn, as well as its ramifications for marital life there.

[5] The scene, which is not further explained in the *Novelle*, has provoked a variety of interpretations. For a brief summary, see Rölleke (340-41). See also note 20 below.

[6] This description applied to Hermann Mergel as a young man and eligible bachelor indicates the degree of "moderate" drinking apparently considered acceptable by the community; the incongruity of "ordentlich" and "Säufer" and the addition of the word "sogenannt" clearly reveals authorial irony.

[7] The question as to how far connubial loyalty should extend is never directly addressed in Droste's works, although the problem is treated ambiguously by her on a number of occasions (cf. *Joseph* and "Der Graf von Thal"). As mentioned above, the issue is raised obliquely in *Die Judenbuche* with regard to Mergel's first wife.

[8] The mother-child relationship is not one that is developed in Droste's works, but its essentially problematic nature is revealed even within the limited treatment it receives in her prose, dramatic fragments, and poetry, as well as in her letters. Motherhood is shown to be inadequate to counter the misery of marriage, and the birth of a child, rather than a happy occasion, is most frequently met with sorrow. The pain of motherhood tends to extend far beyond the early years and frequently includes a struggle with poverty, anguish over the illness and death of the child, and concern for the child's future.

[9] Like Margreth, the wife of the grocer discussed in *Ledwina* (V, 1: 114) also suffers the wrath and indignation of her neighbors—not for anything of her doing, but because of her husband's fiscal irresponsibility and ultimate bankruptcy. Yet, as in *Die Judenbuche*, the situation is not condemned by the narrative voice nor by the fictive figures; no solution for the abused or distraught wife is suggested, and no sympathy for her is expressed.

[10] The tone and portent of the forester's words prove to be a contributing factor in Friedrich's subsequent response which sends Brandis in the direction of the *Blaukittel* and hence to his death.

[11] The description of Margreth as an old woman resembles that of others in Droste's works who have suffered the loss of husband and child. Cf., for example, Lisbeth in *Ledwina*.

[12] Assuming a moralizing tone, the narrator adds with regard to the waning of community support: "wie es denn die Art der Menschen ist, gerade die Hülflosesten zu verlassen, solche, bei denen der Beistand nicht nachhaltig wirkt und die der Hülfe immer gleich bedürftig bleiben" (37). While the remark serves to distance the narrator from the backward inhabitants of rural Westphalia, it is not offered as a personal view of Margreth's plight; here and elsewhere the narrator refrains from any such commentary.

[13] Gössmann, who continues to insist that "Droste die patriarchalische Welt der gutsherrlichen Herrschaft ungemein aufgewertet [hat]," sees both the efforts of the *Gutsherr* and the promise of salvation associated with Christmas eve as

ultimately ineffective in altering the fate of the individual, and concludes: "Wie es den Menschen tatsächlich ergeht, zeigt die Droste am Schicksal der Mutter" (163).

[14] Cf. Moritz, particularly the discussion "Die Lage der Juden" (35-42).

[15] In an earlier version of *Die Judenbuche* there are textual references to Simon's ill-treatment of both his wife and the girl he seduced and abandoned after the birth of her child. Heselhaus, citing Huge's dissertation, notes that the first version of *Die Judenbuche* constitutes "[d]eutlicher als die gedruckte Fassung, eine Sozialstudie, in der die Situation der Frauen in den Dörfern in ziemlicher Deutlichkeit aufgezeigt wird" (153). Cf. the earlier manuscript H^2 HKA V, 2: 258-95).

[16] Although Droste did depict a few successful marriages in her works, her *oeuvre* as a whole attests to the all too frequent unhappy consequences of marriage and reveals the miseries suffered by the wife, regardless of social standing or economic status. Thus the *Reichsgräfin* in *Bertha*, reviewing her married life, exclaims: "o Adelbert / Nur bittre Stunden gabst du mir du hast / Den Leidenskelch gefüllt mir dargereicht / Und ohne Murren trank ich ihn" (VI, 1: 129) and the long-term prognosis for Frau von Benraet, "die arme, gedrückte Nachbarin Mutter und Gattin, und doch verwaißt," provided by Frau von Brenkfelt, is gloomy as well: she "sah sie im Geiste schleichen, alt und verkümmert, in dem dürren, rasselnden Laube ihrer liebsten letzten Hoffnungen" (*Ledwina* V, 1: 118). There are also other cases of both mental and physical abuse in Droste's writings, such as those found in *Walter* and "Der Nachtwandler."

[17] Silz's comment that Margreth "might stand as the type of the decent, well-meaning *individual*" (1949, 680, italics mine) treats her simply as victim *per se* and deprives her of a personal, as well as a gender-specific fate.

[18] Cf. Roebling (1986, 41): "Die Vorstellung vom harmonischen, sanften, liebevollen, pflanzenhaft-naturnahen Charakter der Frau wurde ja von Friedrich Schlegel in seiner Theorie der Weiblichkeit um 1800 aufgenommen, findet sich bei Baader u.v.a. und ist uns auch noch im 20. Jahrhundert nicht ganz fremd."

[19] Although Droste deleted any reference to Margreth's drinking from the final version (apparently when the text was no longer to be part of the longer *Sittengemälde* but rather an independent story dealing with Friedrich and the murder of Aaron), critics have also accused Margreth of heavy alcohol abuse. Henel, for example, refers to the exorcised passages about her drinking and postulates alcohol as an explanation for Margreth's erratic behavior in the garden, suggesting she may have turned to drink for strength "an Tagen, wo ihr Mann sich wüst aufführte" (153-54, 170).

[20] Cf. also McGlathery. Margreth's abuse by Mergel is specifically noted in earlier versions of *Die Judenbuche* (cf. Droste IV, 2: 265, 285). Wells ("Indeterminancy" 479) and Köhler (240), among others, associate Margreth's strange behavior in the garden with her desire not to be seen by the neighbors; Rölleke views her efforts as specifically designed "[i]hre Niederlage...zu

vertuschen...indem sie neugierigen Gaffern bedeuten will, sie sei der Kräuter wegen im Garten" (340).

[21] Brett cites specifically the conversation between mother and son in which Margreth articulates the prejudices of her community, her reactions to the money Friedrich brings home from Simon, and the story of Lumpenmoises and his supposed murder of a certain Aaron (162–65).

[22] Criticism directed at Margreth for allowing Simon to assume the custodianship of her fatherless child fails to take into account that in the world Droste depicts, it was not unusual for the parental role to be taken from the mother and given to a male authority figure ("Der Mutter Wiederkehr") or to have that role assumed by a male—the father (three instances in Droste's early work *Walter* and one in *Joseph*); the grandfather ("Das Hospiz auf dem großen St. Bernhard"); and a male relative (*Joseph*). The subject of child rearing is discussed only by male figures, demonstrated exclusively in terms of father-son relationships, and treated as a purely male concern in Droste's poem "Alte und neue Kinderzucht."

[23] The passage continues:
Um ihrer Dankbarkeit über dieses Lob Ausdruck zu geben, läßt sie sich zu einem Vergleich hinreißen: *Er hat viel von dir, Simon, viel*. Aber schon in der Beurteilung einer Äußerlichkeit straft sie sich selbst Lügen. Als Simon nämlich in seiner Eitelkeit von diesem Vergleich Gebrauch macht, heißt es: *in der Mutter Züge kam ein heimliches, stolzes Lächeln; ihrer Friedrichs blonde Locken und Simons rötliche Bürsten!* (248).

[24] That Simon had denied the paternity of Johannes in the courts is included in earlier manuscripts; the reference to his false oath is the only indication remaining in the final version of *Die Judenbuche*.

[25] The suggestion that Johannes's conception might have been the result of incest alluded to earlier (cf. Kreis [1980] and McGlathery) would also make Margreth as guilty a partner in the neglect and abuse of Johannes as was Simon.

[26] Arend's interest in Droste's use of humor and irony extends beyond her letters to the *Heidebilder*, as well ("Humor and Irony").

[27] The essays published by Niethammer and Belemann include Frederiksen's report "Feministische Ansätze in den späten siebziger und achtziger Jahren am Beispiel der Droste-Rezeption in den USA" (105–23).

[28] In this context particular mention should be made of Friedrichsmeyer's analysis of "Das Spiegelbild" and Peucker's discussion of Droste's use of the double, two works that further illuminate the problematic nature of literary self-expression for Droste—and its significance for her.

Works Cited

Arend, Angelika. "'Es fehlt mir allerdings nicht an einer humoristischen Ader': Zu einem Aspekt des Briefstils der Annette von Droste-Hülshoff." *Monatshefte* 82 (1990): 50-61.

———. "Humor and Irony in Annette von Droste-Hülshoff's 'Heidebilder'-Cycle." *German Quarterly* 63 (1990): 50-58.

Bernd, Clifford Albrecht. "Clarity and Obscurity in Annette von Droste-Hülshoff's *Judenbuche*." *Studies in German Literature of the Nineteenth and Twentieth Centuries: Festschrift for Frederick L. Coenen*. Ed. Siegfried Mews. Chapel Hill: U of North Carolina P, 1970. 64-77.

Brett, Doris. "Friedrich, the Beech, and Margreth in Droste-Hülshoff's 'Judenbuche.'" *Journal of English and Germanic Philology* 84 (1985): 157-65.

Brown, Jane. "The real mystery in Droste-Hülshoff's 'Die Judenbuche.'" *Modern Language Review* 73 (1978): 835-46.

Chick, Edson. "Voices in Discord: Some Observations on *Die Judenbuche*." *German Quarterly* 42 (1969): 147-57.

Coenen, Frederic E. "The 'Idee' in Annette von Droste-Hülshoff's *Die Judenbuche*." *German Quarterly* 12 (1939): 204-09.

Droste-Hülshoff, Annette von. *Bertha oder die Alpen. Historisch-kritische Ausgabe*. Vol. VI, 1: *Dramatische Versuche, Text*. Tübingen: Niemeyer, 1982. 61-224.

———. *Historisch-kritische Ausgabe*. Vol. V, 2: *Prosa, Dokumentation*. Tübingen: Niemeyer, 1984.

———. "Die Judenbuche: Ein Sittengemälde aus dem gebirgigten Westphalen." *Historisch-kritische Ausgabe*. Vol. V, 1: *Prosa, Text*. Tübingen: Niemeyer, 1978. 1-42.

———. *Ledwina. Historisch-kritische Ausgabe*. Vol. V, 1: *Prosa, Text*. Tübingen: Niemeyer, 1978. 77-121.

———. "Westphälische Schilderungen aus einer westphälischen Feder." *Historisch-kritische Ausgabe*. Vol. V, 1: *Prosa, Text*. Tübingen: Niemeyer, 1978. 43-74.

Feise, Ernst. "'Die Judenbuche' von Annette von Droste-Hülshoff." *Monatshefte* 35 (1943): 401-15.

Franzos, Karl Emil. "Eine Novelle und ihre Quellen." *Allgemeine Zeitung des Judenthums* 6 (1897): 609-11, 619-20, 632-33.

Frederiksen, Elke and Monika Shafi. "Annette von Droste-Hülshoff (1797-1848): Konfliktstrukturen im Frühwerk." *Out of Line / Ausgefallen: The Paradox of Marginality in the Writings of Nineteenth-Century German Women*. Ed. Ruth-Ellen Boetcher Joeres and Marianne Burkhard. Amsterdamer Beiträge zur neueren Germanistik 28. Amsterdam: Rodopi, 1989. 115-36.

Freund, Winfried. "Der Mörder des Juden Aaron." *Wirkendes Wort* 19 (1969): 244-53.

Friedrichsmeyer, Sara. "Women's Writing and the Construct of an Integrated Self." *The Enlightenment and its Legacy: Studies in German Literature in Honor of Helga Slessarev*. Ed. Barbara Becker Cantarino and Sara Friedrichsmeyer. Bonn: Bouvier, 1990. 171–80.

Gödden, Walter. *Die andere Annette: Annette von Droste-Hülshoff als Briefschreiberin*. Paderborn: Schöningh, 1991.

Gössmann, Wilhelm. *Annette von Droste-Hülshoff: Ich und Spiegelbild: Zum Verständnis der Dichterin und ihres Werkes*. Düsseldorf: Droste, 1985.

Guthrie, John. *Annette von Droste-Hülshoff: A German Poet between Romanticism and Realism*. Oxford: Berg, 1989.

Hallamore, Joyce. "The Reflected Self in Annette von Droste's Work: A Challenge to Self-Discovery." *Monatshefte* 61 (1969): 58–74.

Heitmann, Felix. *Annette von Droste-Hülshoff als Erzählerin: Realismus und Objektivität in der Judenbuche*. Münster: Aschendorff, 1914.

Henel, Heinrich. "Annette von Droste-Hülshoff: Erzählstil und Wirklichkeit." *Festschrift für Bernhard Blume: Aufsätze zur deutschen und europäischen Literatur*. Ed. Egon Schwarz et al. Göttingen: Vandenhoeck, 1967. 146–72.

Heselhaus, Clemens. "'Die Judenbuche'—Die Sprache der Frau in der Literatur." *Zeitschrift für deutsche Philologie* 99 (1980): 143–60.

King, Janet K. "Conscience and Conviction in 'Die Judenbuche.'" *Monatshefte* 64 (1972): 349–55.

Köhler, Lotte. "Annette von Droste-Hülshoff." *Deutsche Dichter des 19. Jahrhunderts*. Ed. Benno von Wiese. Berlin: Schmidt, 1969. 223–48.

Kreis, Rudolf. "Annette von Droste-Hülshoff: Die Judenbuche." *Die verborgene Geschichte des Kindes in der deutschen Literatur*. Stuttgart: Metzler, 1980. 54–122.

McGlathery, James M. "Fear of Perdition in Droste-Hüllshoff's *Judenbuche*." *Lebendige Form: Festschrift für Heinrich Henel*. Ed. Jeffrey L. Sammons and Ernst Schürer. Munich: Fink, 1970. 229–44.

Morgan, Mary. *Annette von Droste-Hülshoff: A Biography*. Bern: Lang, 1984.

Moritz, Karl Philipp. *Droste Hülshoff: Die Judenbuche*. Paderborn: Schöningh, 1980.

Niethammer, Ortrun and Claudia Belemann, eds. *Ein Gitter aus Musik und Sprache: Feministische Analysen zu Annette von Droste-Hülshoff*. Paderborn: Schöningh, 1992.

Peucker, Brigitte. "Droste-Hülshoff's Ophelia and the Recovery of Voice." *Journal of English and Germanic Philology* 82 (1983): 374–91.

Pongs, Hermann. *Das Bild in der Dichtung*. Vol. 2. Marburg: Elwert, 1939.

Roebling, Irmgard. "Heraldik des Unheimlichen: Annette von Droste-Hülshoff (1797–1848): Auch ein Porträt." *Deutsche Literatur von Frauen*. Vol. 2. Ed. Gisela Brinker-Gabler. Munich: Beck, 1988. 41–68.

———. "Weibliches Schreiben im 19. Jahrhundert: Untersuchungen zur Naturmetaphorik der Droste." *Der Deutschunterricht* 38 (1986): 36–56.

Rölleke, Heinz. "Annette von Droste-Hülshoff: *Die Judenbuche*." *Romane und Erzählungen zwischen Romantik und Realismus*. Ed. Paul Michael Lützeler. Stuttgart: Reclam, 1983. 335-53.
Salmen, Monika. *Annette von Droste-Hülshoff und die moderne Frauenliteratur*. Bernsberger Manuskripte 34. Bernsberg: Thomas-Morus-Akademie, 1987.
Schatzky, Brigitte E. "Annette von Droste-Hülshoff." *German Men of Letters*. Ed. Alex Nathan. London: Wolff, 1961. 79-98.
Schneider, Ronald. "Möglichkeiten und Grenzen des Frührealismus im 'Biedermeier.'" *Der Deutschunterricht* 31 (1979): 85-94.
Silz, Walter. "Problems of 'Weltanschauung' in the works of Annette von Droste-Hülshoff." *PMLA* 64 (1949): 678-701.
———. *Realism and Reality: Studies in the German Novelle of Poetic Realism*. Chapel Hill: U of North Carolina P, 1956.
Staiger, Emil. *Annette von Droste-Hülshoff*. Zürich: Münster, 1933.
Weber, Betty Nance. "Droste's *Judenbuche*: Westphalia in International Context." *Germanic Review* 50 (1975): 203-12.
Wells, Larry D. "Annette von Droste-Hülshoff's Johannes Niemand: Much Ado about Nobody." *Germanic Review* 52 (1977): 109-21.
———. "Indeterminancy as Provocation: The Reader's Role in Annette von Droste-Hülshoff's 'Die Judenbuche.'" *Modern Language Notes* 94 (1979): 475-92.
Whitinger, Raleigh. "From Confusion to Clarity: Further Reflections on the Revelatory Function of Narrative Technique and Symbolism in Annette von Droste-Hülshoff's *Die Judenbuche*." *Deutsche Vierteljahresschrift* 54 (1980): 259-83.
Wolf, Erik. *Vom Wesen des Rechts in deutscher Dichtung*. Frankfurt a.M.: Klostermann, 1946.

Domesticating the Reader: Women and *Die Gartenlaube*

Kirsten Belgum

I argue here that popular reading material in the nineteenth century, besides providing a source of entertainment, also helped create a sense of national identity in its readers, unifying a disparate nation into a cohesive reading audience. In discussing the most popular illustrated magazine of the time, *Die Gartenlaube*, this paper outlines the text's specific strategies for distinguishing between male and female readers. Although the magazine explicitly addressed the entire family, women readers were presented with a restricted, exclusively domestic identity. This analysis of the narrative domestication of women contributes to an understanding of the role of gender both in the conception of the nation and in the creation and consumption of popular culture. (KB)

The last ten years have witnessed a plethora of fascinating theoretical studies on popular, mass-produced texts and their readerships. This growing subfield has explored a wide range of issues, from the possibly subversive pleasure experienced by women readers of romance novels to the role that a general increase in literacy and the broad distribution of written material have played in national identity. Both of these notions, the gendered construction of pleasure and the formation of national identity through popular texts, form the basis of my interest in the nineteenth-century popular family magazine, *Die Gartenlaube*.[1] My discussion focuses on the notion of gender in this magazine for two reasons. In the first place, the magazine's explicitly stated goal was to reach the entire middle-class family. This appeal to the family was a central, but as yet not fully explored, aspect of the magazine's program of becoming a mouthpiece for an emergent "main-stream" German society. And, beyond this, the *Gartenlaube* was a space in which a national identity was constructed and mediated in late nineteenth-century Germany for a broad audience.

Popular written texts and their reading audiences have come to play a major role in the work of several theorists of nineteenth-century nationalism. Benedict Anderson suggests that such texts—as modern products of print-capitalism—were integral to the formation of national "imagined communities" (40-49). Ernest Gellner points to the homogenizing effect universal literacy had on the constitution of a unified national culture in the modern era (39-50), a phenomenon that Eric Hobsbawm has characterized as the nation's self-made "invented tradition" (1-14). These recent critical contributions have been provocative and influential for the analysis of nationalism, but some of their insights have come at the cost of over-generalization. For instance, the notion of gender in popular works and a gender-specific form of reading is surprisingly absent from these discussions. This omission needs to be remedied. Thus, my second reason for focusing on women as gendered readers of the *Gartenlaube* is to suggest a modification of such theoretical approaches to the construction of national identity and, in particular, to explore the significance of gendered reading for the case of German identity in the late nineteenth century. In doing so, my article argues against the facile presumption that the *Gartenlaube*'s entertainment section and pictures were "das sentimentale Reich der Frau" and clearly distinct from the pedagogical objectives of the magazine (Zimmermann 70).[2]

The *Gartenlaube* is particularly interesting and revealing as a "surface manifestation" (Kracauer 67) of the nineteenth century because of its overwhelming popularity. The steady increase in its circulation beginning with its first year of publication suggests it communicated a "message" that many middle-class readers found attractive. According to one source, the magazine had an initial printing of 5,000 in 1853, which increased dramatically to 14,500 by the end of its second year, to 60,000 by the end of its fourth year, to 160,000 by 1863, and to its largest circulation of 382,000 by 1875.[3] In addition, the magazine's appearance in reading rooms, lending libraries, and cafes as well as in the living room of many middle-class families implies that each copy was usually read by several people, a fact that has led some scholars to estimate a *Gartenlaube* readership in the millions.[4] The magazine's wide geographical distribution also attests to its importance as a unified disseminator of ideas and indicator of supra-regional interests; it could be found in all parts of Germany, from Saxony to Baden to Bremen and as far abroad as Brazil and Australia.

A central aspect of the magazine's popularity and broad appeal was no doubt its adoption of the entire middle-class family as its targeted reading audience. The inspiration for the magazine came from its publisher Ernst Keil while he was serving a prison sentence in 1852 for his revolutionary publicist activities. With its initial publication in 1853, the *Gartenlaube* constituted a continuation of the liberal struggle. Keil's objective was to reach and enlighten the broadest possible segment of the German middle classes, because (as an early *Gartenlaube* article put it) freedom is only possible "in einer ziemlich gleichmäßig gebildeten, gleichmäßig tugendhaften Gesellschaft mit gleichen Interessen" (1855, 424).[5] Yet, the conservative post-1848 political climate in Germany severely limited the public form these liberal, democratic ideas could take. Keil's response to the censorship of the restoration period was to cast the intentions of the magazine as neutral and apolitical. Thus, the magazine's self-introduction to its readers on the first page of the first issue appears cautious and tentative: "Fern aller raisonnirenden Politik und allem Meinungsstreit in Religions- und anderen Sachen, wollen wir Euch in wahrhaft guten Erzählungen einführen in die Geschichte des Menschenherzens und der Völker" (1853, 1). The professed apolitical nature of the magazine's content was further tied to the ideal reading context suggested by this introduction. Although the magazine was also available in some public places, it explicitly addressed itself to the middle-class family reading within the privacy of the domestic sphere.[6] The peacefulness of an interior private space or of cultivated nature established the prescribed domestic context of the *Gartenlaube* from its beginning. Over the years, the magazine reaffirmed its program of speaking to the family within the security of the home, or what might be called the "private Öffentlichkeit" of middle-class society.[7]

My argument here is that this domestic agenda was more than a preemptive measure against political censorship in a conservative era. I suggest that the familial or intimate appeal of the *Gartenlaube* was central to its ideological program. In particular, the magazine's success in defining a national and class identity in late nineteenth-century Germany was directly tied to the domestication of its readership. Put another way, the claim to represent the positions of its audience rested upon its ability both to communicate the magazine's interest in the reader and to construct the broadest, most inclusive definition of the reader. Although the *Gartenlaube* could envision the ideal context for reading as "am traulichen Ofen" or in a shady arbor "wenn vom Apfelbaume die weiß und rothen Blüthen fallen" (1853, 1), its programmatic statement was much more vague about just what constituted the reading German family. In part, it obviously envisioned the family as a mixed gender group, an audience of both men and women. The explicit inclusion of women readers was central to its establishment of the middle-class family as the basic building block of German national identity. To understand this project of domestication in the service of the nation, we need to consider the construction of the *Gartenlaube*'s female readership.

As a periodical meant for the whole family, the *Gartenlaube* did not prescriptively identify certain material as intended for female as opposed to male readers. Given the contemporary notions of appropriate reading material for women and their reading preferences, however, the editorial staff most likely had implicit notions concerning the texts that would be read by women. In order to identify the place of the woman reader, one needs to consider the space occupied by women within the texts of the *Gartenlaube*. The essay (including biographical sketches and historical exposés) was the dominant genre in the *Gartenlaube*, focusing primarily on prominent men such as officers, politicians, and poets. When women were featured, it was usually as the wives, sisters, or mothers of notable men. In rare cases, women became the subject of articles and essays independent of men, but then most often in the context of their familial and domestic identity. This emphasis on domesticity even found its way into articles on popular science that presented anthropomorphized familial organization and behavior within the animal kingdom. Finally, articles explicitly addressed to women pertained mostly to feminine, domestic concerns. As we shall later see, even leading figures of the women's movement featured in the *Gartenlaube* were reinscribed within the context of the family.

Thus, judging the magazine solely in terms of thematic frequency, we might conclude that women played a marginal role in the composition of the *Gartenlaube*. But other sources indicate that women were central to the success of the magazine on several levels. Whereas men were often the subject of factual, historical reports, women figured prominently in the magazine's fiction, which highlighted love stories or domestic scenarios. In one sample year (1855), for instance, the fictional tales had such titles as "Die Braut," "Der gestohlene Brautschatz," "Braut und Gattin," "Eine seltene Frau," "Das spanische Mädchen," "Die Stiefmutter," and "Der Diebstahl aus Liebe." Clearly, bringing the family together as a reading audience included appealing to women and their presumed preferences. Although the *Gartenlaube* mastheads from the beginning depicted a grandfather figure reading aloud to a family around the table, it has been suggested that the woman of the house was probably most often responsible for purchasing the magazine.[8] In his outline for the creation of the *Gartenlaube*, Keil explicitly took the woman reader into consideration as the measure for his magazine. It was important to him that the contributions be written "so daß sie die gewöhnlichsten Handwerker, besonders aber die Frauen verstehen können" (Barth 177). The question that remains unanswered here (in terms of the magazine's logic) is whether Keil's goal to make the *Gartenlaube* accessible to women was intended as a way to sell more issues and create more demand (sensing that women had a voice in domestic purchases) or as a way to reach the entire family for the pedagogical goal of educating a self-assured, enlightened middle class.

To contextualize Keil's assessment of women's importance in his project it is instructive to study the topics concerning women that received repeated treatment in the *Gartenlaube* from the mid-1860s to the mid-1880s. This analysis can help us understand both how the woman reader was conceived by the *Gartenlaube* and what role she played in the magazine's project as a whole. The repetition of these topics not only indicates the perceived popularity of the themes with the readership, but also constitutes a textual space in which the magazine can refer to its own earlier positions, thus accentuating its significance both as a mediator of important ideas and as a successful product. Three topics that the *Gartenlaube* editorship apparently considered worth discussing repeatedly were the role of the housewife, women's political emancipation, and women's reading interests.

In the first case, it is significant that there are very few articles that focus on the characteristics of the German housewife. However, although two articles from the 1860s, "Die amerikanische Hausfrau" (1866) and "Zur Charakteristik amerikanischer Frauen" (1867), focus on American women, they are ultimately also about the German housewife or the supposed characteristics of German women, who are addressed in the second person and defined as the audience. This situation is similar to the way the popular anthropological interest of the *Gartenlaube* in Americans on the frontier or Africans in their villages is frequently used to make statements about German society. Identity, be it German identity or German female identity, is often defined by contrast, through comparison with another model.

The articles begin by praising the virtues of the American housewife, generalizing that she is usually attractive, clean, and meticulously concerned about her dress. The American woman is a caring, sometimes overconcerned mother, who takes care of the children's education and is often just as clever and educated as her husband. As a domestic angel, she makes her home as pleasant and attractive as possible, but perhaps her most admirable qualities are her ability to comfort and support her husband in his financial misfortunes and her marital fidelity in times of forced separation (1866, 120–21). The first article goes on to note that American women who are not married have pursued a wide range of occupations which could serve as a model for their European counterparts and that they seem close to achieving the right to vote. But these apparently progressive qualities are qualified at the end of the article when the gradual spread of a sensible household economy in America is credited to the influence of German immigrant women. This move both privileges proper domesticity and ties it to a national ethnic identity, specifically to German domesticity.

More remarkable than this list of ideal characteristics and goals are the strategies by which the magazine 1) presumes reader knowledge, 2) posits the limitations of its female readership and 3) describes women's expectations and desires. The first paragraph of the 1866 article introduces the subject matter: "Die Leserinnen der *Gartenlaube* wissen gewiß schon etwas davon, daß die Stellung der amerikanischen Hausfrau von der

der deutschen nicht unbedeutend verschieden ist, und möchten darüber ein Weiteres erfahren." The article suggests a direct tie between reader desires and needs and the magazine's willingness to satisfy them. The very next sentence apologizes to the women readers for the length of this article that will require them to read longer than they are accustomed to in one sitting. This and similar statements make two assertions. First they presume an exclusively female audience; this initial appeal is repeated throughout the article with each successive address to "unsere deutsche Leserin," or "unsere Leserinnen." In the second place they assert the inferior attention span of women readers. Such condescending remarks, however, ignore the fact that women reading the magazine's fictional contributions dealt with much longer passages than this one that is only just over two pages long.

Such examples of narrative intervention are central to establishing a unity of reading identity and judgment. Each of these forms of address suggests the complicity of the reader with the author of the article and with the *Gartenlaube* as a whole. Ultimately, it assumes agreement among readers by implying that the magazine is simply communicating to the woman reader what she already senses as well as what she wants to know. Thus, these articles reveal that the magazine mediates an identity to female readers through their process of reading, not just by way of the content of a particular passage. Certainly, the similarities and differences between German and American housewives play a role in forming a self-identity in such articles, but the appeal to the identity of the woman as a reader with specific desires and expectations is central to the construction of her identity as a narrative participant. The *Gartenlaube* becomes not only her access to contrastive images of femininity and Germanness, but also a mirror of her own desires, expectations, and abilities.

In addition to the theme of domesticity, the women's movement is a second topic that finds repeated coverage in the *Gartenlaube* over the decades. In general, the woman's question is posed by the magazine in moderate form. An early article on the German "Frauenbewegung" attempts to set it apart from the demands of the older French movement, which it labels decadent and extremist and which supposedly had its roots in the French Revolution. The woman's question of the post-1848 period in Germany is accepted as legitimate precisely because it can be categorized as "eine volksthümliche Erziehungs- und Bildungs-, eine Erwerbs- und Berufsfrage" (1871, 818). The organizations that advocate solutions to this question are tolerable to the author only because they have tried to remain free "von dilletantischer Hereinziehung der hohen Sozialpolitik, von unberechtigter Eitelkeit" (1871, 818). Perhaps the most redeeming quality of this activism, in this author's opinion, is the fact that it has not altered the traditional notion of the German family: "Das innerste Wesen des deutschen Hauses, der deutschen Frau, Ehe und Familie blieb vielmehr unter allen wechselnden Strömungen des neueren Kulturumschwunges was es immer gewesen" (1871, 817).

While the organized women's movement of the 1860s and beyond was subdued in comparison to demands made in the *Vormärz* (Evans 24-30), its coverage in this article additionally dampens the political implications of women's activism. As the author explicitly states, the point of this article is not to present a history of this women's organization, a description of its institutions, or the platform of the "Allgemeiner deutscher Frauenverein" founded in 1865. Rather, the approach is personal: to affirm for its readers the talent, knowledge, education, and especially the "Herzens- und Charakterernst verbunden mit echter Weiblichkeit" of the main female proponents. The author concludes by writing that the *Gartenlaube* believes itself to be serving the interests of its female readers when it presents the portraits of both Auguste Schmidt and Louise Otto-Peters, the two presiding members of the German women's union (1871, 818). Again, the magazine's strategy with respect to a "woman's topic" is to argue that it is merely addressing and affirming pre-existing reader desires.

At the same time, the women's movement is of interest for the magazine as an intimate story. In this way, women's issues, which could potentially serve to divide the overarching class and national goals of the German middle-class family, undergo narrative domestication and personalization in the *Gartenlaube*. An article from 1883 that reports on the thirteenth national convention of the *Allgemeiner deutscher Frauenverein* (1883, 718-22) demonstrates this process. It begins as a veritable celebration of the women's union: "diese Tathsache muß mit aufrichtiger Freude begrüßt werden." But then it mentions the fears within the German male populace ("Was wollen diese fremden Frauen von den unsrigen?") and seeks to allay them by suggesting that the *Gartenlaube* aims to present an objective image of the movement: "Sehen wir uns nun die deutschen Frauen...genauer an, lauschen wir ein Weilchen ihren Vorträgen.... Treten wir also ein in den Versammlungsaal des letzten Düsseldorfer Frauentages!" (1883, 718).

What claims to be an objective overview, however, characterizes this political activity as "die sittlich ernsten Bestrebungen dieser weiblichen Pioniere." In effect, this depiction moderates and contains the changes demanded by the women's movement through two narrative maneuvers. In the first place, it takes a personal look at these women to make them familiar and thus unthreatening. In this representation the women become noteworthy for their positive feminine characteristics: they are "angels" for their husbands in time of need, they are unique beauties, delicate and small, selfless in their dedication to others and, finally, they see their highest happiness in a peaceful, ordered family life and a happy marriage. The novelty of radical demands such as women's right to an education is thus domesticated. Ultimately, despite the advocacy of women's right and duty to work, the most highly valued job seems to be that of the German "Hausfrau." Just as a mother lives not for herself but for her family, so too (this article argues) the women's movement does not seek the betterment of women, but rather the improvement of the German people, i.e., their children and husbands. The article closes by suggesting explicitly: "diese Frauenbewegung, wie wir sie nunmehr kennen gelernt haben, kann nur unsere Sympathien erwecken" (1883, 722).

This assertion of domestic familiarity is accentuated by the second narrative strategy in this article, a strategy that is representative of the *Gartenlaube*'s narration in general. The magazine is self-reflexive whenever possible, reminding the readers of its role in presenting them with new material. An example of this can be found in the repeated announcements that readers have already encountered these members of the women's movement in the pages of the *Gartenlaube*: "Die kleine Frau mit der Brille, an die wir uns jetzt wenden, ist unsern Lesern wohl bekannt, denn in letzter Zeit hat die *Gartenlaube* gelegentlich der Hygiene-Ausstellung auf ihre Verdienste mehrmals hinweisen können" (1883, 720). But the most explicit reference in the article to the work of the *Gartenlaube* itself is the final statement: "und wir schließen mit dem herzlichen Wunsche, daß diese Zeilen dazu beitragen mögen, dies edle Streben deutscher Frauen mehr und mehr zu verbreiten und zu fördern" (1883, 722). This self-reflexive maneuver is a sign of the magazine's role as a creator and former of the German nation, not just a transmitter of others' ideas and values.

In the case of women's issues, the *Gartenlaube* claims to be the servant and advisor of German women for the betterment of the entire German *Volk*. The magazine's notion that its female readers seem to need more advice in order to properly identify themselves as members of the national community becomes evident in the *Gartenlaube*'s presentation of fictional texts. As a magazine that began each weekly issue with a serialized novel or novella, the *Gartenlaube* became active in guiding the literary taste and experience of its female readers. One common approach to this education was the publication of letters from literary figures and critics (such as the liberals Karl Gutzkow and Rudolf Gottschall) to an individual woman who had supposedly requested instruction in the state of the literary arts and in judging literature.

In the case of Gutzkow's letters "an eine deutsche Frau in Paris" about literature, the *Gartenlaube* does not simply document an exchange (be it either real or fictional), but rather acknowledges its own role as the sole mediator of this dialogue. Gutzkow begins his first letter to his female correspondent by mentioning its publication in the *Gartenlaube*: "Nicht nur daß ich die Briefe...wirklich schreibe; Ich umgehe auch die Briefbeförderungsanstalten des kaiserlich französischen

Generalpostmeisters...und schicke Ihnen meine Antworten...durch—die *Gartenlaube*" (1869, 72). This reference alone implies several things. First, it alludes to the magazine's wide distribution, since it presupposes that the German woman to whom he writes subscribes to the *Gartenlaube* or at least reads it regularly in Paris. In addition, the fact that Gutzkow feels compelled to reconstruct the encounter that led to this literary correspondence reveals that, at least in its present form, this letter is intended not only for this particular woman, but for the entire (female) readership of the *Gartenlaube*. Both of these points, the distribution and the communication between two Germans about German literature across a national border, suggest that there is another function to be discovered in the inclusion of a female reading audience for the *Gartenlaube*. In this instance, it gives the excuse for a discussion of German literature in the guise of educating a female reader.

In fact, what is being educated here is a German reader. With the pretext of writing to a "lady," both Gutzkow and Gottschall repeatedly refer to certain characteristics of German literature as explicitly national. These letters use many of the techniques that construct a unified nation found in other texts within the *Gartenlaube*, such as references to typically German landscapes (the sea, oak trees, grape vines, and the Rhine river). In talking about the status and quality of contemporary literature, they also appeal to a common notion of Germanness such as Gottschall's praise of Auerbach's novel *Landhaus am Rhein* as successfully depicting "Die Stimmung der Natur, der Landschaft, des Volkslebens" (1870, 90) while generalizing for his reading audience the romantic associations of the Rhine that he knew as a child: "So steht das flüchtig genossene Rheinpanorama anmuthig vor jeder Erinnerung, auch vor der Ihrigen, Madame!" (1870, 90). Gutzkow sees in his correspondent's renewed encounter (also along this national river) with German spirit the source for her literary interest: "Ja, Sie fühlten wieder die Eigenart Ihres Volkes, unsre Kraft, unsre zähe Ausdauer, die eiserne Festigkeit unsres Willens—! Sie hörten die Quellen wieder rauschen, aus deren Tiefe wir jene Schalen füllen, aus denen sich der Rausch der Begeisterung trinkt!" (1869, 73). Using an erotically charged vocabulary, Gutzkow translates the woman's experience into images of a powerful (masculine) nation. In this way, literature and the nation are continually brought together for the reader in the name of enlightening the uninformed female reader.

The purpose of these contributions in the *Gartenlaube* is, as Gottschall even says of his letters, to give a report now and then on the state of contemporary literature for an interested reader (1869, 745). But a large part of the *Gartenlaube* itself was made up of literature, i.e., novellas and novels serialized for weekly consumption. Indeed, some critics have suggested that the magazine owed part of its success to the popularity of its "star author" Eugenie Marlitt. Marlitt's first big hit in the *Gartenlaube* was her novel *Goldelse,* which appeared in 1866.[9] This work launched the author's long-term collaboration with the *Gartenlaube* and in particular with Ernst Keil, who quickly became an ardent supporter of Marlitt and her work. Indeed, *Goldelse* appealed so strongly to Keil that he chose it for publication even though it was significantly longer than most pieces of fiction accepted at that time. Following *Goldelse,* several other Marlitt novels appeared in quick succession in the *Gartenlaube*: *Das Geheimnis der alten Mamsell* (1867), *Reichsgräfin Gisela* (1869), and *Das Heideprinzeßchen* (1871), all of which were also soon published in record numbers as book editions.[10] The immediate popularity and success of Marlitt's first novel is attested to by the fact that the *Gartenlaube* editors quickly included her name in their December 1866 list, which previewed the contributors for the following year.[11]

For these reasons, *Goldelse* can serve here as a typical, but also exemplary piece of fiction from the *Gartenlaube*. Marlitt's works were not only intended for and read by women; readers' letters from men attested to their appreciation of her as well.[12] However, a careful analysis of this narrative demonstrates the manner in which it privileges a woman's perspective. As we have seen, the political essays in the *Gartenlaube* that discuss the so-called woman's question and women's organizations limit or restrain emancipatory ideas through a reassertion of domesticity. Likewise, the fictional work of Marlitt—a main feature of the magazine in the 1860s and 1870s—also ends up affirming a domestic identity for its female readers. In such novels, however, the force that is controlled through this domestication is not women's political emancipation, but the potentially more disruptive power of female (sexual) desire. Certainly, these fictional stories make reference to the changing social place of women, revealing Marlitt's close political proximity to the liberalism of the *Gartenlaube*'s editor, Ernst Keil.[13] However, the appeal of such texts to (especially younger) female readers seems to be tied to a domestication of the reader.

Goldelse tells the story of Elisabeth Ferber, whose family has been the victim of bad luck: her father lost his job and her mother was meanly denied her inheritance by her aristocratic father for having married into the bourgeoisie. The story begins with Elisabeth working hard to support her parents and younger brother in the face of poverty, thus establishing at the outset her nurturing, mothering nature and her determination and strength. Most importantly, however, it is her domestic abilities and inclination that set the stage for her later path. When her uncle, the prince's forester, arranges a job for her father, the family moves from the city to the old ramshackle castle Frau Ferber was saddled with where, contrary to their expectations, they find comfort and domestic bliss. In this setting as well, Elisabeth (also called Goldelse) proves herself to be in every respect the "angel of the house," a combination of feminine daintiness (elegant, slender white fingers) and domestic energy, doing household chores with her uncle's housekeeper,[14] fetching his pipe and keeping all coffee cups warm and replenished, caring for her younger brother, and supporting her new acquaintance, the young invalid Helene von Walde.

From the beginning, then, the novel depicts the middle-class family as a coherent and stable social group able to overcome financial adversity. The daughter is a skilled domestician whose moral training will guarantee the continuance of the family and its values. Tension mounts when a new threat to the security of this middle-class world appears. This threat is (sexual) desire. The challenge it presents to the coherent family is what creates the narrative suspense and the novel's presumed appeal to the female reader. The story can best be summarized as follows: at the end of the third sequel, Goldelse surveys the region around her new home through a telescope; with this magnifier of the gaze she spots a man, "jung, groß und schlank" (1866, 38). This man, Hollfeld, soon becomes attracted to Goldelse and begins pursuing her, at first genteelly and then agressively, while she, disturbed by his forward behavior, consistently rejects him. Hollfeld's undisguised desire is a threat to Elisabeth's code of modesty, virginity, and domesticity because it expresses itself as uncontrollable lust for the heroine; this is dark, dangerous desire. A brighter form of human passion is the heroine's slowly developing attraction to the hero Rudolph von Walde who, despite his aristocratic identity, exhibits bourgeois restraint and respect. The hero desires Else in return, but, as in most romance novels, both are unaware or are repeatedly made unsure of the other's feelings, so that they run the risk of missing their opportunity to come together.[15]

Both forms of desire increase throughout the novel, but they are constantly paralleled and thus checked by the domestic tendency and activity of the heroine. The tension between the good and bad forces peaks when, in the next to last sequel, the mad woman, Bertha, who had been a real victim of Hollfeld's seduction, comes close to killing Elisabeth. Elisabeth is rescued from this danger by the man she desires: "Die Stimme ging ihr durch Mark und Bein, denn es war *seine* Stimme" (1866, 274). Thus, at the close of the novel, evil in the form of uncontrolled sexual appetite is rejected. The other form of desire (Elisabeth's) is characterized as non-sexual and is placed firmly in the service of domestication as the hero and heroine are united, marry, and found a family. All participants in bad forms of desire are dead or banished from the scene: Hollfeld who is lustful and manipulative and Helene whose love of Hollfeld is blind and whose physical weakness prevents her from fulfilling a domestic role. Middle-class domestic virtue steps in as a cure for a whole host of moral ills. In the epilogue, the reader learns that the arrogant Baroness Lessen, whose hautiness and taste for luxury had wreaked havoc in Lindhof before Rudolf von Walde's return, is punished by having to lead a modest lifestyle that requires her to do her own domestic chores. Bertha—whose sexual disgrace was paralleled throughout the novel by her failure in domestic activities—is given a second chance to behave domestically and morally as a farmwife in America. The absence of domestic responsibility in women leads to aristocratic decadence or immorality; simple domesticity is victorious on every front as the mark of middle-class superiority. In the logic of the novel, domesticity is a form of self-regulation that is (or becomes) an end in itself.

But what is the role of the reader, in particular, of the female reading subject in all of this? Clearly, this story of the victory of upright bourgeois ideals over aristocratic decadence would appeal to a nineteenth-century middle-class audience in principle. But more specifically, in this novel, as in Marlitt's others, the privileged subjective perspective is feminine. The action follows the path of Elisabeth, presenting the reader throughout with the view of the fictional world that is in her purview at any one time. That is to say, the reader is almost always in the same place as Elisabeth; only rarely do we find descriptions that would be beyond her perception. All other characters are introduced through Elisabeth's eyes, and most subjective experiences in the text, such as feeling, recognizing, and seeing, are Elisabeth's. This makes her the dominant source of narrative focalization.[16]

More importantly, however, even the desire that is expressed in the narrative is that of the female gaze. The best example of this is the view the reader gets through the telescope that Elisabeth points at the Lindhof. From the first—"Da rückten die gewaltigen, ernsten Bergkuppen herüber..." (1866, 36)—this gaze is clearly identified as Elisabeth's. Even the randomness or directedness of her gaze is made explicit by the narration: "Hatte Elisabeth das Fernrohr bis dahin rastlos von einem Gegenstande zu dem andern wandern lassen, so suchte sie jetzt einen festen Halt und Stützpunkt für dasselbe; denn sie hatte eine Entdeckung gemacht, die ihr Interesse in hohem Grade fesselte" (1866, 37). The next long paragraph gives a detailed description of the garden at Lindhof, then of the young lady (Helene) reclining there until finally Elisabeth's gaze comes to rest on the object of Helene's view, "das Gesicht eines Mannes" (1866, 38). This is the culmination of the descriptive passage. Here Elisabeth's first contact with and searching description of a man begins a series of instances in which women (in the form of Elisabeth or a focalized female narrator) gaze at men, either with desire or fearful of being desired. In either case, however, the view of the woman is prioritized, her desire is narrated.

However, just as female desire is shut down at the end of the novel, so too is the subjective voice of Elisabeth silenced; she gets her man, she "is happy," but she disappears as the agent of the story, as the focalizing subject. Both she and her desire are domesticated. For the female readers of the *Gartenlaube* then, reading could mean pleasure and the space to explore certain positive and negative, threatening and legitimate forms of desire through fictional heroines. In the end, however, it seems that this desire is explored only to be contained by the power of domestic authority. Indeed, the genius of Marlitt within the context of the *Gartenlaube* is her ability to create these desiring women, figures who are both morally strong and the source of focalization, but who eventually participate in the domestication of desire.

This is not to say that these narrative economies of desire were unique to the *Gartenlaube* or even to late nineteenth-century Germany. Certainly, feminist critics like Tania Modleski and Janice Radway have analyzed the ambiguously empowering function of twentieth-century "mass-produced fantasies for women."[17] Likewise, the German novels of Marlitt were not that different from women's literature in other countries at the time. My discussion of Marlitt is indebted to the work of Nancy Armstrong who has convincingly shown in a wide range of English texts from the eighteenth to nineteenth centuries the gradual domestication of desire. Armstrong suggests that the constructed separation of public from private life that was central to middle-class stability and power can be traced in the history of domestic fiction. The reason for dealing with Marlitt in detail has been to highlight the *Gartenlaube*'s strategy of domesticating its female readership, to insist on the magazine's role in the ideological separation of men and women into distinct public and private spheres in the nineteenth century. My argument is that Marlitt's narrative maneuver helped inscribe the female reader's desire back into the values of middle-class work.[18]

An additional, clearly national function of this gendered narration is stated explicitly in the *Gartenlaube* years later when the magazine interprets the importance of Marlitt, and in particular *Goldelse,* for its readers. Besides the major works of Marlitt, which appeared in quick succession, Marlitt herself and her work were repeatedly the subject of articles in the magazine (three times from 1869 to 1875). An essay entitled "Bei der Verfasserin der *Gold-Else*" from 1869 celebrates the simple, withdrawn lifestyle of this modest lady in the personal tone of an intimate visit in her home. Marlitt is depicted as enduring her rheumatism "mit dem Lächeln echt weiblicher Ergebung und mit der Ruhe einer großen Seele" (1869, 827). Since even one as modest as she cannot deny her success, the article emphasizes that for Marlitt only the pleasure of her readers matters: she is happy if they like her. The inspiration for her writing is described as a drive to make herself useful to the world as best she can, a motherly attitude of service and sacrifice from this woman who was not a biological mother.

A second article, written after the *Reichsgründung* in 1871, affirms both the popularity of Marlitt's novels (and characters) and the social function they acquire because of this success. In this article, the claims that Armstrong has made for the class-affirming function of such texts can be expanded; the domestication of women is used to contribute to the solidification of a national identity as well. "Gold-Else" is depicted as a favorite figure of women readers and is credited with having given innumerable Germans an emotional antidote to the heated conflict of 1866; that was the year *Goldelse* appeared in the *Gartenlaube* and the year of the divisive "Brüderkrieg" between Prussia and Austria. According to the *Gartenlaube*, Marlitt's fictional character had a profound effect on its national readers within that historical context: "ein goldhaariges deutsches Mädchen hatte ein Wunder gewirkt und die zerstreuten Blicke einer wankenden, von leidenschaftlicher Gährung und blutigem Streit erfüllten Welt, auf den schlichten und stillen Glanz ihrer anmuthvollen Erscheinung gelenkt" (1871, 803). The magazine attributes to its feminine fiction a role in the process of national unification when it insists that this virgin symbolized the proud "Kampf des Jahrhunderts, das heitere Siegesbewußtsein der ringenden Zeit- und Volksgedanken."[19] The essay implies that although women are inherently domestic creatures they also contribute to the national cause by appealing to the healthy instinct of the people, i.e., by insisting on the containment of desire while affirming the family and bourgeois values. The *Gartenlaube* thus had given its readers a domestic ideal that it deemed appropriate for the German nation.

In terms of the *Gartenlaube*'s own perceived importance for its readership, this essay is also an advertisement for *Goldelse*. It announces and praises the new illustrated *Prachtausgabe* that will appear just in time for Christmas. But it also advertises (after the fact) its own past role in introducing the German audience to this novel and, in a broader sense, to Marlitt, its author. The article reminds readers that the "chaste story" that brought a ray of sunlight into hearts and homes of the nation was first carried through the world "auf den Schultern der *Gartenlaube*" (1871, 804), estimating that one and a half million people read it in the pages of the magazine. Thus, the subsequent success of the story (that as a book had been published in at least six editions by 1871) is cited as proof of the social good sense of the *Gartenlaube* in identifying the taste of its audience, but also in providing its readership with morally good reading material.

In these articles, the *Gartenlaube* often portrays the woman reader as the grateful beneficiary of the magazine, who also repays this debt by giving testimony for the magazine. One example is an essay that appeared in 1875 to commemorate the *Gartenlaube*'s star-author by describing a so-called "Marlitt-Blatt," a reproduction of a large-format oil painting that depicted the author surrounded by five of her heroines. The article begins by praising the painting, its subject Marlitt, and her model female characters, but then passes the torch to several Marlitt readers, all women, who give their "responses" to Marlitt. This example combines statements from readers with the *Gartenlaube*'s other strategies for treating women: it praises women in a domestic setting, then touches on issues of the women's movement and, finally collapses it back into the domestic sphere by appealing to the activity of reading.

The readers' letters chosen for the article are significant for their appeal to a domestication of reading and a domestication of the potentially radical demands of the women's movement. One reader is identified simply as a "Swiss girl" who first affirms her anti-aristocratic solidarity with Marlitt's female heroines. She then characterizes the enthusiasm of her grandmother and aunts in listening to her read the stories aloud in what is an intimate community of women readers in the idyll of a rural interior setting, an old "Stube." This naive and immediate appreciation of Marlitt is followed by an intellectual woman who was initially skeptical of Marlitt's works because they avoided the "woman's question." But eventually, this reader confesses to her conversion; her involvement with these heroines has convinced her that they are the true models for an emancipation of women. They reveal, she claims, how harmoniously the independence of women can be integrated "mit dem Zauber edelschöner Weiblichkeit" (1875, 70).

Perhaps the most intriguing aspect of this article is again the *Gartenlaube*'s compunction to advertise and sell itself. This is a fundamental element of articles on various themes, but it is particularly prevalent in discussions of female readers. Here, the celebration of the painting—and thus of Marlitt, her stories, and her readers—emphasizes the magazine's importance in creating and maintaining this audience. The essay praises the *Gartenlaube* for playing the biggest role in Marlitt's success. On the one hand, the magazine takes credit for the readers' access to Marlitt: one German women from Ohio testifies, "wenn die *Gartenlaube* kommt, stürze ich darüber her, verschlinge die Fortsetzungen mit wahrem Heißhunger" (1875, 70). On the other hand, in its turn to the readers for affirmation—"wollen wir nicht Diejenigen mitsprechen lassen, deren Briefe meist erst durch die Hand der Redaktion an ihre [Marlitt's] Adresse gelangt sind?" (1875, 68)—the essay insists on the *Gartenlaube*'s role of bringing the readers to Marlitt (not just Marlitt to the readers). Marlitt may be the star, but the *Gartenlaube* is the mediator between her and her audience, in both directions. Indeed, it seems that the wide distribution of her works (the letters included here are from Germany, Switzerland, and America) is a function of their being carried around the globe "on the shoulders" of the *Gartenlaube*. The *Gartenlaube* gives the impression of being an early example of a highly self-conscious commodity, a product aware of the need to refer to its own value. It is not surprising that such an article from the mid-70s coincided with the inclusion, in this and other weekly magazines, of advertising supplements. The magazine simultaneously viewed itself both as a commodity that had to appeal to a public and as the creator of that public.

To return to our point of departure, I suggest we have seen what a discussion of women, domesticity, and commodification in the *Gartenlaube* can contribute to an understanding of the conception of the nation. Theoreticians of nationalism, such as Anderson, Gellner, and Hobsbawm, have proposed that the nation must be understood as a construction in the minds of its members. Anderson, in particular, has coined the term "imagined community" to define the substance of the nation: "It is *imagined* because the members of even the smallest nations will never know most of their fellow-members, meet them, or even hear of them, yet in the minds of each lives the image of their communion" (15). These thinkers all insist, however, that the nation as "imagined" and "invented" is not any less real. For Anderson and for Gellner, the rise of literacy and a large reading public were prerequisites for the modern nationalism that characterizes the nineteenth century.[20] My project on the construction of a national identity in the popular reading materials of nineteenth-century Germany is heavily indebted to Anderson's concept of a community of readers that imagines itself as a coherent nation. According to this notion, each reader envisions him- or herself as just one of thousands (or, in the case of the *Gartenlaube*, millions) of individuals participating in the same exchange of information and images through a common print medium.

Yet, Anderson does not take into account the different reading practices and different modes of address that explicitly separated men and women readers within an otherwise apparently uniform experience. The investigation of women readers within the *Gartenlaube* tells us that the narrative constitution of a national self through reading was not a completely uniform endeavor: gender remained a marker of difference in terms of the magazine's appeal to its readers. By billing itself as a "family magazine," the *Gartenlaube* appealed to the family as an unfractured base upon which to address the entire population as potential participants in an imagined reading community. In this attempt, women were explicitly included, but they were de facto the representative of the domestic sphere. If the family was to remain a stable entity for the construction of national belonging, then women had to bridge the space between the home and the nation. I contend that this happened by domesticating both women as they appeared in the magazine and women as readers of the *Gartenlaube*. The female reader herself was identified in the pages of the magazine as having different capabilities and interests and thus the need and desire to be spoken to in a different way.

This insight is important to understanding the appeal of nineteenth-century popular texts to women. But beyond this, a gender critique of this medium helps us see that, in the final analysis, the *Gartenlaube* can be read as a constant attempt to merge and synthesize disparate groups (here women and men; elsewhere various regional identities and class affiliations) to construct a cohesive, unified national identity. The example of the *Gartenlaube* shows that the nation as an "imagined community" of readers is predicated on certain accepted divisions, divisions that are placed in the service of a narrative of unity. An analysis of the "gendered" premise concerning the family can help us expand on the influential concept of the imagined nation. More generally, gender and the notion of a gendered reader should be central to analyses of popular narratives.

Notes

[1] *Die Gartenlaube* began publication in 1853 under the lead of Ernst Keil. After Keil's death in 1878 the magazine was sold twice (by Keil's widow in 1884 to the Gebrüder Kröner Verlag and again in 1904 to the Scherl Verlag). After its name was changed to the *Neue Gartenlaube* in 1938, it ceased publication in 1944. Despite this longevity, the nineteenth century was the period of the *Gartenlaube*'s greatest success.

[2] Previous work on the *Gartenlaube* includes: Gruppe, Rischke, Rosenstrauch, Sieburg, Wachtel, Wallraf, Zahn, and Zimmermann. Of these existing scholarly discussions, only Rosenstrauch refers to a developed notion of the "reader" (169) and none analyzes in any detail the gender differentiation in the magazine's appeal to male versus female readers.

[3] See Barth, esp. 184–89. Other scholars have cited different numbers. See Rolf Engelsing's figure of 460,000 in the year 1873 (Engelsing 1005). Barth suggests that some of the misguided statistics were already corrected in the pages of the *Gartenlaube* itself, which noticed these overestimates. Despite the variation in actual numbers cited, all scholars agree on the general trend of a remarkable and unprecedented increase in the first twenty years of the magazine's publication.

[4] See Engelsing's statistics on the *Gartenlaube*'s distribution (Engelsing 1005–24). Rosenstrauch estimates a readership of five million by 1876.

[5] Not only was Ernst Keil "ein entschlossener Publizist im Geiste des demokratischen Liberalismus," but numerous editors of the magazine were also members of the liberal-democratic *Nationalverein* (Gruppe 27–33).

[6] Although it quickly became a model for imitations, Keil's magazine was not the first to appeal to the family in the privacy of the home as an audience withdrawn from the noise of public politics. Karl Gutzkow's *Unterhaltungen am häuslichen Herd,* which preceded the *Gartenlaube* by a few years, did the same: "Es gibt Zeiten, wo sich jede Überzeugung in die Familie flüchtet.... Der häusliche Herd ist uns keine gedankenlose Plauderstube... er ist und wird uns bleiben

das sichere Asyl ernster Lebensauffassung...eine allgemeine Vereinigung der Menschen als Menschen, wenn auch Parteiung sie zerrisse" (quoted in Zahn).

[7] The historian Thomas Nipperdey uses this term to describe nineteenth-century associations, but his characterization of these organizations as a space for public discussion of morals and principles distinct from political state institutions also applies to a publication like the *Gartenlaube* (195). This notion is related to what Jürgen Habermas identifies as the literary public sphere in his *Strukturwandel der Öffentlichkeit* (44 ff.). Habermas even makes passing reference to the *Gartenlaube* (196).

[8] Engelsing suggests that the taste of the housewife was the deciding factor in family's subscriptions (1009). His sources for this contention are, however, quite thin, primarily a quote from Peter Hilles's novel *Die Sozialisten*. This is the kind of primary information that is difficult, if not impossible, to locate or verify.

[9] Eugenie John's first submission to the *Gartenlaube* was sent in by her brother under the pseudonym E. Marlitt. Keil approved of the story "Die zwölf Apostel," published it in 1865, and encouraged the "contributor" to write further novels. When her *Goldelse* appeared in serialized form in 1866, the *Gartenlaube* received a rush of enthusiastic letters from readers and experienced a surge in subscriptions. After this extraordinary success, Keil doubled Marlitt's honorarium and guaranteed her a yearly income of 800 Taler (Zimmermann 14). Other women authors (such as Henriette Bissing, Louise Ernesti, Fanny Lewald, and Ottilie Wildermuth) also contributed to the magazine in the 1850s, 60s, and 70s, but at most two or three times and generally short stories rather than full-length novels.

[10] According to Bertha Potthast, *Goldelse* ran to eight book editions by 1871, each of 2,000 to 3,000. Likewise, *Das Geheimnis der alten Mamsell* had six editions in the five years after its publication in the *Gartenlaube* (130-31).

[11] Many critics have argued, as did the magazine itself, that Marlitt played an important role in the *Gartenlaube*'s success (Zahn; Wachtel 10; Sieburg). Indeed, although the exact role her works had in selling issues of the magazine is impossible to ascertain definitively, her contributions did coincide with the sharp and steady increase in subscriptions. Numbers were at 175,000 in 1866, 210,000 in 1867, 250,000 in 1868, 310,000 in 1871, 325,000 in 1874, 360,000 in 1876, and 376,000 in 1878. In many of the final issues for each year Marlitt figured heavily in the announcements for the contributions of the coming year. Obviously, from the point of view of the editor, Marlitt was considered a major selling point.

[12] One letter from an enthusiastic male reader of Marlitt exemplifies her appeal to both sexes: "Als Lehrling war ich verlassen, sie rief mir zu: verzage nicht! Als Handwerksbursch war ich von der Welt verachtet, sie tröstete: verliere das Vertrauen nicht! Und wenn ich als verheirateter Mann mich manchmal in meinen Mußestunden durch das Lesen ihrer schönen Erzählungen

über die Sorgen und Mühen des täglichen Lebens zu erheben suche, so ruft sie stets: hoffe!" (Potthast 21).

[13] See Potthast for a detailed account of their affinity in political and social terms (18–19).

[14] "Elisabeth legte den Reisemantel ab, und war der alten Sabine behülflich, den Kaffeetisch herzurichten" (1866, 19).

"Sabine hatte nicht weit von der Gesellschaft auf einer Rasenbank Platz genommen, um bei der Hand zu sein, wenn man etwas bedürfe. Um nicht ganz müßig zu bleiben, hatte sie ein paar Hände voll junger Möhren aus dem Beete gezogen, die sie eifrig schabte und putzte. Elisabeth setzte sich zu ihr und half bei der Arbeit" (1866, 34).

[15] In her work on popular romances, Tania Modleski has characterized this plot development as common for the male hero. Modleski points out that although the hero is initially contemptuous of or indifferent to the heroine, the reader, familiar with the formula, is "always able to interpret the hero's actions as the result of his increasingly intense love for the heroine" (40).

[16] The narrator even mentions this tie between the story and Elisabeth (as its focalizer) at the end of the first chapter: "Hier nehmen wir den Gang der Erzählung wieder auf und wollen uns die Mühe nicht verdrießen lassen, dem jungen Mädchen zu folgen, das an dem stürmischen Winterabend der elterlichen Wohnung zueilte" (1866, 3).

[17] As part of her goal of deciphering the narrative pleasure women might get from Gothic novels, Harlequin romances, and soap operas, Modleski insists that "the price women pay for their popular entertainment is high, but they may still be getting more than anyone bargained for" (34). Radway rejects the traditional consumption analogy for the interaction with popular literature. By asserting that comprehension while reading is an act of making meaning, she insists that women readers of romance novels are empowered as active reading subjects, even if they also recirculate many notions common to patriarchal society. She suggests that "escape" both refers to conditions left behind and invokes utopian possibility (12).

[18] Just as domesticity is a kind of self-regulation, so too this process of reading constitutes a manner of discipline. In a discussion of the English case, Louis James has suggested that, especially for the female servant, reading can be seen as a "disciplined activity" (353).

[19] Furthermore, according to the article, the enthusiasm of the masses for Marlitt's first novel demonstrated the fact that people recognized the quality and nobility of this work without needing the name of a famous author. The novel's appeal stemmed not from cheap, sensational effects pandering to a feverish thirst for entertainment, but rather from "reifer Lebensanschauung und wärmster Gemüthstiefe" (1871, 804).

[20] For Anderson this includes the economic and market-based changes that made a large reading audience conceivable: "print-capitalism...made it possible for rapidly growing numbers of people to think about themselves, and to relate

themselves to others, in profoundly new ways" (40). Gellner makes a similar argument, but focuses more on the process of educating a uniform readership: "To sum up this argument: a society has emerged based on a high-powered technology and the expectancy of sustained growth, which requires both a mobile division of labour, and sustained, frequent and precise communication between strangers involving a sharing of explicit meaning, transmitted in a standard idiom and in writing when required" (33-34).

Works Cited

Anderson, Benedict. *Imagined Communities: Reflections on the Origin and Spread of Nationalism*. London: Verso, 1983.

Armstrong, Nancy. *Desire and Domestic Fiction: A Political History of the Novel*. Oxford: Oxford UP, 1987.

Barth, Dieter. "Das Familienblatt—ein Phänomen der Unterhaltungspresse des 19. Jahrhunderts: Beispiele zur Gründungs- und Verlagsgeschichte." *Archiv für Geschichte des Buchwesens* 15 (1975): 121-316.

Engelsing, Rolf. "Die Zeitschrift in Nordwestdeutschland: 1850-1914." *Archiv für Geschichte des Buchwesens* 6 (1965): 937-1036.

Evans, Richard J. *The Feminist Movement in Germany 1894-1933*. London: Sage, 1976.

Die Gartenlaube: Illustrirtes Familienblatt. Leipzig: Ernst Keil, 1853-1884.

Gellner, Ernest. *Nations and Nationalism*. Ithaca: Cornell UP, 1983.

Gruppe, Heidemarie. *"Volk" zwischen Politik und Idylle in der "Gartenlaube" 1853-1914*. Frankfurt a.M.: Lang, 1976.

Habermas, Jürgen. *Strukturwandel der Öffentlichkeit: Untersuchungen zu einer Kategorie der bürgerlichen Gesellschaft*. Darmstadt: Luchterhand, 1962.

Hobsbawm, Eric. "Introduction: Inventing Traditions." *The Invention of Tradition*. Ed. Eric Hobsbawm and Terence Ranger. Cambridge: Cambridge UP, 1983. 1-14.

James, Louis. "The Trouble with Betsy: Periodicals and the Common Reader in Mid-Nineteenth-Century England." *The Victorian Periodical Press: Samplings and Soundings*. Ed. Joanne Shattock and Michael Wolff. Toronto: U of Toronto P, 1982. 349-66.

Kracauer, Siegfried. "The Mass Ornament." *New German Critique* 5 (1975): 67-79.

Modleski, Tania. *Loving with a Vengeance: Mass-Produced Fantasies for Women*. New York: Routledge, 1982.

Nipperdey, Thomas. "Verein als soziale Struktur in Deutschland im späten 18. und frühen 19. Jahrhundert: Eine Fallstudie zur Modernisierung I." *Gesellschaft, Kultur, Theorie: Gesammelte Aufsätze zur neueren Geschichte*. Göttingen: Vandenhoeck, 1976.

Potthast, Bertha. *Eugenie Marlitt: Ein Beitrag zur Geschichte des deutschen Frauenromans.* Bielefeld: Rennebohm, 1926.

Radway, Janice A. *Reading the Romance: Women, Patriarchy, and Popular Literature.* Chapel Hill: U of North Carolina P, 1991.

Rischke, Anne-Susanne. *Die Lyrik in der "Gartenlaube" 1853-1903.* Frankfurt a.M.: Lang, 1982.

Rosenstrauch, Hazel E. "Zum Beispiel *Die Gartenlaube.*" *Trivialliteratur.* Ed. Annamaria Rucktäschl and Hans Dieter Zimmermann. Munich: Fink, 1976. 169-89.

Sieburg, Friedrich. "Einleitung." *Facsimile Querschnitt durch die Gartenlaube.* Ed. Heinz Klüter. Stuttgart: Scherz, 1963. n.p.

Wachtel, Joachim, ed. *Heißgeliebte Gartenlaube: Herzerfrischende Wanderungen durch ein deutsches Familienblatt.* Feldafing: Buchheim, 1963.

Wallraf, Karlheinz. *Die "bürgerliche Gesellschaft" im Spiegel deutscher Familienzeitschriften.* Cologne: Orthen, 1939.

Zahn, Eva. "Die Geschichte der 'Gartenlaube.'" *Facsimile Querschnitt durch die Gartenlaube.* Ed. Heinz Klüter. Stuttgart: Scherz, 1963. n.p.

Zimmermann, Magdalene, ed. *Die "Gartenlaube" als Dokument ihrer Zeit.* Munich: Heimeran, 1963.

Equality Decreed:
Dramatizing Gender in East Germany

Katrin Sieg

This essay situates four plays by and about GDR women, written between 1951 and 1963, in relation to the nascent state's gender legislation. The plays register the initially aggressive implementation of gender equality at work and at home that ended with the national and economic crisis created by the cold war. Under pressure, the state expected women to reshoulder domestic responsibilities and concomitant gender roles. Women's drama propagated acceptance of the "double burden," forfeiting feminist politics for family ideology and thereby shaping the contradictory construction of a female, socialist subject. (KS)

When asked what she thought about the future of women in the unified Germany, East Berlin theatre artist Amina Gusner replied: "Die Frauen sind schon zu emanzipiert. Sie sind auf dem Vormarsch, oft aktiver als die Männer, die verunsichert sind, im Osten mehr als im Westen" (Gusner 28). It would be glib to point out the naivety of this remark, dating from October 1990. Rather, I would like to take Gusner's now questionable assumption about the relationship between *Sein* and *Bewußtsein*, which also informs much of Western feminists' thinking, as the point of departure for an examination of material and ideological formulations of gender in East Germany. Despite constitutionally guaranteed legal and economic equality, reproductive rights, affordable day care and other benefits, women in the German Democratic Republic fell short of achieving social (or economic) equality. Moreover, their incursions into traditionally male turf were, with few exceptions, not motivated or sustained by a feminist critique. The majority of East German women were therefore ill-equipped for the epochal encounter with West Germany in the fall of 1989 and the ensuing loss of most of the rights and services the East German state had offered them. Although many participated in the first women's movement to emerge from that country, the interventions of feminists organized in the *Unabhängiger Frauenverband*, founded in February of 1990, came too late and lacked a large, supportive base committed to a long-term political agenda.[1] By now it has become clear that the economic collapse of the former GDR in the wake of reunification has made East German women the losers of the *Wende*.

The *Aufbauzeit* provides the historical context for the following examination of women's plays and gender legislation, which chart the reorganization of male-female relations in the GDR. The term *Aufbauzeit* designates the reconstruction period after World War II, which in most historical accounts ends with the Sixth Party Congress of the SED that declared the arrival of the socialist society. It is also a key period for the understanding of gender relations under socialism. The plays written by and about East German women in the 1950s encode the contradictions between women's material status and the larger socio-semiotic complex we call gender as well as dramatize the tensions within each of these discursive fields. The nascent socialist state's *Frauenpolitik* aggressively set out to change traditional bourgeois gender divisions along the public/private axis. At the same time, the political reorganization around not-so-new sexual hierarchies locked patriarchal structures firmly in place. It produced the specific intermingling of state-socialism and patriarchy that West German feminist Ute Gerhard characterizes as "paternal absolutism" whereby "the GDR regime was able to enforce special privileges and laws that were comparatively favorable to women" (Dölling, "Beitrag" 29).

The reconstruction period was also a time of remarkable activity and opportunity for women in theatre, especially when compared to later decades.[2] In the young socialist republic, the need for ideological production and propaganda attracted many amateur dramatists who often made up for their lack of training with political enthusiasm and commitment. Whereas earlier women playwrights who had addressed gender issues in their work had either been chastised for "impropriety," published under male pen-names, or been denied production (see Giesing), socialism granted many women access to the hallowed halls of the German theatre and supported them in their project to revise gender relations from an egalitarian perspective.

However, what makes the plays from that time interesting is precisely the ways in which they exceed their propagandistic purpose and their socialist closure, the brief moments of insubordinacy and feminist unruliness that betray a history of struggle around socialist gender prescriptions and expectations. The amalgam of "das Ideal sozialer Gleichheit und Gerechtigkeit...mit einem patriarchalisch-paternalistischen Prinzip" described by GDR cultural theorist Irene Dölling complicated notions of opposition or resistance. The imbrication of patriarchal structures with the party hierarchy and state ideology led to the casting of feminism as counter-revolutionary ("Frauenforschung" 42). Accordingly, theatre and drama could accommodate gender questions and conflicts only as long as their formulations remained within preset limits.[3] The handful of women's plays in the 1950s that propagated the *Frau von Morgen,* as one playwright called her, were possible because their message coincided with official policy. The plots of the four plays by and about GDR women that I will discuss here illustrate the boundaries of the medium, which operated as ideological sounding-board. Navigating between central and peripheral contradictions, these plays rehearsed and resisted the disappearance of the Woman of Tomorrow in the New Man of the socialist order. The phrase "Woman of Tomorrow" serves to question the ostensibly gender-neutral notion of the socialist *Neuer Mensch* epitomized by the worker-hero. Depicted as part and partner of the New Man, the Woman of Tomorrow calls attention to male privilege and characterizes their relationship as one of struggle rather than complementary harmony. The term helps to foreground those power relations that the New Man all too easily conceals.[4]

In 1951, the Fifth Plenum of the Central Committee of the Socialist Unity Party (SED) officially sanctioned socialist realism, a decision that emulated the model of soviet theatre.[5] That dramatic style was deemed a congenial vehicle for propagating socialist ideals. Women playwrights took it upon themselves to popularize the socialist program of gender equality. GDR law implemented principles and demands formulated earlier by the proletarian feminist movement led by women such as Rosa Luxemburg and Clara Zetkin. In 1949, the constitution of the new state cancelled "alle im Bürgerlichen Gesetzbuch verankerten familienrechtlichen Regelungen, die die Ungleichheit der Geschlechter absicherten" (Stolt 92), and initiated measures aiming at the ideal of socialized reproduction (child raising and domestic labor).[6] In addition, the gender legislation of the reconstruction period was geared toward the restructuring of the production sphere through women's participation in wage labor. The economic situation of the GDR, weakened by reparations to the USSR, was exacerbated by the shortage of men in the postwar years and by the constant migration of valuable labor into the Western sectors of Germany. These factors facilitated, indeed necessitated, women's integration into the work force.

The energies and fantasies that were mobilized for that purpose contributed to an iconography and tropology of the Woman of Tomorrow that received important impulses from both the workers' movement and the (proletarian and bourgeois) women's movements.[7] Theatre, including drama by and about women, played an important role in the project of ideological production. Socialist realism was exhorted to celebrate the achievements of the young state and to applaud its progress in eradicating pre-socialist vestiges such as outdated gender relations. The comedy form was particularly suited to transmit the decreed optimism with regard to economic recovery and progress, the constitution of a national identity, and the creation of the New Man. While raising problems and obstacles, comedy reassured its spectators that the hurdles on the path towards communism were but minor, that sacrifices would soon pay off, and that historical progress was inevitable.

The aggressive gender legislation of the late 1940s met with resistance on the part of the prisoners of war who, upon their return, demanded the restoration of their positions of superiority (Merkel 87–88). During Soviet occupation, women's committees had called for and enforced equal pay for equal work, the cornerstone of gender equality.[8] In the mid-fifties, women once again appealed to their male comrades to relinquish their privileges in the name of egalitarianism. In 1956, West Germany's joining of NATO and the concomitant loss of hope for German unification precipitated an ideological crisis and prompted a surge of nationalist energies. In the ensuing competition with the West, the utopia of socialized housework was subordinated to the goal of an economic boom. Women's interests had to cede to economic prerogatives, and the female population was expected to reshoulder the burden of reproductive labor; the New Man was played off against the Woman of Tomorrow. The climate of the Cold War turned many of the GDR's accomplishments, such as its progressive gender legislation, into ammunition in the country's defense against the ideological enemy. East Germany's advantages shone all the more brightly when compared to the failings of the Federal Republic of Germany, such as female unemployment, poverty, prostitution, and pornography.

Not all women playwrights were critical of this turn of events. The successful, much-produced playwright Hedda Zinner wrote several plays that revolve around the East-West conflict. The plays are for the most part set in West Germany, which appears as the GDR's negative counter-image and, in the *Sprechchor* play *Das Urteil* (ca. 1960), is characterized as an American colony. The *Epochenwiderspruch* is resolved either through the protagonist's emigration to the GDR or with his/her oath to change conditions in the FRG. The plays expose the notion of freedom that the West appropriated in its rhetoric of democracy as a mystification. The representation of gender roles neatly fits the East-West schema by associating exploitative and strongly hierarchical relations with capitalism, whereas socialist characters are depicted as equal partners who reject Western gender roles as well as the economic order that sustains them. The clever secretary Brieselank in *Der Mann mit dem Vogel* (1952) provides an example of the dilemma of female workers in capitalism in that she constantly has to fend off the sexual advances of her boss who takes advantage of his employee's dependency. In addition, his jealous wife blames the secretary for her husband's escapades. Brieselank rebukes her:

> Mir sind die Westberliner Arbeitslosenziffern nicht ganz unbekannt, gnädige Frau. Aber nun verstehe ich gar nicht mehr, was Sie von mir erwarten? Die

Kollegin Bärbach wurde arbeitslos, weil sie sich weigerte, Ihren Mann auf einer... Geschäftsreise zu begleiten; erwarten Sie nun von mir, daß ich—um nicht ebenfalls arbeitslos zu werden—einer ähnlichen Aufforderung Folge leiste? (13).

The power difference between men and women is rendered as a class difference which, once overcome, will bring about women's liberation, too. Within this orthodox Marxist schema there is no space for female solidarity across classes.

Theatre histories of the GDR have categorized the drama of socialist veterans and returned emigrants, like Zinner, as a transitional phase, a kind of pre-history to socialist national theatre proper as it emerged with the following generation of dramatists (e.g., Funke). The criterion for periodization was the reconfiguration of antagonistic contradictions, such as those that determine Zinner's work. These plays are built around direct confrontation with the ideological enemy through which, as I indicated above, national and gender identity are constituted. Later plays, including those discussed here, refrain from East-West comparisons, but situate contradictions, including those between different gender roles, within the socialist present. The theory of non-antagonistic contradictions rests on the assumption that the cancellation of the primary contradiction in the capitalist order, namely the subject's exploitation in labor relations, results in the instantaneous transformation of all antagonistic into non-antagonistic contradictions in the workers' and farmers' state. Wolfgang Schivelbusch developed the concept of the non-antagonistic contradiction in relation to East German drama, citing the textbook *Grundlagen des Marxismus-Leninismus,* which describes them as

die Widersprüche zwischen den Kräften, die für das Neue kämpfen, und den Kräften, die das Alte verteidigen. Es ist verständlich, daß es ohne die Geburt von Neuem und seine Durchsetzung im Leben, ohne Kampf für das Neue keine Entwicklung geben kann.... Im Kampf um die Lösung der Widersprüche zerbrechen die Menschen die veralteten Ordnungen und Verhältnisse, überwinden Konservativismus und Routine, nehmen neue, kompliziertere Aufgaben in Angriff und schaffen vollkommenere Formen des gesellschaftlichen Lebens (40-41).

Analogous to the worker-heroes of early socialist drama who prevail over reactionary elements in the workplace, the plays by GDR women authors under discussion stage the socialist subject's struggle with and victory over traditional gender roles and relations. They portray the relationship between the liberated, socialist woman and the New Man as a shared learning process, often trying to avoid the implication that men are invested in outmoded gender definitions. For instance, in Lena Foellbach's 1962 play *So eine reizende Familie,* it is actually the husband who persuades his wife to leave bourgeois conventions behind. The play's effort to avoid an antagonistic stance between men and women contrasts conspicuously with the discourse of women's magazines, for instance. Examples of male-chauvinist behavior and instances of men's resistance to women's incursion into domains previously closed to them, especially in the case of highly-qualified positions, were regular subjects of controversy and debate in their pages.[9] Perhaps this discrepancy can be attributed to the different readership/spectatorship of the respective media. The theatre ostensibly spoke to a mixed-gendered audience and showed less willingness to side with the women to whom the magazines addressed themselves.

Five of the twenty-two plays by women that were written between 1951 and 1963 deal with conflicts at home and in the workplace that are generated by changing gender roles.[10] For space considerations, I want to limit my discussion to four of them. Petra Zehlen's comedy *Dramaturgie und Liebe*, written in 1951, attacks the calcified structures that hamper both male-female relations and the theatre/publishing business. The young head editor Kathrin Robert, who champions new, German talents and who is cheered on by two female co-workers, is opposed by her boss who espouses commercial standards and favors foreign dramatists. By chance, a play that Robert had written under a pen name falls into the hands of director Kersten who turns it into a box office hit. With this coup, the editor succeeds in reforming both her boss, who had fired her for incompetence, and Kersten, who believes female inferiority in creative endeavors to be biologically determined. The men are forced to revise their previous attitudes toward women and their intellectual/creative capacities.

In this early play, the front between the sexes neatly separates the progressive female trio from the reactionary males, although Zehlen circumvents all-too-obvious antagonisms by having her heroine fall in love with her arch-chauvinist opponent Kersten. Still, here more than in other plays of the period one is struck by the uppity stance of the female characters, by their pride in having claimed what is rightfully theirs, and by their non-apologetic attitude. Robert not only talks back, but convinces through her actions. Without much ado, she writes a play because she does not like the ones she has read. GDR critic Ina Merkel emphasizes those same attributes in the images in women's magazines: the cockiness of the crane operator leaning out of her cabin, the daring of a photographer riding her motorbike, the exuberance of the farm worker straddling a thresher.[11] Zehlen's protagonist and her unabashed triumphs over male arrogance and backwardness exhibit the same stance. The gendered division between the camps of petit-bourgeois tradition and progressive innovation manifests a militancy that refutes those who now speak so condescendingly of the "alms" the socialist state dispensed to its women citizens and who thus reinscribe female passivity into a history of struggle.

Regina Hastedt's musical *Wer ist hier von gestern? oder Hausfrau gesucht!*, written probably in 1954, arranges the revolution of gender relations as the dialectic three-step of the "Frau von gestern," the "Frau von heute," and the "Frau von morgen." The entrance of Heinz, a mechanical engineer, dressed in an apron, announces dramatic and ideological complications. While he cooks dinner for his wife Hanna, she prepares herself for receiving an award from her brigade. When he hands the whisk back to her, however, she refuses to perform her housewifely duties while he goes to night school, and announces instead her plan to go away to study. The heroine of the play is the secretary Sabine who transforms herself from the exploited Woman of Yesterday into the productive Woman of Tomorrow and restores peace to the household of Heinz, Hanna, and Hanna's brother Paul (with whom she falls in love). As a playwright, she can write librettos for Paul and manage the household for the three of them, so that both Hanna and Heinz are able to study. However, the collectivization of domestic tasks that the play suggests does not herald the end of the unequal distribution of labor and women's exploitation. Although Heinz, who keeps insisting on his rights as a husband, is forced to apologize to the women in the audience, and Hanna declares she will scale down her activism, these characters do not demonstrate a real change of consciousness or behavior. This play makes clear who has to pay the bill for the New Man. When the state does not deliver on its promise of reproductive services, the socialist superwoman is expected to manage job, family, and housework and, on top of it all, retain her feminine charms. The model image of the working activist that other texts propagate is here characterized as an intermediate step, the Woman of Today, on the path toward the Woman of Tomorrow who will recommit herself to additional reproductive labor.

The seemingly progressive gender legislation promised to relieve women from the "petty barbarism" of housework (Lenin) but then turned against them when daycare was not available or the daily procurement of food proved to be an obstacle race. The GDR's *Mangelwirtschaft* required a high degree of compensatory labor on the part of the women (Stolt 94). The propagated ideal of partnership that was based on socio-economic equality and oriented itself to the norm of the working man conversely did not apply to equally shared housework. Women were to be liberated from reproductive labor, rather than burdening the men with it. Consequently, the women's plays of the 1950s often dramatized the resulting contradiction as a marriage crisis.

Berta Waterstradt's drama *Ehesache Lorenz* (1958) reveals contradictions between private and public spheres that erupt in the confrontation between Trude Lorenz, judge in a divorce court, and her husband Willi, an executive. After twenty years of marriage, Trude accidentally finds out about Willi's affair with his young secretary Helga. The crisis in their marriage foregrounds the tenuousness of socialist national identity in the personal realm. Trude must recognize that the difficult early years of her marriage, which was forged in the antifascist resistance, no longer prove to be a solid base for their relationship. When confronted with his unfaithfulness, Willi blames Trude's professional activity as the cause of her neglect of her wifely duties and their estrangement. Willi's affair as well as his accusation signal his ideological regressiveness. His bourgeois manners at the workplace supply further proof of his backwardness, as does the fact that his lover similarly copies pre-socialist behavior patterns. Helga tells Trude that her boss promised her mother to marry her but then left her with an illegitimate child. The troubled, middle-class Lorenzes are contrasted with a model couple, the working-class Schliffkes. The Schliffkes are not only happily married, they are also party members. The play demonstrates that these two conditions are related. Herr Schliffke, Willi Lorenz's chauffeur, tells his superior:

> Viele Frauen halten ihre Männer fest, weil er der Versorger ist, er garantiert ihnen drei Mahlzeiten täglich, Perlonstrümpfe, Halsketten und was sie sonst noch brauchen.... Da nehmen sie Ärger und Aufregung lieber in Kauf. Deine Trude ernährt sich selbst. Da braucht sie sich Deine Zicken nicht gefallen zu lassen. Ist doch ganz einfach (17).

The Schliffkes' example prompts Helga to reconsider her relationship with Lorenz and leave him. In contrast to *Wer ist hier von gestern?*, *Ehesache Lorenz* suggests that it is the man who must change in order to keep up with the new order (and the new women), rather than the other way around. The relatively open ending, which merely hints at Trude's giving in to Willi's wish to stay together, underscores the ongoing formation of identity in everyday life as a series of troublesome, often painful decisions and (self-) reflections. The individual realization of the state's egalitarian doctrine appears as an open-ended process, rather than the acquisition of a fixed position.

Waterstradt's play critically examines the official claim that the equality of the sexes had been attained. Later dramas no longer tend to represent women's self-realization through work as a crucial aspect of female identity—as it was for men—but attempt to combine productive and reproductive functions in the figure of the doubly burdened woman. In contrast, *Ehesache Lorenz* foregrounds the discrepancy between both spheres and exposes the contradiction at the base of socialist gender ideology that fosters women's professional competence but expects of them marital submissiveness. The playwright solves contradictory role expectations through the women's separation from Willi, instead of forcing them into the model image of the double-burdened superwoman. She executes this step twice, and as an act of solidarity between two women. The framing of the play's main action by scenes in the divorce court over which Trude Lorenz presides points to the sphere of production as constitutive for gender identity, instead of anchoring women's identity primarily in the reproductive domain.

Of all the texts considered here, Rosel Willers's play *Gelegenheit macht Liebe,* written in 1963, conforms most to the ideal of a shared and mutual progression of both spouses in the direction of partnership and equality. The stories of two families cross when Elisabeth Helms and Martin Heinz have a brief fling during their vacation. The affair highlights considerable social differences between the partners in both marriages. While the ambitious and successful fashion designer Elisabeth is married to the machinist Paul who also runs the household and (warning signal!) enters dressed in an apron, the division of roles in the Heinz's marriage conforms to a more conventional pattern: Hanni works as a mechanic and manages the home, while Martin has advanced from welder to engineer. Upwardly mobile, he criticizes not only her tired and exhausted appearance, but also her lack of *Bildung.* Understandably, his wife, working two shifts, has little time or energy left for edification in the evening. After their vacation, Elisabeth and Martin return to their respective partners. Their experience leads to profound and lasting changes in the behavior of all four: Paul decides to go back to school and advance his career, Elisabeth takes on her share of the housework, and Martin equally joins in domestic tasks so that Hanni has time to engage in cultural activities in her spare time.

The plays that I have introduced develop a socialist variant of the comedy form that receives its major impulse from the change in gender relations at the center of the comic dynamic. Whereas traditionally, comedy cements the status quo, here it serves to track and foreshadow change. "Sexuality as a productive force" (Morgner), its potential to bring about the socialist conditions and behavior that Peter Hacks dramatized in *Die Sorgen und die Macht* (1965), was recognized by women playwrights as early as the 1950s. Sabine in *Wer ist hier von gestern?* can only inhabit the position of the Woman of Tomorrow after she gives notice to her exploitative boss and falls in love with Paul. *Gelegenheit macht Liebe* demonstrates the instrumentalization of love most clearly: it not only shows the restructuring of the reproductive sphere in analogy to the productive sphere (where equality is achieved), but furthermore enables the ideological colonization of the tertiary realm of leisure and its subsumption under socialist values.

The images of women in plays from the *Aufbauzeit* register and articulate an extremely volatile field of tension between their progressive claim and the perseverance of presocialist gender roles. In 1965, the family code of law was passed, inaugurating a new phase of women's legislation (see Stolt 96-98). That law marked the transformation of *Frauenpolitik,* indicating a certain partiality, to *Familienpolitik,* which was designed to make women available for demographic and economic exigencies. This decision illustrates the lack of fundamental change in regard to the sexual division of labor. The quality of female work shifted "von der unqualifizierten, unkontinuierlichen Erwerbsarbeit...zur qualifizierten, kontinuierlichen Berufsarbeit" (Merkel 174). However, women were still predominantly employed in so-called female professions, which, as in capitalist nations, ranked lower in remuneration and prestige in comparison to men's professions. In addition, they remained largely underrepresented in highly qualified positions. In sum, there continued to be a considerable gap of status and income between men and women.

The rhetoric of egalitarianism mystified the rigidly hierarchical, centralist structure of the one-party state presided over by its general secretary who, particularly in the Stalinist 1950s, was the object of an intense personality cult. The numerous propaganda films sponsored by the Socialist Unity Party during that time emphasize the paternal aspect of political representation and are rife with family narratives and metaphors. They show, for example, Walter Ulbricht teaching his young son to play ping-pong and cultural secretary Johannes R. Becher surrounded by schoolchildren.[12] The political hierarchy that structured social interactions on all levels, from the agrarian collective and the industrial brigade to the GDR's position within the Warsaw pact alliance, had its domestic equivalent in the male-dominated family depicted and somewhat challenged by women's plays. The patriarchal structures in both social spheres served to reinforce each other while reproducing the same contradiction within the public as well as the private realms.

The theoretical underpinnings of the GDR's gender policies dated from the early decades of the century. They were not flexible enough to accommodate the changed circumstances and requirements of the postwar, socialist society. The "revolution" of gender relations was reduced to *sozialpolitische Maßnahmen* aimed at aligning women with norms set by men, rather than throwing open the question of patriarchal power relations. In other words, progress became a quantitative issue rather than a qualitative one (Eifler 36-37). Socialist women were permitted to point out present inequities as long as they remained committed to equality (with men) as the ultimate goal. They were neither allowed to question the methods by which this utopia was to be achieved, nor were they permitted to articulate and criticize the paradoxical appeals to both transgress and conform to traditional roles as anything but a capitalist-bourgeois vestige.

The state implemented a "provider economy"[13] whose "women-friendly" agenda of socialized housework and childcare effected the infantilization of the population, as Dölling has pointed out.[14] The government fostered a passivity that was gender-specific, since men had more opportunities to actively participate in the hierarchical distribution and administration of responsibility and power.

In the women's plays discussed here, the contradictions of socialist gender ideology and the tensions those created were largely solved at the expense of women and could only be overcome through great personal sacrifices. The deferral of the individual's gratification was a common theme in plays by men at the time, and was frequently weighed against the necessity of working for the realization of a communist utopia, which demands sacrifices for the duration of the transitional period of socialism. Ursula Sillge, a longtime lesbian-feminist activist and scholar in East Germany, calls attention to the insidious nexus of disempowerment and hope in what was always declared a transitory structure:

> Das Machtmonopol der SED und die damit verbundene Unüberprüfbarkeit von politischen Entscheidungen erzeugte bei vielen Menschen Verbitterung, das Gefühl der Abhängigkeit und des Ausgeliefertseins. Andererseits hatte die Utopie einer gerechten Gesellschaft eine Faszination, die trotz der Kluft zwischen Theorie und Praxis ihre Anziehungskraft nie ganz verlor (85).

The utopia on which the GDR was founded and which was invoked over and over again in women's plays served to interpolate female subjects into socialism. It bound their energies and desires to a system that demanded their obedience, all the while building the bureaucratic structures and agencies of surveillance to secure their compliance.

In 1963, the Sixth Party Congress of the SED pronounced the final victory of the socialist mode of production in the GDR, thereby closing the historical chapter of the reconstruction and bidding farewell to the myth of the permanent revolution. The party no longer regarded socialism as an intermediate phase on the path toward communism, but as a relatively autonomous socio-economic formation. The arts were assigned the task of representing the developed socialist society. The utopia in whose name women had been asked to subordinate their agendas had moved far into the distance.

Notes

I would like to thank the Henschelverlag, especially the editor Maria Tragelehn, who generously granted me access to their archives and made the research for this piece possible.

[1] This was an evaluation shared by most of the participants at a symposium that took place in Berlin in January of 1991, an event that included women from both East and West Germany and whose proceedings were published in *Wider das schlichte Vergessen*. See esp. Nickel 41–42.

[2] Rather than comparing the number of women's plays to those written by men during the period under consideration (1951-1963), I believe it is more useful to contrast the 22 dramas (not counting children's plays) written by women during the *Aufbauzeit* with the period of inactivity that followed. I found no plays written by women between 1963 and 1974. From 1974 to 1985, still relatively few women's dramas were written, considering the emergence of feminism and feminist literature in the GDR during the 1970s. Of nine scripts published during that time period, two appeared in West Germany. I am at this time unable to discuss the production histories of these plays, or their reception in the GDR—a task still to be accomplished through further research.

[3] As a public medium, the theatre, more than other arts, was politically loaded. It was invested with the now legendary power of an artistic counter-discourse to dominant ideology, the flip-side of which was the institution's high vulnerability to censorship.

[4] Many male playwrights created plays with heroines that embodied the virtues of the *Neuer Mensch*, from Friedrich Wolf's *Bürgermeister Anna* (1950) to Helmut Baierl's *Frau Flinz* (1961) to Volker Braun's dramas. However, just as the *Neuer Mensch* tends to conceal rather than address gender-related tensions within that concept, discussions of feminist heroines in GDR men's plays have tended to efface women playwrights.

[5] The Central Committee declared: "In order to develop realistic art, we orient ourselves to the great example of the socialist Soviet Union, which has created the most progressive culture in the world." Any deviance from this model was deemed "formalist" or "objectivist" and regarded as ideologically suspect (Jarmatz 250). See discussion in Hüttich 26 ff.

[6] The state promised women "die Betreuung und Erziehung der Kinder in gesellschaftlichen Einrichtungen und die weitgehende Auslagerung der Hausarbeit in gesellschaftliche Dienstleistungen (perspektivisch in eine sozialistische hauswirtschaftliche Großindustrie)" (Enders 39).

[7] See Merkel's book, which contains many photographs of women engaged in heavy physical labor in agriculture and industry, as well as a broad spectrum of images of intellectual women in academic contexts.

[8] "Befehl Nr. 253 der Sowjetische Militäradministration in Deutschland, 17. August 1946." *DDR: Dokumente zur Geschichte '84-85.*

[9] Merkel's book documents many such cases which, I would argue, are representative of much more tenacious obstacles than the plays would have one believe.

[10] This figure refers to the plays in the Henschelverlag's archives and does not include the large number of children's plays. Of those 22 plays, 12 alone were written by Hedda Zinner. It should be noted that not all dramas written and performed in the GDR were published by the Henschelverlag. Other sources are the journal *Theater der Zeit*, which occasionally published scripts (and which was owned by Henschelverlag); the *Verband der Theaterschaffenden*; and other publishers such as Aufbau, which published anthologies by major dramatists (but

not by women, to my knowledge). In some cases, theatres produced plays that had not gone through the regular channels of censorship and publication (Hildebrandt 140-41).

[11] See esp. Merkel 90-94 on the image of the *Spitzenmädel*.

[12] These are scenes from the film *Kinder, Kader, Kommandeure*, a montage of DEFA propaganda material that appeared in the summer of 1992.

[13] Christine Kulke coined the term *"Versorgungsökonomie"* (provider economy) (*Wider das schlichte Vergessen* 18).

[14] Women were largely at the receiving end of a quasi-feudal tutelage system "which facilitated the management of both motherhood and career at the same time that it fostered an attitude of grateful acceptance of dependency" (Dölling, "Frauenforschung" 44). See also Dölling's recent article "Alte und neue Dilemmata."

Works Cited

DDR: Dokumente zur Geschichte der Deutschen Demokratischen Republik 1945-1985. Ed. Hermann Weber. München: Deutscher Taschenbuch, 1986.

Dölling, Irene. "Alte und neue Dilemmata: Frauen in der ehemaligen DDR." *Women in German Yearbook 7.* Ed. Jeanette Clausen and Sara Friedrichsmeyer. Lincoln: U of Nebraska P, 1991. 121-36.

———. "Beitrag zum Deutschen Soziologentag." Unpublished ms. cited in Ute Gerhard, "German Women and the Social Costs of Unification." *German Politics and Society* 24 & 25 (Winter 1991-1992).

———. "Frauenforschung mit Fragezeichen? Perspektiven feministischer Wissenschaft." *Wir wollen mehr als ein "Vaterland."*

Eifler, Christine. "Identitätsbruch als Orientierungschance? Zu den Nachwirkungen der (auf)gelösten Frauenfrage in der DDR." *Wider das schlichte Vergessen.*

Enders, Ulrike. *Lebensbedingungen in der DDR: 17. Tagung zum Stand der DDR-Forschung.* Köln: Wissenschaft und Politik, 1984.

Foellbach, Lena. *So eine reizende Familie.* Berlin: Henschelverlag, 1962.

Funke, Christoph, Daniel Hoffmann-Ostwald, and Hans-Gerald Otto. *Theater-Bilanz: 1945-1969.* Berlin: Henschelverlag, 1971.

Giesing, Michaela. "Theater als verweigerter Raum: Dramatikerinnen um die Jahrhundertwende in deutschsprachigen Ländern." *Frauen Literatur Geschichte: Schreibende Frauen vom Mittelalter bis zur Gegenwart.* Ed. Hiltrud Gnüg und Renate Möhrmann. Frankfurt a.M.: Suhrkamp, 1989. 240-59.

Gusner, Amina. "Tango." *Mein Kapital bin ich selber: Gespräche mit Theaterfrauen in Berlin-O 1990-1991.* Ed. Renate Ullrich. Berlin: Zentrum für Theaterdokumentation und -information, 1991.

Hastedt, Regina M. *Wer ist hier von gestern? oder Hausfrau gesucht!* Berlin: Henschelverlag, n.d. (probably 1954).

Hildebrandt, Christel. "Dramatikerinnen in der DDR: Hoffnung auf Veränderung." *Fürs Theater Schreiben: Über zeitgenössische deutschsprachige Theaterautorinnen.* Bremen: Zeichen + Spuren, 1986.

Hüttich, H.G. *Theatre in the Planned Society.* Chapel Hill: U of North Carolina P, 1978.

Jarmatz, Klaus, et al., ed. *Kritik in der Zeit: Der Sozialismus—seine Literatur—ihre Entwicklung.* Halle: Mitteldeutscher Verlag, 1970.

Merkel, Ina. *...Und Du, Frau an der Werkbank! Die DDR in den 50er Jahren.* Berlin: Elefanten, 1990.

Morgner, Irmtraud. "Produktivkraft Sexualität souverän nutzen." Interview by Karin Huffzky. *Grundlagentexte zur Emanzipation der Frau.* Ed. Jutta Menschik. Köln: Pahl-Rugenstein, 1976. 328-35.

Nickel, Hildegard Maria. "Modernisierungsbrüche im Einigungsprozeß—(k)ein einig Volk von Schwestern." *Wider das schlichte Vergessen.*

Schivelbusch, Wolfgang. *Sozialistisches Drama nach Brecht.* Darmstadt: Luchterhand, 1974.

Sillge, Ursula. *Un-Sichtbare Frauen: Lesben und ihre Emanzipation in der DDR.* Berlin: LinksDruck, 1991.

Stolt, Susanne. "Leitbilder—Leidbilder: Zur Frauen- und Familienpolitik der SED." *Irmtraud Morgners Hexische Weltfahrt.* Ed. Kristine von Soden. Berlin: Elefanten, 1991.

Waterstradt, Bertha. *Ehesache Lorenz.* Berlin: Henschelverlag, 1958.

Wider das schlichte Vergessen. Der deutsch-deutsche Einigungsprozess: Frauen im Dialog. Ed. Christine Kulke, Heidi Kopp-Degethoff, and Ulrike Ramming. Berlin: Orlanda, 1992.

Willers, Rosel. *Gelegenheit macht Liebe.* Berlin: Henschelverlag, 1963.

Wir wollen mehr als ein "Vaterland": DDR-Frauen im Aufbruch. Ed. Gislinde Schwarz and Christine Zenner. Reinbek: Rowohlt, 1990.

Zehlen, Petra. *Dramaturgie und Liebe.* Berlin: Henschelverlag, 1951.

Zinner, Hedda. *Der Mann mit dem Vogel.* Berlin: Henschelverlag, 1952.

——. *Das Urteil.* Berlin: Henschelverlag, n.d. (probably 1960).

Political Bodies:
Women and Re/Production in the GDR

Katharina von Ankum

The article analyzes the contradictory positions taken by the SED on the issue of abortion, reflecting the anti-feminist foundation of socialism in the GDR. Throughout the 1950s and 60s the SED engaged in an unabashed pronatalist discourse in an effort to reconstruct the family while simultaneously pulling women into the work force. By 1970, the SED had to acknowledge the failure of its propagandistic and legislative attempts to construct the socialist "working mother." The 1972 decision to legalize abortion resulted from economic constraints and marked a turning point within the SED's strategy to legislate women's place in the GDR, coincidentally providing women with the right of self-determination over their bodies. (KvA)

The 28 May 1993 decision of the *Bundesverfassungsgericht* to declare abortion conditionally *rechtswidrig*, yet *straffrei*, ended the special status of abortion in Germany that had existed since October 1990, rejecting and replacing the legislative compromise reached by the *Bundestag* in 1992.[1] The unification treaty had deferred the resolution of the difference in abortion legislation between the former GDR and the FRG for the two years following unification. The *Fristenlösung* that had existed in the GDR since 1972 allowed for unconditional, free, and legal termination of a pregnancy during the first three months; after the *Bundesverfassungsgericht* had barred similar legislation in the FRG in 1975, West German women were subjected to an *Indikationsmodell*, which permitted legal abortions in medical, ethical, or eugenic emergencies. Abortion in the FRG was also legal if critical social conditions existed; however, the application of the *soziale Indikation* differed widely in the various German states. The *Wohnort/Tatort* principle designed to prevent West German women seeking an abortion from taking advantage of the more liberal conditions in the East drew a new curtain across Germany: it was a woman's legal residence (*Wohnort*) rather than the "scene of the crime"

(*Tatort*) that determined whether she would be prosecuted for terminating a pregnancy.

The Court's decision in 1993 showed blatant disregard for East German women, for whom the personal decision regarding the termination of a pregnancy had become an inalienable right; at the same time it destroyed West German women's hopes that at least some of the GDR's achievements pertaining to the status of women could be salvaged in a united Germany. Effective 16 June 1993, women in unified Germany can obtain legal abortions only if they are able to convince a commission that the required medical, ethical, eugenic or social indicators qualifying them for legal abortion exist.[2] In addition, the Court ruled that the now mandatory consultations cannot be provided by the same organization that performs the abortion, nor are insurance companies required to cover a procedure that has been deemed *rechtswidrig*. In addition, it acknowledged a doctor's right to choose, allowing medical professionals to refuse to assist in a legal abortion. The Court's provisions regarding the mandatory consultations were clearly designed to impress upon women a sense of societal responsibility for the protection of unborn life, thereby supporting governmental efforts to regain control over women's reproductive rights.

In 1993, women throughout Germany were once again reminded of their status as political bodies in a country that modifies women's rights as citizens depending on male-defined national priorities. Political leaders in 1990 had again avoided taking an immediate and definite stand on abortion, as had earlier leaders in 1945. This fact underscores the threat posed to national and capitalist consolidation by liberal reproductive policies.[3] The 1993 abortion law is the single most obvious sign that unification strengthened conservative forces hitherto kept in check by the competition between the two ideological systems. The following analysis demonstrates that even the most progressive abortion legislation in German history was less an expression of the SED state's commitment to women's equality than the result of national, economic, and ideological interest. Such an analysis provides German women in both East and West with an analogous history that must become the basis for joint action.

The "Law for the Protection of Mothers and Children and the Rights of Women" was passed on 27 September 1950, barely a year after the foundation of the GDR (DFD #2). It established women's place in socialist society, laying the groundwork for all subsequent SED-sponsored family legislation. In accordance with the solution to the woman question anticipated by socialist theorists, the legal text anchored women's right to work and to equal pay, and established maternal authority within the family. The SED government committed itself to advancing women's equality in the working world by encouraging their training in traditionally male occupations while simultaneously guaranteeing protective measures for pregnant working women.[4] At the same time, the law established incentives to encourage large families. Unlike West German family legislation of the 1950s that reinforced paternal authority in the family, the SED put mothers at the center of its legislation.[5] By allocating special financial and material assistance to single mothers, assuring a woman's right to care for her children in case of remarriage as well as granting equal legal status to illegitimate children, the law acknowledged and supported the mother-centered family that had resulted from the post-war *Frauenüberschuß*. However, even though the party's support of professional women was laudable and its "matrilocal" family politics progressive, the 1950 law defended unmistakably patriarchal interests. With stagnating population growth due to war losses and emigration to the West, women were as crucial for the continued existence of the GDR state in their functions as child bearers as they were as workers. At the same time that the GDR government facilitated women's entry into the work force, it also wanted to assure itself of the stabilizing force of the family by focusing its social policies on the family's most stable element, the mother.[6] In his speech to the *Volkskammer*, President Otto Grotewohl declared strengthening the family one of the foremost governmental tasks and proclaimed a healthy family one of the pillars of democratic society (Amt). Grotewohl offered East German women a rather uneven bargain, "...das Gesetz soll den Frauen zeigen, was die Regierung alles für sie tut, wenn sie helfen, das Land aufzubauen" (IfGA #6). The 1950 "Law for the Protection of Mothers and Children" was the first example of the *Geschenkpolitik* characteristic of the SED, offering financial incentives to encourage women's engagement in unremunerated household and family work, legislating the double burden and ultimately facilitating "positive" discrimination against women.

With the exception of plans to increase the number of state-supported child-care facilities, the 1950 law included no provisions for socializing household and family work. Not only did the SED government relegate reproduction to the private realm of the family, it also engaged in unabashed pronatalist rhetoric. In his speech, President Grotewohl appealed to women to give birth to more than two children:

> Die Zweikinder-Praxis ist die Praxis einer absterbenden Bevölkerung. Denn da nicht aus jedem geborenen Mädchen eine Mutter wird, die wieder Kinder hat, wird bei dem Zweikindersystem die Bevölkerung nicht einmal stabil gehalten; sie geht vielmehr absolut zurück (11).

Women's reproductive work was consequently established as one of the primary indicators of their ideological commitment to socialism. Motherhood was extolled as patriotic duty, and those who had many children were honored accordingly. With its baby campaign, the GDR government pursued moral as well as economic and political goals. Not only had the surplus of women led to numerous births out of wedlock, it had also denied many women the opportunity for marriage and traditional family life. An increased birth rate, Grotewohl believed, would not only strengthen the state economically and politically, but would accelerate the reconstruction of the traditional nuclear family through a speedy normalization of the ratio between the sexes.

It is hardly surprising that legislation designed to assure maximum exploitation of women's productive and reproductive powers declared abortion illegal. Paragraph 11 of the 1950 law made no attempt to disguise the connection between the government's protection of women and its control over their bodies. The law explicitly stated that legal abortion was restricted in the interest of women's health as well as population growth (DFD #2 1039). In fact, an important task of the family counseling centers instituted by the law was the registration of all pregnant women. Abortion remained legal only in cases of severe medical or eugenic risk.

Discussion of a law defining the status of women had begun as early as 1947, immediately after all but two of the states constituting the Soviet Occupation Zone had replaced §218 with more liberal abortion regulation.[7] However, a revision of the 1947-48 laws had not been addressed in any of the eleven drafts preceding the final one of 17 June 1950. The final version that included the restriction on abortion was the direct outcome of President Grotewohl's objection to the draft of 20 May 1950. The emancipatory focus of this proposal—already apparent in its title "Law for the Advancement of Women"—placed insufficient emphasis on the nuclear family as the core of socialist society and, he feared, established conditions that would "create problems within the families."[8] In *Women under Socialism,* August Bebel had predicted that the emancipation of women under socialism would go hand in hand with a shrinking family size:

> Intelligente und energische Frauen haben—von Ausnahmen abgesehen—in der Regel keine Neigung, einer größeren Anzahl Kinder als einer "Schickung Gottes" das Leben zu geben und die besten ihrer Lebensjahre im Schwangerschaftszustand oder mit dem Kind an der Brust zu verbringen (547-48).

Declaring Bebel's assessment inapplicable for "really existing socialism," Grotewohl demanded a complete revision of the legal text that reflected the government's interest in population growth."[9] The version finally passed in September 1950 marked the SED's betrayal of women's interests in favor of pronatalist national politics. The restriction of legal abortion in §11 was clearly not the result of the hoped-for improvement of economic conditions that the SED had declared as a condition for repealing the *sozial-medizinische Indikation* it had supported in the

1946-47 debate of §218. It was rather part of an attempt to stabilize the patriarchal order in the interest of economic progress by pressuring women to fulfill their traditional family role in addition to their new role in socialist production.

In 1946, the SED had placed itself at the head of the movement demanding a more liberal revision of §218 than the one proposed by the Allied Control Council. In addition to accepting exclusively medical and ethical factors as preconditions for legal abortion, the SED pushed for a wider interpretation of the *medizinische Indikation* to include social factors. Of the two proposals for §2 of the legislation, however, the SED opted for an adaptation of the more cautious one which required a demonstrable connection between the applicant's social conditions and medical risk for mother or child.[10] Abortion would be legal in the event that

> ...die sozialen Verhältnisse der Schwangeren oder ihrer Familie bei einem Austragen des Kindes eine ernste, sich auf die Gesundheit auswirkende Gefährdung für Mutter oder Kind erwarten lassen und der Notlage durch soziale und andere Maßnahmen nicht ausreichend abgeholfen werden kann.[11]

Given the economic conditions of the immediate post-war years, sanctioning social hardship alone as grounds for granting a woman access to legal abortion would effectively have resulted in the complete annulment of §218.[12] However, as legal secretary Hilde Benjamin pointed out, the initial proposal of the Allies made complete abolition of §218 unattainable (6).

The proposal sponsored by the SED in the immediate post-war debate on abortion did not result exclusively from restraints placed on the party by the Allies. It also reflected the anti-feminist tradition and pronatalist tendency of the communist movement. In 1931, the physician, dramatist, and KPD member Friedrich Wolf, one of the most articulate and committed supporters of the KPD's proposal to abolish §218 in Weimar Germany, stated in his brochure *Sturm gegen §218*:

> Die Frage des §218 ist nur eine Teilfrage des ganzen heutigen kapitalistischen Wirtschaftssystems.... Wir wissen, daß unsere Frauen und Mädchen auch in Deutschland wieder freudig Kindern das Leben schenken werden—doch nicht in einem Deutschland des Hungers, des Elends und der Young-Sklaverei [sic], sondern in einem freien, sozialistischen Deutschland! (298)

The KPD supported free and legal abortion primarily in order to alleviate economic pressures on working-class women and assure social justice for women of all classes. Beyond that the existence of blatantly discriminatory abortion legislation served as proof of much-needed fundamental economic and social change. The image of the doubly oppressed proletarian woman, as Käthe Kollwitz had portrayed her in "Down with the Abortion Paragraph" (1924), had become the emblem of capitalist injustice (Grossmann 79). The direct connection between capitalism and the KPD's position on abortion also allowed for a complete reorientation of the communist position once socialism was established. In the words of Karl Kautsky, abortion was a *Tagesfrage* rather than a *Weltanschauungsfrage*.[13]

Given the predominantly female electorate in the Soviet Occupation Zone in the late 1940s, the SED leadership was fully aware of the propagandistic value of supporting legislation favorable to women.[14] In an effort to gain crucial political legitimacy, the SED exploited the discussion of this important and highly visible political issue for its own propagandistic purposes, carefully manipulating documentation of the debate in its publications. In 1946, the SED-friendly women's journals *Für Dich* and *Frau von heute* provided extensive coverage of the abortion debate. *Für Dich* encouraged its readers to explore the question "Welches Verhältnis soll zwischen der persönlichen Verfügungsfreiheit der Frau über ihren Körper und den Forderungen des Staates nach Erhaltung der biologischen und moralischen Grundlagen für das Weiterleben des Volkes bestehen?" ("Paragraph 218"). The fact that an overwhelming number of readers, male and female, spoke up in favor of a woman's right to choose was evidence of the public consensus of the post-war years that, given economic circumstances, legal abortion was a morally permissible act of self-help. In their summary, the editors did not side with their readers' support for uncontrolled access to abortion, but rather advocated a legal compromise identical to the SED proposal. The public debate was thus designed less as a public forum of discussion than as a vehicle to present the SED as the party that presumably most adequately represented women's interests.

At the same time that the SED leadership pursued the construction of the party's image as advocate of women's emancipation consistent with its ideological heritage and political interests, it sustained the pronatalist discourse that had informed the KPD's position on abortion in the 1930s and culminated in the 1950 "Law for the Protection of Mothers and Children." Party media played a crucial role in constructing an image of woman that combined traditional characteristics of motherhood with nontraditional professional skills. The following definition of womanhood is but one example of the rhetoric with which the SED reminded East German women of their central and exclusive responsibility for child rearing and family: "Die Frau will Leben geben, hüten, bewahren. Die Frau ist von der Natur dazu ausersehen, Kinder zu gebären, die die Menschheit daran verhindern, auszusterben. In der Mutterschaft mit allen Sorgen und Mühen findet die Frau Erfüllung ihrer höchsten Lebensaufgabe" ("Das Recht"). In their discussion of the abortion issue, SED publications struck a careful balance between advocacy of liberal abortion rights and encouragement of motherhood. The 1947 article "Für und wider §218" in *Neues Deutschland,* which debated the pros and cons of legalized abortion, was accompanied by a reproduction of Paula Modersohn-Becker's painting *Stillende Mutter* as well as an article on Maria Montessori entitled "Ein Herz schlägt für die Kinder."

In no way did the SED give serious consideration to women's demands for their right to choose. As Maxim Zetkin pointed out in his letter to the *SED-Vorstand,* society has the right to determine the destiny of both mother and child as well as the duty to create humane living conditions for both (IfGA #1). In her discussion of the legal foundations of the debate on §218, Hilde Benjamin insisted that the SED leadership would not go along with isolated feminist demands that placed individual interest over that of society at large, ignoring the "right of the people" to population growth (10). A similar governmental claim on women's reproductive powers underlies the position expressed in a 1947 article in the party publication *Freiheit,* which emphasized that the primary factor in the abortion debate was the preservation of "healthy women and healthy children for the German people" ("Frauen"). The racist overtones of such arguments apparently did cause a certain amount of discomfort among some participants in the debate. However, Benjamin assured her audience that such concerns were groundless due to the different nature and aims of the fascist and socialist German states.

The SED's pronatalist orientation was perhaps most apparent in its contradictory approach to birth control in the post-war years. While communist women and doctors working directly with the female population supported an effective campaign for birth control as the corollary to a more lenient abortion law, women organized in the SED's women's organization *Demokratischer Frauenbund Deutschlands* (DFD) supported the leadership's interests in population growth. When Dr. Annemarie Durand-Wever, a physician and birth control activist from the Weimar years, pleaded with DFD members for more effective implementation of birth control, she was told that rather than being overly concerned with the prevention and interruption of pregnancies, she and her colleagues would be better off maintaining the health of newborns (DFD #1 241–42). Durand-Wever's exile in the West was a welcome opportunity to put her into a questionable ideological light and her slim booklet *Bewußte Mutterschaft* was considered too costly for widespread distribution. Clearly, the SED did not tolerate any active interference with its monopoly over women's bodies. The fact that the party leadership decided to withhold knowledge that would have provided women with the tools to prevent a pregnancy, rather than force them under the authority of state commissions, is perhaps the most blatant evidence of the SED's antifeminist population politics of the 1940s and 50s.

On 9 March 1972, the *Volkskammer* declared abortion in the GDR free and legal. With the exception of a mandatory birth control consultation after the procedure, the state no longer interfered with women's decisions to terminate a pregnancy. The preamble to the law declared "the emancipation of women in educational and professional life, marriage, and family" the prerequisite granting East German women the right to choose. The fact that the law went into effect exactly one day after the celebration of "International Woman's Day" underlined the intended message that unconditional access to abortion was the result of women's increased contribution to the building of socialism.[15] In actuality, the introduction of visa-free travel to Poland, which would have facilitated undesirable abortion tourism, as well as the highly visible struggle of West German women for legal abortion in the early 1970s contributed to the sudden change in GDR abortion legislation ("Ab 1. Januar"). The emphasis on an ideological rationale apparent in the preamble to the law, however, was primarily aimed at concealing the fact that the new abortion law, as previous social legislation pertaining to women, had primarily been the result of economic constraints.

Discussions on the abortion issue in the GDR had resumed again as early as 1961 with the closing of the border to the FRG, resulting in an amendment to §11 of the 1950 "Law for the Protection of Mothers and Children." In consultation with leading gynecologists, the Commission for Family Planning formulated guidelines for the application of §11 to effectively include a *sozial-medizinische Indikation*. As of 21 November 1965, East German women were guaranteed the right to legal termination of a pregnancy if they were physically or psychologically unable to have the child, if they were under sixteen or over forty years of age, if they had more than five children, or if the average time span between the first four pregnancies had been less than fifteen months (DFD #4). This extended interpretation of §11 was designed to remedy the inequities among the standards as applied by regional abortion commissions as well as provide more effective deterrence to illegal abortions. For fear of being turned down by the abortion commission, women had continued to resort to quacks or attempted abortions themselves. Most importantly, however, the changes were motivated by the Commission's findings that, despite existing government incentives, couples without children continued to be better off financially (DFD #10). In addition, labor statistics showed that women were increasingly working shorter hours in order to allow for sufficient time for housework and child care.[16] Ultimately, the government had to acknowledge that exclusive responsibility for the family placed too large a burden on many women and severely curtailed their interest in seeking higher professional qualifications or employment with a greater amount of responsibility. Given the projected development of population growth for the following two decades however, a significant relaxation of the existing abortion legislation was not considered.

The fact that, unlike in 1947, the intended legislative changes were debated only internally and the guidelines published only by the Health Department, suggests that despite the relaxation of §11, the SED government was determined to preserve the emergency character of the legislation. This assessment is supported by evidence that Erich Honecker, then first Secretary of the Central Committee, advised county administrators to use their influence in the selection of abortion committee members to ensure that they would reach decisions in accordance with the goals of SED population politics (DFD #5). Similarly, the series "Fragen an den Frauenarzt" published in *Für Dich* in 1966 not only revealed a willful ignorance regarding reproductive issues, but illustrated the moralistic stand with which the party attempted to coerce women into participation in its baby campaign. The series was not only designed to inform women of their new rights, but to influence their decision-making process. As the "magazine doctor" was quick to point out:

> Die sozialistische Gesellschaft, die von humanistischen Grundsätzen geleitet und erfüllt ist, hat daher kein Verständnis für sexuelle Haltlosigkeit und Entartung und schon gar nicht dafür, das Ergebnis solcher Handlungsweise mit einer Schwangerschaftsunterbrechung aus der Welt schaffen zu wollen. Das sozialistische Bewußtsein verlangt im Prinzip sowohl Sauberkeit als auch Sittlichkeit im Denken und Handeln, ohne dabei etwa übertriebener Zimperlichkeit das Wort zu reden (607).[17]

Such attempts to control public opinion on abortion served the ideological goal of putting socialist East Germany morally ahead of the "degenerate" West, as well as squelching anticipated protest from the SED's only significant opposition, the Church.[18]

Needless to say, the guidelines to §11 did not bring the GDR any closer to recognition of women's rights over their own bodies. The party's exclusively societal perception of reproductive issues is perhaps most apparent in its decision to legalize sterilization. In a discussion with members of the DFD, Health Secretary Dr. Mecklinger defended the highly controversial issue of sterilization as follows:

> Die Verpflichtung jedes Einzelnen, zur biologischen Erhaltung der Gesellschaft beizutragen, muß vorhanden sein, und demjenigen, der offensichtlich für die biologische Erhaltung der Gesellschaft schon genügend getan hat, muß man die Möglichkeit geben, einen Antrag auf Unfruchtbarmachung zu stellen (DFD #6).

This position also comes through in the notion of the much-advocated *gesellschaftliche Indikation,* which granted a woman holding public office the same liberal access to legal abortion as a woman with a medical, ethical, or eugenic emergency. Active political commitment to the party was thus the only work that at least partially exempted women in the GDR from their reproductive duties.

The guidelines to §11 of 1965 seriously affected population growth in the GDR. By 1967, the number of legally terminated pregnancies had increased by 100%, as 88.8% of all petitions based on §11 had been granted (DFD #7). SED health administrators attempted a two-pronged strategy to address this national emergency: an extensive media campaign to convince women of their reproductive responsibilities and a major sex education campaign. Health secretary Dr. Mecklinger rallied for support among DFD representatives, advising them to see their role primarily in exerting positive influence on pregnant women:

> Über 2000 Unterbrechungen im Monat können wir uns wegen des erforderlichen biologischen Wachstums nicht leisten. Dabei werden wir bei einer größeren Anzahl von Mädchen und Frauen nicht auf Verständnis stoßen. Darüber sollte man aber ganz offen sprechen (DFD #6).

The SED's interest in curtailing abortion figures, however, was not exclusively motivated by population statistics, but also by the concern that abortion was rapidly becoming the primary method of birth control. Women cited lack of time to attend family planning sessions as their reason for this dilemma, whereas the government attempted to blame the Western media campaign against the pill for women's reluctance to take it. A very important and very real reason for GDR women's reluctance to use hormonal methods of birth control was the absence of sufficient choice in products. Doctors had called for a wider range of birth control devices as early as 1961. However, the first product *Ovosiston* was not available until 1965, and alternative products like *Nonovosiston, Sequenziston,* and *Tyrikoston* were not developed until 1970.[19] A further handicap to the successful implementation of birth control was the fact that until 1972, prescription of the pill was, at least officially, based on the same restrictions as abortion. Access to birth control was thus effectively denied to the majority of the female population of childbearing age.

Neither of the stop-gap measures devised in reaction to the relaxation of §11 were effective, and in 1969 the death rate exceeded the rate of live births for the first time in GDR history (DFD #13). The November 1970 study commissioned by the GDR-*Ministerrat* identified three main reasons: lack of governmental demographic research and control, failure of the media and cultural apparatus to propagate a positive image (*Leitbild*) of marriage and family, and insufficient governmental support for families. Suggested remedies included an increase in financial incentives for the second and third child, longer vacation time, shorter working hours for mothers, family loans, and preferential access to consumer goods for large families. In conjunction with a comprehensive plan for the "Förderung von Ehe und Familie" discussed by the *Ministerrat*, women's unrestricted right to legal abortion first appeared as part of a legislative package of social and economic measures to encourage young families (DFD #12).

Surprisingly, the DFD's assessment of the situation showed at least a subconscious awareness that such social measures would have only a limited effect. The two crucial factors the DFD identified as responsible for the shrinking family size were the high divorce rate, which discouraged women from taking on responsibility for more children than they could support without the help of a husband, and the generational factor.[20] As the DFD's commentary on the report notes, working mothers with several children were frequently in poor health, and their daughters were simply no longer willing to sacrifice individual health, well-being, and standard of living for the greater benefit of society (DFD #14). While these observation proved the limitations and aberrations of mother-centered family policies, the SED continued ever more forcefully on its path towards "positive" discrimination against women.

The government's inclination towards legal abortion combined with improved benefits for mothers and families was affirmed by the results of a study presented to the Central Committee on 1 December 1971, which showed an increasing tendency towards part time employment among women (IfGA #10). While the study emphasized the undesirable ideological consequences of women's reluctance towards full-time work, it also implied that it was primarily the difficult economic situation of the GDR in the early 1970s that required women's full participation in the work force.

In 1971, the SED government finally had to acknowledge the failure of its concurrent productive and reproductive exploitation of women. The decision to legalize the termination of a pregnancy during the first three months was thus primarily the result of a governmental balancing act attempting to control women's productive and reproductive behavior. It was ultimately decided in favor of production, which happened to coincide with women's right to self-determination. A brief press release on 23 December 1971 informed citizens of the government's decision to legalize abortion ("Gemeinsamer Beschluß").

Over the following two decades, the existence of liberal abortion legislation on the one hand and continuous ideological pressure towards motherhood on the other hand created conflicts for many GDR women that found expression in literary texts long before they could be publicly discussed.[21] In 1970, the DFD had issued the directive that all GDR media should emphasize the positive aspects of GDR family life (DFD #14). Instead, the gradual shift away from the 1950s heroine of production and mother of four toward the single mother torn between the responsibilities of work and child dominated literary texts by GDR women writers in the 1970s and 1980s. Dorothy Rosenberg's observation that from the 1950s onward, GDR-women writers tended to see conflicts between work and family as rooted in individual failings rather than as demanding structural change also holds true for those texts by East German women writers that focus on the issue of abortion (95). Charlotte Worgitzky's short story "Eva" and her subsequent novel *Meine ungeborenen Kinder* (1982) are courageous attempts to break the taboo surrounding abortion. In that respect, they serve a purpose similar to that of the public demonstrations by West German women in 1970. Beyond that, Worgitzky's critique is limited to the timing of the new legislation which comes too late for both her protagonists. In Helga Königsdorf's short story "Unterbrechung" (1978), Monika Helmecke's "Klopfzeichen" (1982) and Maja Wiens's novel *Traumgrenzen* (1983), the protagonists' decisions to terminate a pregnancy vividly illustrate the extreme emotional stress experienced by women caught between the conflicting pressures of childcare and career. Constructing a "concrete utopia" of motherhood, all three texts represent pregnancy and birth as creative forces sacrificed at the altar of the cold pragmatism and male indifference of GDR reality.

Even more powerful testimony of GDR women's (and men's) ambivalence toward abortion than these literary texts is Gabriele Grafenhorst's *Abbruch-Tabu* (1990). Conceived and researched before the fall of the wall, it is a collection of first-person reports that provides a differentiated account of the problems and pressures experienced in a society that offers free and legal access to abortion while silencing any discussion of the issue. Women share their feelings of emotional stress and loneliness when faced with the decision to end a pregnancy and report on the physical and emotional abuse suffered during the procedure. Doctors, on the other hand, voice their frustrations with routinely and anonymously performed abortions.

The fact that the SED regime collapsed just as society began to listen to GDR women's experiences with the existing abortion law—a law that had neither been the result of a democratic process nor the outcome of a societal consensus—may be the reason why the East German women's movement failed to insist immediately on access to free and legal abortion (Rohnstock 70-89). The *Wohnort/Tatort* principle devised by West German politicians in the unification treaty successfully divided and conquered East and West German women, raising false hopes in the West as well as deferring the urgency of the matter in the East. The 1993 decision of the *Bundesverfassungsgericht* provides women throughout Germany with common ground for united outrage and the opportunity to join forces in a protest against the renewed onslaught on their bodies. The women's strike planned for 8 March 1994 in both East and West is a first step in that direction.

Katharina von Ankum 139

Notes

Research for this article was funded by Faculty Research Grants awarded by Scripps College for the summers of 1990 and 1991. The research was conducted at the *Archiv des Demokratischen Frauenbunds Deutschlands* and the *Institut für die Geschichte der Arbeiterbewegung, Zentrales Parteiarchiv der SED* in Berlin. Archival material from these sources will be numbered based on a key provided in the appendices and cited parenthetically in the text, using the following abbreviations:

DFD = Archiv des Demokratischen Frauenbunds Deutschlands

IfGA = Institut für die Geschichte der Arbeiterbewegung, Zentrales Parteiarchiv der SED

Translations are my own.

[1] On the process leading to the 1990 legislative compromise, the so-called *Gruppenantrag,* see Funk (196-97).

[2] The consultant can turn to the opinion of experts and family members to evaluate whether a woman's claim to medical, ethical, or social hardship is justified and it is s/he who decides at what point the consultation is concluded. These regulations remain in place for a transitional period, until the *Bundestag* passes a revised abortion law based on the Court's directives.

[3] On 30 January 1946, the Allies had repealed all legislation introduced during the Third Reich with the exception of §218 and §219, the paragraphs pertaining to abortion (Thietz 25).

[4] It is notable however that, unlike the suggestions submitted by the DFD to President Grotewohl on 7 March 1950 and the 20 May 1950 proposal, the final version of the law did not set a specific quota for female trainees, providing the government with greater flexibility in implementing its plans and granting women less leverage in achieving equality in the work place (DFD #3, IfGA #5).

[5] In the West, child allowances (*Kindergeld*), for example, were paid out to the male head of the family, even if both parents were working (Moeller 153).

[6] Ursula Heukenkamp observes a similar emphasis on women's return to traditional female roles in the work of GDR women dramatists of the 1950s. While this may have been partially the result of propagandistic influence on the authors, it may also point to the fact that women themselves considered their traditional roles a welcome stabilizing factor in their otherwise chaotic lives.

[7] By February 1948, all states in the Soviet Occupation Zone had declared abortion legal if a medical or ethical indication existed. Sachsen, Thüringen, and Mecklenburg also accepted the *soziale Indikation,* which in Brandenburg was considered part of the medical considerations. In addition, Mecklenburg recognized a eugenic indication. Sachsen-Anhalt did not accept the *soziale Indikation*, but a resolution of 7 February 1948 introduced special support with food and clothing for pregnant women and newborn babies (IfGA #3).

[8] In its preamble, the proposal stated "Die Verwirklichung der Gleichberechtigung der Frau ist entscheidend abhängig von der Anteilnahme der Frau

an der produktiven Arbeit. Durch die gesellschaftliche Arbeit und die berufliche Tätigkeit werden Können und Kräfte entwickelt, die das Selbstbewußtsein stärken und die Frauen befähigen, um von dem Recht auf Gleichberechtigung einen ständig besseren Gebrauch zu machen" (IfGA #5).

[9] Grotewohl's commentary suggests that he acted primarily in anticipation of protest from the Soviet Military Administration (SMAD), which had to authorize the legislative proposal. This, however, cannot be adequately documented until the SMAD files are publicly accessible.

[10] The undated letter of the Central Commission of Education to the SED Frauensekretariat quotes the two versions that became the basis for discussion of the SED proposal on abortion legislation: "Weil die sozialen Verhältnisse der Schwangeren oder ihrer Familie so liegen, dass sich aus dem Austragen des Kindes ernste gesundheitliche Schädigungen für Mutter und Kind erwarten lassen und der Notlage durch soziale und fürsorgerische Massnahmen nicht ausreichend abgeholfen werden kann" (Hamann, September 1946, IfGA #7). "Weil die sozialen Verhältnisse der Schwangeren oder ihrer Familie bei einem Austragen des Kindes eine ernste wirtschaftliche Gefährdung für Mutter und Kind erwarten lassen und der Notlage durch soziale und fürsorgerische Massnahmen nicht ausreichend abgeholfen werden kann" (Maxim Zetkin, 2. October 1946, IfGA #7).

[11] The SED proposal was attacked from within the party as well as by members of the CDU. A letter from the Department of Justice to the Department on Women's Affairs pointed out that the SED proposal lagged behind that of the SPD that suggested unconditional and legal access to abortion for an interim period of two years. Ethical reservations raised by the Christian Democrats were considered invalid, since they pertained to an individual's conscience, which could and should not be regulated by the state. However, an individual's conscious decision against abortion was respected very little, as became clear in the case of a Thüringen doctor who had refused to perform abortions based on the *soziale Indikation*. It was recommended that he leave the profession, since his actions demonstrated that he had been infiltrated by the class enemy and was threatening the basis of democracy in the Soviet Occupation Zone (IfGA #2, #4).

[12] As it was, many women made fraudulent use of the *ethische Indikation* claiming they had been raped by Soviet soldiers (Johr 61). For a discussion of the different abortion policies in all Allied Occupation Zones during the immediate post-war years, see Poutrus.

[13] For a detailed discussion of the positions taken by the political left in the Weimar debate on abortion, see Hagemann (220-305).

[14] According to the census taken in the Soviet Occupation Zone in December 1945, out of a total population of 16,194,626, there were 9,612,647 women. The total "excess" of women amounted to 3 million, with 100 men for every 146 women (Merkel 17). After the 1946 elections, the SED held 57.1 percent of the votes throughout the Soviet Occupation Zone (Childs 19).

[15] The connection between the presumably attained high level of societal development and abortion legislation had always been central to the discussion of reproductive policies in the GDR. The fact that the GDR did not follow suit when abortion was legalized in all other countries of the Eastern block in 1956 was explained with the different degree of socialism existing in these societies.

Undoubtedly, the fact that the GDR continued to lose considerable numbers of people to its Western neighbor even after the erection of the Berlin wall played a major role in the construction of this rhetoric.

[16] "Seit 1961 gehen die berufstätigen Frauen immer mehr zur verkürzten Arbeitszeit über...30% der arbeitsfähigen Frauen sind nicht berufstätig, nur 15,5 der Frauen sind Facharbeiterinnen im Gegensatz zu 70,2% Männer" (IfGA #8).

[17] Similarly, the decision to extend the prescription of birth control pills to girls under the age of 18 was justified with the argument that teenage pregnancies reflected poorly on socialist society (DFD #6, #9).

[18] A letter to Helmut Axen, editor in chief of *Neues Deutschland,* refers to an Associated Press news release of 30 November 1965 regarding the support of Anglican bishops for more liberal abortion legislation in Great Britain, and suggests reprinting this article in conjunction with the information on §11 to prevent protest from the church (IfGA #9).

[19] The Health Department consistently denied the possibility that birth control pills contained carcinogenic substances. The fact that the FRG had taken six products off the market that contained the same active ingredients as *Ovosiston* was belittled as "capitalist marketing strategy" (DFD #8). Despite the fact that studies had shown that two-thirds of all women had problems with the product, *Ovosiston* was heavily marketed (DFD #7). One reason for this was the failure of planned socialist economy. The pharmaceutical industry had to pay a fine for medication it had not been able to sell. Women's reluctance to take the pill thus interfered not only with the state's reproductive policy, but with economic planning as well. Birth control focused exclusively on women reinforced the notion that women alone were responsible for reproductive and family issues. Condoms were mentioned only once as an alternative method of contraception with the remark that the quality of the rubber had to be improved, a fact that in and of itself should have been an argument in support of legal abortion (DFD #11).

[20] Fathers were not required to pay child support in case of remarriage if the mother of the children was working, a law designed to encourage men to found more than one family.

[21] For a brief analysis of abortion statistics after 1972, see Aresin (93-94).

Works Cited

"Ab 1. Januar: Reiseverkehr mit Polen visafrei." *Neues Deutschland* 23 Dec. 1971.

Amt für Information der Regierung der Deutschen Demokratischen Republik. *Gesunde Familie-Glückliche Zukunft.* Berlin: Deutscher Zentralverlag, 1950.

Aresin, Lyke. "Schwangerschaftsabbruch in der DDR." *Unter anderen Umständen: Zur Geschichte der Abtreibung.* Berlin: Argon/Dresden: Hygienemuseum, 1993. 86-95.

Bebel, August. *Die Frau und der Sozialismus.* Berlin: Dietz, 1990.

Benjamin, Hilde. "Juristische Grundlagen für die Diskussion über §218." *Mitteilungen der Juristischen Arbeitskommission im Zentralen Frauenausschuss*, 3. Folge. 25 December 1947.
Childs, David. *The GDR: Moscow's German Ally*. London: Allen, 1983.
Durand-Wever, Annemarie. *Bewußte Mutterschaft*. Rudolstadt: Greifenverlag, 1948.
"Fragen an den Frauenarzt." *Für Dich* 4, 1966.
Frauen in die Offensive. Berlin: Dietz, 1990. 70-89.
"Frauen und Mütter, das geht Euch an!" *Freiheit* 20 June 1947.
Funk, Nanette. "Abortion and German Unification." *Gender Politics and Postcommunism*. Ed. Nanette Funk and Magda Mueller. New York: Routledge, 1993. 194-99.
"Für und wider §218." *Neues Deutschland* 4 January 1947.
"Gemeinsamer Beschluß des Politbüros des ZK der SED und des Ministerrates der DDR." *Neues Deutschland* 23 December 1971.
Grafenhorst, Gabriele. *Abbruch-Tabu*. Berlin: Neues Leben, 1990.
Grossmann, Atina. "Abortion and Economic Crisis." *When Biology Became Destiny: Women in Weimar and Nazi Germany*. Ed. Renate Bridenthal et.al. New York: Monthly Review, 1984. 66-86.
Hagemann, Karen. *Frauenalltag und Männerpolitik*. Bonn: Dietz, 1990.
Helmecke, Monika. "Klopfzeichen." *Im Kreislauf der Windeln*. Ed. Horst Heidtmann. Weinheim: Beltz, 1982. 201-17.
Heukenkamp, Ursula. "Die Geschlechterverhältnisse in der politischen Kultur der DDR." *Wen kümmert's wer spricht?* Ed. Inge Stephan, Sigrid Weigel, and Karin Wilhelm. Köln: Böhlau, 1991.
Johr, Barbara. "Die Ereignisse in Zahlen." *BeFreier und Befreite*. Ed. Helke Sander and Barbara Johr. München: Kunstmann, 1992. 46-57.
Königsdorf, Helga "Unterbrechung." *Die geschlossenen Türen am Abend*. Frankfurt a.M.: Luchterhand, 1989. 7-26.
Merkel, Ina. *...und Du, Frau an der Werkbank*. Berlin: Elefanten, 1990.
Moeller, Robert. "Reconstructing the Family in Reconstruction Germany: Women in Social Policy in the Federal Republic 1949-55." *Feminist Studies* 15.1 (Spring 1989): 137-69.
"Paragraph 218." *Für Dich* 1, 17, 1946.
Poutrus, Kirsten. "Ein Staat, der seine Kinder nicht ernähren kann, hat nicht das Recht, ihre Geburt zu fordern: Abtreibung in der Nachkriegszeit 1945-1950." *Unter anderen Umständen: Zur Geschichte der Abtreibung*. Berlin: Argon/Dresden: Hygienemuseum, 1993. 73-85.
"Das Recht auf Mutterschaft." *Neues Deutschland* 30 April 1946.
Rohnstock, Kathrin, ed. *Frauen in die Offensive*. Berlin: Dietz, 1990.
Rosenberg, Dorothy. "On Beyond Superwoman: The Conflict Between Work and Family Roles in GDR Literature." *Studies in GDR Culture and Society* 3. Ed. Margy Gerber et al. Lanham, MD: UP of America, 1983. 87-100.
Thietz, Kirsten. *Das Ende der Selbstverständlichkeit*. Berlin: Basisdruck, 1992.

Wiens, Maja. *Traumgrenzen*. Berlin: Neues Leben, 1983.
Wolf, Conni, ed. *Cyankali von Friedrich Wolf—Eine Dokumentation*. Berlin: Aufbau, 1978.
Worgitzky, Charlotte. "Eva." *Im Kreislauf der Windeln*. Ed. Horst Heidtmann. Weinheim: Beltz, 1982. 136-48.
——. *Meine ungeborenen Kinder*. Berlin: Der Morgen, 1982.

Appendix I
Documents from the *Archiv des Demokratischen Frauenbunds Deutschlands* (DFD)

#1 Protokoll der Sitzung des DFD-Bundesausschusses, 24 September 1948.
#2 Gesetzblatt der Deutschen Demokratischen Republik, no. 111, 1 October 1950.
#3 Vorschläge des Demokratischen Frauenbundes Deutschlands zur Förderung der Frauen.
#4 Ministerium für Gesundheitswesen: Instruktion zur Anwendung des §11 des Gesetzes über den Mutter- und Kinderschutz und die Rechte der Frau vom 27.9.1950.
#5 Brief Erich Honeckers an die 1. Sekretäre der Bezirks- und Kreisleitungen, 26 March 1965.
#6 Protokoll über die Sitzung mit den vom DFD in die Indikationsausschüsse delegierten Freundinnen, 16 December 1966.
#7 Information über die bisherige Tätigkeit der Vertreterinnen des DFD in den Indikationsausschüssen der Bezirke, 3 January 1967.
#8 Beratung der Zentralen Kommission für Familienplanung, 22 January 1971.
#9 Beratung der Zentralen Kommission für Familienplanung, 2 June 1967.
#10 Untersuchung der Ursachen für den Rückgang der Anzahl der Geborenen, 1970. Anlage 2, Artikel 4.
#11 Beratung der Zentralen Kommission für Familienplanung, 16 April 1970.
#12 Brief des Ministerrates der DDR an Ilse Thiele, 12 October 1971.
#13 Abteilung Frauen, Abteilung Gesundheitspolitik, "Information über die Geburtenentwicklung und Tendenzen der Schwangerschaftsunterbrechung seit Annahme des Gesetzes," 11 June 1974.
#14 DFD-Bundessekretariat, "Gedanken und Vorschläge zur Bevölkerungsentwicklung," 29 November 1970.

Appendix II

Documents from the *Institut für die Geschichte der Arbeiterbewegung, Zentrales Parteiarchiv der SED* (IfGA)

Archival documentation is given in brackets.

#1 Maxim Zetkin. "Über §218," Brief an den Vorstand der SED, 2 Oct. 1946. [IfGA ZPA IV 2/17/28]

#2 Brief der Abt. Justiz an das Frauensekretariat betreffend der Änderungsvorschläge zur Schwangerschaftsunterbrechung, 27 Nov. 1946. [IfGA ZPA IV 2/17/28]

#3 Zentralsekretariat der SED, "Betr. Die neue Gesetzgebung zur Schwangerschaftsverhütung in der sowjetischen Besatzungzone." [IfGA ZPA IV/2/17/28]

#4 Brief an den Kreisvorstand der SED Abt. Arbeit und Sozialfürsorge vom Landesvorstand Thüringen, 23 April 1948. [IfGA ZPA IV 1/17/28]

#5 Entwurf: Gesetz zur Förderung der Frau vom 20. Mai 1950. [IfGA ZPA J IV/2/12/137]

#6 Aktennotiz über die Besprechung beim Ministerpräsidenten Otto Grotewohl, 9 June 1950. [IfGA ZPA I IV/2/12/1370]

#7 Undatierter Brief der Zentralen Kommission für Erziehung an das Frauensekretariat der SED. [IfGA ZPA IV/2/17/28]

#8 Vorschläge zur Förderung der Geburtenentwicklung, Anlage 2, Artikel II, 27 May 1964. [IfGA ZPA IV/As/17/83]

#9 Brief an Helmut Axen, 30 November 1965. [IfGA ZPA IV As/19/22]

#10 Protokoll der ZK-Sitzung, "Bericht über die Entwicklung der Beschäftigung der Frau in der Produktion." [IfGA ZPA J IV 2/3/181]

At the Margins of East Berlin's "Counter-Culture": Elke Erb's *Winkelzüge* and Gabriele Kachold's *zügel los*

Friederike Eigler

This article introduces Elke Erb and Gabriele Kachold by first looking at the positions they occupied within East Berlin's "counter-culture" in Prenzlauer Berg. I then explore the experimental features of Erb's *Winkelzüge* and Kachold's *zügel los,* both of which challenge previously held views of GDR literature. I argue that these features are not a substitute for but an integral part of social issues such as gender and power relations. Thus, the article concludes, these texts may help to call into question the presumed incompatibility of *engagierte Literatur*—frequently associated with the East—and form-oriented (post)modern literature—frequently associated with the West. (FE)

Since the *Wende* in 1989, our previously held views of the GDR and of GDR literature have come under scrutiny. As Patricia Herminghouse, Wolfgang Emmerich, and others have recently pointed out, our image of GDR literature was shaped not only by selective publication practices in the East (i.e., censorship) but also by selective reception practices in the West. Most scholars and critics interpreted GDR literature in its relation to GDR cultural politics and thus favored content over form. While most critics in the East focused on support of the socialist ideology and many critics in the West on its critique, we all tended to detach GDR literature from other literatures and cultures and often neglected artistic dimensions. Karen Jankowsky has discussed how feminist scholars participated in this selective reception process by often limiting their interest to a few women authors like Christa Wolf or Irmtraud Morgner.

These recent reflections contrast with the self-serving statements by a number of prominent critics in the West German media. In the context of the "Christa Wolf controversy" just after the opening of the wall, critics like Greiner, Schirrmacher, and Bohrer dismissed East German authors as proponents of a *"Gesinnungsästhetik."*[1] I would like to argue that instead of dismissing an entire literature—some of which was celebrated in the West before the *Wende*—we need to critically examine our earlier approaches to this literature and explore works by previously marginalized authors.

The issue of cultural marginalization within the GDR is often associated with the alternative cultural movements that emerged in the late seventies in numerous East German cities such as Berlin, Leipzig, Dresden, Erfurt, and Halle. The largest, best-known, and by now most controversial emerged in the Berlin district "Prenzlauer Berg" and included painters, musicians, poets, and multi-media artists. For the most part, these young artists had turned away from socialist ideology as well as from political activities criticizing or opposing "real existing Socialism" (G. Wolf, "gegen sprache"). The discovery that two main figures of the Prenzlauer Berg circle were also informers for the *Stasi*, however, indicates that these counter-cultures were entangled in the very system from which they sought to retreat. The news of Sascha Anderson's and Rainer Schedlinski's *Stasi* activities drew media attention even after the *Wende* to those people who had dominated the Prenzlauer Berg. Consequently, the contributions of others continue to remain obscured.

In a postscript to a critical statement, Peter Böthig—an insider of the Prenzlauer Berg circle and a victim of the *Stasi*—acknowledges that the Prenzlauer Berg culture was a "Männerszene" and calls for a study of the political and aesthetic implications of the marginal role played by women writers ("Politik").[2] While Böthig is moving in the right direction, I suggest also looking at the writings of women who had some interaction with the Prenzlauer Berg circle. Elke Erb and Gabriele Kachold[3] are among the few women writers who were loosely associated with the group. While Erb participated to a limited extent in the cultural life of the Prenzlauer Berg, Kachold was acutely aware and personally affected by the situation described by Böthig.

In this article, I would like to introduce these two women authors by first looking more closely at the positions Erb and Kachold occupied within the GDR in general and the Prenzlauer Berg circle in particular. In my analysis of recent publications by Erb and Kachold, I then explore their innovative use of stylistic and linguistic features that deviate from our previously held images of GDR literature. I argue that these linguistic experiments are not a substitute for, but an integral part of, social issues such as education, identity formation, and gender relations.

Elke Erb, born in 1938, represents an older generation and is better known for her association with a group of poets that one of its members, Adolf Endler, humorously called the *"Sächsische Dichterschule."* This "school" was comprised of poets such as Karl Mickel, Volker Braun, Rainer and Sarah Kirsch, and Adolf Endler, who began transgressing aesthetic and ideological rules in their poetry during the sixties and seventies (G. Wolf, "Laudatio" 116–17; Emmerich 216–32). Later Erb was one of the few writers of her generation to become actively involved with the mostly younger poets in Prenzlauer Berg who were more daring in their artistic experiments and seemed more radical in their political disengagement.[4] In her interactions with the Prenzlauer Berg circle, Erb not only continued to develop her own brand of "poetic prose," but was also active as mentor and editor. In 1984, she and Sascha Anderson edited *Berührung ist nur eine Randerscheinung*, a collection of innovative poems and prose texts by approximately thirty authors who generally were unable to get published in the GDR. Since Erb and Anderson did not find an East German publisher, it was published in the West and became the first volume to introduce this "other" literature from the GDR to a West German audience.[5] Presumably because of her age and her editorial work, West German critics have described Elke Erb as the "mother of the Prenzlauer Berg circle." Erb rejects this label that falsely attributes to her a leading position and obscures her own creative work.

The writer and performance artist Gabriele Kachold, born in 1953, lives in Erfurt and is part of a women's group that is involved in collective art projects (G. Wolf, "Gabriele Kachold"; Kyselka and Stötzer). She also spent time in Berlin with the artists in Prenzlauer Berg, but her relationship to this group was far more ambivalent than Erb's. Kachold belongs to the younger generation of the counter-culture and shares their rejection of a society that seemed impervious to change. Kachold's text "An die 40jährigen" from the mid-eighties (included in *zügel los*) demonstrates in radical terms her break with the previous generation and its political and economic achievements:

> das ist das gedicht einer 30jährigen, ohne vers, ohne reim, ohne maß, damit ist schon alles gesagt oder vieles. wir sind die zu spät gekommenen, ein klein wenig zu spät für eure ordnung, um eintritt zu finden dazu, zutritt in den raum der geregelten abläufe. ihr hattet noch zeit euch einzurichten, in das land, in das leben, in die zeit.... als ich geboren wurde, war alles aufgebaut, war alles fertig, perfekt, ein schillerndes förderband mit der richtung nach oben. die ideologie war sicher, der weg war sicher, die häuser, die wohnungen, die rente war sicher.... wir horden uns in gruppen und stehn an den rändern eurer welt. wir finden keinen einlaß, wir suchen keinen einlaß, wir haben keine angst. wir haben keinen mut, wir haben keine zukunft, wir haben keinen platz, wir haben keine hoffnung, wir haben kein ziel.... wir sind rastlos, wir sind heimatlos, mit euren ländern verbinden uns nur eure grenzen (*zügel los* 79-80).

The publication of *zügel los*—written in an uncompromising language previously not heard in the GDR—coincided with the political events of 1989 and the collapse of the socialist system. Indeed, in retrospect this text sounds like a necrology that depicts both in form and in content the fossilization of the state versus the lively anger and frustration of the younger generation. The sentence structure consists of a repetitive parataxis that conveys a sense of impatience and urgency. The emphatic juxtaposition of "we" versus "you" also illustrates disparity with the attitudes of the previous generation of writers. East German authors such as Christa Wolf, Irmtraud Morgner, Helga Schütz, Stefan Heym, Volker Braun, and others were often critical of the GDR but continued to believe in the socialist project and in the political impact of art (Kaufmann). An unnamed young writer modeled after Kachold is mentioned in Christa Wolf's *Was bleibt* (1990).[6] The narrator expresses admiration for the woman's daring writings, anxieties about the woman's future and frustration with her own inability to further protect or support this young writer (52–55).

Kachold's harsh criticism of the social order was shared by many in Prenzlauer Berg, but she has turned her criticism also to the power structures within the Prenzlauer Berg circle. Shortly after Biermann revealed that Anderson had been a *Stasi* informant for fifteen years, Kachold, in a published interview, addressed the restricted entry and rigid order that prevailed in the Prenzlauer Berg circle. In particular, she mentions the disregard for her own feminist projects and claims that Anderson, especially, was unable to see her texts other than in terms of competition to his writings (Kachold, "Interview"; cf. also "Frauenszene"). These critical comments challenge the idealized image of a counter-culture as it was promoted not only by its major representatives in the East but also by intellectuals in the West (Arnold 9–13; Meyer-Gosau).

Beyond the more general question of the counter-culture's complicity with the power structures it claimed to oppose, Kachold's comments give a rare glimpse into the gender relations within this alternative cultural circle. Cornelia Sachse, who belongs to the youngest generation of writers and critics raised in the GDR, provides a similar account of the "counter-culture":

> Das U-Boot im Untergrund, der freie Sprachraum im Abseits, ausschließlich ausgestattet mit Matrosen, Mannschaftscrew und Käptn, bleibt ein Spiegelbild staatlicher Ordnung, wie auf den Flotten der staatlichen Armada, auch wenn sie im folgenden die Piraterie der Autorinnen als einen gewaltsamen Angriff auf dieses Schiff unter See definiert hätte ("Die Orange" 403).

These personal accounts correspond to the relative absence of women's voices in the publications of the Prenzlauer Berg circle. Most of the unofficial journals that were printed in small numbers in Prenzlauer Berg and elsewhere during the eighties were edited exlusively by men (Sachse, "Vage Zagenvragen" 402).

The anthology *Vogel oder Käfig sein* includes a cross-section of contributions from these unofficial journals, most of which combined poetry and short prose with paintings and graphic art. The journal

Ariadnefabrik, published 1986-1990 in Prenzlauer Berg, focused on poetological and theoretical issues. Many different essays in *Ariadnefabrik* challenge traditional concepts of language and of the subject, often drawing on various postmodern and poststructuralist theories.[7] Yet by and large the issue of gender is absent from any discussion of language and identity. What feminist scholars have argued in the West also applies to the reception of poststructuralist theories in the East: The critique of traditional concepts of the subject is potentially useful for exploring the construction of gendered identities but does not automatically result in breaking with an androcentric approach (de Lauretis 21-26; Goodman; Walker; Schulz).

The contributions to the journal *Ariadnefabrik* are a case study of how potentially liberating critiques of language and of the subject can become exclusionary and repressive when the category of gender is ignored. This is most evident in the satirical piece "Autodafé" published in 1987 in *Ariadnefabrik* under the pseudonym V. Toth (94-106). "Autodafé" casts the battle between different aesthetic positions as a judicial hearing. A representative of the "Maxie-Wander-Workshop" sues a representative of the "Konterliteratur" for betraying the social mission of art. In this satirical depiction, the "Maxie-Wander-Workshop" disregards questions of aesthetic style and form and instead attributes an exclusively social and therapeutic function to literature that is addressed to "depressiven und vereinsamten Frauen, Homosexuellen [und] Invaliden aller Art" (100). The author of "Autodafé" thus clearly aims at ridiculing the presumably realist literature of the "Maxie-Wander-Workshop" and identifies instead with the "counter-literature" of the defendant. In the process of pitting a socially committed realist literature against the experimental literature of the counter-culture, the author deliberately conflates realist with conformist literature (104).

This contribution to the avant-garde journal *Ariadnefabrik* expresses an extreme degree of intolerance towards deviating aesthetic positions. It is true that the state agencies in the GDR were overly skeptical of the experimental art in the "counter-culture," but the author of "Autodafé" displays a reverse paranoia by identifying the realist literature of the "Maxie-Wander-Workshop" with the state authorities.[8] Maxie Wander seems a particularly inappropriate target for such claims because her book *Guten Morgen, du Schöne* in fact challenged conformist views of society by illustrating the discrepancies between the GDR's official claim for gender equality and the persistence of traditional gender roles in everyday life.

While it may have been coincidental that the author of "Autodafé" chose the "Maxie-Wander-Workshop" as the representative of socially committed literature, this text illustrates two problematic tendencies within the journal *Ariadnefabrik,* the theoretical "voice" of the Prenzlauer

Berg circle: first, the elimination of differently gendered perspectives, and second, the attack on those who continue to believe that art can contribute to social and political change.

Recent publications by Erb and Kachold illustrate that the critique of traditional concepts of language and the subject do not necessarily preclude dealing with social questions. Kachold's *zügel los,* a collection of short texts, many of them autobiographical, was first published in 1989 by Aufbau. Unfortunately, the insightful commentary by the editor Gerhard Wolf has been omitted in the 1990 Luchterhand edition. Elke Erb published her literary autobiography *Winkelzüge oder nicht vermutete aufschlußreiche Verhältnisse* with the newly founded publishing house Galrev in Prenzlauer Berg.[9] While issues of gender are present but not dominant in Erb's text, Kachold's writing provides challenging perspectives on gender identity and the question of individual responsibility.

Although Erb's *Winkelzüge* and Kachold's *zügel los* are very different in style, content, and scope, they have some central features in common. Both authors question a clear distinction between the autobiographical and the fictional. The integration of the visual arts into these texts highlights the creative dimension: Erb includes drawings by the artist Angela Hampel; Kachold includes photos of her own performance art. Neither of these texts follows a consistent story line or chronology. The identity of the writing subject is not fixed or stable, but rather part of the subject matter of these texts, that is, in part a product of the writing process itself. Thus both texts challenge traditional "male" concepts of autobiography, i.e., the chronological and teleological account of a pre-established identity (Smith 3–19). For Kachold, the processes of writing and reconstituting her identity are closely linked to her socialization in and confrontation with the East German state, while Erb refers to social and political conditions only indirectly. Both *Winkelzüge* and *zügel los* have as recurring theme a failed love relationship and both attempt to come to terms with the past through the process of writing. Both titles consist of rather unusual expressions but they suggest different emphases: *zügel los* refers to feelings of rage, anger, and frustration and their effects on (body) language. *Winkelzüge* follows the reverse path: by exploring multiple meanings of words and phrases, Erb traces complex (de)formations of the writing subject.

Erb rejects what she calls a "consumer attitude" not only of the reader but also of the author; i.e., she believes the author should go beyond already existing syntactic and semantic structures (G. Wolf, "Laudatio" 119). Therefore many of Erb's texts are not readily accessible. Her unique writing style, which Gerhard Wolf has termed "prozessuales Schreiben" ("Vexierbild" 104), requires the active involvement of the reader. Erb has captured two different ways to read: "Zwei entgegengesetzte Arten zu lesen.... Zu welchem Leben führen die Worte?... Wie sind die Worte zum Leben gebracht?" ("Brötchenholen" 79). The first type of reading corresponds to a concept of language as a reflection of "reality." The second corresponds to a modern Saussurian concept of language that considers the relation of signifier and signified to be unstable. Erb's writing adheres to this latter concept that allows for the metonymic use of language and the destabilization of conventional meanings.[10]

In *Winkelzüge*, Erb questions traditional concepts of writing and author(izing) by turning the narrative voice into the reader and commentator of her own texts.[11] She frequently returns to earlier passages and uses them for new explorations of related themes. This results in a circular rather than linear style of writing. In the first part of *Winkelzüge*, she performs this writing in progress in an exemplary manner as a "workshop" (20-27). The narrator quotes one of her earlier texts in italics and adds corrections and comments she made in the process of revising the text. "Verwandelte Korrektur" (445), a phrase Erb uses at the very end of *Winkelzüge*, accurately describes her writing in respect to both content and style.[12]

Erb writes an autobiography as a process of reading her previous life and texts. She thus makes the processes of selection and interpretation—that underlie every autobiography—visible as structuring elements of her text. Likewise, Erb tries to involve the reader as active participant in the formation of the text, i.e., as co-author of the evolving text:

> Die Betrachter (Autor und Leser) werden, / was sie gewahren und was ihnen in den Sinn kommt, / der Heldin sofort zukommen lassen müssen, // wollen sie ein Erbe nicht schmälern, das sie antreten, / wenn die gestellte Frage ihnen am Ende des Textes / die Heldenrolle übergibt (*Winkelzüge* 15).

The question mentioned in this excerpt is spelled out at the beginning of *Winkelzüge*: "Aber werde ich denn noch lieben?" (9). This question refers to a failed love relationship and generates processes of painful re-vision and self-assertion of the writing subject.[13]

While the term "Heldin" is usually associated with fiction, the following passage draws attention to the autobiographical dimension of the text: "Die Heldin, von ihrer Geschichte / (nicht vom Autor, denn sie ist nicht erfunden) / so ungewiß geführt, / daß sie sich weder in der Gegenwart / noch in der Zukunft ausweisen konnte..." (*Winkelzüge* 13). By privileging the story over the author—"Die Heldin / Von ihrer Geschichte so ungewiß geführt"—Erb foregrounds the role of language, which constitutes rather than merely represents this life-story. The multiple meanings of the term "Geschichte" add to the oscillation between the fictional and the autobiographical. "Geschichte" refers to the story/text in progress, as well as to her life story ("sie ist nicht erfunden"), and last but not least to collective history.

Similarly, the expression "mir stehen schwarze S/Zeiten bevor," which reappears numerous times throughout the text (21, 68, 95, for example), refers to the "dark," i.e., uncertain and yet unwritten future of both the text and the writing subject. While traditional autobiography is directed towards a telos and therefore tends to eclipse the present and future of its author, *Winkelzüge* captures the open-ended process of reworking the past and its continuous impact on the writing subject.

Winkelzüge includes surprisingly few direct references to the social situation in the eighties and the political upheavals preceding the events of the fall of 1989 (which coincided with the final revisions of *Winkelzüge*). Erb thus consistently frustrates expectations to which readers in East and West have become accustomed when reading East German literature. And here she offers perhaps the greatest challenge to scholars of GDR literature who are used to reading texts in relationship to or as a reflection of the political situation. I agree with Simpson that Erb's writing has social implications despite the lack of explicit references (174–75). For instance, Erb does not merely juxtapose the generational conflict—as does Kachold in the excerpt quoted above. Erb critically examines the institution of the school as the central (de)forming force of her generation. The teaching methods in school privileged the objective, a "dead" past and a predetermined future ("Alleinherrschaft des Ziels") (342–55, 383–401) instead of the subjective and the individual past to which we can relate (360). This critique of the stifling effects of school refers primarily but not exclusively to the GDR's educational system.[14]

Winkelzüge reconstructs the long process of "unlearning" the life-shaping school lessons. The school had prepared the author for a didactic writing style that disseminates "die Lehre" (presumably of socialism); instead, she started searching for a language different from the prefabricated phrases of the newspaper or the predetermined messages of fiction (362–63). Erb's translation of the Russian author Marina Zwetajewa became the starting point (her "Gesellenstück") for this transformation; the process of translation forced her to work through the "rubble" ("Schutt") of her own language (388). This linguistic transformation is closely linked to a different view of her self and other people. The process of liberation led eventually to her attraction to the younger generation in general and the experimental artists of the Prenzlauer Berg in particular. "Andere hatten schon als Kinder verstanden, / was da auf sie zukam, schon als Kinder sich gewehrt, / Gegenwelten entworfen, in Gegentexte übersetzt! // Und, oft gerade bei Frauen, / welche Selbständigkeit der Ansichten, / Kühnheit des Überblicks, des "Zusammenfassens" (429). The depiction of independent, daring women applies, among others, to Gabriele Kachold.

Erb is more overtly concerned with linguistic dimensions and the process of (de)constructing meanings than Kachold. But they both consider their particular writing "styles" to be the reaction to (and the partial solution of) existential crises. Kachold describes a crisis that was triggered by political events: she was imprisoned following her protests of Biermann's expatriation in 1976. One of the personal crises Erb mentions was intensified by her political disillusionment following the "Biermann-affair."[15] In a chapter titled "das nichterschriebene Grauen," the writing subject describes how she failed to write *about* the stages of horror she experienced following the end of a relationship and how she later overcame this state of paralysis by discovering language's potential to generate new and unexpected perspectives and meanings (262-63)—a "discovery" that would shape Erb's new writing style.

In a similar manner, Kachold posits the fundamental identity crisis that she experienced while in prison as the origin of her urge to express herself in writing. Kachold's book *zügel los* includes a variety of different writing styles. The texts in the first part of her book deal mostly with her prison experiences. These texts are unconventional in style but more coherent than the excerpts from a journal in the second part of *zügel los*; the increasingly unconventional use of orthography, syntax, and semantics make some of the journal entries less accessible. Kachold adopts the term "automatisches Schreiben" from surrealism and attempts to access the subconscious and the body—as the material manifestation of multiple injuries and unfulfilled yearnings—through writing (*Sprachblätter* 153-58). While Erb extends existing linguistic rules in a sometimes playful manner, Kachold often ignores or violates these rules; she writes, for instance, exclusively in lower-case letters.

Kachold portrays the initial interrogations in the aftermath of the "Biermann-affair" as a battle over language, as the futile attempt to hold on to her truth, that is, to her formulations and to her identity: "wenn ich nicht um sie [die Wahrheit] kämpfte, verlor ich sie; mit ihr verlor ich mich" (*zügel los* 57). In this passage, Kachold links her identity to the moral responsibility to tell the "truth" and to resist the state authorities who attempt to impose their "truth" on her. Her unwillingness to give in and the impossibility of entering into a meaningful dialogue resulted in a confusion over who and where she was: "aber wer war ich und wo war ich...im niemandsland" (60).[16]

This confusion over identity stands in stark contrast to Sascha Anderson's evasive play with multiple identities when he was questioned about his *Stasi* activities ("Das ist gar nicht so einfach") or to Schedlinski's extensive commentary about the *Stasi*, which refrains from addressing issues of personal responsibility ("Die Unzuständigkeit der Macht"). Comparing Kachold's ethical considerations with the apologetic or abstract nature of Anderson's and Schedlinski's comments sheds light on potential dangers of the postmodern "dissolution of the subject." Reactions such as

Anderson's and, to a lesser degree, Schedlinski's illustrate the danger of disconnecting identity from individual responsibility (Eigler).[17]

Gerhard Wolf has called Kachold one of the most courageous young writers since she did not give in to those in charge of the definition of "truth" ("Gabriele Kachold" 157). When Kachold refused to sign a false protocol that would have been an admission of guilt, she received a one-year prison term. In *zügel los*, she describes how the experiences of helplessness and isolation in prison threatened her identity as a woman, an identity which she had taken for granted until then. A series of painfully repetitive phrases capture her estrangement from her self and from her body, deprived as it was from any meaningful sexuality: "du bist schon lang keine Frau, ein biologischer notzustand." This powerful text closes with the appeal, "treibt die frau nicht hinter eine wand" (19).

In another text dealing with her life in prison, the narrator initially adopts the de-humanized language of the prison when she refers to herself with the cell number, "die zelle nummer 5 erhielt eine neue insassin" (*zügel los* 65). This text describes how the new inmate breaks through Kachold's complete isolation and introduces her to a community of women prisoners whose interaction with one another creates some kind of counter order to the official order: "es war erstaunlich, mit welcher leichtigkeit sie die mauern durchbrachen, diese wesenslos machten, wenn sie zueinander sprachen" (67). "Breaking through walls" refers to the prison walls separating the inmates, but the real boundaries are those of the ego. The words Kachold chooses to describe the interaction of the imprisoned women evoke, often simultaneously, dimensions of verbal, emotional, and erotic involvement.

One could argue that this is an idealized or utopian image of an all-women's community—reminiscent of the women's enclave in Christa Wolf's *Kassandra*. Wolf, however, portrays a retreat from the world of war into nature, implying that there is a place "outside" of the social power structures (Wilke). By contrast, Kachold's community exists within a prison, i.e., within the center of the GDR's disciplinary system which, according to Foucault's more general discussion of power, mirrors the power structure of modern societies. Kachold does not claim that a retreat from society is possible. She portrays this "other order" of women inmates as her way to survive within oppressive power structures without compromising her own political and ethical convictions.[18]

In retrospect, Kachold realizes that she had initially accepted the totalizing claims of the official order and ignored the existence of "another order" of life. By trying to convince her interrogators of her position, she had already entered an order whose rules were entirely out of her control. By juxtaposing this official order represented by men with a community of women, this text also draws attention to the relationship of the politics of gender and the politics of identity and difference

(Cornell and Thurschwell). The official disregard for difference that Kachold experienced during the interrogations is mirrored in texts dealing with heterosexual relationships. These comparable (but not identical) experiences in the political and personal realms emphasize the extent to which gender-related power structures were not limited to the official state authorities but even pervaded her personal life in the "counter-culture."[19]

Kachold's accounts of her personal life illustrate her own conflicting positions: the internalization of societal images of a desirable woman, on the one hand, and the attempts to liberate herself from relationships to men that do not respect her emotional and sexual needs, on the other. The uncontrolled and sometimes inaccessible flow of language in the second part of her book indicates the painful and paralyzing effects of this dilemma. By contrast, Erb faced no such gender-related conflicts within the "counter-culture" but describes her interaction with the young artists as liberating. These diverging experiences may be due in part to Erb's age. The special position she occupied within the Prenzlauer Berg circle, which resulted from her being older than most, made it perhaps easier for her to negotiate her identities as a woman and as an artist.[20]

Curiously, some of Kachold's accounts of her prison experiences seem less oppressive than the accounts that deal with experiences in the outside world. Unlike the conflicting and paralyzing positions she occupies in the "real" world, in prison she holds on to her "deviant" position and eventually finds support from fellow women inmates. Yet, Kachold neither implies that there was an absence of aggression in the community of incarcerated women nor that this community could make up entirely for the initial disorientation and ensuing identity crisis she experienced in prison.

As one example of the destructive and self-destructive tendencies she developed while being in prison, Kachold describes the urge to destroy every glass door she passed once she was released. Glass panes reappear in a different context in this book and assume symbolic significance: they represent Kachold's artistic activities as attempts to reconstruct a shattered sense of identity. Included in *zügel los* is a series of photos showing the author naked behind a pane of glass on which she paints with her fingers. This scene—involving her body as subject and object of painting—recalls and at the same time cancels the traditional pose of a naked woman serving as model for the male artist.[21] Kachold does not simply reverse this relationship (as is done, for instance, in the recent French film *La Belle Noisette* when the female model assumes control over the male painter); she rather involves her own body in the creative process. Her sometimes dancing movements and the act of painting itself appear liberating and empowering. This impression is contrasted with the painting she creates, which obscures and crosses out the body behind the glass. She thus captures what the art critic Darcy Grimaldo Grigsby has called the "dilemma of visibility": woman artists who represent the female body have the chance to take "responsibility for what it is to make bodies visible," but they also risk perpetuating the "history of women's objectification and oppression" (100). Kachold stages this dilemma through the act of making her body *in*visible, a message that corresponds to the content of many of her texts. These texts describe memories of betrayal, competition, and distrust in a past relationship and yearn for a different kind of sensuality and sexuality.

The discrepancy between the often painful content of her writing on the one hand and the liberating act of writing and painting on the other is confirmed by the closure of *zügel los* (168-69), which sounds surprisingly content and forward-looking: "Ich habe etwas geborgen. / kein geld keinen hasen keine streunende katze / aber mich." The last lines speaks of a new beginning: "das leben wird nie wieder so sein wie es war / von dieser minute an."

In a similar manner, Erb closes *Winkelzüge* by talking about a new direction in her life/writing that liberates her from a law that calls for "Tilgen, Töten und Leugnen" (445). For Erb, this liberation is closely connected to embracing multiple subject positions: "Ich denke, ich werde nur noch um meine Heldin / ein wenig herumgehen. // Sie ist an vielen Orten in dieser Erörterung angekommen, / aber ich denke, daß sie wohl nirgendwo die Antwort erhielt / die sie ursprünglich meinte" (*Winkelzüge* 437). Both Erb and Kachold reconstitute in their texts a sense of identity—not as a fixed entity but as ongoing process—by working through painful experiences in the past and they do so with often puzzling and striking linguistic means. Neither Kachold nor Erb hold on to a fixed concept of the subject; at the same time, however, they do not detach the question of identity(ies) from social contexts.

The accounts of Kachold's experiences in prison exemplify what may well have been the greatest harm the GDR did to its citizens: In the name of a future society that would supposedly be more humane, the socialist regime legitimized the systematic control of individuals in the present and left little room for dissent or for individual responsibility. It is in this context that I see the critical dimension of Kachold's writings: in *zügel los*, Kachold links her sense of identity to the responsibility to tell her "truth." She contrasts this identity with the *Stasi*'s efforts to control and manipulate its "subjects." By positing identity as a necessary construct for assuming responsibility, Kachold exposes and subverts the state's ideology.

In *Winkelzüge*, the writing subject is concerned with the inability to relate to her self and her past after experiencing the failure of an important relationship. Against the backdrop of a society aimed at "educating" and thus controlling its people with prefabricated phrases, *Winkelzüge* questions concepts of language and the subject that are based on the exclusion and negation of that which is unconscious, different, or contradictory. Without being overtly political—as are some passages in *zügel los*—the writing subject in *Winkelzüge* attempts to re-cover a sense of her self and of language that is less confined by multiple rules and control mechanisms. Although both *Winkelzüge* and *zügel los* refer to the situation in the GDR, the pertinence of the issues they address, such as responsibility, power, gender, and identity, extends to all modern societies regardless of ideology or political system.

Written before the *Wende*, *Winkelzüge* and *zügel los* technically belong to GDR literature. But the experimental character of *Winkelzüge* and the uncompromising language of *zügel los* challenge previously held views that GDR literature is primarily content-oriented. Thus, writers like Erb and Kachold may help to call into question the presumed incompatibility of *engagierte Literatur*—frequently associated with the East—and form-oriented (post)modern literature—frequently associated with the West.

Notes

[1] "Gesinnungsästhetik" is frequently used as a pejorative term for all politically or socially committed art ("engagierte Literatur"). I refer here only to the reviews by West German critics of Christa Wolf's controversial book *Was bleibt* and the ensuing controversy about GDR literature in general (cf. Anz).

[2] There are however several women *painters* and *artists* who contributed regularly to the journals published in the Prenzlauer Berg; among the most prominent are Angela Hampel, Cornelia Schleime, Helge Leiberg, and Christine Schlegel (cf. *Vogel oder Käfig* 429-43).

[3] Throughout this article, I refer to "Gabriele Kachold" since she published *zügel los* under this name (i.e., her name by marriage). In the meantime, she has readopted her maiden name "Stötzer."

[4] Not all of her older colleagues approved of this transition. Volker Braun, for instance, in a critical essay about the Prenzlauer Berg artists, called her "Flip-Out Elke" (Emmerich 436).

[5] Klaus Michael has documented the long history of the anthology's obstructed publication in the GDR (*MachtSpiele* 202-16).

[6] Therese Hörnigk and Anna Kuhn who both know Wolf personally have indicated to me in conversations that the young writer in *Was bleibt* was modeled after Gabriele Kachold.

[7] I have dealt more extensively with the journal *Ariadnefabrik* and the reception of postmodern and poststructuralist concepts within the social context of the GDR in my article "The Responsibility of the Intellectual: The Case of the East Berlin 'Counter-Culture.'"

[8] "Autodafé" is in a peculiar way reminiscent of a passage in Monika Maron's novel *Die Überläuferin*. In a dream-like scene (153-59), a representative of the "Association of Writing Men," who values language more than life,

announces capital punishment for the woman writer Martha, one of the novel's main protagonists. He maintains that language is no playground for "Feministengeplapper" and that her frequent use of words like hope, longing, pain, etc. threatens the 'tower of genuine poetry' ("Turm der Dichtung"). This dream included in Maron's novel is based on the long history of the exclusion or marginalization of women's writings. By contrast, Toth's text reverses this constellation and falsely attributes claims of universality to the "Maxie-Wander-Workshop." This overreaction may be due to the author's own marginal position in the GDR. It is nevertheless significant that Toth turns against Maxie Wander rather than against a writer who clearly supported the repressive political system.

[9] Schedlinski and Anderson are the main entrepreneurs of this newly founded publishing house Galrev (reversal of "Verlag"). *Winkelzüge* was published just before Anderson's and Schedlinski's involvement with the *Stasi* became known. Nevertheless, Erb's choice of the Galrev press is an indication that her relationship to the Prenzlauer Berg circle was closer and less ambivalent than Kachold's. Erb told me recently that she will no longer publish with Galrev since Anderson continues to avoid addressing his past.

[10] For a brief discussion of the implications of metaphor versus metonymy for feminist literature, see Renate Lachmann.

[11] Helen Fehervary observes a similar phenomenon in Christa Wolf's prose. She maintains that "a narrative voice that is at once a reader and writer" results in "the relinquishment of the authorial ego in favor of reciprocal involvement" (80).

[12] Patricia Anne Simpson has explored the evolution of this circular writing style in Erb's earlier publications (272).

[13] The term "heroine" does not refer to a person but to the central question ("Werde ich denn noch lieben?") that has shaped *Winkelzüge*.

[14] This aspect has an interesting autobiographical twist: Erb moved with her parents to East Germany when she was eleven, i.e., after having attended school for five years in the West; in *Winkelzüge* she does not explicitly distinguish between her experiences in East and West.

[15] Her separation from her husband, Adolf Endler, coincided with her "separation" from the state due to the political events in the late seventies (G. Wolf, "Laudatio" 111).

[16] The author Jürgen Fuchs describes a similar confusion over identity in *Vernehmungsprotokolle*. A friend of Wolf Biermann, Fuchs was imprisoned immediately after Biermann was expatriated. By threatening repercussions for his family and friends, the *Stasi* manipulated Fuchs into signing a statement in which he 'voluntarily' gave up his citizenship and agreed to leave East Germany. "Ich unterschreibe / ja, ich habe unterschrieben / wie groß muß eine Demütigung sein, von der man sich nicht mehr erholt? / Wann ist man klug? / Wann schlau? / Wann vernünftig? / Und wann ein Verräter?" (222).

[17] I do not primarily refer here to their *Stasi*-activities in the GDR, which may well have occurred under the immense psychological pressure Schedlinski has described in his initial commentary, "Dem Druck, immer mehr sagen zu sollen, hielt ich nicht stand." Rather, I mean the absence of any real dialogue

after their activities for the *Stasi* had been revealed and confirmed (cf. contributions to *Machtspiele,* especially Drawert's essay).

[18] After she was released from prison, Kachold established a women's group in Erfurt that is involved in collective art projects but that also serves as a support group ("Frauenszene" 135-36).

[19] Indeed, there is evidence that the large majority of secret informers—"IMs" or "inoffizielle Mitarbeiter"—who regularly reported to the *Stasi* on Kachold, Erb, and many others were men; according to Kachold, this is just another expression of the partriachal power structures that pervaded the GDR ("Frauenszene" 130).

[20] I am not implying that in Erb's case gender-related conflicts do not exist, but that they express themselves differently. Cornelia Sachse has observed that the question in *Winkelzüge,* "Aber werde ich denn noch lieben?," may reflect the loneliness many women artists face ("Die Orange" 403).

[21] The book cover consists of a different but related series of photos. They show transformations of Stötzer Kachold's face: the process of putting mascara on her eyelashes turns into images in which dark color (which looks like blood) runs down from her eyes. The image of culturally determined female beautification is contrasted with an injured or distorted mask-like face.

Works Cited

Abriß der Ariadnefabrik. Ed. Andreas Koziol and Rainer Schedlinski. Berlin: Galrev, 1990.

Die andere Sprache: Neue DDR-Literatur der 80er Jahre. Special issue of *TEXT + KRITIK.* Ed. Heinz Ludwig Arnold. Munich: text + kritik, 1990.

Anderson, Sascha. Interview with Iris Radisch. "Das ist nicht so einfach." *Die Zeit* 1 November 1991.

Anz, Thomas, ed. "Es geht nicht um Christa Wolf." *Der Literaturstreit im vereinten Deutschland.* Munich: Spangenberg, 1991.

Biermann, Wolf. "Über Georg Büchner: Der Lichtblick im gräßlichen Fatalismus der Geschichte." *Die Zeit* 25 October 1991.

Böthig, Peter. "Politik und Ironie: 12 Punkte zur literarischen Infrastruktur des Prenzlauer Berges." Unpublished manuscript of a paper presented February 1992.

Cornell, Drucilla and Adam Thurschwell. "Feminism, Negativity, Intersubjectivity." *Feminism as Critique: Essays on the Politics of Gender in Late-Capitalist Societies.* Ed. Seyla Benhabib and Drucilla Cornell. Cambridge: Polity, 1987. 144-89.

Cultural Transformations in the New Germany: American and German Perspectives. Ed. Friederike Eigler and Peter Pfeiffer. Columbia, SC: Camden, 1993.

de Lauretis, Teresa. *Technologies of Gender.* Bloomington: Indiana UP, 1987.

Drawert, Kurt. "Sie schweigen. Oder sie lügen. Von der Beschaffenheit einer gescheiterten Elite." *MachtSpiele.* 74-83.

Eigler, Friederike. "The Responsibility of the Intellectual: The Case of the East Berlin 'Counter-Culture.'" *Cultural Transformations*. 157-71.

Emmerich, Wolfgang. "Do We Need to Rewrite German Literary History Since 1945?" *Cultural Transformations*. 117-31.

——. *Kleine Literaturgeschichte der DDR: 1945-1988*. Frankfurt a.M.: Luchterhand, 1989.

Erb, Elke. "Brötchenholen." *Abriß der Ariadnefabrik*.

——. *Winkelzüge oder nicht vermutete aufschlußreiche Verhältnisse*. Berlin: Galrev, 1991.

Erb, Elke, and Sascha Anderson, eds. *Berührung ist nur eine Randerscheinung*. Cologne: Kiepenheuer & Witsch, 1985.

Fehervary, Helen. "Christa Wolf's Prose: A Landscape of Masks." *New German Critique* 27 (1982): 57-87.

Fuchs, Jürgen. *Gedächtnisprotokolle. Vernehmungsprotokolle*. Reinbek: Rowohlt, 1977.

Goodman, Katherine. *Dis/Closures: Women's Autobiography in Germany Between 1790 and 1914*. Frankfurt a.M.: Lang, 1986.

Grigsby, Darcy Grimaldo. "Dilemmas of Visibility: Contemporary Women Artists' Representations of Female Bodies." *The Female Body: Figures, Styles, Speculations*. Ed. Laurence Goldstein. Ann Arbor: U of Michigan P, 1991. 83-102.

Herminghouse, Patricia. "New Contexts for GDR Literature." *Cultural Transformations*. 93-101.

Jankowsky, Karen. "Canons Crumble Just Like Walls: Discovering the Works of GDR Women Writers." *Cultural Transformations*. 102-16.

Kachold, Gabriele. *zügel los: Prosa*. Berlin: Aufbau, 1989. (Page numbers refer to the Luchterhand edition: Frankfurt a.M.: Luchterhand, 1990.)

(Kachold) Stötzer, Gabriele. "Frauenszene und Frauen in der Szene." *MachtSpiele*. 129-37.

Kachold, Gabriele (Stötzer). Interview with Christel Lautert. "Denn wir haben uns doch nur bekämpft und verletzt." *Freitag* 3 January 1992.

Kaufmann, Eva. "DDR-Schiftstellerinnen, die Widersprüche und die Utopie." *Women in German Yearbook 7*. Ed. Jeanette Clausen and Sara Friedrichsmeyer. Lincoln: U of Nebraska P, 1991. 109-20.

Kyselka, Verena and Gabriele Stötzer (Kachold). *Multimedialistinnen: Internationale Performerinnenwoche 14.11.-22.11.92*. Erfurt: Kunsthausverlag, 1993.

Lachmann, Renate. "Thesen zu einer weiblichen Ästhetik." *Weiblichkeit oder Feminismus? Beiträge zur interdisziplinären Frauentag Konstanz 1983*. Ed. Claudia Opitz. Weingarten: Drumlin, 1984. 181-94.

MachtSpiele: Literatur und Staatssicherheit im Fokus Prenzlauer Berg. Ed. Peter Böthig and Klaus Michael. Leipzig: Reclam, 1993.

Maron, Monika. *Die Überläuferin*. Frankfurt a.M.: Fischer, 1986.

Meyer-Gosau, Frauke. "Zu Markte getragen: Texte vom Prenzlauer Berg in der BRD." *Die andere Sprache*. 244–49.
Michael, Klaus. "Eine verschollene Anthologie: Zentralkomitee, Staatssicherheit und die Geschichte eines Buches." *MachtSpiele*. 202–16.
Sachse, Cornelia. "Vage Zagenvragen" and "Die Orange leben." *Vogel oder Käfig sein*. 401–04.
Schedlinski, Rainer. "Dem Druck, immer mehr sagen zu sollen, hielt ich nicht stand." *Frankfurter Allgemeiner Zeitung* 14 January 1992.
———. "Die Unzuständigkeit der Macht." *Neue deutsche Literatur* 6 (1992): 75–105.
Schulz, Genia. "Anmerkungen zum Verschwinden des Autors und zum Erscheinen der Autorin." *'Wen kümmert's, wer spricht.' Zur Literatur und Kulturgeschichte von Frauen aus Ost und West*. Ed. Inge Stephan, Sigrid Weigel, and Kerstin Wilhelms. Cologne: Böhlau, 1991. 57–62.
Simpson, Patricia Anne. "Die Sprache der Geduld: Produzierendes Denken bei Elke Erb." *Zwischen gestern und heute: Schriftstellerinnen der DDR aus amerikanischer Sicht*. Ed. Ute Brandes. Berlin: Lang, 1992. 263–76.
Smith, Sidonie. *A Poetics of Women's Autobiography: Marginality and the Fiction of Self-Representation*. Bloomington: Indiana UP, 1987.
Toth, Vvinzton (pseudonym). "Autodafé der Sanctae Literae." *Abriß der Ariadnefabrik*. 94–106.
Vogel oder Käfig sein: Kunst und Literatur aus unabhängigen Zeitschriften in der DDR 1979–1989. Ed. Klaus Michael and Thomas Wohlfahrt. Berlin: Galrev, 1992.
Walker, Cheryl. "Feminist Literary Criticism and the Author." *Critical Inquiry* 16 (1990): 551–71.
Wander, Maxie. *Guten Morgen, du Schöne: Frauen in der DDR. Protokolle*. Berlin: Aufbau, 1977.
Wilke, Sabine. "'Kreuz- und Wendepunkte unserer Zivilisation nach-denken': Christa Wolfs Stellung im Umfeld der zeitgenössischen Mythos-Diskussion." *German Quarterly* 61.2 (1988): 213–28.
Wolf, Christa. *Kassandra: Erzählung*. Darmstadt: Luchterhand, 1983.
———. *Was bleibt*. Berlin: Aufbau, 1990.
Wolf, Gerhard. "Elke Erbs Vexierblick." *Sprachblätter*. 104–09.
———. "gegen sprache mit sprache—mit-sprache gegen-sprache: Thesen mit Zitaten und Notizen zu einem literarischen Prozeß." *Die andere Sprache*. 15–25.
———. "Die selbsterlittene Geschichte mit dem Lob: Laudatio für Elke Erb und Adolf Endler." *Sprachblätter*. 110–125.
———. *Sprachblätter Wortwechsel: Im Dialog mit Dichtern*. Leipzig: Reclam, 1992.
———. "Vor-Sätze außer der Reihe—zu Gabriele Kachold: zügel los." *Sprachblätter*. 153–58.

Christa Wolf's *Kassandra*: Refashioning National Imagination Beyond the Nation

Karin Eysel

This essay traces Wolf's uncoupling of the classical Cassandra figure from national allegiances. I argue that from a modern, psychological, and female perspective Wolf not only lays bare the politics of nationalism, she also imagines a different community, transnational in character. Returning to the cradle of Western civilization, Wolf rewrites the legend of the siege and destruction of Troy in order to refashion the national imagination of the past and to imagine a new community beyond the nation. (KE)

The former East Germany presented a unique paradigm, situated as it was between East and West and constructed out of Cold War politics. Until the 1970s, however, this socio-economic / political-ideological genesis of the GDR out of post-war occupation was largely repressed in its national culture.[1] In the GDR's formative years, the emergence of a national popular movement composed largely of intellectuals was the inspiration to create, to use Benedict Anderson's famous phrase, an "imagined community." Based on socialist principles, the imagining of this community coincided with the formation of a separate German state. The GDR intellectuals of Wolf's generation were driven by what I want to discuss here as a sense of nationalism, which Harro Segeberg, in his article "Nationalismus als Literatur," understands to mean "idealtypisch eine kollektive soziale Bewegung, die das Bewußtsein der eigenen Nationalität mit der Forderung nach politischer Partizipation verbindet" (298). Seizing the opportunity in the aesthetic realm to forge a specific East German identity, many intellectuals fashioned a myth of origin for a separate German nation. In their works they constructed a teleological historical narrative that would suture the gap between the present and the still-to-be realized fatherland and reconnect this ideal to the preexisting anti-imperialist and anti-fascist tradition.[2] Transcending historically specific and different war experiences in order to establish an undisturbed organic continuity in its national heritage, GDR literature created "a reconciliatory center of national unity" (75) that David Lloyd and others have identified as an essential feature of national discourse.[3] Circumventing the fascist history that it shared with West Germany, this new nation reserved the theme of liberation and resistance for itself in order to justify its radical rupture with the ever-present imperialist forces in the West (cf. Silberman). The intellectuals' initially emancipating impetus to create an "imagined community" built on socialist principles was thus put aside in the face of the more immediate need to establish a national identity and justify a separate German state.

Forging a political union out of a heterogeneous population, the national literature of the GDR fostered, as David Lloyd has discussed in the context of Irish nationalism, a "second-level identification with the paternal spirit of the nation" (76), cast predominantly in the form of a family romance.[4] Nationalism, finding its expression in the narratives of an ideal community and presuming to speak for a collective identity, degenerated into, as Lloyd observes, a "normalizing function that the new literature performed" (74), absolving GDR citizens from reflecting upon the history they shared with West Germany as well as the origins of their new nation. The proclaimed national unity overshadowed and indeed covered up the dependence between the two sides in the Cold War conflict, each needing the other to disguise its own self-interests.

The question of nationalism as a movement forging a common identity and allegiance in the face of an imperial rule in order to achieve self-government has come under close scrutiny in post-colonial discourse. Although, as Edward Said has pointed out, "a great deal...of the resistance to imperialism was conducted in the name of nationalism" (8), this political ideology remains deeply implicated in imperialist thinking; for as Said further observes, "the cultural horizons of nationalism are fatally limited by the common history of colonizer and colonized assumed by the nationalist movement itself" (9). The works of Said, Partha Chatterjee, and Lloyd have uncovered the complicity between nationalist and imperialist discourses.[5] In their struggle for independence, the nationalists opposed colonialism in the name of Reason by asserting their ability to modernize their "backward" country into becoming a sovereign nation-state and joining the family of nations. As if one could measure all peoples by one system of thought, Chatterjee objects, the nationalists set out to conform to the post-Enlightenment thematic of universal history, the ideal of linear progress. "Why is it," he asks, "that non-European colonial countries have no historical alternative but to try to approximate the given attributes of modernity when that very process of approximation means their continued subjection under a world order which only sets their task for them and over which they have no control?" (10). The national narratives attempted to assimilate and homogenize the various communities within the nation to the project of modernity.[6] However, as Lloyd has made clear, if the national culture was to instill a "feeling of nationality in the citizens" through a "model of cultural identification," it at the same time accepted a "universal narrative of development," a gradual process of assimilation and homogenization of its citizens to a "normative humanity which was the nation's collective goal" (76). Paradoxically, Lloyd continues, the writers "reproduced in their very opposition to the Empire a narrative of universal development that is fundamental to the legitimation of imperialism" (76).

While post-colonial theorists speak from a perspective of decolonization and resistance to Western imperialism, their insights are nevertheless pertinent here.[7] Apart from articulating the interdependence of nationalism and imperialism, more recently these theorists have begun to denaturalize the nation-state—conceived in the West along the lines of a common history, language, and culture—as the "dominant organizational form" (Gupta 73), that is, as no longer forming the basis for imagining communities.[8]

In the years during which the GDR sought to establish its identity, the national narrative unfolded by a logic of cultural essentialism.[9] But given the absence of genuine socialism and democracy, the nation defined in modernist terms came increasingly under attack. In her Cassandra project Christa Wolf lays bare the politics of nationalism.[10] From a distinctly modern, psychological, social, and female perspective, Wolf traces the prophetess's disassociation from her society as she remembers and reflects upon the establishment of a totalitarian regime and the rise of a nationalist consciousness in a wartime Troy that represented itself as a victim of outside aggression.[11] Returning to the cradle of Western civilization for source materials, Wolf focuses on two classical plays in which Cassandra speaks to the two founding principles for modern nations: patriarchy and imperialism. Situating her imaginative reconstruction of Troy at the seam between a matriarchal and a patriarchal society, Wolf combines both concerns, casting them in a family romance in which she depicts Cassandra's gradual severing of her paternal/national ties. In *Kassandra* Wolf imagines a different community, transnational in character, that, because it refuses to be incorporated and contained within the national narrative, no longer constructs identity according to nationality. Rather than obliterate the history of violence inscribed in the documents of Western civilization, she rewrites the legend of the siege and destruction of Troy from a female perspective in order to refashion the national imagination of the past and to imagine a new community beyond the nation.

In the *Oresteia,* Aeschylus utilizes Cassandra's voice to give validity to the triumph of patriarchy over matriarchy.[12] Aeschylus inserts

Cassandra's voice just before Agamemnon walks into Clytemnestra's death trap. Sympathizing with Agamemnon's fate Cassandra cries out, "What outrage—the woman kills the man!" (Aeschylus l. 1241).[13] With the power struggle between male and female at the core of the *Oresteia,* Aeschylus uses Cassandra to support the need for a wife's subordination. For Aeschylus, Clytemnestra is clearly out of bounds when she chooses her own husband, rules by her own decree, and avenges her daughter's death. She thus represents a source of anarchy in the male-controlled polis. Froma Zeitlin has argued:

> ...the *Oresteia*'s program is to trace the evolution of civilization by placing the polis at the center of its vision.... If Aeschylus is concerned with world-building, the cornerstone of his architecture is the control of women, the social and cultural prerequisite for the construction of civilization (150).

If the exclusion of women from the public sphere is one of the founding principles of a city/nation, Wolf uncovers an increasing violence against women as its consequence. In her imaginative revision of Trojan society, Wolf depicts the objectification of women as tied to the rise of a war mentality. Not only are the women as pawns in the war increasingly subjected to male aggression, they are also degraded to commodities for the men's perverted desires. First Hecuba is excluded from the council, then Briseis is declared a traitor. The council entices Polyxena to spy on the Greeks' war plans by offering herself to Achilles, and later she is used as a bait to kill him. And Cassandra is married off in order to gain military-political advantage over the Greeks. Attempting to resist male domination, Penthesilea takes up her arms against all men, a separatist vision that allows for no dialogue. The battle between the sexes takes on a parallel configuration in the confrontation between nations, a topic Wolf uncovers in her revision of Euripides's play.

Euripides's *The Trojan Women* portrays two nations at war. Classical scholars generally consider it an anti-war play that condemns Greek imperialism. Euripides depicts the brutality of the Greeks from the point of view of the suffering survivors of the war. He presents Cassandra among the Trojan women before they are taken away by their captors after the fall of Troy. Well aware that she is to be Agamemnon's concubine, Cassandra carries a flaming torch and invites the women to dance in ecstasy, in mad celebration of her unwanted marriage. Cassandra sees herself as a martyr, for through her marriage she herself can avenge Greek aggression. Euripides's Cassandra commemorates and praises her fellow Trojans as heroes who have died at the hands of the Greeks: "The Trojans have that glory which is loveliest: they died for their own country" (ll. 385–86). Ideally, Euripides's Greek spectators are meant to feel shame, pity, and remorse for the destruction they have inflicted on Troy.

While in Euripides's play Cassandra holds on to her national pride, in Wolf's narrative Cassandra no longer defends her people; she pledges no such allegiance to her country. By taking revenge in order to defend her nation, Euripides's Cassandra remains trapped in a vicious cycle of endless aggression and counter-aggression. Rather than engage in a politics of blame, Wolf's Cassandra protests against a sense of nationhood that constructs a national pride based on enmity to the Greeks. How the Trojans imagine the "other" in Wolf's work becomes a crucial mechanism through which Trojans define their national identity. Once the Trojans have defined the Greeks as their enemy, this self/other relationship extends to exclusionary social practices at home. Mistrusting the Greeks, Trojans begin to mistrust each other. Yet Cassandra will discover that what the Trojans perceive as foreign and a threat to their culture is at least in part based on a projection of their own internal fears and dislikes onto the other/Greeks.[14]

Standing in front of the gates of Mycenae, Cassandra gives testimony about Trojan history in the years before and during the war. The Troy Cassandra recalls is a culture in transition from a matriarchal to a patriarchal society in which the patriarchal gods are displacing the female gods (Pickle 33). The struggle in the cultural realm to shape the collective imagination is simultaneously carried out in the political sphere. As Cassandra awaits her death, she reflects upon the emergence of a war-mentality in Troy. Long before the war started, the Trojans revealed themselves to be similar to the Greeks. Just as Agamemnon sacrificed Iphigenie to ensure a safe seaway to Troy, Priam, out of fear that Paris might dethrone him, has ordered his son to be killed in the countryside (57–59). Priam's insecurity over his political authority helps prepare Eumelos's appearance on the scene in Troy. Deemed "ein fähiger Mann am rechten Platz" (64), Eumelos, head of the palace guard, maneuvers himself into the highest position of power at the court. From there he reinforces and cements a new hierarchy of values, conjuring up an atmosphere in which war appears to become necessary and inevitable. Priam entrusts Eumelos with fending off and eradicating those voices he believes to be against his rule.

Eumelos fosters the imposition of a new code in Troy through his awareness that language creates reality; he consciously engages in a "Sprachkrieg" (Risse 24–33) in order to prepare the Trojans for the war, now named an attack.

"Die Leute des Eumelos waren an der Arbeit. Sie hatten Anhänger unter Palastschreibern und Tempeldienern gewonnen. Auch geistig müßten wir gerüstet sein, wenn der Grieche uns angreife. Die geistige Rüstung bestand in der Schmähung des Feindes (von 'Feind' war schon die Rede, eh noch ein einziger Grieche das Schiff bestiegen hatte)" (73).

The effect of Eumelos's "Sprachkrieg" is to polarize Trojan society into those who support and those who oppose the war. After Cassandra has proposed stopping hostilities, Priam cries: "Seine Tochter! Sie, von allen sie mußte es sein, die hier im Rat von Troia für die Feinde sprach. Anstatt eindeutig, öffentlich und laut...für Troia zu sprechen." "Ich sprach für Troia" (87), Cassandra replies. Ruling by decree, Priam demands absolute submission and self-sacrifice for the greater cause of the nation.

Anchises unmasks Eumelos's new logic: "Er setzt voraus, was er erst schaffen mußte: Krieg. Ist er soweit gekommen, nimmt er diesen Krieg als das Normale und setzt voraus, aus ihm führt nur ein Weg, der heißt: der Sieg. Dann allerdings diktiert der Feind, was dir zu tun bleibt" (120). Anchises observes that as soon as the Trojans internalize the need to win—that is, as soon as the Trojans take their antagonistic relationship to the other/Greeks as the natural state of affairs—Trojans become encircled in a totalized world. By accepting the premise that the Greeks are the aggressors, Trojans perceive the alien culture to be intruding into their own lives; Trojans begin to define and protect their identity in terms dictated by the enemy.

Eumelos runs a para-military group, a state within the state that exhibits allusions to both National Socialism and the *Stasi*. Eumelos successfully creates an outer (Greek) and inner (internal opposition) enemy. Pondering why the Trojans consent to Eumelos's divisive politics, Cassandra concludes that they are willing to be deceived—a willingness symbolized in the narrative through the voyages of the three ships.[15] With hindsight Cassandra warns: "Wann Krieg beginnt, das kann man wissen, aber wann beginnt der Vorkrieg. Falls es da Regeln gäbe, müßte man sie weitersagen. In Ton, in Stein eingraben, überliefern. Was da stünde...: Laßt Euch nicht von den Eignen täuschen" (76–77). Accepting Eumelos's new logic as the natural state of affairs, Trojans let themselves be deceived by their own government. This only becomes possible, however, when they cast themselves in the role of victims of either outside aggression or internal repression, as is the case with Cassandra. In doing so, she arrives at one of her central insights into her own ambivalence: "Nur, was ich damals nicht begriff und nicht begreifen wollte: daß manche nicht nur von außen, auch aus sich selbst heraus zum Opfer vorbereitet waren" (111).

Cassandra gradually recognizes that inhabiting the position of victim only serves the master-narrative of Trojan nationalistic politics. Once Cassandra discovers that Helen does not exist in Troy and that she only exists as a phantom to rally support for the war,[16] she at first wants to escape into madness. It is behind this phantom that Priam disguises and tries to cover up Troy's own territorial claims. Torn between her loyalty to her father/nation and her own inner aversion to the war, Cassandra must confront the self-deception for which Arisbe reproaches her:

"Schluß mit dem Selbstmitleid" (71). Because Cassandra conceived of herself as a victim rather than an engaged subject, she had in fact become complicit with the politics of the palace: "Der Eumelos in mir verbot es mir. Ihn, der mich im Palast erwartete, ihn schrie ich an: Es gibt keine Helena!, aber er wußte es ja" (79-80). Fearing the loss of popular support for the war, Priam elicited Cassandra's promise not to reveal the "Staatsgeheimnis"; nevertheless he imprisoned Cassandra in order to silence her.

Cassandra never goes public with her knowledge that Helen is not in Troy. There is a reason, I believe, why Cassandra chooses silence and a peaceful opposition to the ruthlessly nationalistic thinking at the palace. For just as Cassandra must overcome her early desire to conform to those in power in order to pursue the painful path of inner resistance, the people of Troy must find their own voice. If Cassandra were to assume the responsibility for a public conscience by revealing the "Staatsgeheimnis" and becoming a spokesperson for an oppositional politics, she would inadvertently abet Eumelos's war game. By pushing Cassandra into a defensive position as she tries to oppose his logic, Eumelos entraps her in his new logic. The dominant political order in Troy, embodied by Eumelos, has thus built into its system the capacity to "contain apparently subversive gestures, or even to produce them precisely in order to contain them" (Montrose 402). Within the framework of his new logic, Eumelos assigns to Cassandra her position of resistance to the war. By dictating to her the terms of her resistance, Eumelos in fact attempts to manage and absorb her refusal to partake in the war. Summarizing the limits of a subjective or collective agency against forms of domination, Montrose observes: "The binary logic of subversion-containment produces a closed conceptual structure of reciprocally defining and dependent terms, terms that are complementary and mutually complicit" (402). Cassandra is quite aware of how her public opposition would aid Eumelos's ends: "Dem Volk hätt ich es sagen müssen. Das hieß: Ich, Seherin, gehörte zum Palast. Und Eumelos war sich ganz klar darüber" (80). As Anchises has explained to Cassandra, only by stepping outside of Eumelos's new logic and searching for a third way, a third language, can Cassandra resist Eumelos's new logic. While Cassandra enacts her own painful struggle to find her own way of resisting the nationalist policies in Troy, she at the same time enlists the reader to participate symbolically in her psychological journey.

Keenly aware of how the palace could appropriate Cassandra's voice into the institutionalized relations of power, Wolf attempts to design a narrative structure in which a critical self-reflective subject remembers her path to a politics of subjective resistance. Telling her own story from the margin of her society becomes a balancing act between not succumbing to the palace's attempts to silence her and refusing to act as a public spokesperson for an oppositional politics. Cassandra thus does not straddle, as Leslie Adelson suggests, "the fine line between the palace circle and the cave community" (510),[17] but one between resistance to the structures of victimization and the constant threat of containment and appropriation of that resistance in her position as palace priestess. Nevertheless, the more Cassandra breaks away from the repressive politics of the palace, the more she begins to defy it and to speak in her own voice. In fact, she refuses to support the plan to use Polyxena as a decoy for the murder of Achilles and she actively intervenes on behalf of Greek prisoners:

> In zitternder Stille standen die Troer und die gefangenen Griechen sich gegenüber, zwischen ihnen der Abgrund eines Schrittes, über dem Abgrund der Troer blanke Messer. Da trat ich, ohne Priesterkleid, in diesen schmalen Zwischenraum, ging ihn, vom heißen Atem der Griechen, von den kalten Messern der Troer gestreift, Schritt für Schritt entlang, von der einen Wand zur andern. Alles still. Hinter mir sanken die Messer der Troer. Die Griechen weinten. Wie liebte ich meine Landsleut. Paris vertrat mir den Ausgang. Du also, Priesterin, gestattest meinen Leuten nicht, Gleiches mit Gleichem zu vergelten.—Ich sagte: Nein (129-30).

On her painful path toward autonomy Cassandra finally comes to resist the war, the patriarchal and insistently hierarchical order of the "Zitadelle," the new Trojan state, in short, everything "was ich 'Vater' nannte" (146). Freeing herself from the palace's structures of victimization,[18] Cassandra finds a new "home" in the counter-culture at Mount Ida. Before she can feel fully part of this new community, however, she must first dissolve her emotional ties to the palace.

Kathleen Komar has commented on "memory's dynamic process of reconstructing personal identity and deconstructing gender roles" in Christa Wolf's works. Because the female protagonists not only "remember, literally reassemble, their individual identities," but re-integrate themselves into new communities, memory becomes essentially "communal and not private" (42). Komar has observed that, similar to many other female protagonists in Wolf's writing, Cassandra

> must find the discrete self that is so often lost to categories and labels...[in] a hostile outer world.... Kassandra...must struggle to locate this individual self before she can move on to the next level of selfhood. Second, however, one must give this unencumbered, individual self that has escaped externally imposed role definitions a new potential for development by reintegrating into a meaningful community. Kassandra comes to realize this as she looks for a new "we" to complete her "I."... Kassandra comes to realize this necessity for community as she joins the society of women who dwell in the caves along the Scamander River (49-50).

At the beginning of her narrative Cassandra notes her self-alienation, which she connotes as "diese fremde Stimme" (46). Once she has immmersed herself in the community at Mount Ida, Cassandra asserts that she has found her own voice: "Da entstand ein Schweigen, in das meine Stimme paßte; nun hatte sie genau den Raum gefunden, der für sie vorgesehen war" (140). Finding her new identity thus coincides with her feeling part of the cave community: "Da, endlich, hatte ich mein 'Wir'" (141). This new community gives Cassandra the resolve to reject the world of the "Zitadelle," which becomes most explicit when Priamos asks Cassandra for support in the scheme to use Polyxena as bait: "Zehn-, hundertmal habe ich vor Priamos gestanden, hundertmal versucht, auf sein Gebot, ihm zuzustimmen, mit Ja zu antworten. Hundertmal habe ich wieder nein gesagt. Mein Leben, meine Stimme, mein Körper gaben keine andre Antwort her" (148).

In her remembrance Cassandra searches for a new language and a third way beyond the dualisms of Greeks/Trojans, matriarchy/patriarchy, east/west. While the Trojans want to portray themselves officially as victims of an outside/Greek aggression, the cave community along the Scamander River looks beyond these false alternatives. "Fantasy, sensitivity, and subjectivity," Edith Waldstein asserts, "characterize Cassandra's attempt at a new discourse" (195). In contrast to the palace, which stands, as Waldstein maintains, "for hierarchy, insensitivity and violence," the "Gegenwelt" at the caves represents Wolf's utopian model for society, an "alternative collective" (196). This new society "has yet to be created (both aesthetically and socially)—a utopia that Christa Wolf purposely only shades in, leaving the outline to be drawn by us and future readers" (197).[19] What is nonetheless striking is that Cassandra can imagine the contours of a new community created in the imagination and thus forms an identity from within the popular domain of a sub-culture that exists outside of the official nation-state in Troy. Life in this alternative culture is based on dialogue and the peaceful coexistence of different groups of people transcending social class, gender, and national boundaries—a community Wolf in her *Voraussetzungen* calls "sozial und ethnisch heterogen" (96). In the cave community female slaves from the Greek camp, scattered Amazons, and noble women such as Hecuba and Cassandra find refuge. Anchises, his son Aeneas, and men searching for nurturance while recovering from their war-wounds also form part of the subculture that gathers at the Scamander river. The alternative community had originally emerged in response to the marginalization of the old female goddesses before the war. Escaping oppression, the women had congregated to celebrate Cybele and offer her sacrifices. As a foil against which to measure the prevailing developments in Troy, the utopian community is marked by the inclusion rather than exclusion of all kinds of peoples and the "absence of hierarchy" (Kuhn 204). However radical the language of this utopian community might be, its existence is limited to a short time span during the war. This counter-culture not only remains impotent in preventing the destruction of Troy, it will also become entangled in yet another history of imperialism.[20]

Cassandra reflects on her choice of captivity and death over following Aeneas in his "verräterische Entschlüsse" (7) to create a new nation. In retrospect, Cassandra creates an imagined conversation with Aeneas: "Wir hatten nicht die Zeit über meine Weigerung, mit ihm zu gehn, die nicht die Vergangenheit betraf, sondern die Zukunft" (108). Because Cassandra rejects building a nation that relies on violence either against another nation or against its own people, she comes to the recognition that Aeneas will be no exception in history:

> Du hast mich verstanden, lange eh du's zugabst. Es war ja klar: Allen, die überlebten, würden die neuen Herren ihr Gesetz diktieren. Die Erde war nicht groß genug, ihnen zu entgehen (156).

Not only does Aeneas himself become an invader of a foreign land, he will also impose a new homogeneity onto that foreign culture. Aeneas's desire to found a new Troy based on non-patriarchal and egalitarian ideals will be imbricated in those destructive patterns from which he is trying to escape. And as Aeneas and his supporters were to some extent shaped by the very society he tried to flee, he will replace and reproduce old social structures in new national terms, inaugurating the assimilation of others to his universal vision of a better humanity and thus repeating the imperialist gesture. Aeneas cannot reassure Cassandra that he will succeed without forging a new nation-state based on a hegemonic political vision.[21]

Cassandra's refusal to join Aeneas in his flight to found a new nation has been interpreted as her inability to let go of her relationship to her father and the palace. "Kassandra perceives this third way in the cave-dwellers but does not succeed in appropriating it as her own.... Kassandra remains, even in death, daughter of the palace" (Adelson 511).[22] Because she does not follow Aeneas, Cassandra presumably rejects the ideals of the cave community and thus seems to reaffirm a nationalistic Trojan identity. Yet, to equate Cassandra's refusal to join Aeneas in his flight with a rejection of the ideals by which the cave-dwellers live in Troy is to be guilty of ideological slippage. That she refuses to leave Troy does not necessarily mean she espouses the politics of the palace. To flee, in fact, does not solve the problems of a politics of domination and reification that Cassandra has identified for both sides—for Greece and Troy—and in which Rome will follow suit. Speculations in Troy abound as to why Panthoos had once left Greece to come to Troy.[23] Cassandra comes to the conclusion: "Als ich Troia wirklich kannte, meinen Mittelpunkt, verstand ich ihn. Nicht Neugier wärs gewesen, die mich weggetrieben hätte: Entsetzen. Doch wohin hätte ich, mit welchem Schiff, noch fahren solln?" (40).

That Cassandra chooses death over fleeing with Aeneas also does not imply that she reaffirms a Trojan identity rooted in the palace. Throughout her narrative Cassandra speaks in many different voices and assumes different roles in order to let the reader participate in the transformation of her various identities. In a passage at the beginning of her narrative, Cassandra reflects upon how her personal identity and history are interwoven with the stories of Troy; in the context of the writing and rewriting of Troy's history, the narrative shifts to Cassandra's personal history—from her childhood fascination with the stories of the inner circles that initially shaped her identity to her exclusion from the inner circles of the palace.[24] Just as Troy's history changes, so does Cassandra's story. "Nicht durch Geburt, durch die Erzählungen in den Innenhöfen bin ich Troerin geworden. Durch das Geraune der Münder am Gucklock, als ich im Korb saß, habe ich aufgehört, es zu sein" (40). From the point of view of public perception, especially from that of the inner circles of the palace, she is no longer a true Trojan but an insane traitor; but because Cassandra states in her own voice, "ich habe aufgehört, es zu sein," she cannot be claimed and subsumed under Troy's history of self-destruction. In her remembrance Cassandra rewrites the history of Troy and recounts the history of her "Befreiung" (41). After she has rewritten her story and Troy has fallen, Cassandra reclaims her identity. "Jetzt, da es Troia nicht mehr gibt, bin ich es wieder: Troerin. Nichts sonst" (40).[25] From the perspective of a contemporary reader, Cassandra has rewritten her inscription in the Western mythical and literary tradition. With hindsight Cassandra thus reclaims her identity as a product of, as well as her critical engagement with, Trojan history.

On first reading, her statement—"Jetzt, da es Troia nicht mehr gibt, bin ich es wieder: Troerin. Nichts sonst"—appears to contradict my assertion that Cassandra embraces a transnational identity. To embrace a transnational identity, however, does not mean that Cassandra has to reject or deny her personal history. It is not a matter of exchanging one for the other; rather her past lives in a transformed way in her new selfhood. More importantly, Cassandra's personal history as she tells it in her remembrance should not so easily be incorporated and subsumed under a homogeneous story of Trojan society. To place Cassandra firmly within Trojan palace society is to situate her personal history in Troy's national agenda. After all, by giving Cassandra a personal history for the years before and during the war in order to unearth Cassandra from the male-heroic tradition in which she has been inscribed, Wolf attempts to portray a differentiated picture of Troy and its internal cultural and political struggles. Having told the story of her emancipation from Troy's patriarchal, nationalist, and war history, Cassandra at the end of her path has recreated from within a sub-culture of Trojan society a transnational identity. The cave community, too, refuses to partake in Eumelos's "us versus them" politics. Speaking from a position within the alternative society, Cassandra nonetheless refers to the other Trojans as "unsre[r] Troer" (152). The community thus practices a politics of difference without being exclusive. "Mich erstaunte, daß eine jede von den Frauen am Skamander, so sehr verschieden wir auch voneinader waren, fühlte, daß wir etwas ausprobierten. Und daß es nicht darauf ankam, wieviel Zeit wir hatten. Oder ob wir die Mehrzahl unsrer Troer, die selbstverständlich in der düstern Stadt verblieben, überzeugten" (152). In this transnational culture in which Cassandra finds a sense of belonging lies the utopian vision of the "Troerin."[26]

As Judith Ryan has observed, the "utopian impetus that outlives the prophetess herself" survives not only in the readers who "rethink, with Cassandra, the seeming inevitability of the events it recounts," but it also comes alive in the consciousness of the narrator (321). While Cassandra herself dies, her utopian model for forming transnational identities might not. For Cassandra and the narrator, the act of remembering becomes a radical act of cultural criticism. In Komar's words: "Immersing herself in Kassandra's consciousness, Wolf merges her personal memory with that of her subject. Together, the modern narrator and her classical character re-member the cultural tradition itself; and they dis-member many of the institutions of heroism and valor associated with war" (43).

"Hier war es," the opening paragraph begins. In the last two lines Wolf returns to a modern setting. "Hier ist es." The narrator thus literally carries, to speak in Benjamin's words, the traces of a "history of barbarism" (256) within her voice. Transposing a contemporary consciousness to the cradle of occidental civilization through her narrative technique, Wolf suggests here as she has in other works that the past lives in the present. The temporal shifts invite a comparison between the ancient Troy and Wolf's contemporary world.[27] Looking back into history the narrator portrays the ancestors of modern nations to be rooted in the tradition that unfolded in Troy. Wolf relies on the legend in which Rome imagined its origins as Trojan. "Whereas the victorious Greeks," Brown argues,

> provided the intellectual and cultural basis for Western civilization, the defeated Trojans are imagined to be the physical ancestors of modern European nations, Italy, Germany, and England. Christa Wolf's innovation is to view Troy, in its pre-war phase, which she imagines to have been a matriarchal society, as a superior ideological model, as well, with the destruction of Troy leading to thousands of years of patriarchal oppression (118).

Cassandra witnesses the demise of what the women of Troy could still remember and envision to be a non-patriarchal society. Could the narrator perhaps be also specifically reimagining the origin of her own sense of nation and trying to confront the distortion of an ideal she had once hoped to create? The allusion to Rome evokes Hitler and the Third Reich and implies a subtle reference to the emergence of the GDR out of the Cold War. Just as the image of the enemy united Trojans behind a national front, the former GDR built its national consciousness in enmity to the West. And just as Troy portrayed itself as a victim of imperialist aggression, the former GDR represented itself as being on the defensive in the East/West conflict.[28] Significantly, Wolf constructed her narrative from within a country that exploited an alleged position of victimization to form a national consciousness which she then deconstructed in order to uncover its expansionist politics.

In her lectures on poetics accompanying the narrative *Kassandra,* Wolf describes what attracted her to Cassandra: "daß sie imstande war, sich so weit außerhalb des eigenen Volks zu stellen, daß sie sein unheilvolles Schicksal 'sah'" (*Voraussetzungen* 16–17). Severing her relation to her religion, state, and family, Cassandra forgoes her national identity in order to be able to speak her truth and gain self-knowledge, in spite of the guilt and pain Wolf believes Cassandra must have experienced. Wolf can identify with Cassandra's pain, recognizing the psychological burden of feeling alien in her own culture. In the narrative web of the lectures Wolf repeatedly raises the questions of "Heimatlosigkeit" and "Exil." Reflections on the figure Cassandra often intermingle with reflections on Wolf's personal fears. She contemplates "die Frage nach dem Zeitpunkt, an dem Heimatgefühl verlorenging." Wolf answers her generally posed question from Cassandra's point of view: "(Der Augenblick, der in Kassandras Leben die Einsicht bedeutet haben muß, daß ihre Warnungen sinnlos waren, weil es das Troia, das sie retten wollte, gar nicht gab.)" (*Voraussetzungen* 26). Albeit in a different context, Wolf openly acknowledges the pain her own people have inflicted on her. While her friend N., who has returned to Greece from exile in the hope of rebuilding his nation, "kann nicht zulassen, daß ein Symbol, ein Traum verfällt," Wolf has already found a way to cope with her own disillusionment: "Unstillbar, das weiß man doch, ist der Schmerz, den die Eignen einem antun, es sei denn, man verwandelt sie oder sich selbst in Fremde..." (*Voraussetzungen* 37). Like Cassandra, Wolf had to choose either self-estrangement by assimilating to her society or her integrity by disassociating herself from her culture; and like Cassandra, Wolf has made strangers of her people.

In an interview conducted by Theresa Hörnigk in June 1987 Wolf more openly acknowledges: "Meine Generation hat früh eine Ideologie gegen eine andere ausgetauscht, sie ist spät, zögernd, teilweise gar nicht erwachsen geworden, will sagen: reif, autonom" (*Dialog* 26). Speaking for her generation, Wolf has redefined the national identity through which they had originally marked themselves during the early years of GDR history. Rather than being different from their Western counterparts, they in fact shared a common history. Invoking a largely mythical past as a way to imagine themselves into a nation, many GDR intellectuals had participated in creating a myth of origin in their narratives. "What is," Slavoj Zizek observes, "'national heritage' if not a kind of ideological fossil created retroactively by the ruling ideology in order to blur its present antagonism" (49)? In *Kassandra* Wolf uncovers the antagonism, the fantasy of the enemy, which held together the nation-state. At the same time she creates a powerful new narrative similar in its vision to Kirstie McClure's theoretical treatises on imagining communities that look beyond the "state as a privileged expression of political community, and hence as the principle and necessarily privileged site of political action." Instead of locating political identities within the confines of the "modern state as a singular and sovereign adjudicator and enforcer of rights within a bounded and definite 'society'" (110), McClure suggests that formulating an identity politics ('subjects of rights') along the axis of differences from within a sub-culture "may imply potential solidarities not only within but beyond the domestic context or territorial confines of the national state" (112). Forging a transnational identity from within a diverse community, Cassandra resists a disciplining in the name of the nation. Her narrative gestures towards imagined communities beyond national, gender, and class divisions—communities in which nationality no longer constitutes citizenship.

Notes

I would like to thank Katherine King for her helpful comments and suggestions on an earlier draft of this essay.

[1] For a detailed survey of the historical background in relation to the GDR's cultural politics see Wolfgang Emmerich.

[2] On this topic see John Borneman. He observes: "By claiming that fascism is a problem of capitalism, and not necessarily of German history alone, the GDR universalized and abstracted the Third Reich. Fascism became a universal problem of an abstract, nonlocal nature, attributable to a virulent form of capitalism and class conflict that could, theoretically, exist anywhere in the world" (51).

[3] Lloyd discusses the rise of Irish nationalism and in that context presents a more general analysis of a national discourse ("Writing in the Shit"). Much of this discussion on nation and nationalism comes out of English studies and post-colonial discourse. See also Paul Gilroy, Tom Nairn, and Homi Bhabha.

[4] I am thinking here particularly of Christa Wolf's early novel *Der geteilte Himmel*, in which Rita chooses her "nation" over her love for Manfred who deserts to the West.

[5] Lloyd makes the case that "while nationalism is a progressive and even necessary political movement at one stage in its history, it tends at a later stage to become entirely reactionary, both by virtue of its obsession with a deliberately exclusive concept of racial identity and, more importantly, by virtue of its *formal* identity with imperial ideology" (*Nationalism* ix-x); see also Partha Chatterjee.

[6] Here is where many feminist critiques of nationalist discourses set in, for invariably the politics of nationalism ghettoizes and subordinates women's politics to the periphery. On this topic see the works by Kumkum Sangari and Sudesh Vaid and by R. Radhakrishnan.

[7] A point of clarification is in order. I am not denying the emancipating nature of nationalism in anti-colonial struggles in the Third-World or its counterforce in many places today. In fact, in "Yeats and Decolonization" Said argues "nationalist anti-imperialism...formed the initial basis of the second moment...the idea of liberation, a strong new post-nationalist theme" (10).

[8] Gupta further writes: "The displacement of identity and culture from 'the nation' not only forces us to reevaluate our ideas about culture and identity but also enables us to denaturalize the nation as the hegemonic form of organizing space" (74). See also Said and Chatterjee.

[9] I am thinking here of Socialist Realist aesthetics that in order to facilitate and consolidate socialism demanded a mimetic representation of social dynamics and conflicts from the perspective of the ultimate triumph of socialism.

[10] Those critics who after the demise of the GDR state accuse Wolf of having been complicit with its oppressive practices by calling her "Staatsdichterin" falsely equate the author with the GDR's national politics and in fact overlook how their own thinking falls prey to and participates in West Germany's national discourse.

[11] Brown argues that the "Trojan War story is retold three thousand years later from the losing side and, more significantly, from a woman's side. The ancient versions were created by the victors, the Greeks, and by men, centuries after the historical war" (115).

[12] I base my discussion of the *Oresteia* on Froma Zeitlin's excellent femininst reading of Aeschylus's trilogy. She shows how the plays "assert the primacy of the male through appeal to the primacy of the father.... The denial of matriarchy is achieved by the denial of *mater*." Through "a new forum, namely, the law court, the city's device which admits the use of logical argument and debate..." (168) the plays legitimate "a new justice" (169).

[13] The various translations vary slightly in formulation. I have chosen the most explicit, but will cite other translations for comparison. "So far her daring reaches: / the woman will murder the man" (Grene ll. 1230-31). "No, this is daring when the female shall strike down the male. What can I call her and be right?" (Lattimore ll. 1231-32).

[14] For a discussion of the mechanisms of nationalism from a Lacanian point of view see Salecl and Zizek.

[15] On this topic see Anna Kuhn (198-202). Also see Anke Bennholdt-Thomsen, who has established a connection between *Kassandra* and *Kindheitsmuster* through the motif of the ship (53-60). While in *Kindheitsmuster* the white ship represents the "Kriegsangst der Erwachsenen," in *Kassandra* the ships symbolize "Vorkrieg." Through the ship motif Wolf makes a subtle link between World War II and the myth: "Das Schiff vermittelt wie selbstverständlich zwischen Mythos und Geschichte" (57).

[16] "Um aber dem Krieg zujubeln zu können, hatten sie diesen Namen gebraucht" (78).

[17] I further disagree with Adelson when she claims that Cassandra, having to choose between the palace and the cave-dwellers, remains a daughter of the palace. Cassandra never invalidates the life at Mt. Ida, even though she does not follow Aeneas. To me, her death has a positive meaning because it signifies her resistance to an incorporation of the life in the caves into another nation-state, as she predicts will happen. Her vision stays alive although she dies. Adelson's interpretation appears to be motivated by a desire for a "Leben" (presumably with Aeneas) that denies Cassandra's most fundamental insight: the danger of appropriation and cooptation of her vision into new national narratives.

[18] See Adelson for an excellent discussion of Cassandra's process of "Subjektwerdung" (508-12).

[19] Waldstein views the cave community as primarily a female place; she thus does not take into account the central role Anchises plays in that sub-culture.

[20] Wolf is alluding to Virgil's *Aeneid*. His patriotic and national epic celebrates Aeneas's bloody struggles to found the Roman nation. The legend has it that the emperor Augustus is a direct descendant of Aeneas.

[21] Aeneas threw "den Schlangenring ins Meer" (56), thus symbolizing his break with the matriarchal tradition. Furthermore, he will be unable to adhere to values that Wolf proposes in the form of questions as fundamental to a new community: "Ein Verzicht auf die Beherrschung und Unterwerfung der Natur, Verzicht auf Kolonialisierung andrer Völker und Erdteile, aber auch auf die Kolonialisierung der Frau durch den Mann? Es ist eine Lust zu leben—vorausgesetzt man ist nicht Herr der Welt und strebt auch nicht an, es zu sein" (*Voraussetzungen* 117-18).

[22] In order to make this argument Adelson has to discredit Cassandra's search for autonomy, "freedom from objectification," as "unglaubwürdig," a judgment that the text in my view does not support.

[23] That escaping to another place is useless and not a viable option to the problems in Western culture that Cassandra describes in her narrative is in fact foreshadowed in the Panthoos episode.

[24] This passage is often quoted out of context to bolster the argument that Cassandra does not truly disassociate herself from the palace. In my perception, the passage begins on page 37, when Anchises teaches Cassandra Trojan history, particularly how the history of the first ship and of Panthoos's appearance in Troy have been written and rewritten. This notion of history corresponds to Wolf's agenda of revising the Cassandra myth. Thus Cassandra during her childhood first believed in the official, public version of the first expedition (this in itself undergoes several rewritings in the passage), then hears Hektor's discussion of it in the palace, and finally Anchises's revision.

[25] The "nichts sonst" I take to mean her refusal to be once again, after she has retold and redefined her identity, appropriated in a patriarchal (Aeschylus) or nationalist discourse.

[26] In the *Voraussetzungen* Wolf writes: "Das Troia, das mir vor Augen steht, ist—viel eher als eine rückgewandte Beschreibung—ein Modell für eine Art von Utopie" (83).

[27] Wolf invites such a comparison by calling her narrative "eine Schlüsselerzählung" (*Voraussetzungen* 119).

[28] Peter J. Graves discusses the specific passages from the work that were not printed in the GDR and their political implications for GDR sensitivity (944-56).

Works Cited

Adelson, Leslie A. "The Bomb and I: Peter Sloterdijk, Botho Strauß, and Christa Wolf." *Monatshefte* 4 (1986): 508-12.

Aeschylus. *Oresteia*. Trans. Robert Fagles. New York: Viking, 1966.

Anderson, Benedict. *Imagined Communities*. London: Verso, 1983.

Bathrick, David. "The End of the Wall Before the End of the Wall." *German Studies Review* 2 (1991): 297-311.

Benjamin, Walter. *Illuminations*. Trans. Harry Zohn. New York: Schocken, 1978.

Bennhodt-Thomsen, Anke. "Die Schiffe in Christa Wolf's *Kassandra* und die Verfahrungsweise des poetischen Geistes." *Literatur für Leser* 2 (1986): 53-60.

Bhabha, Homi. *Nation and Narration*. New York: Routledge, 1990.

Borneman, John. "State, Territory, and Identity Formation in the Postwar Berlins, 1945-1989." *Cultural Anthropology* 1 (1992): 45-62.

Brown, Russell E. "The *Kassandra* of Christa Wolf." *Classical and Modern Literature* 2 (1989): 115-23.

Chatterjee, Partha. *Nationalist Thought and the Colonial World: A Derivative Discourse*. London: ZED Books, 1986.

Emmerich, Wolfgang. *Kleine Literaturgeschichte der DDR*. Darmstadt: Luchterhand, 1984.

Euripides. *The Trojan Women*. Ed. David Green and Richard Lattimore. *The Complete Greek Tragedies. Volume III*. Chicago: U of Chicago P, 1958.

Gilroy, Paul. *There Ain't No Black in the Union Jack*. London: Hutchinson, 1987.

Graves, Peter J. "Christa Wolf's *Kassandra*: The Censoring of the GDR Edition." *Modern Language Review* 81 (1986): 944-56.

Grene, David and Wendy Doniger O'Flaherty. *The Oresteia*. Chicago: U of Chicago P, 1989.

Gupta, Akhil. "The Song of the Nonaligned World: Transnational Identities and the Reinscription of Space in Late Capitalism." *Cultural Anthropology* 1 (1992): 63-79.

Huyssen, Andreas. "After the Wall: The Failure of German Intellectuals." *New German Critique* 52 (Winter 1991): 109-43.

Komar, Kathleen. "The Communal Self: Re-Membering Female Identity in the Works of Christa Wolf and Monique Wittig." *Comparative Literature* 44 (Winter 1992): 42-58.

Kuhn, Anna K. *Christa Wolf's Utopian Vision: From Marxism to Feminism*. New York: Cambridge UP, 1988.

Lattimore, Richmond, trans. *The Oresteia*. Chicago: U of Chicago P, 1953.

Lloyd, David. *Nationalism and Minor Literature: James Clarence Mangan and the Emergence of Irish Cultural Nationalism*. Berkeley: U of California P, 1987.

———. "Writing in the Shit: Beckett, Nationalism, and the Colonial Subject." *Modern Fiction Studies* 35 (1989): 71-86.

Maisch, Christine. *Ein schmaler Streifen Zukunft: Christa Wolf's Erzählung Kassandra*. Würzburg: Königshausen, 1986.

Mauser, Wolfram, ed. *Erinnerte Zukunft: 11 Studien zum Werk Christa Wolfs*. Würzburg: Königshausen, 1985.

McClure, Kirstie. "On the Subject of Rights: Pluralism, Plurality and Political Identity." *Dimemsions of Radical Democracy: Pluralism, Citizenship, Community*. Ed. Chantal Mouffe. London: Verso, 1992.

Minnerup, Gunter. "East Germany's Frozen Revolution." *New Left Review* (May/April 1982): 5-32.

Montrose, Louise. "New Historicism." *Redrawing the Boundaries*. Ed. Stephen Greenblatt and Giles Gunn. New York: MLA, 1992.

Nairn, Tom. *The Break-up of Britain*. London: Verso, 1981.

Nicolai, Rosemarie. "Christa Wolfs *Kassandra*: Quellenstudien und Interpretationsansätze." *Literatur für Leser* 2 (1985): 137-55.

Pickle, Linda Schelbitzki. "Scratching Away the Male Tradition: Christa Wolf's *Kassandra*." *Contemporary Literature* 1 (1986): 32-47.

Radhakrishnan, R. "Nationalism, Gender, and the Narrative of Identity." *Nationalisms and Sexualities*. Ed. Andrew Parker, Mary Russo, Doris Sommer, and Patricia Yaeger. New York: Routledge, 1992.

Risse, Stefanie. *Wahrnehmung und Erkennen in Christa Wolf's Erzählung Kassandra*. Pfaffenweiler: Centaurus, 1986.

Ryan, Judith. "Twilight Zones: Myth, Fairy Tale, and Utopia in *No Place on Earth* and *Cassandra*." *Responses to Christa Wolf*. Ed. Marilyn Sibley Fries. Detroit: Wayne State UP, 1989.

Said, Edward. "Yeats and Decolonization." *Nationalism, Colonialism and Literature*. Lawrence Hill: Field Day Pamphlet, 1988.

Salecl, Renata. "Nationalism, Anti-Semitism, and Anti-Feminism in Eastern Europe." *New German Critique* 57 (Fall 1992): 51-65.

Sangari, Kumkum and Sudesh Vaid, eds. *Recasting Women: Essays in Indian Colonial History*. New Brunswick, NJ: Rutgers UP, 1990.

Segeberg, Harro. "Nationalismus als Literatur: Literarisches Leben, nationale Tendenzen und Frühformen eines literarischen Nationalismus in Deutschland (1770-1805)." *Polyperspektivik in der literarischen Moderne*. Ed. Harro Segeberg and Jörg Schönert. Bern: Lang, 1988.

Silberman, Marc. "Writing What—for Whom? Vergangenheitsbewältigung in GDR Literature." *German Studies Review* 3 (1987): 527-38.

Stephan, Alexander. "Frieden, Frauen und Kassandra." *Wolf: Darstellung, Deutung, Diskussion*. Ed. Manfred Jürgensen. Bern: Francke, 1984.

Waldstein, Edith. "Prophecy in Search of a Voice: Silence in Christa Wolf's *Kassandra*." *Germanic Review* 4 (1987): 194-98.

Wolf, Christa. *Im Dialog*. Berlin and Weimar: Luchterhand, 1990.

——. *Kassandra*. Darmstadt: Luchterhand, 1983.

——. *Voraussetzungen einer Erzählung: Kassandra*. Darmstadt: Luchterhand, 1983.

Zeitlin, Froma. "The Dynamics of Misogyny: Myth and Mythmaking in the *Oresteia*." *Arethusa* 11 (1978): 149-83.

Zizek, Slavoj. "Eastern European Liberalism and its Discontents." *New German Critique* 57 (Fall 1992): 25-49.

Auseinandersetzung mit dem Abendlanddenken: Gisela von Wysockis *Abendlandleben*

Petra Waschescio

The article examines Gisela von Wysocki's innovative first drama *Abendlandleben* (1987), in which she does away almost entirely with the dialogue structure of classical theatre and avoids familiar modes of individual self-exploration and -analysis. Instead, the self-determined bourgeois subject becomes a conglomerate of diverse social rules and ways of thinking that assign a separate status to women. They, like the "savages" in masculinist Enlightenment discourse, have become surfaces for the projection of unassimilatable desires. By illuminating Wysocki's *modus operandi,* the article aims to establish a basis for further scholarly discussion of her work. (JC)

Gisela von Wysocki ist eine Essayistin, Lyrikerin, Hörspiel- und Theaterautorin, die bisher trotz der Bandbreite ihrer Fähigkeiten kaum breitere Bekanntheit erlangt hat. Im Zentrum dieses Beitrags steht Wysockis erste, umfangreiche und bisher kaum aufgeführte Theaterarbeit *Abendlandleben oder Apollinaires Gedächtnis: Spiele aus Neu Glück* (1987). In ihr bündelt sie Ergebnisse vorangegangener Essays zu einer systematischen Kritik unserer modernen westlichen Kultur und Selbstdefinition. Mit dieser exemplarischen Betrachtung des Textes soll der Versuch unternommen werden, eine erste Grundlage für eine weitere wissenschaftliche Auseinandersetzung mit den Werken Wysockis zu schaffen.

Gegenstand der Analyse von *Abendlandleben* soll sein, welche Kriterien die Autorin diesem Abendland zuordnet, ob und welche Kausalität sie der Entwicklung des modernen Europas zugrundelegt und welche Bedeutung sie dabei der Differenzierung der Geschlechterrollen beimißt. Im Einzelnen wird in den Abschnitten "Wissenschaftliche Weltaneignung," "Vernunftherrschaft und Herrschaft der Technik" und "Geschlechterdifferenz" anhand einer Analyse der *Spiele* die Frage nach den Grundlagen der abendländischen Gesellschaft und ihren Auswirkungen im Verständnis Wysockis ("Aufklärung als Prozeß der Kolonisierung") gestellt. "Durchkreuzung der Polaritäten" schließlich skizziert den aus dem Text interpolierten Ansatz zu einer dem dichotomisierenden Denken entgegengesetzten Bewegung.

Der Kritik und Teilen der Frauenbewegung ist Wysocki mit ihrem zweiten Essayband *Die Fröste der Freiheit* (1981) aufgefallen, einer Sammlung von sechs Porträts unterschiedlichster Frauen, deren Gemeinsamkeit im Aufbruch in eine frauenunspezifische Sphäre lag: die Teilhabe an der Kulturindustrie als Produzentinnen oder Darstellerinnen. Bei nahezu allen Rezensenten ist es primär die Sprache der Autorin, die Aufmerksamkeit erweckt. Eine "Sprachbesessene" ("Gisela von Wysocki"), mit "Scharfsinn und Sprachmacht" (Henrichs) sei hier am Werk, deren "Kühnheit und Schönheit der Sprache atemlos" mache (Schwarz). An ihr wird neben "analytischem Scharfsinn" (Henrichs)—gar "messerscharfer, fast eisiger Präzision"—auch eine "poetische, leuchtende Sprache" (Freier) hervorgehoben. Abgesehen von manchen zweifelhaften Etikettierungen wie "helle Vernunft" und "dunkler Zauber" (Henrichs), ist es wohl genau diese Oszillation zwischen analytischer Präzision und ungebundener Phantasie, die sie nicht nur auf der sprachlichen, sondern auch auf der inhaltlichen Ebene aus dem Gros der frauenbewegten Schriften der siebziger Jahre hervorhebt. So vermerkt Inge Nordhoff positiv, daß die Autorin in ihren Porträts "von psychoanalytischen, gesellschaftlichen oder literaturwissenschaftlichen Deutungsmustern" absieht. Bedingungen würden zwar "skizziert, aber nicht zum alleinigen Ausgangspunkt der Anschauung gemacht" (Schwartz).

Wysockis Schreiben markiert eine Abkehr von sozialpsychologischer Bekenntnis- und Selbstverwirklichungsliteratur, die in ihrer Tendenz an einer folgerichtigen, linearen Persönlichkeitsentwicklung festhält, damit aber auch eine Bestimmung des Weiblichen als Opfer, deren Darstellung sicher auch notwendig ist, festschreibt. Wysocki ist im Urteil der Kritik eine Autorin, die kraft ihres Intellekts sich selbst und auch die porträtierten Frauen über den Status der Unterdrückten erheben kann. Sie nennt ihre Essays "Prozeßakten" weiblicher Deserteure (1981, 8). Flüchtige aus einer Zwangsmaschinerie, die den Tod nicht über sich ergehen lassen wollen und die gleichzeitig bei Bewußtsein einer Strafe zum Tode fliehen, aber mit der Hoffnung, ihm zu entkommen. So wird denn der selbstbestimmte Tod dreier ihrer Akteurinnen nur knapp beschrieben; beiläufig, fast lakonisch wird er vermerkt (1981, 32, 51, 55 f.).

Wesentlich ist nicht das tragische Scheitern. Gisela von Wysocki sucht nach Rissen auf der glatten und teilweise, im Falle der Filmdiven Marlene Dietrich und Greta Garbo, glanzvollen Oberfläche unserer patriarchalen Kultur. Sie sucht in den Gesichtern inszenierter Weiblichkeit nach Resten, die auf eine andere, verdrängte Daseinsform weisen.

Benjamin Henrichs spricht davon, die *Fröste der Freiheit* seien nicht als "Rekonstruktionen" konkreter weiblicher Lebensläufe sondern eher als

"Entwürfe" zu einer "Idee des Weiblichen" zu lesen. Die Porträtierten veränderten sich nach seinen Beobachtungen in der Beschreibung durch Wysocki. So etwa verzichte sie darauf, dem Rückzug Marie Luise Fleißers in die Ehe und das provinzielle Ingolstadt angemessen Raum zu geben. Übrig bleibe statt der "ungelenken" Sprache Fleißers die gelenkig-souveräne Wysockis. Das klingt nach bewußter Heldenproduktion weiblicher Provenienz. Doch gerade die Herstellung der Einheit der Person gelingt den weiblichen Deserteuren bei Wysocki nicht.

Sowenig Wysockis Blick allein auf das weibliche Opfer gerichtet ist, soweit ist sie davon entfernt, die Widersprüche und Kapitulationen zu verschweigen. Alle Portraits des Essaybandes sind konzentriert auf die Unangemessenheit der (vorgegebenen) Formen, in denen die Erfahrungen der (eigenen) Fremde und Zerstückelung überwunden werden soll. Gerade in den Lebensläufen der außergewöhnlichen Frauen legt Wysocki die Macht traditioneller Weiblichkeitsbilder frei. Sie entwickelt in den *Frösten der Freiheit* keine positive Idee, sondern Ansätze zu einer Typologie des Weiblichen, die sie erst später in *Weiblichkeit und Modernität: Über Virginia Woolf* (1982) oder *Abendlandleben oder Apollinaires Gedächtnis: Spiele aus Neu Glück* (1987) ausweitet zu einer Typologie des abendländischen Menschen. Dort erst werden auch Spezifika des abendländischen Denkens auf die Geschlechter verteilt, so daß eine Idee des Weiblichen dahinter sichtbar werden kann.

Die Essays erscheinen eher als Vorstudien zu einer grundsätzlichen, in *Abendlandleben* geführten Auseinandersetzung um die Tauglichkeit des Subjektbegriffs, dem die Wirksamkeit kulturell verbindlicher Grundmuster entgegenzustehen scheint. Menschliche Individualität wird schon in den Essays, noch vorrangig erprobt an der weiblichen Realität, als Konglomerat kultureller Ablagerungen offengelegt.

I. *Abendlandleben oder Apollinaires Gedächtnis: Spiele aus Neu Glück*

Abendlandleben ist Wysockis erstes Theaterstück. Es ist 1987 erschienen, uraufgeführt, und mit dem Theaterpreis der Autorenstiftung ausgezeichnet. Christina Weiß definiert den Text als eine "multimediale und darin postmoderne," mit Heiner Müllers *Hamletmaschine* vergleichbare Assemblage. Sibylle Cramer spricht von *Abendlandleben* als einem "Gesamtkunstwerk-Versuch." Beide Rezensionen lassen—stellvertretend—die Schwierigkeit erkennen, die Komplexität des Stücks zu erfassen. Auch ich werde in meiner Analyse nur einen Teil der darin enthaltenen Aspekte behandeln können. Zu ausgeprägt ist zum Beispiel Wysockis Verwendung von fremden Versatzstücken im eigenen Text. Diesen vollständig nachzuspüren, wäre Aufgabe einer eigenständigen Studie. Obwohl Form und Inhalt in diesem Theaterstück in einer sehr engen, fast programmatisch zu nennenden Verbindung stehen, möchte ich mich zunächst von "außen" dem Text nähern und den Rahmen, innerhalb dessen das Stück seinen Verlauf nimmt, beschreiben. Wie der Titel bereits anzeigt, nimmt Wysocki den französischen Dichter Guillaume Apollinaire[1] zum Ausgangspunkt ihres Stückes. Am 17. März 1916 wurde Apollinaire kriegsbedingt von einem Granatsplitter verletzt, der seine Schädeldecke durchdrang (*Oeuvres* 4, 661). Eine Schädelbohrung sollte die Entfernung des Splitters ermöglichen. Wysocki geht von diesem Vorgang der realen Operation aus—die Öffnung des Kopfes und Freilegung des Gehirns—und deutet ihn um in eine Freilegung des Gedächtnisses. Auf diese Weise konstruiert sie einen Innenraum, den sie als "Zimmertheater" bezeichnet (10),[2] als Ort für Vorgänge, die im Verlauf des Stückes von Außen betrachtet werden können.

Aufgebaut hat Wysocki das "Zimmertheater" als Abfolge dreier in ihrer Struktur ähnlicher "Bilder." Sie beginnen jeweils mit der Bildbeschreibung eines auch im Text abgebildeten Kunstwerks:

1. Salvador Dali, *Banlieue de la ville paranoiaque-critique; après-midi sur la lisière de l'histoire européenne* [Außenbezirk der paranoisch-kritischen Stadt; Nachmittag am Rand der europäischen Geschichte] (Ausschnitt) 1936, Öl auf Holz, 46x66.
2. Pablo Picasso, *Le repas frugale* [Das kärgliche Mahl] Radierung, 1904, das Wysocki mit dem nicht belegten Titel "Die Trinker" angibt.
3. Edward Hopper, *Excursion into Philosophy,* Öl auf Leinwand, 1959.

Die "Bilder" gehen dann über in einen rhythmischen Wechsel von Figurenrede und Sequenzen sogenannter "Spiele." Die Sequenzen umfassen jeweils vier bis sechs Spiele.

Diese Spiele sind die optisch herausragenden Bestandteile des Textes. Insgesamt hat Wysocki zwanzig verschiedene entworfen. Sie werden jeweils in den zwei folgenden Bildern in veränderter Zusammenstellung wiederholt. Der Umfang der einzelnen Spiele ist bereits im ersten Bild festgelegt. Jedoch enthält jeder Text zunächst Lücken, die von Durchgang zu Durchgang komplettiert werden. Wysocki beschreibt diese Vervollständigung als kontinuierlich sich verbessernde Arbeit des freigelegten Gedächtnisses; zunächst "stockend. NOCH ohne Blick für Zusammenhänge" (25), stabilisiert es sich (51), bis es am Ende "repariert," "auf seiner Höhe" einen "mühelosen Bilderstrom" erzeugt (85, 100, 105).

Doch verweist der Titel über das individuelle Schicksal hinaus; der Bezug auf Apollinaire erfolgt nur im Untertitel. Vorrangig, die Fettschrift des Wortes auf dem Buchdeckel legt es nahe, ist dies ein Text, der sich mit dem Kulturraum "Abendland" auseinandersetzt: Apollinaires Gedächtnis wird zum Museum, in dem Europa ausgestellt wird.

Nun, nach dem Einschuß der Granate, liegt unter dem Operationsspiegel sein Gedächtnis frei. Die chirurgischen Schnitte zeichnen Linien nach, die

Umrisse einer unterirdischen Ordnung.... Schneiden, tiefer. Schälen Bilder heraus, patterns, Pläne. Den Aufbau einer uns fernstehenden Menschheit. Urbilder des EUROPI (11).

Der Zugang zum Kulturraum Europa erfolgt durch eine "Kolonialistische Tür" (19), d.h., der Blick von Außen bleibt gewahrt, wird nun aber definiert als ethnographische Perspektive.

Vier Figuren—Lady und Fredy, die allerdings in der zweiten Bildbeschreibung auch Gegenstand der Betrachtung sind, und Stimmen 1 und 2—fungieren als Betrachter der fremden Kultur.

Stimme 1 Irgendetwas war es
Stimme 2 Irgendetwas in ihren langen Hosen
Stimme 1 Irgendetwas verstecken sie da
Stimme 2 Entweder ihre Exkremente... Oder Ihre Genitalien (97).

Die sukzessive Reparatur des Gedächtnisses meint damit nicht allein die Wiederherstellung individueller Erinnerung, die Operation dient ebenso der Wiederherstellung kollektiver Erinnerung. Die dezentrale Betrachterperspektive, ebenso wie etwa das literarische Mittel des Zeitsprungs, ist dabei Möglichkeit, selbstverständlichen Konventionen unserer Kultur die Aura des Natürlichen zu nehmen und sie damit der Kritik zugänglich zu machen.

DER ZUSCHAUER KANN SICH NIEMALS SICHER SEIN, OB ER EINER JAHRTAUSENDEALTEN UNBEKANNTEN MENSCHENART ZUSIEHT ODER DER EIGENEN SPEZIES (13).

II. Neu Glück

Die Autorin beginnt hinter dem Inhaltsverzeichnis mit dem Abschnitt "NEU GLÜCK, Biographische Notiz." Auch wenn sich Daten und Inhalt vorrangig auf Apollinaire beziehen, so ist es grammatisch durchaus möglich, diese biographische Notiz auch auf NEU GLÜCK zu beziehen. Wysocki selbst legt nahe, die aus Apollinaires Biographie und Werken herausgegriffenen Aspekte, Modernität und Kriegsbegeisterung,[3] als über das Individuelle hinausgehende Merkmale zu begreifen.

> Er [Apollinaire] ist das Phänomen des historisch überdeterminierten Europi, in dem sich alles staut und verdichtet—ganz Europa ist da sozusagen auf den Beinen (Roeder 131).

Was also ist NEU GLÜCK, abgesehen davon, daß es der Name einer tatsächlich existierenden Villa ist, in der Apollinaire in den Jahren 1901 und 1902 als Privatlehrer tätig war? NEU GLÜCK, so scheint es, ist auch der Name dessen, was die individuelle und kollektive Erinnerung allmählich, im Verlauf des Stücks, reproduziert: "Er kann in aller Ruhe sein

Gedächtnis / betrachten.... / Von oben sickert Licht herein, fällt auf.... Abdrücke, Fährten. / Auf die heiße Spur von Neu Glück" (10).

Wysocki exponiert gleich zu Anfang zwei Eckpfeiler von Neu Glück: Zum einen lesen wir: "Die Natur ist eine Kübelpalme" (9). Die Natur ist hier als exotisches Gewächs auf einen Blumentopf reduziert, vom Menschen gepflegt, aber auch kontrolliert. Natur, definiert als "ohne Zutun des Menschen Existierendes, Sich-Entwickelndes" (*Fremdwörterduden* 516), existiert nicht mehr. Die Kräfte der Natur sind gebändigt, "kultiviert." Der Mensch ist nicht mehr Teil dieser Natur, sondern sie ist schmückendes Beiwerk des menschlichen Kulturraums. Zum anderen heißt es: "Die Menschen gehen als Croupiers" (9). Mit diesem Satz erfaßt Wysocki gleich zwei wesentliche Aspekte: Croupiers sind im Roulett die Stellvertreter des Bankhalters; sie scheinen das Schicksal der Spieler in der Hand zu halten, indem sie die Kugel ins Rollen bringen, die über Sieg oder Niederlage entscheidet. Doch ist ihr Einfluß begrenzt; sie sind weder in der Lage, Weg und Ziel der Kugel zu kontrollieren, noch gar die Regeln des Spiels zu verändern. Beanspruchen die Menschen aus "Neu Glück" die Rolle dieser stellvertretenden Bankhalter, so langen sie—"Spiel" in "Leben" übersetzt—nach der scheinbaren Macht, das Schicksal zu bestimmen, nach der Macht über die Wirklichkeit also. Doch tatsächlich sind auch sie nicht in der Lage, Ausgang oder Regeln zu bestimmen. Nicht Produzenten der Wirklichkeit sind sie, allenfalls deren Verwalter. Der zweite Aspekt dieses Satzes liegt in dem Prädikat "[sie] gehen als," indem es auf eine Verschiebung hinweist: Die Menschen sind nicht das, als was sie erscheinen, sondern sie geben nur vor, etwas zu sein.

Dieses Rollen-Spielen präzisiert Wysocki im weiteren Text anhand der dort auftretenden Figuren, die wechselnde Rollen übernehmen: Apollinaires Gedächtnis als His Masters Voice, Fantomas als Guillaume Apollinaire, Marie als Anna O. (20, 40, 79). Doch führt sie dieses Spielen mit Identitäten noch weiter. Das Individuum ist in *Abendlandleben* keineswegs, wie sein Name sagt, unteilbar. Die Figuren erscheinen im Gegenteil jeweils vervierfacht; jede einzelne Teilfigur kann dabei unabhängig oder in Wahlpartnerschaften neue Rollen übernehmen. Während etwa Fantomas 1 und 2 auf der Suche nach einem passenden Kopf sind (74 f.), erscheinen Fantomas 3 und 4 als Albert Camus (77).

Die Identität des Einzelnen verschwindet hinter Kostümierungen, wobei allerdings fraglich ist, ob sie überhaupt als invarianter Kern existiert. Für Guillaume Apollinaire lautet die Anweisung im Stück: "vollständig übersetzt in das Material eines Abendanzugs" (11). Hier verbleibt kein unveränderlicher Rest unter einer Hülle. Der Mensch ist die jeweilige Rolle. Es gibt keine verläßliche, verborgene Größe; weder die Vorstellung der Identität hat eine Entsprechung in der Wirklichkeit noch die der Natur des Menschen, denn es existiert unter der Hülle auch kein Körper mehr. Die Welt des Menschen aus NEU GLÜCK ist eine "Welt ohne Haut und Fleisch" (11). Überlagert von Kostümierungen ist keine Natur auszumachen. Die Geschichte der Europi beginnt bei Wysocki bereits mit der zweiten Natur, der Kultur also. Der Mensch ist damit auch nicht als Teil einer ursprünglichen Natur vorstellbar. Doch wird mit dem Mangel an "Haut und Fleisch" ebenso—analog zu dem Bild der auf den Blumentopf reduzierten Natur—auch die Reduktion des Menschen um seine über den Körper vermittelte, sinnliche Wahrnehmungsfähigkeit angedeutet.

Die progressive Ausprägung dieser Merkmale NEU GLÜCKS korrespondiert mit einer beständig voranschreitenden Lichtwerdung im Stück: Zum einen wird die sich verbessernde Arbeit des Gedächtnisses begleitet von einer immer perfekteren Ausleuchtung des Hirninnenraums.

Das GEDÄCHTNIS zeigt NOCH Zufälliges.... Einzelnes lebt auf.... Anderes bleibt im Dunkeln (37).

Das GEDÄCHTNIS arbeitet NOCH immer disfunktional. Verstecke. Dunkle Zonen, die chirurgisch NOCH unerschlossen sind (41).

Das GEDÄCHTNIS, VOM Licht der Operationslampe strahlend erfaßt. Alle Winkel glücklich ausgeleuchtet (109).

Zum anderen zeigen aber auch die Spieldurchgänge eine vergleichbare Vorwärtsbewegung. Im Verlauf des Stücks wird auch die Welt der Europi immer heller ausgeleuchtet. Wysocki spricht im ersten Bild von der "Schwärze des Anfangs" und einem unaufhaltsam blauer werdenden Himmel, an dem stetig neue Sonnen aufsteigen (19, 31, 36, 40, 73, 92, 94, 119).

120.000 Lux. Eine verdurstende Natur. Die Stube der Menschheit...steht blank und häuslich da.... Die EUROPI sind von ihrer Kindheit geheilt, von den vegetativen Lauten der Fischer und Jäger, vom Nisten Lauern Fallenstellen (68).

Um die Bedeutung des Prozesses des Hellerwerdens zu klären, bedarf es nicht einmal der metaphorischen Ausdeutung, es reicht ein Blick auf eine andere europäische Sprache. "Enlightenment" im Englischen erfaßt sowohl wörtlich den deutschen Begriff "Lichtwerdung" als auch den deutschen Begriff "Aufklärung." Wysocki bestimmt NEU GLÜCK damit als Europa seit der Aufklärung und die ersten beiden Sätze der "biographischen Notiz" sind nun deutlich einzuordnen als Zustandsbeschreibungen des Abendlandes in der Folge des Aufklärungsgedankens.

III. Gesellschaftsspiele

Entgegen der Idee der Autonomie des Ich eröffnet Wysockis theatralische Operation der Kopföffnung einen Einblick in die Regel-Haftigkeit der Persönlichkeitsentwicklung (Roeder 132), die vor den Augen des durch ihren Kunstgriff außen gehaltenen Betrachters "spielerisch" trainiert wird. Dabei dokumentiert nicht allein die drei- bis viermalige Wiederholung die Serialität des Geschehens, sondern auch die Benennung der Textpassagen als "Spiele." Denn im allgemeinen ist Gesellschafts-Spielen ein fester Regelkorpus inhärent, der einen immer gleichen Rahmen für die wechselnden Spieler festlegt. Auch der bereits von Anfang an vorgegebene Umfang der einzelnen "Spiele" unterstützt die Vorstellung eines festen Umrisses. Die mit jedem Durchgang erfolgende Auffüllung der Textlücken ist eine Vervollständigung, die die Grenzen unberührt läßt und deshalb auch nicht innovativ wirken kann. Die "Spiele" geben den Hintergrund für die Akteure Fantomas, Billy, Mariezibill und Marie im Vordergrund. Sie sind die Determinanten eines augenblicklichen Geschehens und stellen somit die handelnden Akteure als abhängig von unbewußten gesellschaftlichen Strukturen aus: "Ihr Zusammenspiel folgt einer dramatischen Syntax...einer szenischen Überschreitung, die eine Traumdeutung wäre" (14).

Wysocki entwirft zwanzig verschiedene "Spiele," die sie mit teilweise fiktiven, teilweise realen Personen der politischen und kulturellen Geschichte ausstattet, und die unterschiedliche Themenschwerpunkte aufgreifen. So gibt es eine erste Gruppe von vier "Spielen," die versucht, die allgemeinen Grundlagen des aufgeklärten Abendlandes und die Methoden seiner Weltaneignung zu bestimmen; eine zweite Gruppe mit zehn "Spielen" thematisiert die Auswirkungen dieser Grundlagen auf das menschliche Selbstverständnis und die menschliche Lebenswelt, eine dritte Gruppe schließlich konzentriert sich auf die Darstellung der Geschlechter und ihr Zusammenspiel.

IV. Wissenschaftliche Weltaneignung

Das "Schließlich wurde das Modell von Descartes noch übertroffen" Spiel ist der zeitlich größte Rückgriff, den Wysocki in *Abendlandleben* in die Kulturgeschichte vornimmt. Dies legt nahe anzunehmen, daß es den Beginn der im Stück thematisierten Entwicklung der Europi markiert: Descartes ist im Allgemeinwissen gespeichert als der "erste systematische Denker der Neuzeit" (*Konversationslexikon* 278) und damit als Wegbereiter einer veränderten Weltsicht, der modernen Wissenschaft. Als deren Charakteristika gelten Systemdenken (= Herausarbeiten von Kategorien und Methoden), Universalität (= nichts kann sich auf Dauer dem untersuchenden Zugriff entziehen), das Unfertige (= dem der Fortschrittsgedanke inhärent ist), Allgemeingültigkeit und damit verbunden die Forderung nach der zwingenden Gewißheit der Erkenntnis, zu der notwendig auch die jederzeitige Nachprüfbarkeit durch Dritte gehört (Jaspers 83 ff.).

Der Grundsatz der zwingenden Gewißheit und Nachprüfbarkeit macht die über die Sinne des Einzelnen wahrgenommene äußere Erscheinung der

Dinge fragwürdig (Jaspers 86). Sie ist ein bisher nicht ins System integrierbarer Rest, der als "Natur" (100) definiert wird. Soll er das System nicht irritieren, muß er zunächst ausgegliedert werden, indem man ihn als unwesentlich disqualifiziert.

> Das ist neu. Neuzeitlich. Das Dunkle zu verstecken hinten in der Dunkelheit. Es genügt ja, UNWESENTLICHES EINFACH WEGZUDENKEN. FARBE HÄRTE GESTALT TON UND TEMPERATUR. Descartes stellt fest, ohne diese Banalitäten sind sie wirklicher DIE DINGE (100 f.).

Um eine wahre Aussage (wahr im Sinne des wissenschaftlichen Denkens) über die Dinge treffen zu können, bedarf es also zweier paralleler Operationen: Zum einen muß von der sinnlichen Qualität der Dinge abstrahiert werden, zum anderen aber auch von der sinnlichen Wahrnehmungsfähigkeit des Menschen. Die Konsequenz ist die Entsinnlichung der Natur und damit auch des Menschen als Natur. "Descartes ein heiterer Entbehrungskünstler, wendet nun seine Methode auch auf sich selber an. Descartes: als reine Substanz. Tonlos farblos gestaltlos" (101).

Das Modell Descartes' und seine Perfektionierung ist, wie Foucault es beschreibt, der Übergang der mechanischen Berechenbarkeit zur Berechenbarkeit des Lebendigen (1978, 165). "Ich denke, also bin ich," die Vorherrschaft des Geistes über den Körper, ist die Voraussetzung für die Entwicklung einer Erkenntnisform, die, absehend von der äußeren Erscheinung und der subjektiven Wahrnehmung, sich unter die Oberfläche der Gegenstände ihrer Untersuchung gräbt. "Die Forscher blicken durch ihre Gläser.... Den Fröschen wird ein neues Futter gereicht. Gehirne atmen.... Lange Tabellen wachsen aus ihren Lungen heraus. Aus Mündern und Hälsen. Die laufenden Füße lassen Zahlenreihen hinter sich zurück" (107).

Das "Embryo in Spiritus" Spiel führt vor, daß die Erscheinung als Gesamtheit in Frage gestellt wird, und so auch die Intaktheit der Oberfläche nicht mehr zwingend ist.

> Sie betrachten kleine Frösche und notieren ihre Werte. Die Frösche stehen aufrecht da.... Sie trippeln rhythmisch. STELZEN. GALOPPIEREN.... Ihre Pupillen sind stark geweitet, ihr Nervennetz angespannt. In der Nähe ihrer Gelenke riecht es nach Spiritus. Eine Knochenschere schneidet sehr vergnügt (107).

Der Weg der Erkenntnis, das Denken gegen den Augenschein, das ins Innere der Erscheinungen vordringen will, ist bei Wysocki direkt ins Bild gesetzt als Zerschneiden eines intakten Körpers. "Wahre" wissenschaftliche Erkenntnis erfolgt danach also nur im Töten des Lebendigen. Natur ist als eigene Qualität verlorengegangen. Sie ist nur noch als für den Menschen gemachte, instrumentalisierte Größe denkbar.

Dem gleichen systematischen Zugriff entspringt die Idee einer sich beständig perfektionierenden Natur, die Wysocki im "Man vergleiche unsere Hand mit der Delphinflosse, mit den Flügeln der Fledermaus, mit der Grabklaue des Maulwurfs" Spiel aufgreift.

Die Darstellung homologer Organe gehört zu den obligaten Veranschaulichungen der Evolutionstheorie im Schulunterricht (z.B. Lindner 301). Sie soll im Blick auf Baupläne den Beweis für die Differenzierung einer einheitlichen Ausgangsstruktur erbringen. Doch gilt es, nicht allein Differenzierung im allgemeinen darzustellen, sondern die Entwicklung zu "immer höher differenzierten und umweltunabhängigeren Formen" (Lindner 292). Wenn Wysocki also schreibt: "Man erkennt schon die Züge des heutigen EUROPI QUER DURCH DIE REPTIL- UND SÄUGETIERSYSTEME" (102) so beinhaltet das zwei Konsequenzen.

Zum einen erscheint im Rückblick die Entwicklung als kontinuierlich und zielgerichtet. Evolution wäre danach der Ausdruck einer an Vernunft- und Ordnungskriterien orientierten Natur. Zum anderen scheint, daß mit dem Menschen als "höchstentwickeltem und umweltunabhängigstem" Wesen, der (vorläufige) Endpunkt der Entwicklung erreicht ist. Doch ist auch diese Erkenntnis nur um den Preis des Todes der zu betrachtenden Natur zu erlangen: Erst der Vergleich der Skelette gibt Aufschluß über eine Gleichartigkeit der Strukturen. Die wissenschaftliche Weltaneignung und die ihr zugeschriebene Bedeutung für die Freiheit des Menschen wird also dargestellt als Prozeß fortschreitender Distanzierung von der Natur und schließlich der Vernichtung des Lebens.

Mit dem "Plastik als Bilderrätsel" Spiel beschreibt Wysocki den Endpunkt des oben skizzierten Prozesses.[4]

Koffer Bürste Autokarosserie Spielzeug Stoff Röhre Schlüssel Eimer Folie Schmuckstück: ALS SKALA DER ERFINDUNGEN. Hier fühlt man sie wieder, die magische Wirkung der Gegenstände. Ihre Einheit. Den Schauer der Identität.... Immer auf's neue wird es von Hitzebädern überrascht (103).

Spricht Wysocki hier von der magischen Wirkung der Gegenstände, so beschreibt Roland Barthes die Herstellung der unterschiedlichsten Gegenstände aus Plastik als "magische Operation par excellence" (79). Sie führt die Umwandlung von Materie als Schöpfungsakt vor. Ohne die Notwendigkeit, Stadien der Entwicklung durchlaufen zu müssen, entstehen die Dinge aus einem gemeinsamen Ursprung.

Was über die wissenschaftlichen Analysen, die Sezierung des Lebens, verlorengegangen ist, reproduziert der Mensch mit Hilfe von Plastik. Mit Plastik hat er eine Materie entwickelt, anhand derer ein genuiner Schöpfungsakt rekonstruiert/reproduziert werden kann, wobei die neue "Urmaterie" wesentliche Merkmale besitzt, die die Selbstdefinition der modernen, wissenschaftlich denkenden Menschen nicht in Frage stellen: Plastik, so Barthes, ist Ausdruck einer neuen Ebene der Imitation, die darauf verzichtet, an das ursprüngliche Maß der Imitation, den mineralischen oder animalischen Ursprung, zu erinnern (81).

Die Dinge gehen in ihrem Gebrauch auf. Plastik erfüllt die Voraussetzung von Materie, aus der alles hervorgehen kann, ohne an die Herkunft des Menschen aus der Natur zu erinnern. Und indem es unter der Einwirkung des Menschen und seiner Technik metamorphisch seine Gestalt wandelt, kann sich der Mensch schließlich als neuer, göttergleicher Schöpfer nicht allein der Wirklichkeit, sondern des Lebens allgemein imaginieren. "Die Hierarchie der Substanzen ist zerstört, eine einzige ersetzt sie alle: die ganze Welt kann plastifiziert werden, und sogar das Lebendige selbst, denn...[man] beginnt schon Aorten aus Plastik herzustellen" (Barthes 81). An diesem Punkt jedoch geht Wysocki über Barthes hinaus und hebt die dialektische Bewegung dieses anscheinend geradlinigen Emanzipationsprozesses hervor. Die Konsequenz der wissenschaftlichen Weltaneignung, die über die empirische Erfassung der Natur(-gesetze) die Natur für den Menschen dienstbar machen will, ist eben nicht allein die Distanzierung, sondern die Zerstörung. Im modernen Krieg des Menschen gegen sich selbst und seine Lebensbedingungen wird die künstliche Substanz überleben. Im Evolutionsprozeß ist sie die "Umweltunabhängigste."

V. Vernunftherrschaft und Herrschaft der Technik

Zwei Konsequenzen des Aufklärungsgedankens, die Bergfleth in seinen vehement anti-aufklärerischen Thesen konstatiert, werden ebenfalls in *Abendlandleben* thematisiert. Sie sind Gegenstand der zweiten Gruppe von "Spielen."

...die größte Vernunft verendet in der Vernunftherrschaft, die ihrerseits verendet in der Herrschaftsvernunft der Technokratie.... Die Aufklärung hat sich nämlich klamm und heimlich weiterentwickelt zur technokratischen Rationalisierung, die unsere gesamte wissenschaftlich-technische Umwelt bestimmt (Bergfleth 10, 9).

Die Gefahr der Verkehrung einer emanzipativen in eine restriktive, Herrschaft ausübende Vernunft wird unter anderem aus Systemdenken und dem Anspruch auf Universalität hergeleitet (u.a. Adorno/Horkheimer 19). Die Suche nach Gesetzmäßigkeiten birgt notwendig auch die Differenzierung in Norm und Abweichung, d.h., die Ausgrenzung von nicht in das System integrierbaren Phänomenen. Am augenfälligsten wird der Aspekt einer repressiven Vernunft sicher gerade an der Verbegrifflichung und einer damit kontrastierenden Trennung von Vernunft und Wahnsinn (Foucault 1977; Nitschke). Die von der Vernunft abweichende Realitätswahrnehmung wird im Begriff Wahnsinn stigmatisiert und muß, soll sie das System nicht gefährden, aus der Gesellschaft ausgeschlossen und interniert werden. "Die Irren lernen die REIHE kennen, ihre erste Lektion....

Die Psyche turnt. Sie muß sich noch an vieles gewöhnen. An Scheinwerfer, Wachposten, Wachtürme, an Staub und sengende Sonne" (118). Die Reihe als Bild der Gleichmäßigkeit gegenüber der ungleichmäßig arbeitenden Wahrnehmung, der "turnenden" Psyche der Irren, braucht die Gewalt der Internierungslager, um sich zu behaupten; sie wird zur Komplizin totalitärer Herrschaft.[5] Doch zeigt Wysocki, daß der Mechanismus nicht nur an den Orten offener Gewalt sichtbar wird, sondern auch dort wirksam ist, wo die Hoffnung auf Veränderung in den letzten zwei Jahrhunderten ihren Platz fand: in der kommunistischen Utopie. Diese Utopie aber ist soweit schematisiert und systematisiert, daß ihr Inhalt über Gesetzmäßigkeiten eilig übermittelt werden kann:

> Tasse Teller und Frühstücksbrötchen in ihrem HISTORISCHEN CHARAKTER SEHR AUGENFÄLLIG.... Lenins Arbeitszimmer öffnet sich jetzt für die Besucher aus Frankreich. Eilig macht er sie mit den Gesetzmäßigkeiten des Bolschewismus vertraut (109).

Tasse, Teller, Frühstücksbrötchen existieren weder in ihrer Gegenständlichkeit noch in ihrem Gebrauchswert für den Menschen. Von Funktion und Körperlichkeit abstrahiert erscheint ihre Einordnung nach überindividuellen Maßstäben zwanghaft. Als die Utopie zur Wissenschaft wurde, ist aus dem "Nicht-Ort" ein fester Ort im System geworden, der keine revolutionäre Energie auf sich vereinigen kann, sondern im Gegenteil systemerhaltend zu wirken scheint.[6]

Das "Apollinaire vor einem Tonaufnahmegerät" Spiel skizziert nur umrißartig den Vorgang der Tonaufnahme selbst—ein großer Teil des Spiels wird von Apollinaires Gedicht "Les Colchiques" eingenommen. Das Hauptaugenmerk scheint auf der Umwandlung der menschlichen Stimme in die technisch gebannte Stimme "His Masters Voice" zu liegen, wobei das Bild des in der Trichteröffnung des technischen Apparates verschwindenden Kopfes die Aussage des Spieles verdeutlicht. Identifiziert man üblicherweise diesen in der Trichteröffnung verschwindenden Kopf nach dem Emblem der Plattenfirma Electrola als Kopf eines Hundes, so arrangiert Wysocki den Text allerdings so, daß der Kopf nun als der Kopf des vor dem Aufnahmegerät stehenden Menschen vorgestellt werden kann.

"Das Kunstwerk im Zeitalter seiner technischen Reproduzierbarkeit" erlaubt zwar die weite Verbreitung der Kunst, doch es nimmt der künstlerischen Darbietung gleichzeitig die "Aura des Hier und Jetzt" (Benjamin 29). Die Fixierung des Kunstwerks auf reproduzierbare Trägermedien gibt dem Originalitätsgedanken den Abschied. Doch was möglicherweise auch als Chance zu einer veränderten, vom Subjektideal abgekehrten, Sicht auf die Welt durch die Kunst begriffen werden kann, wird hier von Wysocki im Falle Apollinaires als Einsaugen des Menschen in die Technik ins Bild gesetzt. Gerade der Kopf, Körperteil, in dem die

Vernunft vermutet wird und das die Technik kreiert hat, wird verschlungen von seiner Schöpfung: "His Masters Voice"—Allegorie des mechanisierten Menschen. Nicht mehr die Technik steht im Dienst des Menschen, sondern der Mensch im Dienst der Technik.

Eine Lok, Symbol des wissenschaftlich-technischen Fortschritts und Bild der grenzüberschreitenden Bewegung des Menschen, steht im Mittelpunkt des "Wie man eine Eisenbahn rentabel gestaltet" Spiels.

> Hitze-Insekten. Jeder erledigt seinen Handgriff, in regelmäßigen Intervallen.... Das tägliche Ritual: die Lok wird reisefertig gemacht. Alles wird wie immer durch Hände und Zangen zügig geregelt.... Man erfindet immer komplexere Muster. (Trotz mehrjähriger Untersuchung hat man nicht feststellen können, daß repetitive Arbeit schädigt.... Die Handgriffe werden immer heiterer (110).

Doch die Menschen machen die Lok nur täglich reisefertig, sie fährt nicht ab, um die Menschen mitzunehmen. Wie eine riesige Bienenkönigin thront die Maschine im Zentrum dieses Spiels. Die Menschen sind spezialisierte Arbeiter, jeder notwendig, doch ohne Einsicht in den Gesamtzusammenhang wiederholen sie immer die gleichen Handgriffe.

Die Bedienung des in der Lok manifest gewordenen Fortschritts erfordert keine Kreativität, sondern eine durch Spezialisierung repetitive Arbeit. Die "komplexeren Muster" beziehen sich auf die Organisation des Zusammenspiels, das immer differenzierter wird, die Handgriffe des einzelnen dagegen müssen sich immer stärker vereinfachen. Der wissenschaftlich-technische Fortschritt ist das System, er zeigt keinen Weg über die Grenzen des Bestehenden hinaus. Die Rationalisierung der Arbeit hat die Menschen zu Werkzeugen funktionalisiert: Die "Hände" scheinen sich von den "Zangen" kaum mehr zu unterscheiden.

VI. Geschlechterdifferenz

Die dritte Gruppe von "Spielen" thematisiert Erscheinungsweisen des "Männlichen" bzw. "Weiblichen."

> TREPANATION UND BESICHTIGUNG DER KÖPFE. Man erwartete kein rotes Blut.... Und doch überrascht die azurne Fassung des Gehirns.... In winzigen Hautlappen ist die Entstehung der Arten untergebracht. Alles so wohnlich und angenehm wie im CHAMBRE SÉPARÉE (105).

Das freigelegte Gedächtnis spiegelt die ordnende Kraft der Vernunft. Eingehüllt in die azurne Fassung erscheint das Gehirn des Helden als eine von einer Atmosphäre umhüllte, eigene Welt, in der die menschlichen Erfahrungen und menschheitsgeschichtlichen Traditionen einer bestimmten Ordnung folgend aufgeteilt und abgespeichert sind. Die Ordnung des Gedächtnisses scheint die Ordnung der Welt nur zu spiegeln. Doch wird der Mann im "Er liebt daß Ordnung ist" Spiel als "Bewohner und

Bewahrer des Musée de l'Homme" vorgestellt (101), dessen Kopf die Kategorien der Einordnung produziert: "Er notiert. Protokolliert. Erfindet neue Ordnungsmuster" (101). Mit dem Wort "erfinden" erscheint Ordnung als zufälliges, willkürliches Produkt subjektiver Phantasie und keineswegs als unverrückbar und von Zufällen unabhängig. Der Mann ist Fantomas, das Phantom-As, wie Wysocki am Anfang des Stückes die Namensfindung erklärt (17). Er ist nicht nur Meister der Erfindung einer außerhalb von ihm existierenden Welt, sondern der Mensch/Mann[7] als selbstbestimmtes Wesen selbst ist die größte Fiktion innerhalb einer imaginierten Welt (112 f.).

Zerstörung, Auflösung von Zusammenhängen und in deren Folge die Marginalisierung von Mensch und Natur wurden als Konsequenzen des wissenschaftlich-technischen Fortschritts und der Herrschaft der Technik vorgestellt. Doch werden sie im Stück auch in die Sphäre männlicher Erotik versetzt, etwa im "Wie man eine Eisenbahn rentabel gestaltet" Spiel: "Und eine Lok.... Gewichst und gebürstet, ein voluminöses Organ" (110).[8] Nicht nur die phallische Form der Lok, sondern auch das umgangssprachliche Wort "gewichst," verweisen Ordnungs- und Fortschrittsdenken in den Bereich der männlichen Selbstbefriedigung (106).

Jede Figur aus der "Vordergrundebene" des Stücks hat eine Passage zur Verfügung, die allein der Selbstdarstellung vorbehalten ist (*Abendlandleben* 35–37 [Fantomas], 28–30 [Mariezibill], 61–63 [Billy], 79–80 [Marie]). Die Passage des Fantomas ist überschrieben mit dem Titel "Stammesentwicklung." Fantomas 1–4 skizzieren darin mit verteilten Rollen eine weitergedachte Evolutionsgeschichte.

> Ganz MEIN KULTURELL, die Gelenke streckten sich, dann gaben sie nach und rissen aus.... Die Hände stellten sich auf Propeller um, die Arme festigten sich zu Eisenteilen, das Blut gefror, so gefiele mir das Blut, Memoire setzte aus.... Der Himmel war so blau, das Genital flachte ich ab, die Beine warf ich wie Flügel um.... Ein monotones Rauschen legte los.... Das Herz...schlug regelmäßig an und plötzlich heulte ein Motor in mir auf...sonnte sich das symmetrische Fleisch, ein Rhythmus für Götter (36).

Gliedmaßen, Augen und Geschlechtsorgan werden im Verlauf dieser Evolution keine sinnlichen, sondern maschinelle Aufgaben zugewiesen: Hände tasten nicht mehr, sie drehen als Propeller, das Genital muß aus aerodynamischen Gesichtspunkten abgeflacht werden. Der hier beschriebene Prozeß ist die Entwicklung zur Maschine. Doch wird deutlich, da es die Selbstpräsentation der Figuren Fantomas 1–4 ist, daß Wysocki diese als männlich identifiziert. Sie greift damit eine Typisierung des Mannes auf, die sie bereits in ihrem Essay "Weiblichkeit und Modernität" am Beispiel von Virginia Woolfs Vater, Leslie Stephenson, entwickelt hatte: den Flieger (24), und läßt sie in der Flugmaschine kulminieren.

Mit der Maschinisierung des Mannes, der Umwandlung des Fliegers zur Flugmaschine, kehrt Wysocki zu den Basisstrukturen zurück, die sie in den "Spielen" entwickelt hat: Ordnungs- und Systemdenken, Gleichmaß und Technisierung. Der maschinelle Rhythmus ersetzt die fließende Bewegung des Lebens: "Das Blut gefror." Am Ende des Prozesses der zunehmenden Erhebung des Menschen über die Natur, die natürlich auch im Bild des fliegenden Menschen gefaßt ist, steht die Erhebung der Maschine über den Menschen. Die Technik als Instrument der Herrschaft über die Natur hat dann ganz zu sich selbst gefunden: Sie ist Instrument einer unmenschlichen Herrschaft.

Fantomas, kurz vor seinem Tod, am Ende des Stückes an der Schnur der Rolläden hängend, hat den Kontakt zum Boden verloren, das Licht, das nun unschwer als Licht der Aufklärung gedeutet werden kann, ist nicht mehr abzuschalten, es zwingt zu ununterbrochenem Wachsein. Der Schlaf und Traum, als Territorium der Unvernunft und Unlogik und mit Elisabeth Lenk notwendiger Bereich des Ausgleichs (14), existiert nicht mehr. Das Licht der Aufklärung, das die Emanzipation des Menschen aus der Unfreiheit bringen sollte, ist zur Folter geworden.

Im "Flieger grüß mir die Sonne" Spiel öffnet sich über das Bild des Fliegers und seiner Selbstapotheose durch die Umwandlung zur Maschine jedoch zusätzlich eine konkrete politische Dimension: Die dort genannten Flieger-"Asse," teils dem Film, teils der Realität entnommen, waren allesamt, ungeachtet nachträglicher Zurechtrückungen, mit dem NS-Staat verbunden: Hans Albers (als Flieger in "FP1 antwortet nicht"), Heinz Rühmann (als "Quax") in der Filmindustrie und damit in die Propaganda-Absichten des Staates verwoben, Ernst Udet, ehemaliger Jagdflieger des ersten Weltkriegs und Generalluftzeugmeister (1938) sowie Rudolf Hess, als Stellvertreter Adolf Hitlers, der mit seinem legendären Flug nach Schottland Friedensverhandlungen mit Großbritannien führen wollte, um danach zu einer gemeinsamen Politik gegen die UdSSR zu finden.

Wysocki zeigt mit der Anspielung auf den Faschismus eine mögliche aktuelle Konkretisierung der anerkannt wirksamen Strukturen. Der Faschismus erscheint danach als Konsequenz einer männlich dominierten Weltaneignung und keinesfalls als "Rückfall in die Barbarei" und als Auflodern archaischer Unvernunft, sondern als Konsequenz eines Übermaßes an instrumenteller Vernunft (immer natürlich orientiert an den Kriterien, die Wysocki in den "Methoden-Spielen" an die Hand gibt).

Den "Frauen-Spielen" ordne ich "Das Flieger grüß mir die Sonne Spiel," "Das Strip Tease" Spiel sowie das "Amour fou und keep smiling" Spiel zu. Namentlich vertreten sind in diesen "Spielen" nur zwei der drei weiblichen Figuren: Billy und Mariezibill. Marie erscheint dagegen nur auf der Vordergrundebene. Alle drei werden gleichermaßen als Bräute bezeichnet: Billy, die mechanische Braut; Mariezibill, die vamp-iristische Braut; und Marie, die hysterische Braut. Legt man Wysockis Bestimmung der "Braut" aus den Essays zugrunde, so sind die einzelnen Frauentypen, ungeachtet ihrer unterschiedlichen Erscheinungsweise, primär definiert über ihre Bezogenheit auf den Mann. Eine Collage von Hannah Höch aus den zwanziger Jahren kommentierend sagt Wysocki in den *Frösten der Freiheit*: "Die Braut ist die Frau als Geführte" (14).

Die Bräute Billy und Mariezibill repräsentieren zwei Typen, die Wysocki bereits in den Essays als Grundmuster patriarchaler Weiblichkeit aufgenommen hatte und auf die sie ihre porträtierten Frauen wieder abgefragt hat: Das College-Girl/die Angestellte und die Femme fatale (den Vamp). Billy ist die Angestellte, deren beruflicher Erfolg die Schattenseiten des Systems vergessen läßt: "KURZ UND GUT. HEPP UND HOPP. / BILLY TRAUMLOS IM GALOPP" (62).

Wie Fantomas kurz vor seinem Tod den Schlaf der Vernunft entbehrend—traumlos—hat sie sich ganz dem Fortschritt verschrieben und die technokratische Leistungsnorm verinnerlicht. Was zählt ist die Perfektion: Pünktlichkeit, Diensteifrigkeit, der perfekt durchtrainierte und gewartete Körper (62 f.). Doch spitzt die Autorin diesen Typus weiter zu. Indem sie ihn auf der "Spiele"-Ebene mit dem des männlichen "Fliegers" koppelt, wird die "mechanische Braut" zur Mittäterin. "...diese Girl-Maschinen. Teil eines Menschenstroms in einem unaufhörlichen Vorwärts. Aufwärts. Himmelwärts. Billy hat den Blick für das 'höhere Wesen' des Mannes. ER IST DIE FIRMA UND DAS FIRMAMENT" (116). Billys Blick nach oben umfaßt gleichermaßen die Ausrichtung auf den Mann, die Annäherung an sein System, wie auch die mitvollzogene Distanzierung von der Natur. Bedenkt man die politische Konsequenz, die in der Nennung der Flieger-Namen angedeutet war, so wird sie—wie Wysocki dies auch im Riefenstahl-Essay zeigt (1981, 77 f.)—auch zur politischen Komplizin bei der Errichtung totalitärer Herrschaft.

Die Selbstdarstellung der "vamp-iristischen Braut" Mariezibill zielt ganz auf die bekannten Phantasien zum Vamp bzw. zur Femme fatale: Die pelzumhüllte Frau, mit ihrer blutrünstigen Lust am Männermord. Ich möchte auf diesen Aspekt nicht weiter eingehen, zumal diese Phantasien bereits mehrfach aufgearbeitet worden sind.[9] Wichtig dagegen scheint mir ein genauer Blick auf das "Strip Tease" Spiel. Wysocki erweitert dort den Rahmen dieses Typus über die erwähnten Charakteristika hinaus. Zum einen wird schon durch die Beschreibung Mariezibills die Femme fatale als Artefakt und keineswegs als weibliche Natur kenntlich gemacht (117). Zum anderen lehnt sich die Autorin, ähnlich wie im Fall des "Plastik als Bilderrätsel" Spiel, sogar bis hin zum Titel an den Essay Roland Barthes "Strip Tease" an.

> Mariezibill schaut an ihrem Aufzug herunter. Sie kann sich nur als Pflanze betrachten. Als BLÄTTERUNDBLÜTEN. In DIAMANTFORM.... Oder

als Tierleib.... Als FEDERUNDFLÜGEL. Als PELZUNDPERLEN-KETTE. Eine Zigarettenspitze wächst aus ihrer Hand, krallenartig. Schwarze Strumpfbänder sitzen tief im Fleisch der Schenkel (117).

Der Exotismus der Umhüllungen entrückt die reale Frau so sehr dem menschlichen Zugriff, daß sie auch entkleidet von den Accessoires ihrer Ausstellung noch tief durchdrungen bleibt (Barthes 68). An anderer Stelle hat Barthes in diesem Zusammenhang den Begriff des "Luxusobjekts" gebraucht und als immer mit der Natur verbunden, an seinen mineralischen oder animalischen Ursprung erinnernd, definiert. Mariezibill als "FederundFlügel," mit dem diamantengeschmückten Geschlecht—das, wie Barthes schreibt, immer den Endpunkt des Strip tease darstellt (70)—ist in ihrer Verhüllung Verweis auf die Natur. Als Tierleib stellt sie Natur dar und ist damit, nach der von Wysocki aufgezeigten Logik, Objekt der wissenschaftlichen Weltaneignung, deren Methode auf Beherrschung und Überwindung zielt. Die Entblößung des Körpers steht dazu nur in scheinbarem Gegensatz. "Mariezibill bei dem Versuch, ihre Umhüllungen loszuwerden. Eine Sisyphosarbeit: Die Haut wächst immer wieder zu.... Ihre wirkliche Haut hat sie nie gesehen, nicht eine einzige Stelle ihres Körpers" (117).

"Strip Tease" erinnert an das immer wieder nachwachsende Fleisch des verwundeten Prometheus: Die zerstörerische Macht liegt nicht allein im Angriff, sondern im immerwährenden Kreislauf von Unversehrtheit und Verwundung, der gerade darin absolute Herrschaft offenbart, daß kein Ausweg, und sei es im Tod, besteht. So sind auch nicht die Entkleidungen der Ausdruck männlicher Herrschaft im Voyeurismus, die die Frau als Objekt der Lust verfügbar machen, sondern die nachwachsenden Umhüllungen sind es, die die Wiederinbesitznahme des eigenen Körpers und seiner Repräsentationen verhindern, damit aber den Status eines ebenbürtigen Gegenübers verweigern. "Strip Tease" ist sowohl das Bild für die männliche Kolonisierung des weiblichen Ich als auch für die Domestizierung des Körpers und der Sexualität, also auch der sinnlichen Erfahrung, indem die Frau, als ambivalente Natur bedrohlich, aber im Ritual der Ein- und Entkleidung gleichzeitig gebannt, ausgestellt wird.

VII. Auflärung als Prozeß der Kolonisierung

Im einleitenden Kapitel II "Entfernungen," in dem Wysocki technische Hinweise für die Aufführung des Stücks gibt, definiert sie das "Gedächtnis" als bestehend aus einer Hintergrundebene, den "Spielen," und einer Vordergrundebene, dem "Musée de l'Homme."

Das Museum ist erreichbar durch eine Tür, die sie als "kolonialistisch" bezeichnet. Gleichzeitig verbindet sie in einer Regieanweisung diese Tür mit der allmählichen Erhellung des Gedächtnisses bzw. des Abendlandes. Der Gedanke der Aufklärung wird hier also mit einer auf

Eroberung zielenden Perspektive korreliert. Die Reisen der Forscher und Entdecker erwecken nur auf den ersten Blick den Eindruck, mit fremden Kulturen bekannt machen zu wollen. Der Besuch der Fremde dient weniger dem Verständnis fremder Kulturen, als der Konstituierung des eigenen Ich. "Besonders deutlich ist diese Subsumierung des Fremden unter die Perspektive des Eigenen in den Versuchen, die Wilden als Repräsentanten eines früheren Zustandes in der eigenen Geschichte zu betrachten: die Wilden als Vorstufe bzw. Ursprung der Zivilisation" (Weigel 182). Was in den "Spielen" der Blick unter die Oberfläche war, nämlich die Suche nach einheitlichen Grundbausteinen, aus denen ein gemeinsamer Ursprung des Lebens und die herausragende Stellung des Menschen abgeleitet werden sollte, ist im Blick auf die menschheitsgeschichtliche Entwicklung die Einordnung fremder Kulturen in einen linearen Prozeß: Sie negiert qualitative Unterschiede zugunsten der Geschlossenheit des eigenen Erkenntnissystems. Die abweichende Erscheinung muß aus dieser Perspektive notwendig als insuffiziente Variante des Eigenen betrachtet werden. Der Prozeß der Vereinnahmung bedingt gleichzeitig die Festschreibung als Abweichung. Die gleiche Tendenz sieht Weigel im Umgang mit "Weiblichkeit," die ebenfalls mit der Aufklärung ihre bis heute gültigen Grundlagen bekam. "Die Frauen unterliegen einer epidemischen Wildheit.... Sie sind zwar äußerlich zivilisierter als wir, aber innerlich sind sie wahre Wilde geblieben" (Diderot, in Weigel 171).

Diesen Satz Diderots, den Weigel an den Anfang ihres Vortrags gestellt hat, offenbart die Ideologisierung des "Weiblichen" als zutiefst ambivalente Erscheinung. Nach außen dem Mann an Zivilisiertheit überlegen, verbirgt sich unter der Oberfläche eine nur mühsam zurückgestaute Wildheit. Da jedoch die Frauen ebenso wie die Wilden in die einheitliche Perspektive auf die Welt integriert werden, rücken sie, wie diese, als Repräsentanten eines früheren Stadiums der Zivilisation, das der Mann als Betrachter bereits hinter sich wähnt, näher an den Zustand der Ursprünglichkeit, der ja auch als unmittelbare Nähe zur Natur definiert wird.

> Die Wilden in der Ferne bilden den Ort des Fremden, zu dem sich der europäische Mensch in eine historische Beziehung setzt, er besetzt dabei die Position des Fortschritts. Die Frau in der Nähe bildet den Ort des Anderen zu dem sich der Mensch=Mann in eine moralisch geistige Beziehung setzt, wobei er die Position des höhergestellten vernünftigen Subjekts einnimmt (Weigel 179).

Ziel also muß es sein, die in der Frau noch wirksamen, unbeherrschten Kräfte der Natur, manifest in der Sexualität, einzudämmen. Die Folge ist, daß die Frau aus dieser Perspektive ebenfalls aufgrund dessen definiert wird, was ihr "mangelt im Vergleich zum 'Zivilisierten,' zum Mann" (Weigel 174).

Diese Thesen zur Verknüpfung von "wilden Kulturen" und "Weiblichkeit" unter dem Aspekt der Herrschaft einer vereinheitlichenden Vernunft greift Wysocki in der Darstellung der dritten weiblichen Figur auf. Marie 1-4, als Anna O., führen dort die Geschichte einer Krankheit, der Hysterie, und ihrer Heilung vor, während Fantomas 1-4, Billy und Mariezibill die Darstellung kommentieren (79 f., 83-85, 95 f.). Hinter Anna O. verbirgt sich Berta Pappenheim, deren Krankengeschichte für die Hysterieforschung exemplarische Bedeutung bekam, zumal hier durch Freud erstmals der Sexualität als ausschlaggebendem Faktor konsequent Rechnung getragen worden ist.[10]

Wysocki überschreibt die Passage "Anna O. oder die Belichtung des dunklen Kontinents" und hebt damit zwei Aspekte dieser Krankengeschichte hervor: Zum einen wird Hysterie mit dem Begriff "dunkler Kontinent" assoziiert, der von Freud direkt für die weibliche Sexualität gebraucht wurde (Weigel 175), d.h., daß Hysterie zwar nicht als direkter, so aber doch als verschobener Ausbruch der ungezähmten Natur in der Frau begriffen wird.[11] Zum anderen wird mit diesem Begriff oder auch dem von Fantomas verwendeten, "terra incognita" (84), die Frau der abendländischen Norm weiter entrückt und als "Fremde" definiert. Damit aber wird auch der Mechanismus der Kolonisierung aktiv. Das "Entrée der Frau ins Abendland" (79) erfolgt über die Subsumierung der weiblichen Sexualität unter die Ökonomie der männlichen:

Fantomas 1:
ICH DARF GAR NICHT DARAN DENKEN.... An deine unverheilten Tragödien.... An deine ganze kleine ekelhafte Anatomie. Du bist ja noch eine Baby-Mensch. Eine Drüse.... Noch ist das alles nicht mehr als eine Dauerentzündung. Ein ausgefallenes Geschlecht hast du da (84).

Das Adjektiv "ausgefallen" beschreibt dabei in doppelter Hinsicht den Mechanismus der Kolonisierung: Da das weibliche Geschlecht "ausgefallen" ist, also aus dem Rahmen der normsetzenden "Männlichkeit" fällt, wird es auch als eigenständige Qualität negiert, "ausgefallen" dann im Sinne von "nicht existent." Das weibliche Geschlecht bezeichnet nur noch den Ort des Mangels, die "Wunde" (79).

Die Psychoanalyse erscheint als eine der geographischen Kolonisierung vergleichbare Form der Inbesitznahme und gleichzeitig der Enteignung der Kolonisierten.[12] So vollzieht sich am Ende des Auftritts von Marie als Anna O. ein Übergang: Das Menstruationsblut wird ersetzt durch die Attribute der Braut (85). Die weibliche Sexualität ist nun nur noch in ihrer Beziehung zum Mann definierbar. Sie ist als "Beutestück" (97) in das Museum des Mannes eingegangen. Doch wird Marie auch als Hoppers Frau bezeichnet (vgl. 95). Wysocki verbindet die Geschichte dieser Kolonisierung so mit dem Bild Edward Hoppers, dessen Beschreibung sie im Stück auf die Polarisierung von geometrischen Formen/lesendem

Mann und nacktem Frauenkörper/"Wildheit des Haares und der Landschaft" im Fenster zuspitzt. Die Methode der Psychoanalyse ist eben auch die Integration von Sexualität in die wissenschaftliche Weltaneignung. Wysocki schreibt dazu: "...die Psychoanalyse organisiert die in der Krankheit zur Darstellung gebrachten unbewußten Phantasien zur Logik einer 'Fallgeschichte'" (1986, 48).

Dadurch jedoch, daß diese Aneignung sich am Körper der Frau vollzieht, wird auch sie, wie die "Wilden," als Ort des Anderen nun wissenschaftlich festgeschrieben. Der moderne Blick auf die "Weiblichkeit" hat die Realität so weit entkernt, daß sie zur idealen Projektionsfläche männlicher Phantasien geworden ist. Wysocki offenbart so die weiblichen Selbstdarstellungen bzw. die in den Essays herausgearbeiteten Grundtypen nicht nur als wirkende Strukturen, sondern auch als Ausdrucksformen patriarchaler Machtverhältnisse.

VIII. Durchkreuzung der Polaritäten

Mit *Abendlandleben* markiert Wysocki die Eckpunkte einer mit dem aufklärerischen Vernunftideal einsetzenden Entwicklung der europäischen Gesellschaften. Das (wissenschaftliche) Denken gegen den Augenschein bereitete danach den Weg zur Zerstörung von Zusammenhängen des Lebendigen und zur Emanzipation der Technik vom Menschen. Sein Anspruch auf Ausschließlichkeit und Eindeutigkeit, so wurde mit den "Spielen" deutlich, war Antrieb für eine Ausgrenzung der von der Norm abweichenden Erscheinung oder Wahrnehmung.

Parallel zu dieser Entwicklung gestaltet Wysocki die allmähliche formale Vervollständigung der "Spiele." Am Ende des Stücks sind die anfänglichen Textlücken geschlossen. Die—im wörtlichen Sinn—Freiräume sind beseitigt, d.h., die sukzessive Schichtung ist nicht mehr erkennbar. Der Regelbestand des Gesellschafts-Spiels *Abendlandleben* ist endgültig formuliert. Die Spiele erscheinen so heute, am vorläufigen Endpunkt der skizzierten Entwicklung, als ewige, nicht mehr hinterfragbare Bestandteile einer homogenen Kultur. Die wissenschaftliche Weltaneignung wird nicht mehr als eine spezielle Ausprägung gewertet, die Trennung von Subjekt und Objekt, von Vernunft und Unvernunft bzw. Wahnsinn, von männlicher Rolle und weiblicher gelten nicht mehr als Ergebnis einer geschichtlichen Entwicklung. Sie erscheinen als natürlich, als selbstverständlich. Wysocki definiert die "Spiele" auch als "Einübungen von Abendland. Es sind Exerzitien" (Roeder 130). Ihr ritueller Charakter setzt auf die Wiederholung anstatt auf die Erklärung. Nicht zufällig jedoch spricht Wysocki im Zusammenhang mit kulturell wirksamen Strukturen von "Geschichtetem." Das allmähliche Auffüllen der Textlücken ebenso wie der gemeinsame Wortstamm von "Geschichte" und "Geschichtetem" soll uns gerade die Einsicht in die historische Bedingtheit der eigenen Kultur ermöglichen. Die Analyse der "Spiele"

ergab zudem, daß Wysocki wesentliche Merkmale dieser Entwicklung als Produkte einer männlich dominierten Gesellschaft verstanden hat. Dennoch sucht Wysocki die Lösung nicht im Gegenstück zum Bestehenden, d.h., bei den Frauen bzw. im "Weiblichen."
Nachdem der Auftritt der letzten Frauenfigur beendet ist, gibt Wysocki eine Regieanweisung, die zeigt, daß beide Geschlechter einer Verschiebung von etwas "Authentischem" unterworfen sind: "MÄNNER und FRAUEN. Bilder und Bildesbilder..." (96). Die Männerfiguren sind beherrscht durch die Spiele der wissenschaftlichen Weltaneignung. Das war versinnbildlicht im Dienst des Mannes an der Maschine und seine letztendliche Umwandlung zur Maschine. Die Frauenfiguren dagegen sind sowohl beherrscht durch die Spiele der wissenschaftlichen Weltaneignung, als auch durch die männlichen Kolonisateure. Das aber bedeutet, daß auch mit der Frau das Leben keinen Ort außerhalb der Kultur hat, d.h., "Weiblichkeit" nicht als Folie für Utopien einer unschuldigen Menschheit dienen kann. Gerade in der Figur der Marie zeigt Wysocki, daß die Assoziierung von "Weiblichkeit" und Natur Ausdruck männlichen Subjekt- und Weltverständnisses ist, daß es sich damit also verbietet, "Weiblichkeit" in dieser Form als Ausweg aus einer Herrschaft der Vernunft zu imaginieren. Dennoch sieht Wysocki eine Chance, die bei den Frauen liegt.

> Die Fähigkeit, sich neben diesen Kopf zu stellen, der ja unser eigener ist und in ihn hineinzuschauen wie in ein fremdes Universum, ist dem weiblichen Autor möglicherweise leichter gegeben, weil wir in unserer Geschichte niemals die Gewißheit haben konnten, im Zentrum dieser Abläufe zu stehen (Roeder 132).

Vom "äußeren Rande der europäischen Geschichte," wie das einleitende Bild Dalis im Stück den Standpunkt der Frau festlegt, ist dem gesellschaftlichen Geschehen der Anschein des Selbstverständlichen zu nehmen. Nur der dezentrale Blick auf die Wirklichkeit erlaubt, ihre Struktur und Funktionsweisen zu erkennen. D.h., nur die Negierung von tradionellen Gegensatzpaaren, wie sie in *Abendlandleben* thematisiert wurden, könnte die Mechanismen der Ausgrenzung außer Kraft setzen.

Anmerkungen

Dieser Artikel ist eine überarbeitete Fassung des Gisela von Wysocki gewidmeten Kapitels meiner Studie *Vernunftkritik und Patriarchatskritik: Mythische Modelle in der deutschsprachigen Literatur der 80er Jahre* (Bielefield: Aisthesis, 1993).

[1] Apollinaire wurde am 26.8.1880 in Rom geboren und starb am 9.11.1918 in Paris an den Folgen einer Kriegsverletzung.

[2] Angaben im Text, die ausschließlich Seitenzahlen enthalten, beziehen sich immer auf *Abendlandleben*.

[3] Detailliertere Angaben zu Wysockis Umgang mit Apollinaire finden sich in meiner Studie *Vernunftkritik und Patriarchatskritik: Mythische Modelle in der neuesten Literatur*. Diss. Marburg, 1991.

[4] Wesentliche Gedanken, teilweise wörtlich, entnimmt Wysocki dem Abschnitt "Plastik" Roland Barthes aus *Mythen des Alltags* (79–81), wobei sie sich allerdings auf die Beschreibungen und Definitionen Barthes konzentriert und seine interpretatorischen Ausführungen beiseite läßt. Da für mich darin jedoch keine Absicht erkennbar wird, sich von der inhaltlichen Aussage Barthes kritisch zu distanzieren, werde ich mich in der Deutung des Spiels an den Reflexionen Barthes orientieren. Es widerspräche auch der Definition der Spiele, deren ritueller Charakter gerade auf Erklärungen verzichten muß.

[5] Möglicherweise zieht Wysocki hier eine direkte Parallele zwischen faschistischer Herrschaft und der Herrschaft der Befreier: Ezra Pound, den sie in dieses Spiel aufgenommen hat, galt als Befürworter des Faschismus in Italien und wird nach dem Krieg von den Amerikanern interniert, später in eine psychiatrische Anstalt eingewiesen.

[6] Auch das "Spiel vom siebenjährigen Mozart" gehört in den Rahmen dieses zwanghaften Integrationsstrebens des System- und Normdenkens. Das "Faites votre yeux" Spiel dagegen kann als Reaktion auf eine Alleinherrschaft der Vernunft gedeutet werden, nach der das Bedürfnis nach Irrationalität und religiösem/magischem Erleben in dem Maße wächst, in dem die Welt auf die rationale Erkenntnis reduziert wird.

[7] Ich möchte keinesfalls hier die Identifikation von Mensch und Mann fortschreiben. Doch Wysocki gebraucht den Terminus "Musée de l'Homme" sicherlich zum einen als "Museum der Menschheit," macht aber, indem sie den Mann zu seinem Bewahrer einsetzt, deutlich, daß es auch ein "Museum des Mannes" ist, d.h., die Geschichte, die dort ausgestellt ist, eine männlich dominierte ist.

[8] Besonders in den Apollinaire-Zitaten Wysockis wird die Erotisierung der Technik im Krieg deutlich, vgl. meine Studie "Vernunftkritik und Patriarchatskritik" 184 f.).

[9] Für eine Zusammenstellung einschlägiger literarischer Texte mit einem einleitenden Vorwort, siehe Stein, Gauthier und Täger.

[10] Vgl. Freud und Breuer; ebenfalls Gay.
[11] Vgl. Geitner zur Problematik "Hysterieforschung."
[12] Wysocki bezieht sich hier auf die grundlegende feministische Arbeit Luce Irigarays zur Psychoanalyse.

Zitierte Werke

Adorno, Theodor W. and Max Horkheimer. *Dialektik der Aufklärung*. Frankfurt a.M.: Fischer, 1986.
Apollinaire, Guillaume. *Oeuvres complètes*. Ed. Michel Décaudin. Vol. 1-4. Paris: Balland, 1965-1966.
Barthes, Roland. *Die Mythen des Alltags*. Trans. Helmut Scheffel. Frankfurt a.M.: Suhrkamp, 1964.
Benjamin, Walter. *Das Kunstwerk im Zeitalter seiner technischen Reproduzierbarkeit*. Frankfurt a.M.: Suhrkamp, 1976.
Bergfleth, Gerd et al. *Kritik der palavernden Aufklärung*. München: Matthes, 1984.
Bloch, George. *Pablo Picasso: Catalogue de l'oeuvre gravé et litographié 1904-1967*. Kat. Nr. 1, Tome I. Bern: Kornfeld, 1968. 21.
Cramer, Sibylle. "Das Gedächnis als Gesamtkunstwerk: Gisela von Wysockis Herausforderung des Theaters: Abendlandleben." *Frankfurter Rundschau* 1 Dec. 1987.
Dali, Salvador. *Retrospektive 1920-1980: Gemälde. Zeichnungen. Grafiken. Objekte. Filme. Schriften*. Trans. Heinrich Dechamps. München: Prestel, 1980. 293.
Foucault, Michel. *Die Ordnung der Dinge*. Trans. Ulrich Köppen. Frankfurt a.M.: Suhrkamp, 1978.
———. *Wahnsinn und Gesellschaft*. Trans. Walter Seitter. Frankfurt a.M.: Suhrkamp, 1977.
Freier, Barbara. "Feststellung der Fremdheit: Zu Gisela von Wysocki, Auf Schwarzmärkten." *Süddeutsche Zeitung* 30 March 1983.
Fremdwörterbuch. Vol. 5. Mannheim: Duden, 1982.
Freud, Sigmund and Josef Breuer. *Studien zur Hysterie (1895)*. Frankfurt a.M.: Fischer, 1985.
Gauthier, Xavière. *Surréalismus und Sexualität: Inszenierungen der Weiblichkeit*. Trans. Heiner Noger. Berlin: Medusa, 1980.
Gay, Peter. *Freud: Eine Biographie für unsere Zeit*. Frankfurt a.M.: Fischer, 1989.
Geitner, Ursula. "Passio Hysterika: Die alltägliche Sorge um das Selbst. Zum Zusammenhang von Literatur, Pathologie und Weiblichkeit im 18. Jahrhundert." *Frauen—Weiblichkeit—Schrift*. Ed. Renate Berger. Berlin: Argument, 1985.
"Gisela von Wysocki—Essayistin." *Neue Zürcher Zeitung* 14 Apr. 1987.

Henrichs, Benjamin. "Die Haut blickt, das Auge fühlt, im Gehen denkt der Körper (Aufbruchsphantasien: Gisela von Wysockis außerordentliche Essays 'Die Fröste der Freiheit')." *Die Zeit* 19 June 1981: 38.

Irigaray, Luce. *Speculum: Spiegel des anderen Geschlechts*. Trans. Xenia Rajewski et al. Frankfurt a.M.: Suhrkamp, 1980.

Jaspers, Karl. *Vom Ursprung und Ziel der Geschichte*. Frankfurt a.M.: Fischer, 1956.

Konversationslexikon in 20 Bdn. Vol. 3. München: dtv-Lexikon, 1980.

Lenk, Elisabeth. *Die unbewußte Gesellschaft: Über die mimetische Grundstruktur in der Literatur und im Traum*. München: Matthes, 1983.

Levin, Gail. *Edward Hopper: 1882-1967. Gemälde und Zeichnungen*. Trans. Karin Stempel. München: Schirmer, 1981.

Lindner, Hermann. *Biologie*. Stuttgart: Metzler, 1971.

Nitschke, Bernd. *Die Zerstörung der Sinnlichkeit*. München: Matthes, 1981.

Nordhoff, Inge. "Angst vor der Verführung: Gisela von Wysockis Auswahl kreativer Frauen." Rev. of *Fröste der Freiheit*. *Stuttgarter Zeitung* 24 Oct. 1981.

Roeder, Anke. "Abendlandspiele—Abschiedsspiele: Gespräch mit Gisela von Wysocki." *Autorinnen: Herausforderungen an das Theater*. Ed. Anke Roeder. Frankfurt a.M.: Suhrkamp, 1989. 123-39.

Schwartz, Leonore. "Gespräch mit der Mutter." Rev. of Gisela von Wysocki, *Die Fröste der Freiheit*. *Deutsches Allgemeines Sonntagsblatt* 7 Feb. 1982.

Stein, Gerd. *Femme fatale—Vamp—Blaustrumpf: Sexualität und Herrschaft. Kulturfiguren und Sozialcharaktere des 19. und 20. Jahrhunderts*. Frankfurt a.M.: Fischer, 1985.

Täger, Annemarie. *Die Kunst, Medusa zu töten: Zum Bild der Frau in der Literatur der Jahrhundertwende*. Bielefeld: Aisthesis, 1987.

Weigel, Sigrid. "Die nahe Fremde—Das Territorium des 'Weiblichen': Zum Verhältnis von 'Wilden' und 'Frauen' im Diskurs der Aufklärung." *Die andere Welt: Studien zum Exotismus*. Ed. Thomas Koebner and Gerhard Pickerodt. Frankfurt a.M.: Athenäum, 1987. 171-99.

Weiss, Christina. "'Ich öffne Ihren Kopf, Monsieur.' Gisela von Wysocki's Textmaschine *Abendlandleben*." *Süddeutsche Zeitung* 1-2 Aug. 1987.

Wysocki, Gisela von. *Abendlandleben oder Apollinaires Gedächtnis: Spiele aus Neu Glück*. Frankfurt a.M.: Qumran, 1987.

———. *Die Fröste der Freiheit: Aufbruchsphantasien*. Frankfurt a.M.: Syndikat, 1981.

———. *Peter Altenberg: Bilder und Geschichten des befreiten Lebens*. Frankfurt a.M.: Fischer, 1986.

———. *Weiblichkeit und Modernität: Über Virginia Woolf*. Frankfurt a.M.: Qumran, 1982.

Memory and Criticism: Ruth Klüger's *weiter leben*

Dagmar C.G. Lorenz

Klüger's autobiography is a literary account of an Auschwitz survivor, an immigrant to the United States and a professor of German literature. *weiter leben* is also a metadiscourse on earlier accounts and studies of the Holocaust and the exile experience. Klüger's familiarity with international Holocaust literature and Fascism theory lends this very personal work, with its close-up descriptions of concentration camp life and insights into the experience of a Jewish woman scholar in contemporary Germany, a multi-dimensional, critical perspective and an unusual scope and depth. Klüger confronts the present with her own recollections and her generation's collective memory. (DCGL)

Ruth Klüger's autobiography, written in the late 1980s and published in 1992, represents a landmark between early and recent representations of the Holocaust written in German. While Klüger's account of her survival of Auschwitz and Theresienstadt challenges commonly held notions, it positions itself nevertheless in the context of 20th-century literary and critical history and responds to the international Holocaust discourse. At a time when several German and Austrian Jewish women such as Jeanette Lander, Lea Fleischmann, Nadja Seelich, Ruth Beckermann, and Barbara Honigmann, most of whom were born after 1945, set out on a quest to define themselves as writers, filmmakers, and intellectuals, wanting to compromise neither their Jewish identity nor their status as emancipated women, Ruth Klüger establishes a tenuous affinity with Germany, reclaiming as a Jewish writer her native German language and making Göttingen her second residence.

In Göttingen, a medium-size university city in Lower Saxony where she spent several years as the director of the University of California Studies Abroad program, Klüger is a foreigner, an *Ausländerin*, with all the traditional negative and liberating connotations implied by this term. Göttingen and its language generate a vague sense of alienation that causes Klüger to assume the part of a critical observer. A similar attitude sets the tone of many exile writers' memoirs, but Holocaust survivors who intended to resume their life in Germany generally express no such detachment. They want to bear witness, to reestablish their shattered identity, if not their lives, by revising their accounts time after time to create the illusion of biographical continuity (cf. Spies and Edel). *weiter leben* combines autobiography and a critical metadiscourse integrating feminist theory, Holocaust studies, theories of fascism, and history. Its approach more closely resembles that of the autobiographies written in the 1970s and 1980s by exile writers than that of typical Holocaust memoirs.

Since most of the Holocaust survivors of Klüger's and earlier generations have died or stopped writing, *weiter leben* marks the final point of a tradition of survivors' correspondences and memoirs, as well as that of literary and scholarly works about the Holocaust. With some notable exceptions such as Jean Améry's and H.G. Adler's works, sophisticated intellectual superstructures are uncharacteristic of Holocaust texts based primarily on personal experience. The complex narrative and theoretical structures of *weiter leben*, prose interspersed with lyric poetry, the earliest dating back to Auschwitz and the latest written just before the completion of the book, show Klüger to be an accomplished author and critic.

weiter leben is a work about *Vergangenheitsbewältigung*. It documents a Jewish feminist's attempt to integrate her at least two biographies and her perceptions formed in different languages and eras. Gentile critics such as Alexander and Margarete Mitscherlich and Klaus Theweleit contended that the Germans must accept their responsibility for Nazi crimes individually and collectively, while Jewish writers such as H.G. Adler, Peter Weiss, Jean Améry, Jeanette Lander, Hannah Lévy-Hass, and Ruth Beckermann suggested that mourning and coping with the past are important tasks that face the Nazi victims and their children as well. In keeping with the theses advanced by these writers and theorists, *weiter leben* challenges the notion that the Nazi legacy concerns only the German mainstream. Klüger's work illustrates that Jews too need to come to terms with their past, with the Holocaust, with Germany, and with the Germans.

Klüger's autobiography is a document of healing and self-realization despite its focus on attacks on the narrator's and author's individuality, freedom, health, and life. Vienna, Theresienstadt, Auschwitz, and Groß-Rosen are the places of Klüger's suffering. Bavaria of the 1940s and Göttingen of the 1980s witness her physical and emotional recovery after her narrow escapes from death. The last recovery is closely associated with the German language as spoken in Northern Germany, an idiom distinctly different from the author's native Viennese. Inserted are impressions from Klüger's university studies, her marriage and motherhood, and her career, all of which took place in the United States and were mediated by the English language.

As a scholar and critic, Klüger is conversant with German and international Holocaust literature. She bases her theoretical assessments on both her research and her first-hand experience. Her allusions to historical and philosophical discussions suggest profound critical insights that are impossible to articulate in the framework of her autobiography. The amount of factual and theoretical information contained in Klüger's candid account makes for great textual intensity. Klüger clearly chose her material carefully, subjecting it to a rigorous selection in order to preserve the simplicity of her narrative voice, a voice that appears spontaneous but is in reality the result of reflection, study, teaching, writing, and rewriting.

One debate that Klüger bypasses is the one about the representation of the Holocaust, which Berel Lang aptly summarizes as follows:

> Is the enormity of the Holocaust at all capable of literary representation? And what would be the justification for attempting such representation even if it were possible? In his much-quoted statement condemning the "barbarism" of writing poetry after Auschwitz, Theodor Adorno suggests a larger boundary-question for *any* writing that takes the Holocaust as its subject: Placed in the balance with the artifice that inevitably enters the work of even the most scrupulous author, what warrant—moral or theoretical or aesthetic—is there for writing about the Holocaust at all? (2).

At no point does Klüger address the question raised by Lawrence Langer "whether an unmediated text about the Holocaust experience is ever achievable" (26). Saul Friedländer too argues that reality since World War I "became so extreme as to outstrip language's capacity to represent it altogether" (Young 16). But Klüger simply does not enter the debate about the limitations of language and the aesthetics of the Holocaust. For an expert in the field of Holocaust studies such as Klüger, the avoidance of this entire discourse from Adorno to Hilberg must have been deliberate.[1]

Klüger's attitude is reminiscent of Jurek Becker's implicit dismissal of Bertolt Brecht's criticism of nature poetry in "finsteren Zeiten." The theoretical deliberations in Becker's novel *Jakob der Lügner* suggest that Becker considered Brecht's assessment irrelevant for a Holocaust survivor (Lorenz 181 ff.). In much the same way Klüger dismisses the theories about the representation of the Holocaust because most of them were forged by critics and scholars who had never been in a death camp.[2] Many of them attempted to capture the atmosphere by visiting well-known sites such as Auschwitz, Dachau, Buchenwald, and Mauthausen, which after the war were built up as memorials and museums (Milton).

In her earlier review of Claude Lanzmann's film *Shoah*, Klüger set her experience as a Holocaust survivor apart from the views of "outsiders," including critics and artists:

> I don't believe in going back. Lanzmann does. The museum culture that has sprung up around the concentration camps is based on a sense of *spiritus loci*

which I lack. What was done there could be repeated elsewhere, I have argued, conceived as it was by human minds, carried out by human hands, somewhere on earth, the place irrelevant, so why single out the sites that now look like so many others? I don't go back to where I've been. I have escaped. Lanzmann goes back to where he has never been.... Like all survivors I know that Auschwitz, when the Nazis killed Jews there, felt like a crater of the moon, a place only peripherally connected with the human world. It is this "otherness" of the death camps that we have such difficulty conveying. But once the killing stopped these former camps became a piece of our inhabited earth again (250).

Here and elsewhere Klüger distances herself from much of the critical discourse discussing Holocaust literature in prescriptive and moralistic terms. From the start critics on both the Left and the Right have measured Holocaust literature with a different yardstick, demanding that it be of higher quality than "ordinary" texts, thereby deliberately or accidentally repressing literature and memoirs written by many Holocaust survivors.[3] Intended Nazi-victims who asserted their right to define their position independent of the critical mainstream became the object of violent controversies, for example Edgar Hilsenrath, Erich Fried, or Fania Fénelon.

The most outspoken critics involved in the debate about representations of the Shoah, for example Theodor Adorno and Bruno Bettelheim, were themselves not Holocaust survivors. The same is true for many filmmakers, including Lanzmann, who have problematized the representation of the Holocaust. Jean Améry, who had been a prisoner in Auschwitz, does not even raise the issue of "representability," and the Holocaust survivor Alain Resnais, director of the film *Night and Fog*, used original footage from the death camps, certain that it could and should be shown on screen. While the majority of the critics and filmmakers dealing with the Holocaust were in one way or another biographically affected by the Nazi atrocities, it could be argued that those who did not experience the death camps have no way of judging which representations are fitting and which ones are not. Klüger does not even bother to take issue with their opinions.

What distinguishes Klüger's point of view from that of exile writers or authors born after 1945 is the fact that she has been where their imagination fails to take them. As late as 1986, the autobiographical protagonist of forty-three-year-old painter and writer Barbara Honigmann's *Roman von einem Kinde* refers to Auschwitz as "her location" in an allusion to Peter Weiss (28). But Klüger's memory extends even into the time before the invasion of Vienna and the Holocaust.

> Heute gibt es Leute, die mich fragen: "Aber Sie waren doch viel zu jung, um sich an diese schreckliche Zeit erinnern zu können." Oder vielmehr, sie

fragen nicht einmal, sie behaupten es mit Bestimmtheit. Ich denke dann, die wollen mir mein Leben nehmen, denn das Leben ist doch nur die verbrachte Zeit, das einzige, was wir haben, das machen sie mir streitig, wenn sie mir das Recht des Erinnerns in Frage stellen (73).

Because of her ability to remember, she feels no need to search for the lost culture and revisit the death camps. Experience has taught her that only memory transcends time and space, and she disputes the notion that landscapes and buildings can retain history.

Lander, Honigmann, and Beckermann reach the same conclusion *after* their trips to Eastern Europe. Klüger explains:

> Es liegt dieser Museumskultur ein tiefer Aberglaube zugrunde, nämlich daß die Gespenster gerade dort zu fassen seien, wo sie als Lebende aufhörten zu sein. Oder vielmehr kein tiefer, sondern eher ein seichter Aberglaube, wie ihn auch die Grusel- und Gespensterhäuser in aller Welt vermitteln (76).

Klüger does not repeat the known descriptions of the concentration camps and makes no attempt to depict the details of the prisoners' daily routine. These topics have been discussed *in extenso* by Raul Hilberg, H.G. Adler, Käthe Starcke, and others. Klüger builds on their texts as well as on those of Tadeusz Borowski, Primo Levi, Elie Wiesel, Peter Weiss, Günter Anders, Theodor Adorno, and Hannah Arendt, just to name a few. They provide her with a framework of references.

As a feminist Klüger finds herself often in disagreement with views commonly advanced in Holocaust literature and scholarship. She denounces the discrimination of women in all Western cultures, including Judaism. According to her, misogyny is the reason why Holocaust texts by prominent authors such as Elie Wiesel omit or misrepresent the concentration and death camp experience of women and distort pre-Holocaust society. While critical studies, as Klüger points out, often diminish the plight of women, some Holocaust fiction goes even further, representing women's experiences with prurient overtones or as outright pornography: "Es gibt ja eine Pornographie der KZs, die Vorstellung der absoluten Macht über andere erweckt Lustgefühle" (236).[4]

By introducing a critical feminist voice to the multifaceted Holocaust discourse Klüger's book expands the scope of Holocaust literature that admonishes posterity never to forget. She emphasizes this continuity through frequent references to such works as Peter Weiss's *Die Ermittlung,* a drama based on the Auschwitz-trials; the account of his visit to Auschwitz, *Meine Ortschaft;* or to Lanzmann's *Shoah.* This type of intertextuality is common among Jewish exile authors and survivors: Weiss's report of his journey to Auschwitz is a dialogue with an earlier text by Stephan Hermlin, *Auschwitz ist unvergessen* (1953), in which Hermlin defined Auschwitz as his major psychological reference point (85–89). Erich Fried's *Meine Puppe in Auschwitz* responds to both earlier visitors (106–16), and Barbara Honigmann in *Roman von einem Kinde* indicates her solidarity with the older writers (28).

There also exists a similarity between Klüger and contemporary women writers who are concerned with the issue of memory. *weiter leben* shares the Janus-like perspective of their works, looking with one eye towards the past and with the other towards the future; it conveys similar perceptions as Christa Wolf's *Kindheitsmuster*, Jeanette Lander's *Die Töchter*, Lea Fleischmann's *Dies ist nicht mein Land*, and Ruth Beckermann's film *Die papierene Brücke* and her autobiographical essay *Unzugehörig*. However, in intent and outlook, *weiter leben* is closest to Fleischmann, Lander, and Beckermann who engage in a search for their identity because they feel incompatible with their contemporary German or Austrian culture.

Klüger has achieved greater distance, albeit not greater impartiality, than younger Jewish authors such as Fleischmann and Beckermann. She explores the terror of her early childhood among apprehensive, persecuted adults and her adolescence amidst the chaos of genocide. She also discusses political and social developments, the historical background for her and her family's suffering. Her narrative represents subjective impressions and historical processes side by side and occasionally as intimately intertwined as in Peter Weiss's, Manès Sperber's, and Elias Canetti's well-known autobiographies. Yet Klüger's account is free of the nostalgia that characterizes, at least in part, the autobiographical texts of exile authors. Despite her precise rendering of the past, the focus of her book is the present.

All texts are constructed of the same material, language, and are part of specific historical and discursive traditions. The same conventions shape autobiographical and literary texts in general as well as Holocaust memoirs (Langer 26–27) and literature. Hence the same critical standards ought to apply no matter what subject matter a text is concerned with, including the Holocaust. Nowhere in Klüger's autobiography is there a hint that she expects any special consideration for her work, nowhere does she suggest that her autobiography is extraordinary because of its content. On the contrary, she doubts whether a book like hers would have any relevance for the present generations. It is precisely this matter-of-factness and humility, which Detlev Claussen observes in the case of other Holocaust texts as well (62–63), which distinguish *weiter leben* from popular sentimental depictions of Auschwitz.

weiter leben does not restrict itself to the author's youth, as the subtitle leads the readers to expect, unless the time spent in Göttingen be understood as a symbolic rebirth brought on by Klüger's accident, an experience as disruptive as it was healing. An uncanny synchronization, this event recapitulates and reenacts Klüger's confrontation with the German soldiers in 1938 whom she first encountered in Vienna: "die...sprachen deutsch, aber nicht wie wir, und anfänglich glaubte ich noch, die gehören nicht so hierher wie ich" (22). In Göttingen a collision also takes place:

> ...Metall, wie Scheinwerfer über Stacheldraht, ich will mich wehren, ihn zurückschieben, beide Arme ausgestreckt, der Anprall, Deutschland, ein Augenblick wie ein Handgemenge, *den* Kampf verlier ich, Metall, nochmals Deutschland, was mach ich denn hier, wozu bin ich zurückgekommen, war ich je fort.... Und diese Vorstellung, oder auch nur Einbildung, daß mich der Sechzehnjährige aus Aggression umgefahren hat. Nicht aus aggressivem Denken, wohl aber aus aggressivem Instinkt, wie die Buben hinterm Steuerrad der Autos, Herrschaft über die Maschine, eine Art Trunkenheit. Schließt nicht aus, daß es ihm nachher leid getan hat (272).

Passages like these are indicative of the complexity of Klüger's narrative. Multiple layers of facts are scrutinized in light of different levels of awareness and cultural assumptions. On one level the accident is a replay of the narrator's past, on another this is clearly not the case: the boy criticized so severely was not a native of Germany, but a young Vietnamese, the adopted son of a German couple who, ironically, belonged to Klüger's circle of colleagues. Most importantly, however, the later event is an accident rather than premeditated, wholesale persecution.

weiter leben portrays Klüger's experiences and perceptions past and present in a lively, colorful fashion. She describes her childhood from the point of view of the adult narrator who is aware of facts that she did not know at the time. The tension created by this dual perspective determines the structure of her autobiography. Bi-polarization is also characteristic of other memoir literature, for example Nina Weilovà's unpublished memoir "71978 Jude: Erinnerungen," Benedikt Kautsky's book *Teufel und Verdammte*, and Rahel Behrend's autobiography *Verfemt und verfolgt*, as well as in other works thematizing persecution, life in hiding, and deportation such as the autobiographical novels by Peter Edel and Ilse Aichinger, *Schwester der Nacht* and *Die größere Hoffnung*. However, the interval between Klüger's concentration camp experience and her writing of *weiter leben* is much longer than in the above-mentioned works. Thus she repeatedly undercuts the apparent clarity suggested in the stark contrasts by introducing more balanced viewpoints.

With a sensitivity for nuances, the author evokes ideological and historical contexts, moods, atmospheres, and individual characters as if in bold brush strokes, by using key words and phrases. Austrian expressions and sayings, the Viennese timbre, and occasional Yiddish vocabulary evoke an impression of life in the conservative Viennese Jewish middle class during the 1930s. Klüger depicts herself as a rebellious young girl, within and in contrast to this environment; she was attracted to Zionism and insisted on changing her name from Susanna to Ruth in order to better express her personality (40).

Klüger integrates her subjective perceptions into critically processed material, thus creating a reflective text whose tone is characteristic of accounts and films produced considerably after the Holocaust. Despite the difference in genre, the content and perspective of *weiter leben* recalls such films as Kitty Hart's *Return to Auschwitz*, a documentary about a woman's revisiting Auschwitz together with her son, or Ruth Beckermann's *Die papierene Brücke*, a poetic and at the same time critical film in which the daughter of Holocaust survivors attempts to bridge the gap between past and present by exploring the remnants of Jewish culture in Vienna and Romania. As the memory of the Holocaust faded, Jewish authors and filmmakers felt the need to authenticate their past in documentary and biographical works. Many of them, like Klüger addressing a predominantly Gentile public, revealed how history continued to affect their lives. They described the long-range impact of the Holocaust on the survivors and the following generations.

In more than three decades of reflection, Klüger achieved mastery of her autobiographical material and the confidence to draw conclusions without arguing every point. Suggesting that even imperfect texts convey meaning worth communicating, Klüger, who wrote her first poems in Auschwitz, supports any serious attempt to articulate the "unspeakable" regardless of the form (36). By including some of her earliest poetry, she validates her own struggle to articulate the fate of her family and community and her own survival.

Klüger reflects on the process of writing and remembering as she discusses her creative process and her writing tools, formerly the pen and typewriter, now the computer (25–27). Having been denied access to writing implements in the concentration camps, she takes nothing for granted, least of all the material basis for her work. Beyond creativity and self-motivation as important aspects of authorship, she displays an acute awareness that the powers of the individual are limited. By revealing the factors upon which she depends as a writer, she shows that the realization of "talent" or "genius" depends on circumstances beyond the individual's control. Her accident in, of all places, Göttingen's Jüdenstraße is one example of her powerlessness. She describes its profound effects on her mental processes. Her reorientation during her reconvalescence necessitates her confrontation with the "Gespenster" of the past with whom, as she states, she had been familiar for a long time. She has to struggle to integrate the shattered thoughts (279) that she experienced "nicht als Kontinuum, sondern als Glasscherben" (278).

As an aspect of identity, language also proves to be elusive and uncontrollable. Klüger discusses her experience with the four major languages in her life, Viennese, Yiddish, English, and German. She associates her native Viennese dialect with her family and childhood friends. She is born into this idiom, which remains her language of intimacy and still colors her literary diction. Yiddish, on the other hand, is associated with the Holocaust. Klüger picked it up as the *lingua franca* of the camps, a necessary tool for survival. Through it she acquired an identity that she later suppressed (cf. 176). Yiddish evokes the extinct shtetl culture, the tenderness and the wit of Eastern European Jews, and above all, genocide (208-09). Not without irony does Klüger point out that her Yiddish is quite different from the Yiddish presently *en vogue* in Germany.

English and Standard German are the media of Klüger's profession, *Germanistik*. In "High German," which Austrians have to learn almost like a foreign language, Klüger confronts the German intelligentsia of the 1980s. Equipped with only a fragmentary knowledge of Nazi and Holocaust history, and a special vocabulary and body language reserved for these topics, they fail to achieve the much-debated *Vergangenheitsbewältigung*, although the past has been the topic of public debates throughout the postwar decades.

> Ich hatte mich erkundigt, wieviele Juden es denn in dieser Gesellschaft gäbe, und man hatte mir seufzend den Namen eines älteren Ehepaars genannt, das in einer bescheidenen Wohnung von einer kleinen Rente lebte. Man war froh, daß man in der neuen Direktorin des Studienzentrums zufällig nicht nur eine Jüdin, sondern noch dazu eine "Betroffene" hatte, also eine biographisch geeignete Rednerin [i.e., for a presentation commemorating the "Kristallnacht"] (269).

Klüger characterizes the mentality she encounters in Germans both in the United States and in Germany in Wolf Biermann's words: "Sie haben uns alles verziehn / Was sie uns angetan haben" (269). Without the distance from her country and language of origin and her "collision" with the past in Göttingen, Klüger could not have achieved the detachment that allowed her to write *weiter leben*.[5] The confrontation in Göttingen with the perpetrators' language after years of living in the USA seems to have been the precondition for the writing of her memoirs.

weiter leben engages its reader's intellectual and emotional faculties simultaneously. The contrasting modes of poetry and prose captivate the imagination in different ways as the narrator moves from one time frame to another. Klüger's favorite devices are sudden switches from a global perspective to an intimate look at the situation at hand, from serious reflection to irony. She has a talent for conceits, witticism, and puns. One example is her variation on the term "kinderfeindlich" in her description of Vienna, the cradle of anti-Semitism: "judenkinderfeindlich." The book's opening sentence is another example. It immediately establishes an unsettling ambiance that remains characteristic of the entire book: "Der Tod, nicht Sex war das Geheimnis, worüber die Erwachsenen tuschelten, wovon man gern mehr gehört hätte" (7). Statements like these expose a reversal of values with which the narrator wrestles throughout the text.

Klüger's perspective can best be described in terms of shifting camera angles. In her panoramic views, different moods fluctuate, creating mental images of changing colors and lighting, while stark close-ups bring feelings and ideas into focus. Subjective and factual information merge, seemingly without transition. Characters such as the narrator's father are singled out from the larger social spectrum and examined in great detail. Flashbacks and previews enable the narrative voice to connect different events, to travel in time and between the cultures. The chronological structure suggested in the table of contents is merely a blueprint on which a network of associations and cross-references is superimposed.

Klüger likens her approach to the "unerase" capability of a computer, which allows the user to recall information as long as it has not been overwritten with new information (271). This metaphor indicates the place the past occupies in her mind: the memories of her childhood in Vienna and the Holocaust have remained intact, because no later experience was powerful enough to "overwrite" and erase them.

There is no doubt about the narrator's identity or the authenticity of her insights. The person telling her story may have changed and grown, but she has remained in touch with her earlier self despite the vastly different conditions under which she lived in the course of her lifetime. She describes her inner development from a position of certainty, for example her discussion of Theresienstadt as the place where she developed her interactive social skills. Her lack of self-doubt is surprising in a postmodern literary environment where identity and the construction of self are frequently problematized. Klüger's narrator does not claim to know the whole truth but she does achieve objectivity by disclosing the basis for her views and contextualizing herself: "Man sieht schon, diese Aufzeichnungen handeln fast gar nicht von den Nazis, über die ich wenig aussagen kann, sondern von den schwierigen, neurotischen Menschen, auf die sie stießen, Familien, die ebensowenig wie ihre christlichen Nachbarn ein ideales Leben geführt hatten" (54).

Klüger's identity rests primarily on her Jewishness. She describes her family as "emanzipiert, aber nicht assimiliert" (41). Before her stay in Göttingen, she explains, she lived "nicht ausschließlich, aber doch weitgehend" as "Jüdin unter Juden" (269). This was true for her life in Vienna, in the concentration camps, and in the United States (61, 269). Feeling herself an insider and not, as Hannah Arendt defined the status of Jewish women in German society, a "pariah" or "parvenu" de-problematizes the issue of Jewish identity in *weiter leben*: it is a given rather than a "question."[6] Klüger's innermost convictions spring from her Jewish identity, which is confirmed in her being accepted by other Jews as well as by the hostility of anti-Semites.

In this respect Klüger's experience differs markedly from that of assimilated Jews or individuals with only one Jewish parent, for example

Lotte Paepcke, Ingeborg Hecht, and Peter Edel. They were caught between the cultures and their identity was shaped largely by the rejection and discrimination on the part of the hostile mainstream, while Klüger experienced her gender and ethnicity as positive forces. She portrays them as the source of her political views, her love of justice, her compassion with the oppressed, her rejection of violence, and her circumspection. The author of *weiter leben* displays both pride and a keen awareness of her vulnerability as a Jew and a woman. Her unprecedented isolation in Göttingen as a Jew among Gentiles may, in fact, be an additional factor that prompted her to write.

Being a woman is the second important aspect of Klüger's identity. Neither the Holocaust nor the experience of aging (283) have eased her rebellion against the religious and social conventions in Jewish society that relegate women to an inferior position. Klüger mentions in particular the fact that as a woman she is denied the right to mourn her father by reciting *Kaddish*, the prayer for the dead. She also criticizes the fact that Judaism reduces women to the position of domestic help-mates:

> Wär's anders und ich könnte sozusagen offiziell um meine Gespenster trauern, zum Beispiel für meinen Vater Kaddisch sagen, dann könnte ich mich eventuell mit dieser Religion anfreunden, die die Gottesliebe ihrer Töchter zur Hilfsfunktion der Männer erniedrigt und ihre geistlichen Bedürfnisse im Häuslichen eindämmt, sie zum Beispiel mit Kochrezepten für gefilte fish abspeist (23).

Citing numerous examples she eloquently exposes the double standard that denies them social experience and freedom equal to that of men: "Du unterschätzt die Rolle der Frau im Judentum, sagen mir die Leute. Sie darf die Sabbatkerzen anzünden am gedeckten Tisch, eine wichtige Funktion. Ich will keine Tische decken und Sabbatkerzen anzünden, Kaddisch möchte ich sagen. Sonst bleib ich bei meinen Gedichten" (23).

Yet her criticism of traditional Judaism is clearly that of an insider; its goal is change within her culture, reform rather than abolition. Unlike Otto Weininger in his unsuccessful attempt to proclaim himself an honorary "Aryan," Klüger in no way rejects her Jewish identity. Without internalized anti-Semitism or self-hatred, Klüger proposes feminist interpretations of biblical texts emphasizing instances of female bonding in the Thora, for example the Biblical Ruth's loyalty to her mother-in-law Naomi.[7]

After Klüger's account of the persecution to which she was exposed as a Jewish woman in Central Europe, the passages of her acculturation in the United States read almost effortlessly. Klüger minimizes the rejection and discrimination that she encountered as an immigrant woman—she expected them. Neither they, nor the acquisition of a new language, are problematized. Klüger reports that after her admittance to New York's

Hunter College soon after her arrival, she began writing in English. Her success as a student and her ensuing career as a professor of German demonstrate her ability to overcome cultural and intellectual barriers (231).

However, Klüger also integrates the memory of the Holocaust, the third important facet of her identity, into her new nationality and language. It clearly affects the complex and ambivalent relationships portrayed in *weiter leben*. The foremost examples are the love-hate relationship between Klüger, her mother, and her step-sister and the life-long codependency between her, her mother, and this Holocaust survivor who had become like family because she shared their death camp experience. The disputes within this exclusive group do not preclude emotional closeness and mutual understanding.

On the other hand, the misunderstandings between Jews and German Gentiles, "die Deutschen" (23), occur because these groups share no common ground. She intimates, however, that the lack of communication is one-sided: the Jews understand the Germans all too well, while most Germans remain caught up in denial. As the most blatant example she introduces a woman Gisela who, short of denying the Holocaust altogether, trivializes it by her arrogant, ill-informed statements about concentration camps and exile. "Theresienstadt sei ja nicht so schlimm gewesen, informierte mich die deutsche Frau eines Kollegen in Princeton, die sich der Gnade der späten Geburt erfreute" (84). This Gisela later equates her own father's death as a soldier in World War II with the murder of Klüger's father in a death camp (85, 92). Gisela's revisionist and crypto-fascist statements indict the victims and exonerate the Germans. The character of Gisela illustrates the gulf separating the victims from the perpetrators and their allies. Another example is a young Jew about to marry a German woman. In a bout of defensiveness and self-hatred he accuses the survivors of the Holocaust of opportunism: "Ihr seid über Leichen gegangen" (72).

In Klüger's observations about the behavior of women concentration camp prisoners and guards, her feminism comes to the fore. In contrast to Fania Fénelon, Klüger differentiates between the behavior of men and women, asserting that sadism among women was the exception rather than the rule. Examining gender roles among prisoners and perpetrators, she exposes the stereotype of the brutal women Capos (women prisoners put in charge of other prisoners) as male fantasies. According to Klüger, "SS-women" never existed despite their popularity in TV series and films.

> Von der Grausamkeit der Aufseherinnen wird viel geredet und wenig geforscht. Nicht daß man sie in Schutz nehmen soll, aber sie werden überschätzt. Sie kamen aus kleinen Verhältnissen, und man steckte sie in Uniformen, denn irgendwas mußten sie ja tragen und natürlich nicht Zivil

für diesen Dienst in Arbeitslager und KZ. Ich glaube auf Grund dessen, was ich gelesen, gehört und selbst erfahren habe, daß sie im Durchschnitt weniger brutal waren als die Männer, und wenn man sie heute in gleichem Maße wie die Männer verurteilt, so dient ein solches Urteil als Alibi für die eigentlichen Verantwortlichen" (146-47).[8]

Klüger's notions about women differ from the overly idealistic views of authors such as Hanna Lévy-Hass and Joan Ringelheim (741-61), who suggest that love and nurturing are innate to the female psyche. Klüger emphasizes that mutual support greatly increased chances for survival, particularly in the generally neglected women's camps, but she does not consider solidarity among women or "feminist" behavior to be biologically pre-determined. However, she concurs with feminist sociologists who believe that women prisoners have a greater capacity for endurance and collaboration (and thus survival) than men because of gender-specific socialization. "Ich glaube fest, obwohl die Männer es unbegreiflicherweise bestritten, daß Frauen lebensfähiger als Männer sind" (237, 128).

Klüger also approaches the topic of anti-Semitism with a critical attitude. In pointed statements she refutes common misapprehensions about Jews and Judaism that most Germans continue to adhere to: "Die Juden haben alle Geld gehabt, die waren wohlhabend. Außer den Armen" (24). She tolerates clichés neither about Jews nor about German Gentiles, disputing, for example, the simplistic view that the Nazis were primitive barbarians (148). This misconception, she believes, provides easy answers and Hollywood-style interpretations of the Holocaust, but fails to take into account historical fact.

Klüger writes with affectionate and tolerant criticism about her residence of choice, Orange County, USA. But as the tone of her remarks suggests, Northern Germany, rather than California, engages her fascination.[9] Germany at the time of unification, with its debates about the country's future, provided the impetus for *weiter leben*. In an atmosphere where the "jüngste Vergangenheit," the "most recent" past—a German euphemism for the Nazi era—seemed to be washed away in a wave of renewed national pride, remembrance seemed more important than ever before.[10] In her daily contact with the language most closely associated with Prussian militarism and German National Socialism, Klüger was confronted with the civilization that had perpetrated the destruction of the European Jews. The fact that *weiter leben* was, perhaps by necessity, written in Germany is no contradiction to Klüger's aversion to revisiting the places of the past. What matters in *weiter leben* is not Germany's *genius loci*, but its language and the aggressive vitality of its contemporary cultural environment, which Klüger views generally with optimism and occasionally with concern (269-70).

The positive reception of *weiter leben* proves that despite everything that has been written about the persecution of the Jews, the Nazi era, and the genocide, this most recent Holocaust autobiography addresses concerns that also affect unified Germany. Within a few weeks, Klüger's autobiography held the first place on the prestigious *Bestenliste* of the *Südwestdeutscher Rundfunk*. Soon thereafter it was discussed by the *Literarisches Quartett* on German Television, perhaps the most influential literary forum in Germany today, and the author was invited for readings and interviews in Germany and Austria. She was awarded the 1992 Rauhstein prize of the City of Linz.

Throughout her work Klüger underscores that the barriers between German gentiles and Jews do not signify a moral difference—being victimized does not presuppose superiority—but a different sensibility arising from the admission of one's vulnerability. While Auschwitz, as Klüger explains to her students in Germany, was not a training ground for humanity and tolerance, it created two categories of people, intended victims and perpetrators. Klüger believes that the Holocaust survivors and the students in today's Germany speak a different language.[11]

Despite the imposing intellectual and emotional force that propels Klüger's book, humility emanates from every page of her account. She explains her fate in terms of coincidence, *Zufall*, rather than providence (73). Her awareness of human frailty introduces an intellectual and spiritual honesty into her text, lending it an aura of grace that shines through in her attitude towards her former enemies.

> Mut aus Gewissensgründen kann man nicht verlangen, denn der ist eine Tugend; wäre er selbstverständlich, dann bräuchten wir ihn nicht als vorbildlich zu bewundern. Daher sei Feigheit auch kein verächtlicher Grund für Handlungsunfähigkeit. Das Normale ist Feigheit, und man soll keinen für normales Benehmen verurteilen. Nur kann man nicht gleichzeitig behaupten, wir haben nichts von den Gewalttaten der Nazis gewußt, und wir haben aus Furcht oder Feigheit nichts dagegen unternommen (184).

Rather than calling for an indiscriminate reconciliation between Jews and Germans, an unqualified "forgiving and forgetting," as many Gentile authors have done, Klüger insists on historical accuracy, demarcations, and differences which, if adhered to, could possibly bring about the kind of tolerance that Moses Mendelssohn advocated in vain two centuries ago.

Notes

[1] Hilberg elaborates: "Schließlich könnte ein dritter Schwerpunkt der Frage sein, wie man überhaupt, innerhalb oder auch außerhalb Deutschlands über den Holocaust sprechen kann, inwiefern der Genozid an den Juden, der Versuch der Nationalsozialisten, das jüdische Volk auszulöschen, nicht nur besonderer Methoden bedarf, sondern eine eigene Sprache, vielleicht sogar eine eigene Ästhetik erfordert" (Hilberg and Söllner 175).

[2] The author of *weiter leben* exercises what James E. Young calls "the right to invoke the empirical bond that has indeed existed between a writer and events in his narrative...the right to invoke the experiences as one's own" (24).

[3] One reason why Holocaust scholars and writers were overly critical of Holocaust literature may be the fact that the reality of the Holocaust has been questioned time and again in revisionist and anti-Semitic literature. Failure to recognize, as Young points out, "the difference between narrative that fabricates its authenticity as part of its fiction and that which attempts to salvage, however tenuously, an authentic empirical connection between text, writer, and experience" (24) may have led to the categorical rejection of representations deviating from what any given school of thought had come to consider as "fact."

[4] Klüger establishes unequivocal priorities in statements like the following: "Auch kamen Leute mit Bordellphantasien zu mir und wollten wissen, ob ich vergewaltigt worden sei. Dann sagte ich, nein, aber fast umgebracht haben sie mich, und erklärte den Begriff der Rassenschande, weil ich es interessant finde, daß ein bösartiger Begriff ein weitgehendes, wenn auch kein absolutes Schutzmittel für Jüdinnen gewesen ist. Wenn das Interesse erlahmte, wußte man, daß die intime Frage einem falschen Interesse gedient hat" (236). In Holocaust fiction and recollections such those by Ka-Tzetnik 135633, Leonard Frank, but also in such memoirs as Norbert Troller's documents, in the Leo Baeck Institute of New York, sexual exploitation of women and rape occupy the writer's imagination to an extraordinary extent.

[5] America, she writes, "Das ist ein Land, dessen Geschichte darin besteht, daß seine Einwohner hierher flohen, um der Geschichte zu entrinnen, der europäischen und der asiatischen, und schließlich auch der amerikanischen Geschichte, sofern sie sich weiter östlich zugetragen hat. Die Häuser in Orange County sind aus Holz gebaut, auch die teuren. Keine gemeinsame Vergangenheit bindet uns, darum ist jede Vergangenheit persönlich, betrifft nur den einen, der daran zu schleppen hat.... Ich lebe gern hier. Diese von Erdbeben bedrohte Meer- und Wüstenlandschaft, mit Sonne gesegnet, von Wassernot geplagt, hat sich die törichte, tragische Aufgabe gestellt, die Vergangenheit abzuschaffen, indem man sie abstreitet, in dem man die Gegenwart durch eine andere Gegenwart ersetzt, bevor die erste alt werden kann. Das geht nicht, darum ist es töricht. Das rächt sich, darum ist es tragisch" (280–82).

[6] Douglas Hauer convincingly argues that Arendt uses the biography of Rahel Levin Varnhagen to reflect on her own identity, that of a German Jewish woman and exile writer (2).

[7] In her novel *Der Brautpreis* Grete Weil engages in a similar undertaking trying to reinterpret parts of the Thora from a feminist point of view.

[8] "Man wendet ein, Nazi-Frauen hatten einfach weniger Gelegenheit, Verbrechen zu begehen als Männer. Bleibt noch immer die Tatsache, daß die deutschen Frauen, sogar die Nazi-Frauen, nachprüfbar weniger verbrochen haben als die Männer. Man verurteilt einen Menschen ja nicht für das, was er unter Umständen tun würde oder könnte, sondern dafür, was er tatsächlich getan hat.... Kann es nicht sein, daß sich die berühmten Beispiele weiblicher Grausamkeit in den Lagern auf immer dieselbe relativ kleine Gruppe von Aufseherinnen beziehen? Wird nicht immer dieselbe Ilse Koch beim Namen

genannt?... In Ermangelung von exaktem Material stelle ich die These auf, daß es in den Frauenlagern im Durchschnitt weniger brutal zuging als in den Männerlagern" (146).

[9] As other Holocaust accounts show, for example Salo Beckermann's statements in Ruth Beckermann's film *Die papierene Brücke*, the perception of German and Austrian culture and language on the part of survivors depends on where the individual person experienced persecution and mass murder. Beckermann encountered anti-Semitism and persecution predominantly at the hands of Rumanian Nazis and considered Vienna and Austria after 1945 as a safe haven and the place of his liberation.

[10] "Über die Geschichte der sogenannten 'jüngsten Vergangenheit' (die mit den Jahren nicht älter zu werden scheint und daher irgendwie so zeitlos ist wie das Jüngste Gericht) ist so viel geforscht und geschrieben worden, daß wir sie langsam zu kennen meinen, während die Geschichte der Vergangenheitsbewältigung noch aussteht" (198). In this context it is important to consider that the date of the unification, which some choose to refer to as "re-unification," coincided with that of the Kristallnacht pogrom of 1938 only fifty years earlier.

[11] Hans Thalberg expressed it this way in his memoirs (cf. Lorenz 139).

Works Cited

Aichinger, Ilse. *Die größere Hoffnung*. Wien: Bermann-Fischer, 1948.

Angress, Ruth Klüger. "Lanzmann's *Shoah* and Its Audience." *Simon Wiesenthal Center Annual* 3 (1986): 249–60.

Arendt, Hannah. *Rahel Varnhagen: Lebensgeschichte einer deutschen Jüdin aus der Romantik*. München: Piper, 1962.

Beckermann, Ruth. *Unzugehörig*. Wien: Löcker, 1989.

———, director. *Die papierene Brücke*. Wien: filmladen, 1989.

Behrend, Rahel. *Verfemt und verfolgt*. Zürich: Büchergilde Gutenberg, 1945.

Behrend-Rosenfeld, Else R. *Ich stand nicht allein: Erlebnisse einer Jüdin in Deutschland 1933-45*. Frankfurt: Europäische Verlagsanstalt, 1964.

Canetti, Elias. *Das Augenspiel*. München: Hanser, 1985.

———. *Die Fackel im Ohr*. München: Hanser, 1980.

———. *Die gerettete Zunge*. München: Hanser, 1977.

Claussen, Detlev. "Nach Auschwitz." *Zivilisationsbruch: Denken nach Auschwitz*. Ed. Dan Diner. Frankfurt a.M.: Fischer, 1988. 54–68.

Edel, Peter. *Die Bilder des Zeugen Schattmann*. Frankfurt a.M.: Röderberg, 1972.

———. *Schwester der Nacht*. Wien: Müller, 1947.

———. *Wenn es ans Leben geht: Meine Geschichte*. Frankfurt a.M.: Röderberg, 1979.

Fénelon, Fania. *Das Mädchenorchester von Auschwitz*. München: dtv, 1981.

Frank, Leonard. *Die Jünger Jesu. Gesammelte Werke* II. Berlin: Aufbau, 1959.
Fried, Erich. "Meine Puppe in Auschwitz." *Fast alles Mögliche.* Berlin: Wagenbach, 1975. 106-16.
Hart, Kitty. *Aber ich lebe.* Hamburg: Claassen, 1961; *I am Alive.* London: Schumann, 1961.
Hauer, Douglas. *Resistance and Survival and Jewish Identity in Germany*, Masters Thesis, Ohio State U, 1993.
Hermlin, Stephan. "Auschwitz ist unvergessen." *Äußerungen.* Berlin: Aufbau, 1983. 85-89.
Hilberg, Raul and Alfons Söllner. "Das Schweigen zum Sprechen bringen." *Zivilisationsbruch: Denken nach Auschwitz.* Ed. Dan Diner. Frankfurt a.M.: Fischer, 1988. 175-200.
Honigmann, Barbara. *Roman von einem Kinde.* Darmstadt: Luchterhand, 1986.
Ka-Tzetnik 135633. *House of Dolls.* London: Muller, 1956.
Kautsky, Benedikt. *Teufel und Verdammte: Erfahrungen und Erkenntnisse aus sieben Jahren in deutschen Konzentrationslagern.* Zürich: Büchergilde Gutenberg, 1946.
Klüger, Ruth. *weiter leben: Eine Jugend.* Göttingen: Wallstein, 1992.
Lander, Jeanette. *Die Töchter.* Frankfurt a.M.: Insel, 1976.
Lang, Berel, ed. *Writing and the Holocaust.* New York: Holmes, 1988.
Langer, Lawrence. "Interpreting Survivor Testimony." *Writing and the Holocaust.* Ed. Lang. 26-39.
Lévy-Hass, Hanna. *Vielleicht war das alles erst der Anfang.* Berlin: Rotbuch, 1979.
Lorenz, Dagmar C.G. *Verfolgung bis zum Massenmord: Holocaust-Diskurse in deutscher Sprache aus der Sicht der Verfolgten.* New York: Lang, 1992.
Milton, Sybil. *In Fitting Memory.* Detroit: Wayne State UP, 1991.
Morley, Peter, director. *Kitty: Return to Auschwitz* [Kitty Felix Hart]. Yorkshire Television, 1979.
Ringelheim, Joan. "Women and the Holocaust: A Reconsideration of Research." *Signs* 10.4 (1985): 741-61.
Sperber, Manès. *All das Vergangene....* Wien: Europa, 1983. ["Die Wasserträger Gottes"; "Die vergebliche Warnung"; "Bis man mir Scherben auf die Augen legt".]
Spies, Gerty. *Drei Jahre Theresienstadt.* München: Kaiser, 1984.
———. *Ein Stück Weges (ein Gedanke an Jahre schmerzvoller Reifung).* Ms. New York: Leo Baeck Institute Archive, n.d.
———. *Theresienstadt: Gedichte.* München: Freitag, 1948.
Thalberg, Hans. *Von der Kunst, Österreicher zu sein.* Wien: Böhlau, 1984.
Troller, Norbert. Portfolio. Leo Baeck Institute Archive, New York.
Weil, Grete. *Der Brautpreis.* Zürich: Nagel, 1988.
Weilovà, Nina. "71978 Jude: Erinnerungen." Ms. Wien: Österreichisches Dokumentationsarchiv der Widerstandsbewegung, n.d.
Weininger, Otto. *Geschlecht und Charakter.* Wien: Braumüller, 1906.

Weiss, Peter. *Die Ästhetik des Widerstands*. Frankfurt: Suhrkamp, 1975.
——. "Meine Ortschaft." *Rapporte*. Frankfurt a.M.: Suhrkamp, 1968. 113-24.
Wolf, Christa. *Kindheitsmuster*. Berlin: Aufbau, 1976.
Young, James E. "On Rereading Holocaust Diaries and Memoirs." *Writing and Rewriting the Holocaust*. Bloomington: Indiana UP, 1988. 15-39.

Antiracist Feminism in Germany: Introduction to Dagmar Schultz and Ika Hügel

Sara Lennox

In September 1991 German skinheads attacked Vietnamese and Mozambican workers in the small East German town of Hoyerswerda as its townspeople watched and applauded. The events of Hoyerswerda vividly documented the rise in racist violence in Germany since 1989 and a more broad-based support for racism among the German people. Hoyerswerda also cast its shadow over the November 1991 Women in German conference and was responsible for WiG members' decision to focus the 1992 WiG conference on two guest speakers who had played a central role in German antiracist feminism, Dagmar Schultz, a white Christian woman, and Ika Hügel, an Afro-German woman. Their talks at the 1992 conference, slightly revised to account for developments in Germany since then, are printed in this volume. As the number of attacks on foreigners in Germany continues to mount (6300 in 1992 [Buchsteiner]) and the names of other German towns—Hünxe, Rostock, Mölln, Solingen—have also become emblematic for escalating racist violence, the issues that Schultz and Hügel raise here remain of utmost urgency.

In their essays, Schultz and Hügel draw on their many years of active engagement in antiracist struggle within the women's movement. Schultz, active in the German women's movement from its beginnings, was one of the founders of Berlin's *Feministisches Gesundheitszentrum,* and her name may be familiar to WiG members as a coeditor of the 1984 collection *German Feminism* (and author or editor of six other books). As she explains here, her own antiracist politics were forged in the American civil rights movement and still reveal their American origins, evident in the moral rigor with which she demands accountability from herself and others (particularly vis-à-vis white skin privilege), her emphasis upon differences among women, and her commitment to coalition-building. With typical modesty, Schultz does not reveal the major role her own often unacknowledged efforts have played in making racism a central concern of German feminism. She herself may have initiated the discussion of racism within the German women's movement with an article in the October 1981 issue of the feminist journal *Courage,* where she reported on the 1981 National Women's Studies Association convention, focused on racism within the American women's movement, and then explored the relevance of the NWSA debates for German feminism. One of the most important vehicles for Schultz's antiracist work has been the Orlanda Frauenverlag, which she helped to found in 1972 and has directed since 1982. In 1983 Orlanda's publication of *Macht und Sinnlichkeit*, a collection of poetry and prose by Audre Lorde and Adrienne Rich (the keynote speakers at the NWSA conference) opened a broader discussion of racism within the German women's movement; in 1987 Christina Thürmer-Rohr's *Vagabundinnen*, also an Orlanda product, dared to propose that women were not just victims of patriarchy but might also play some role in oppression themselves. In the eighties, Orlanda published a wide array of books dealing with the concerns of Jewish women and women of color within and outside of Germany, and its spring 1993 publication of *Entfernte Verbindungen: Rassismus, Antisemitismus, Klassenunterdrückung*, a polemical collection of essays edited by Hügel, Schultz, and four other women associated with Orlanda, is sure to provoke further vigorous discussion. As Schultz notes, Orlanda's commitment to racial equity has been practical as well as intellectual: half of its paid positions are held by women of color, and it was to fill one of those positions that Ika Hügel joined Orlanda in 1990 as its *Pressereferentin*.

Hügel's life, and that of other Afro-Germans in Germany, was profoundly transformed by one of Schultz's antiracist initiatives, her invitation to the African-American poet Audre Lorde to teach in the spring semester 1984 at the Freie Universität in Berlin. In 1984 and during her subsequent visits to Germany, Lorde helped Afro-German women to identify and organize around their commonalities—indeed, the very term "Afro-German" appears to be her coinage. One of the earliest and most exciting manifestations of Lorde's influence was *Farbe bekennen: Afro-deutsche Frauen auf den Spuren ihrer Geschichte*, published by Orlanda in 1986 (and in English translation by the University of Massachusetts Press in 1992 as *Showing Our Colors: Afro-German Women Speak Out*). *Farbe bekennen* led to the formation of the Initiative Schwarze Deutsche, a political action group that embraces all Germans of color. It also gave Afro-German women the confidence to make common cause with immigrant and Jewish women in Germany, to demand that white Christian feminists confront the racism of their own movement, and to launch the many initiatives on their own behalf that Hügel tells us about in her essay. Hügel's encounter with the writing and person of Audre Lorde deeply influenced her politics and changed her life. She and Schultz became close friends of Lorde and her partner Gloria Joseph, and they were at Lorde's bedside when she died in St. Croix on 17 November 1992. Within the Afro-German women's movement, Hügel's own work has focused on several areas. She has emphasized that the current German wave of violence is not merely *Ausländerfeindlichkeit*, but racism, since it is also directed against Germans of color like herself. Like other Afro-Germans, she has vigorously laid claim to the German identity many white Germans want to deny her. (That white German rejection was pithily summarized in the message on an anonymous postcard sent to the filmmaker Christel Priemer as she was preparing a television film on Afro-Germans: "Deutsche sind weiß. Neger können keine Deutschen sein!") Hügel has collaborated on the project of establishing positive definitions of Afro-German identity, while she simultaneously insists, as in her recent contribution to *Entfernte Verbindungen*, a discussion with a much younger Afro-German woman, on exploring differences between Afro-Germans of varying generations and backgrounds. She has tried to forge links to other men and women of the African diaspora and in August 1993 was able to celebrate her own Black American roots in a joyful first meeting with the African-American father she had never known. An active participant in coalitions of Black German women, Jewish women, and immigrant women with white Christian women, Hügel has worked to make German feminism a movement that serves the interests of all women.

Can the German women's movement embrace the presence of many different kinds of women in Germany and work for a transformation of Germany (or even the world) that would benefit all of them? In the summer of 1993, the verdict is still out. As Schultz reports, racism is now a popular topic within German feminism. Since 1989, racism, antisemitism, and xenophobia have been the focus of a series of explosive conferences—Bremen, November 1989; Cologne, November 1990; Berlin, October 1991—and several feminist publications, including special issues of *Beiträge zur feministischen Theorie und Praxis* and *Feministische Studien*, while a number of German feminists have begun to undertake a variety of more or less visible antiracist initiatives and projects. On the other hand, *Entfernte Verbindungen* attests again and again to the opposition that Black, Jewish, and immigrant women encounter when they try to raise the issue of racism, the reluctance of white German feminists to engage in antiracist work, and their efforts to exempt themselves from responsibility for German racism and xenophobia. Schulz alludes to the strategy of the editors of the special issue of *Feministische Studien*, who want to speak merely of "kulturelle und sexuelle Differenzen" and argue that categories like "racism" and "sexism" remain within a moralizing discourse founded on a problematical hierarchization of oppressions. But as Helma Lutz points out in *Entfernte Verbindungen*, refusing to use those analytical concepts makes it virtually impossible to talk about the power structures that terms like "racism" and "sexism" designate (139–40), nor is it an act of moralism to point out that within those structures certain people have more power than others. Alice Schwarzer's strategy for avoiding a substantive discussion of racism within feminism is even more ingenious. In *Emma*, she maintains that recent attention to racist violence (for which men alone are to blame) is a hypocritical attempt by men to deflect attention away from the violence against women that should be the real object of feminist concern. Some other German feminists have argued that they are so exhausted by their attempts to defend the interests of German women that it is unreasonable to expect them to concern themselves with the problems of foreigners, too. But, as Schultz argues here, even if German feminists were determined to mount a campaign against racism, the structure of the movement itself, organized in tiny projects with little connection to one another, militates against such an effort. Thus the prognosis for the future of feminist antiracism in Germany that both Schulz and Hügel offer is mostly quite grim.

Might American feminist Germanists play some role in the struggle against racism in Germany? Though I fear I may exaggerate our influence, I think there are some interventions we as scholars and teachers of German literature and culture might make. We can insist on integrating the presence and accomplishments of people of color in Germany into our teaching at all levels, attempting to transform the canon of German literature which, as Russell Berman has argued, "still gives priority to 'the white boys of Weimar' or subsequent authors who fit that mold" (Seyhan 5). We can undertake the even more unpopular task of exploring to what degree German national identity and culture might rest upon ethnocentric and white supremacist first principles. We can investigate the relationship of German colonialism to National Socialism to present debates around German national identity, the ideological or actual role that women may have played in the successes of German racism, and the ways in which the constitution of German racism, nationalism, and national identity is similar to or differs from that of other countries, including the USA. As American feminists, we can try to transmit to the German women's movement our own accomplishments and mistakes in attempting to understand diversity among women and build cross-racial coalitions, as we simultaneously refrain from imposing our own models on the quite different German situation, and we can publicize German efforts to advance and implement an antiracist analysis. Many Women in German members are already engaged in such projects, and WiG's invitation to Hügel and Schultz and its publication of their essays here continue that important antiracist work.

Works Cited

Beiträge zur feministischen Theorie und Praxis [Geteilter Feminismus: Rassismus, Antisemitismus, Fremdenhaß] 27 (1990).

Buchsteiner, Jochen. "'Die spüren, daß wir da sind.'" *Die Zeit* 9 July 1993: 5.

Feministische Studien [Kulturelle und sexuelle Differenzen] 9.2 (Nov. 1991).

Hügel, Ika, Chris Lange, May Ayim, Ilona Bubeck, Gülsen Aktas, and Dagmar Schultz. *Entfernte Verbindungen: Rassismus, Antisemitismus, Klassenunterdrückung*. Berlin: Orlanda Frauenverlag, 1993.

Opitz, May, Katharina Oguntoye, and Dagmar Schultz. *Farbe bekennnen: Afro-deutsche Frauen auf den Spuren ihrer Geschichte*. Berlin: Orlanda Frauenverlag, 1986. English trans. *Showing Our Colors: Afro-German Women Speak Out*. Trans. Anne V. Adams. Amherst: U of Massachusetts P, 1992.

Priemer, Christel. "Deutsche sind weiß: Neger können keine Deutschen sein!" Fernsehfilm für den Saarländischen Rundfunk, 1986.

Schultz, Dagmar. "Dem Rassismus in sich begegnen." *Courage* (Oct. 1981): 17–22.

Schwarzer, Alice. "Editorial." *Emma* (Jan. 1993).

Seyhan, Azade. "Introduction: Special Issue on Minorities in German Culture." *New German Critique* 16.1 (Winter 1989): 3–9.

Thürmer-Rohr, Christina. *Vagabundinnen: Feministische Essays*. Berlin: Orlanda Frauenverlag, 1987.

Wir kämpfen seit es uns gibt

Ika Hügel

Mein Name ist Ika Hügel, ich bin 1947 in der Bundesrepublik Deutschland geboren und aufgewachsen. Meine Mutter ist weiße Deutsche, mein Vater afro-Amerikaner. Ich habe ihn nie kennengelernt. Aufgewachsen bin ich in einer Kleinstadt in Bayern. Sowohl in unserem Haus, in der Umgebung, im Kindergarten und in der Schule war ich die einzige mit einer anderen Hautfarbe. Rassismus und Diskriminierungen begannen für meine Mutter nach meiner Geburt. Sie wurde aus der katholischen Kirche ausgeschlossen und von vielen als "Negerhure" betitelt. Selbst vom engsten Familienkreise (außer von meiner Großmutter) wurde sie verachtet und in keiner Weise unterstützt. Sie war vom Tag meiner Geburt an ausgeschlossen aus der Gesellschaft. Zu der damaligen Zeit (nach 1945) schalteten sich auch die zuständigen Jugendämter als Unterstützung in der Form ein, in dem sie zielgerichtet den Müttern von afro-deutschen Kindern nahelegten, sie in einer Pflegefamilie oder in einem Heim unterzubringen. Im Bundestag wurde die Gruppe der Afro-Deutschen als "Sonderproblem" beurteilt:

> Eine besondere Gruppe unter den Besatzungskindern bilden die 3.093 Negermischlinge, die ein menschliches und rassisches Problem besonderer Art darstellen.... Die verantwortlichen Stellen der freien behördlichen Jugendpflege haben sich bereits seit Jahren Gedanken über das Schicksal dieser Mischlinge gemacht, denen schon allein die klimatischen Bedingungen in unserem Lande nicht gemäß sind. Man hat erwogen, ob es nicht besser für sie sei, wenn man sie in das Heimatland ihrer Väter verbrächte... (*Das Parlament*, 19.3.1952, zitiert in *Farbe bekennen* [100]).

Als Resultat der damaligen Politik der Jugendämter wurde ich von meinem siebten Lebensjahr an bis zu meinem fünfzehnten Lebensjahr in einem christlichen Heim weit weg von meiner Familie untergebracht. Ich wurde gequält, meine noch junge Persönlichkeit vernichtet und mein Selbstbewußtsein zerstört. Mir ist es wichtig an dieser Stelle zu erwähnen, daß nicht nur ich, aber gerade meine Generation (die also nach dem zweiten Weltkrieg) die Auswirkungen von Rassismus und die einhergehende Isolation and Ausgrenzung am spürbarsten zu tragen hatten. Generationen vor uns, auch wenn die Schwarzen Väter nicht anwesend waren, konnten doch von ihren Landleuten sprechen, von Kameradinnen und Kameraden, von gemeinsamen Treffpunkten und Unternehmungen. Als Beispiel zitiere ich Friede P., 1920 einem schwarzen afrikanischen Vater und einer weißen Deutschen geboren:

> ...ab '38 bin ich zu den Filmen nach Berlin gekommen. Da lernte ich dann die Landsleute kennen—Landsleute—, so bezeichnen wir Alten uns noch heute. Vorher kannte ich ja keine.
> Bei der Filmerei war es sehr gemütlich. In den Pausen nahmen die Afrikaner oft ihre Trommeln, und wir sangen vor den Ateliers. Aus allen Produktionen kamen die Leute gelaufen und hörten begeistert zu.
> Nach 1933 waren kaum Afrikaner und Afrikanerinnen zurückgekehrt. Was sollten sie in Afrika? Wer hätte ihnen die Fahrt bezahlt?...
> Wir waren alle zusammen—jüngere und ältere Afrikaner/innen, die heute überall verstreut in Deutschland leben. Viele sind auch in den Kriegsjahren umgekommen (*Farbe bekennen* 77-78).

Kinder von GIs waren gewöhnlich abgeschnitten vom Land des Vaters, da diese alle wieder zurückgingen oder wieder zurückbeordert wurden. So erfuhr auch mein Vater nie, daß ich geboren wurde. Ein Bezug zu Afrika herzustellen war deshalb kaum möglich, da ja noch nicht einmal der Kontakt zu den USA da war. Die Generation nach uns, in den siebziger Jahren, hatte vorwiegend Väter aus afrikanischen Ländern. Sie kamen als Studenten nach Deutschland, meist nach und während der Unabhängigkeitskriegen. Die meisten Afro-Deutschen in dieser Zeit hatten und haben Kontakt mit ihren Vätern und viele lernten das Heimatland kennen.

1985 fand das erste afro-deutsche Treffen in der Bundesrepublik Deutschland statt. Ich war 39 Jahre alt, als ich das erste Mal andere Afro-Deutsche und Schwarze Menschen kennenlernte. Ich zitiere aus meinem Text, *Entfernte Verbindungen*:

> Ich kann mich sehr gut erinnern, daß sich etwas in meinem Bewußtsein und in meiner Persönlichkeit verändert hat, als ich Schwarze Deutsche kennengelernt habe. Mir wurde klar, daß ich mich bisher immer nur von Weißen unterschieden habe, und die waren in der Regel immer "besser" als ich. Sie waren mir in allem überlegen, wurden geachtet, mir gegenüber bevorzugt, brauchten sich nicht in Frage zu stellen, und viele genossen all die Selbstverständlichkeiten, für die Afro-Deutsche hart kämpfen mußten und noch immer müssen. Die Mehrzahl der Weißen konnte sich eher mit den angenehmen und interessanten Dingen im Leben beschäftigen. Diese Vielfalt des Lebens bot sich den meisten von uns nicht.
> Als ich Afro-Deutsche kennenlernte, entdeckte ich zum ersten Mal Unterschiede, die nicht trennen, sondern in erster Linie verbinden. Gemeinsam erkannten wir unsere Stärken und Schwächen, jede und jeder für sich und all auf ihre Weise. Unsere Hautfarbe und der Kampf des Überlebens ließen uns

Nähe verspüren, die wir bis dahin unter Weißen nie gefühlt haben. Ich war nicht mehr allein auf der einen Seite dieser Welt. Es gab eine Gruppe, der ich angehörte und die mich brauchte. Ab diesem Zeitpunkt fing ich Schritt für Schritt an, meinen Weg zu mir selbst zu finden, zu sehen, wer ich war und auf was ich stolz sein konnte. Ich konnte mich anders wahrnehmen, mich anders spüren. Distanz und Grenzen, die stets zwischen mir und Weißen existierten, gab es zwischen uns Afro-Deutschen nicht, dafür sicherlich andere, aber niemals solche, die ausgrenzten, einengten und die mich nicht atmen und leben ließen. Diese gewonnene Sicherheit erlaubte mir nun endlich, Empörung und Wut zu empfinden (*Entfernte Verbindungen*).

Afro-Deutsche in der BRD wollen *ihre* Schwarze Geschichte schaffen, weiter entwickeln und für alle Menschen, Schwarz und weiß, sichtbar machen. Sehr wichtig ist die Initiative Schwarze Deutsche (ISD), 1985 gegründet und heute in jeder größeren Stadt vertreten.

Für viele bot die ISD die erste Kontaktmöglichkeit mit anderen schwarzen Frauen und Männern, insbesondere für schwarze Deutsche, die nach Kriegsende geboren wurden. [Wir] wuchsen bis dahin meist völlig isoliert und ohne jegliche Verbindung zu schwarzen Menschen auf. [Wir] waren es auch letztlich, die die schwarze deutsche Geschichte sichtbar zu machen begannen. Mittlerweile finden in einzelnen Städten wie auch überregional regelmäßige Treffen statt. Seit 1988 werden vierteljährlich zwei Zeitschriften herausgegeben: *Afrekete, Zeitung für afro-deutsche und schwarze Frauen*, und *Afro-Look, Zeitschrift von schwarzen Deutschen*. Vor ca. vier Jahren gründete sich die afro-deutsche Frauengruppe (ADEFRA). [Diese] Arbeit trug dazu bei, weitere afro-deutsche Frauengruppen in anderen Städten der BRD zu initiieren. Das Buch *Farbe bekennen* regte afro-deutsche Frauen aus den neuen Bundesländern an, die Spuren ihrer eigenen Geschichte zu suchen. Mit einem Dokumentarfilm über das Leben der Afrikanerin Machbuba, die vor hundertfünfzig Jahren in Begleitung des Fürsten Pückler nach Müskau, in der Nähe von Cottbus kam, machten sie den Anfang.

Auf internationaler Ebene wurde ein Netzwerk schwarzer Frauen u.a. durch das 5. Interkulturelle Sommerseminar für Schwarze Frauenstudien gefördert, das 1991 drei Wochen lang in Deutschland stattfand. Daran beteiligte Afro-Amerikanerinnen, wie z.B. Andrée Nicola McLaughlin, gründeten in Reaktion auf ihren Aufenthalt in Deutschland das Afro-German/Afro-American Friendship Committee. Diese Organization will u.a. interessierten afro-deutschen Frauen dabei behilflich sein, ihre Väter und Verwandten in den USA zu finden (Hügel, *Lesben Liebe Leidenschaft*).

Seit einigen Jahren wird der "Black History Month" von der ISD organisiert und durchgeführt.

In den letzten zwei Jahren fanden Kongreße in Bremen und in Berlin ausschließlich für Schwarze Frauen, Immigrantinnen und jüdische Frauen statt. Bei diesen Treffen erlebten wir zum ersten mal, daß wir nicht die

Minderheit waren, nicht mehr allein und voneinander isoliert. Wir hatten lange um einen Platz und um Gehör in der Frauenbewegung gekämpft. Wir hatten das "wohlgemeinte" und "oberflächliche" Verständnis der weißen christlich säkularisierten Frauen uns gegenüber satt. Wir wollten weder ihre anhaltende Betroffenheit noch ihre Schuldbekenntnisse. Während wir ständig um ein Miteinander kämpften, begegneten sie uns beständig mit Ignoranz und stehlen sich noch heute aus der Verantwortung. Eine Versöhnung mit uns, ohne Konsequenzen, und Harmonie um der Harmonie willen wollten wir nicht mehr. Ihre Ausreden, ihre trostsuchenden Tränen, ihre Feigheit und ihre gleichzeitige Überheblichkeit nahmen wir nicht länger hin. Ob bei diesen, oder anderen Veranstaltungen, wir waren ausschließlich in der Rolle der Aufklärenden und gingen aus solchen Veranstaltungen nie gestärkt heraus.

Ohne die Erfahrungen und Erlebnisse mit Schwarzen Frauen, ohne meine afro-deutschen Schwestern und Brüder, ohne die Begegnung und Freundschaft mit Schwarzen Frauen, besonders die mit Audre Lorde und Gloria Joseph, wäre ich nicht das was ich heute bin: Eine lebensfrohe, starke selbstbewußte Kämpferin, glücklich darüber, ein Teil der Schwarzen Bewegung zu sein. Ich bin stolz auf meine Hautfarbe, die mir, und uns anderen Schwarzen Menschen, wieder im Jahre 1992 das Leben kosten kann.

Am 9. November 1989 fiel die Mauer in Berlin. Meine Gedanken, Gefühle und Beobachtungen, die ich damals niederschrieb, wurden in *Beiträge zur feministischen Theorie und Praxis,* Köln, in der Zeitschrift *Ashe* und im *MS* Magazin New York unter dem Titel "Begegnungen mit Grenzen" veröffentlicht. Ich zitiere aus diesem Text:

> "Ich hab' dich mittlerweile so gut kennengelernt, und du bist mir so vertraut geworden, daß ich gar nicht mehr merke, daß du schwarz bist. Rassismus, ist das denn wirklich dein Thema, was verstehst du denn als schwarze Deutsche darunter und vor allem, wie lebst du damit?"
>
> Solche Aussagen und Fragen und noch viele andere werden häufig an mich herangetragen, und die verblüfften Gesichter von weißen deutschen Frauen, wenn ich sie frage, was macht Rassismus mit euch, wie könnt ihr damit leben, sind oftmals erschreckend. Sie bewegen sich selbstverständlich auf der anderen Seite, denn Rassismus markiert eine Trennungslinie, weist also Grenzen auf. Unter Grenzen leiden am meisten die, die ausgegrenzt werden. Die größten Verluste erleiden letztlich jene, die sich abgrenzen, sich nicht öffnen, den Blickwinkel nicht wechseln, die andere Seite und unser Schwarz-sein nicht wahrnehmen oder auch die eigene Perspektive nicht in Frage stellen.
>
> Ich denke oft in den letzten Tagen an meinen kurzen Aufenthalt in Berlin, an diese Grenze, diese Mauer, die bis dahin diese riesige Stadt teilte. Doch wer wäre besser in der Lage, eine Grenze zu verstehen, mit einer Grenze zu leben, als schwarze Deutsche? Nicht ohne Ergriffenheit erlebte ich mit, wie

diese Mauer ihre Macht verlor und die Menschen auf der anderen Seite zu Tausenden herüberkamen. Ich sah in ihre Gesichter, und manch ablehnender Blick, prüfend in voller Unkenntnis, auch ich könnte deutsch sein und sie willkommen heißen, traf mich. Grenzen sind schlimm, und man kann sich leider an ein Leben mit einer Grenze gewöhnen, ohne wahrzunehmen, wie sehr man durch ihre bloße Existenz betroffen wird. Mitten unter all den Menschen spürst du, wie stolz Westberliner sind, keine Ostberliner zu sein, sowie Bayern keine Preußen sein wollen und umgekehrt, vor allem aber wollen Weiße niemals Schwarze sein. Erschreckend war mein Gefühl, und ich wurde erneut überrumpelt von der Gewißheit, alle tragen ihre Grenzen mit sich herum. Deutlichen Ausdruck finden Grenzen in der Bildung von Vorurteilen und Angstgefühlen.

In dieser Stadt, mitten in Berlin, dachte ich immerzu, wie es sein kann, Grenzen zu überschreiten. Ich sah mir die Menschen an und wünschte mir, daß in jedem dieser Herzen die eigenen Grenzen auch zu überwinden wären. Mir fiel auf, wie freundlich alle miteinander umgingen, wohlwissend, ihre Gesten schließen mich nicht mit ein. Glückwünsche und Umarmungen; soviele Hände streckten sich entgegen, und ich war gerührt. Nur für eine Sekunde lang hätte ich mir gewünscht, so willkommen zu sein, ich, wir, die nicht deutsch aussehen, es aber sind.

Besonders problematisch und schmerzlich sind dann schließlich die Mauern, die man dann selbst um sich herum aufbaut und die Grenzen, die mitten durch das eigene Selbst hindurchgehen und die eigene Identität im eigenen Land in Frage stellen. Besonders in dieser Nacht spürte ich um einiges schmerzhafter wie es ist, Fremde im eigenen Land zu sein.

Mitten in diesem Freudentaumel von Gefühlen wurde auch ich mitgerissen. Niemanden, außer die Freundin neben mir, kannte ich. Die meisten kannten sich nicht länger als nur einen Augenblick. Dennoch konnte ich soviel Menschliches sehen. Vieles an dieser Freude konnte ich nicht teilen, wollte mich schämen dafür, doch wohin mit diesem Wissen, Wissen darüber, es gibt sie überall die Grenzen, überall kann ich sie sehen und fühlen, und manchmal ziehe ich sie selbst. (Kommt es nicht oft darauf an, wie streng die Grenzen bewacht werden?)

Mit dem Wunsch noch einmal die Mauer zu sehen, stieg ich aus dem Auto, stand sprachlos da und schloß meine Augen. Es ist ein Ort der mich verraten könnte, mein "Anders-sein". Ich will diese Mauer, diese Grenze nicht sehen, auch nicht das Stück Niemandsland.

Erinnerungen!—Erinnerungen an jene, die immer wollten, daß ich Lebewohl sage. Ich spüre den Schweiß an meinen Händen und die Verkrampfung meines Magens, obwohl ich weiß, es ist alles in Ordnung, du bist auf der richtigen Seite. Alles ist in Ordnung, nur mit meiner Wut stimmt etwas nicht.

Überschrittene Grenzen sind nicht überwundene Grenzen.

Und so lief ich noch lange durch die menschenüberfüllten Straßen. Suchte hilflos, wo ich stehenbleiben konnte. Will nicht mehr wissen, was ich für sie alle bin, deutsch? Meine Stimme, mein Schrei nach Freiheit und Heimat birgt das Geheimnis einer Liebe in einer Welt, die freundlich nicht für all ist.

Und jetzt?

Meine Erfahrungen als schwarze Deutsche und die tägliche Konfrontation mit Rassismus in diesem Land, zwingen mich immer wieder aufs neue, meine Wut nicht zu ignorieren, sonder laut heraus zu schreien. Doch wohin mit all dieser Wut, wenn es genau die treffen muß, in deren Mitte wir uns verunsichert und isoliert bewegen und die uns mit jedem noch so kleinen Wutausbruch mit erneuter Ausgrenzung bestrafen? Tatsache ist, Weiße müssen sich eben nicht mit Rassismus auseinandersetzen, müssen nicht ihre Werte und Identität in Frage stellen. Ganz im Gegenteil, denn für sie bedeutet in Frage stellen (also antirassistisches Engagement), ihre Privilegien in Frage stellen, und wer kann und will sich das auf Dauer schon leisten.

Privilegien in Frage stellen bedeutet ebenso Grenzen wahrnehmen und über Grenzen gehen.

Die Gesellschaft um mich herum ist noch weit entfernt von der Erkenntnis, daß überschrittene Grenzen, wie am Beispiel Berlins, nicht überwundene Grenzen sind, solange Erfahrungen nur an nationale Grenzen gebunden bleiben. Für viele bleiben die inneren Grenzen eine lebenslange Behinderung, Belastung und Bedrohung.

Wenn wir gemeinsam etwas bewegen wollen, müssen wir wohl oder übel Grenzen überschreiten, um zu einer neuen Bündnispolitik zu kommen, die *alle* Menschen miteinschließt.

1990 war ich nach Berlin umgezogen, um als Pressereferentin im Orlanda Frauenverlag meine Arbeit zu beginnen.

Kaum daß ich, wir, Zeit hatten, den Fall der Mauer und die damit erneut aufkommende rassistische Gewalt zu überleben, Ängste zuzulassen, darüber zu sprechen, afro-deutsche Schwestern und Brüder zu trösten (besonders die aus den neuen Bundesländern), begann schon die Diskussion über die Vereinigung Europas. Noch während wir auf die alltägliche rassistische Gewaltverbrechen reagierten, Schwarzen und Afro-Deutschen bei der Flucht aus dem Osten (nicht anders kann man es bezeichnen) halfen und ihnen für längere und auch kurze Zeit unsere Wohnungen als Schutz zur Verfügung stellten, diskutierten und stritten weiße Frauen über angemessenes Reagieren und Handeln, und verfielen erneut in Hilflosigkeit. In einigen Städten im Osten, so z.B. in Dresden, Leipzig und Cottbus was das Leben für Schwarze Menschen kaum noch möglich. Rechtsradikale beschmierten ihre Wohnungstüren mit Hakenkreuzen oder riefen ihnen hinterher: "Dich schwarze Negersau kriegen wir auch noch hier raus. Deutschland den Deutschen." In dieser Zeit schrieb May Ayim, eine meiner besten Freundinnen in Berlin, Mithauptautorin des Buches

Farbe bekennen, in einem Aufsatz (ebenfalls in *Beiträge zur feministischen Theorie und Praxis* veröffentlicht unter dem Titel "Die Fremdheit nimmt ab, die Feindlichkeit zu") folgendes. Ich zitiere:

1992 soll die Vereinigung Europas vollzogen sein, und allseits werden Vorbereitungen getroffen, um Staatsgrenzen zwischen den einzelnen europäischen Ländern abzubauen. Mit der Vereinigung nach innen geht, wie auch im bereits vereinten Deutschland, eine zunehmende Abgrenzung nach außen einher: Während innerhalb Europas Reise- und Arbeitsbeschränkungen aufgehoben werden, werden ImmigrantInnen und Flüchtlinge aus anderen Kontinenten einer verstärkt restriktiven Einwanderungs- und Asylgesetzgebung unterworfen, und der alltägliche Rassismus bedroht auch das Leben derer, die nicht die eigene Ausweisung und Abschiebung zu fürchten haben. Offensichtlich wollen sich diejenigen, die sich durch Ausplünderung und Unterdrückung bereichert haben, nun gemeinsam hinter neuen Mauern verschanzen, um die Beute und den erkauften Frieden ungestört genießen zu können. Die Armut soll vor den Toren Europas bleiben und dort haltmachen.

Es ist eine wiederkehrende Erfahrung, daß wir als Menschen schwarzer und weißer Herkunft von kleinauf mit Rassismus infiziert werden und dies in dieser Gesellschaft in einer konsequenten und subtilen Weise geschieht, die vor allem die potentiellen Mit-TäterInnen selten aufschreckt.

In der Schule erfuhren wir—und mit wir meine ich so ziemlich alle von uns, die in der Bundesrepublik aufgewachsen sind—nichts über das Leben von ImmigrantInnen in der Bundesrepublik und schon gar nichts über Schwarze Menschen in diesem Land.

Wir erfuhren nicht, daß der einmillionste Immigrant, ein Portugiese, bei seiner Einreise in die Bundesrepublik ein Motorrad geschenkt bekam und wilkommen geheißen wurde. Wir erfuhren nicht, wann und warum sich die (geheuchelte) Anfangs-Freundlichkeit gegenüber ImmigrantInnen in offene Feindseligkeit verwandelte.

Wir erfuhren nicht, daß sich einige Lebenswege von AfrikanerInnen in Deutschland bis in die Zeit des Mittelalters und noch weiter zurück dokumentieren lassen.

Wir erfuhren nicht, daß der erste afrikanische Student mit einer juristischen Arbeit über Schwarze in Europa promovierte—und die nicht im Jahre 1967, sondern im Jahre 1729! Und wir erfuhren nicht, daß Schwarze Deutsche in der Nazizeit verfolgt, zwangssterilisiert, vertrieben und umgebracht wurden.

Die rassistische Gewalt erfahren wir tagtäglich. Schwarze Menschen können nur noch in bestimmten Gegenden mit S- und U-Bahn fahren. Nach 18 Uhr, vor Einbruch der Dunkelheit trauen sie sich nicht mehr auf die Straße. Viele Mütter bringen ihre Kinder aus Angst vor rassistischen Übergriffen nicht mehr in den Kindergarten. Schwarze Menschen werden auf offener Straße zusammengeschlagen, so wie auch der Angolaner

Antonio Amadeo, der an den Folgen eines rassistischen Überfalls durch Rechtsextremisten starb. Einem Mann, polnischer Herkunft, wurde von Skinheads mit einer Schere ein Stück der Zunge abgeschnitten. Jüdische Friedhöfe und Denkmäler werden verwüstet: zuletzt die Gedenkstätte in Sachsenhausen (eine Baracke die als Museum und zu unser aller Erinnerung und Mahnung erhalten wurde, in der jüdische Menschen gelebt haben und vergast wurden).

Fast täglich werden Asylheime mit Steinen und Molotowcocktails beworfen und in Brand gesetzt. Zwei afro-deutsche Frauen wurden bei der Rückreise aus dem Ausland an Flughäfen einer demütigenden und rassistischen Leibesvisitation unterzogen. Eine Flughafenangestellte machte folgende Bemerkung dazu: "Man sortiert hier neuerdings nach Farbe".

Die rassistische Gewalt herrscht in der gesamten Bundesrepublik, jedoch verstärkt in den neuen Bundesländern.

Viele von uns Afro-Deutschen haben bereits die Bundesrepublik, das heißt, ihre Heimat, verlassen. Sie haben die Situation in der BRD nicht mehr ausgehalten. Wir kämpfen seit es uns gibt (und uns gibt es schon sehr lange) um einen Platz in unserer Gesellschaft, um den Platz, der uns zusteht. Für viele, die dennoch gegangen sind, war dieser Schritt nicht leicht, und schmerzvoll für diejenigen die blieben.

Trotz der rassistischen Gewalt kämpfen wir weiter und geben nicht auf. Nur wir können eine Schwarze Geschichte in Deutschland schaffen, die notwendig und wichtig ist für alle die nach uns kommen. Es ist schwer, tagtäglich ums Überleben zu kämpfen und gleichzeitig Schwarze Geschichte sichtbar zu machen. Wir tun es dennoch, und es kostet uns oft mehr Kraft, als wir überhaupt zur Verfügung haben. Wir organisieren Lesungen von Afro-Deutschen für Afro-Deutsche. Die ISD Berlin hat eine Kinder- und Jugendgruppe, ein Platz, wo sie Kontak haben und Freundschaften mit anderen Afro-Deutschen und Schwarzen schließen können. In einem bisher weißen Frauenprojekt haben es afro-deutsche Frauen in monatlichen Auseinandersetzungen und Kämpfen geschafft, das dazugehörige Cafe in Eigenregie zu übernehmen. Die Schwarze Lesbengruppe organisiert Ausstellungen über Kunst von Schwarzen Frauen in Berlin, München, Frankfurt, in allen größeren Städten der BRD.

May Ayim schreibt zur Zeit an ihrer Dissertation zum Thema "Rassismus im Therapiebereich" und wird ihren ersten Gedicht- und Prosaband im Orlanda Frauenverlag veröffentlichen. Gemeinsam haben May und ich Lehraufträge an der Freien und Technischen Universität in Berlin zum Thema: Antirassismus, persönliche Bewußtseins- und politische Bildungsarbeit. Ich selbst unterrichte Schwarze Frauen, jüdische Frauen und Immigrantinnen in Selbstverteidigung. Seit einiger Zeit bin ich dabei, mein eigenes Buch zu schreiben, das Texte enthält, die sich mit dem Überleben als Schwarze Frau in einer weißen Gesellschaft auseinandersetzt.

Viele Afro-Deutsche tragen ihren Teil zur Schwarzen Geschichte bei, und nicht alle kann ich hier erwähnen. Ich bin besonders stolz auf alle Afrodeutschen und Schwarzen Menschen die in der BRD leben. Von ihrem Mut und ihren Überlebenskämpfen können alle Menschen profitieren, Schwarz und weiß.

Audre Lorde ist mein Vorbild und meine Freundin. Ich möchte mit einigen Gedichtzeilen aus ihrem Gedicht "Outlines" enden:

Wir haben einander gewählt
und die Schärfe unserer jeweiligen Kämpfe
der Krieg ist derselbe
wenn wir verlieren
wird eines Tages das Blut der Frauen erstarren
auf einem toten Planeten
wenn wir siegen ist nichts abzusehen
wir suchen über die Geschichte hinaus nach einer neuen und möglichen Begegnung.

Berlin, Dezember 1992

Nachdem ich diesen Text an der Women in German Tagung 1992 vorgetragen hatte, bot mir Sara Lennox an, meinen Vater zu suchen. Ich hatte ein gutes und sicheres Gefühl, denn ich wußte, Sara Lennox wird nicht eher mit der Suche aufhören, bis sie ihn bzw. meine schwarze Familie gefunden hat.

Am 19. Mai 1993 um ca. 7,30 Uhr europäischer Zeit erhielt ich einen Anruf von Sara Lennox: "Ika, ich habe Deinen Vater gefunden!"

Am 24. Mai 1993 schickte ich den ersten Brief, Fotos von mir und meiner Mutter an meinen Vater.

Am 25. Juni erhielt ich den ersten (vierseitenlangen) Brief (mit Fotos) von meinem Vater.

Am 21./22. August 1993 habe ich im Alter von 46 Jahren meinen nun 75jährigen Vater in Chicago besucht. (Er und seine Familie haben sich sehr auf mich gefreut. Ich habe noch zwei Schwestern und drei Brüder.)

Ich habe mit Hilfe und Unterstützung von Sara Lennox nun alle meine Wurzeln gefunden, meine schwarze Familie, und ich nenne mich stolz—afroamerikanisch-deutsch.

Mein Empfinden und meinen Dank an Sara Lennox kann ich noch nicht in Worte fassen. Danke!

Ich bin unbeschreiblich glücklich!

Ika Hügel/Marshall
August 1993

Zitierte Werke

Ayim, May. "Die Fremdheit nimmt ab, die Feindlichkeit nimmt zu." *Beiträge zur feministischen Theorie und Praxis* [Feministische Öffentlichkeit-Patriarchale Medienwelt] 30/31: 211–16.

Farbe bekennen: Afro-deutsche Frauen auf den Spuren ihrer Geschichte. Ed. Katharina Oguntoye, May Opitz, and Dagmar Schultz. Berlin: Orlanda Frauenverlag, 1986.

Hügel, Ika. "Begegnungen mit Grenzen: Geteilter Feminismus, Rassismus, Antisemitismus, Fremdenhaß." *Beiträge zur feministischen Theorie und Praxis* 27: 93–94.

———. "Lesbischsein läßt sich verleugnen, schwarzsein nicht." Ed. JoAnn Loulan et al. *Lesben Liebe Leidenschaft.* Berlin: Orlanda Frauenverlag, 1992.

Hügel, Ika, Chris Lange, May Opitz, Ilona Bubeck, Gülsen Aktas, and Dagmar Schultz, eds. *Entfernte Verbindungen: Rassismus, Antisemitismus, Klassenunterdrückung.* Berlin: Orlanda Frauenverlag, 1993.

Racism in the New Germany and the Reaction of White Women

Dagmar Schultz

My subject is not a pleasant one. Racism and antisemitism in the new Germany are a frightening and shameful specter, and I wish I had better news to bring to this country. We find ourselves living in times that demand an ever-intensified struggle against negative powers on many levels—the government, an internationally linked Right-wing movement propelled by violence, stupidity, and inhumanity, and a large part of the population that is at best unconcerned, and at worst condones or supports destructive forces.

I want to begin by giving some information about my own development as a white Christian woman in Germany. When I talk of "white Christian," this is to distinguish between Christian and Jewish and does not pertain to religious practice. I will then present some information about the white women's movement in Germany, focusing on its relationship or lack thereof to concerns dealing with racism and antisemitism. Finally I will address the present situation in Germany.

I was born in 1941 in Berlin. In 1943, my father had in vain applied for a release from the army and reinstatement in his civilian job. When refused, he returned belatedly to Russia, where he was sentenced for desertion and ostensibly committed suicide. I grew up with my grandmother, my mother, and my sister and was able to finish high school. My school years took place during the 1950s, the era of the Cold War during which the "economic miracle" of the western part of Germany was constructed with the help of the Marshall Plan. Twice we went through world history and twice our teachers stopped at the year 1930. I learned almost nothing about the political movements of the time, for example, the movement against the remilitarization of Germany. This meant that I was part of the post-war generation that was not taught about the past. We had to acquire the knowledge on our own and figure out for ourselves how to deal with the guilt of our parents and grandparents.

When the German Left began to evolve in the early 1960s, I left Germany to study in the United States. In Ann Arbor, Michigan and later in Mississippi, Puerto Rico, Madison, Wisconsin, and Chicago I worked in the civil rights movement. This is where and how I received my political education. I had the opportunity to learn from the struggles of Black people, which, in the United States, form the basis for all other progressive political movements, including the women's movement. In the course of my political activities and my personal friendships, I learned about differences and commonalities between my interests as a white middle-class woman and those of women of other class and ethnic backgrounds. Once I returned to Germany in 1973, translating these experiences to activism in the German situation turned out to be difficult. The more I recognized, however, that the absence of these "other" women in the movement was not accidental, but formed an integral part of white women's identification and of their political work, the more uneasy I felt.

The Development of the White Women's Movement in Germany and its Relation to Racism and Antisemitism

As in other countries, the white women's movement emerged in the early 1970s by drawing its strength from a consciousness of women as victims. As important as this collective self-analysis may have been initially, it also contributed to the blurring of differences between the realities and power relations of women of varying backgrounds. Viewing oneself as victim also fulfilled the function of not having to deal with the role white women played and are playing in supporting the patriarchal system. A first breakthrough of this perspective was the concept of women's complicity in the white man's patriarchy developed by Christina Thürmer-Rohr and presented in her book *Vagabundinnen,* published in English translation as *Vagabonding: Feminist Thinking Cut Loose* (1991).

Only during the 1980s did women begin to confront themselves with the historical and present role of white Christian women as perpetrators during the period of German colonialism, during National Socialism, and in relation to racism and antisemitism in present-day Germany. Martha Mamozai initiated with her books *Schwarze Frau, Weiße Herrin* (*Black Woman, White Master*) (1989) and *Komplizinnen* (*Accomplices*) (1990) the discussion on the part white German women played in colonialism. The discourse about women as victims of National Socialism took on new forms: until the 1980s white Christian women had been considered involuntary supporters. Some historians had declared their abilities to survive daily life during the war to be a sort of resistance. Now women began to raise uncomfortable questions such as whether it is not a lie and self-deceptive to believe that the system did not and does not leave any choice to women, that women are racist only in a "secondary" way, that men are the real perpetrators.

These questions could not have been posed without the theoretical and practical work of Jewish women and Black women, and these questions are still subjects for research and discussion. Many political activists as well as academicians still resist asking them, just as a great part of the white non-Jewish society in general avoids accepting guilt and shame or transcending those feelings by responsible action. In academic discourse, the concept of "difference" is now emerging—a concept that again tends to deny power relations by arguing that emphasis on cultural differences results in each group being a "stranger" to the other. Women academics of this orientation consider racism and antisemitism as "concepts" that prevent a scientific discourse by being "moralizing" and caught in hierarchies of oppression (Schilling and Weigel).

Thus the discussion on racism and antisemitism had a late and slow start in the white German women's movement. During the rise of the women's movement and the parallel growth of the immigrant communities, for a long time called "guest workers," projects for immigrant women, especially Turkish women, developed in the mid 1970s. White women participated in these projects, frequently with paid positions. From the perspective of the women's movement these projects remained marginal. This was true also for feminist research: research on immigrant women or by them was largely delegated to the realm of social work and was not integrated into feminist theory.

The first major conference that brought immigrant women, Black women, and white women together for an exchange about causes of and experiences with racism and discrimination within and outside of the movement took place in 1984 in Frankfurt. It was a historic event. Although the need for solidarity and action had become very obvious, the conference had little after-effect in the white women's movement. For immigrant women it was, however, the beginning of a strengthened organization among themselves.

White Christian women in Germany could distance themselves from dealing with racism and antisemitism much longer than their sisters in, for example, the United States and Britain, since they were much less frequently confronted by Black and Jewish women. They refused to recognize immigrant women as feminists and rather adhered to stereotypical ideas, especially about Islamic women as backward and submissive to men. White Christian women still today have the tendency to judge women of other cultures by their religious affiliation, denying the influence of Christianity on their own socialization and on German culture and society. They were, until recently, oblivious to the existence of Black German women, and accepted the political significance of a Black German women's community only with great resistance. It was just as difficult for Jewish women to assert their position within the white women's movement. Jews are less visible than immigrants and Black Germans. Beyond that, it takes a lot of courage and strength to identify oneself as Jewish in Germany. White Christian women were and are far from providing a space for Jewish women where an exchange can take place and Jewish women can feel relatively safe. The lesbian-feminist

Shabbes-circle, a Berlin group of Jewish and non-Jewish women who worked on antisemitism and Jewish women in history from 1984 to 1989, was for years the only group that addressed antisemitism in the white women's movement at many conferences and other occasions.

The interaction of white Christian women with Jewish women distinguishes itself from that with immigrant and Black women. The encounter with Jewish women is marked much more by guilt and rejection of guilt, and the entanglement of these feelings with the family history of white Christian women. As one white Christian writer expressed it: "Was z.B. eine jüdische Frau konkret sagt, ist nicht entscheidend. Ausschlaggebend für die Überflutung mit Scham- und Schuldgefühlen ist die Wucht der historischen Dimension, verbunden mit unverarbeiteten Gefühlen, der sich die christliche Deutsche nicht entziehen kann..." (Koppert).

The attitudes of white women toward Black women are, in my opinion, less influenced by guilt feelings. In part, this has to do with the fact that German colonial history is considered insignificant on account of its shorter duration and because we do not learn anything about it in schools and in the family. Therefore, white women develop no guilt feelings about it, but also no feeling of responsibility. We can grow up in Germany without learning that apartheid and the pass laws in South Africa were originally developed and used by Germans in German-Southwest Africa, that Germans who emigrated to Namibia to avoid retribution for crimes they committed during National Socialism still live there, adhering to the principles of contempt for Black people and of the National Socialist race hatred. We can go to school in Germany and study at the university without ever knowing that descendants of Africans, namely Afro-Germans, underwent forced sterilization and/or were murdered in concentration camps. The confrontation with antisemitism is loaded with guilt feelings; the one with racism expresses, however, the loathing of having to deal with a problem area that white German women had up to now relegated to the United States or other western European countries.

In 1984, I was able to invite Audre Lorde as a guest professor to the Free University of Berlin. A year earlier, I had edited *Macht und Sinnlichkeit (Power and Sensuality)*, a volume of prose and poetry by Audre Lorde and Adrienne Rich, published by our press, Orlanda Frauenverlag. This turned out to be one of the first books that initiated intense discussions on racism and antisemitism in Germany. From 1984 to 1992, Audre Lorde and Gloria Joseph, formerly a professor at Hampshire College, spent time annually in Berlin. In readings and discussion with both of them, white women were challenged to acknowledge racist structures in society and in their own political context. Afro-German women began to work on their own history and present with the encouragement of Audre Lorde, the result being the book *Farbe Bekennen: Afrodeutsche Frauen auf den Spuren ihrer Geschichte* (English translation:

Showing Our Colors: Afro-German Women Speak Out, 1991). We published this book with a preface by Audre Lorde in 1986 shortly after the founding of the Initiative of Black Germans. The authors made themselves visible as Afro-German women in readings and political activities. White women for the first time had to deal concretely with the fact that racism in Germany cannot be covered with the euphemism "hostility toward foreigners." Racism has to do with skin color and affects Black Germans just as much as immigrants of color. "Hostility toward foreigners" is, therefore, also incorrect insofar as this hostility is not directed against white foreigners.

The concept of racism entered linguistic and colloquial usage in Germany only recently. One explanation given for this fact is that because the term "racism" was used in Germany after 1945 for the analysis of the exclusion, discrimination, and systematic murder of non-Aryan Germans, its application to present-day circumstances would signify a parallelization and, therefore, simplification and devaluation of the Shoa (Lutz). After all, most white Christian women shared the view of the majority that a development such as National Socialism could never occur again. To avoid encountering racism in Germany and their own participation in it, the concept of hostility against foreigners was a welcome one.

Since 1989, racism has become a popular topic in response to Black and immigrant women's confrontation, and a series of conferences and women's events have been devoted to its discussion. A kind of competition developed between "racism" and "antisemitism" (Jacobi and Magiriba Mlwanga, 1990). When antisemitism was part of the discussion, situations developed in which white Christian women publicly accused themselves of being guilty, probably in the hope of achieving a kind of therapeutic cleansing. Reactions to Black women raising the issue of racism were far more rejective or aggressive. During such conferences, the whole repertoire of defenses, mistrust, and imputations came to the fore and repeatedly led to women of color and Jewish women leaving the event in anger, and finally organizing their own conferences.

German unification in 1989 unfortunately was not used as an occasion for a critical reflection of nationalistic feelings that spread across the country, nor of the close connection between these feelings and racism and antisemitism. Instead, white Christian women quickly organized an "East-West festival"—not an "East-West-North-South festival." At the East-West Congress, which took place in Berlin in 1990, a small group of immigrant and white women had to fight to make racism, antisemitism, and the new restrictive law on foreigners a topic of discussion. At this point, the differences between white women in the West and in the East became noticeable: the eastern women bitterly complained about the arrogance of western feminists, who communicated to them that they had nothing to offer and had better adopt feminism western-style.

nately, however, women of color could not expect much solidarity from white eastern women either. Most of them were preoccupied with their own situation, i.e., the threat of unemployment. 95% of all employable women in the East had been in the workforce before unification. Now, 65% of all unemployed persons (15%) in the East are women. Work had taken a central place in the lives and identities of women in the East, and this development has disastrous consequences for many of them. On the other hand, the experience of living in a socialist system had not sensitized white women to racism, and only few have seen a connection between their own plight and that of foreign women losing their jobs and having to leave the country.

The resistance against cooperation on an equal base with Jewish women and women of color has continued. Only a few of these women find the possibility of working in a project like SUSI (*Solidarisch, Unabhängig, Sozial, International*), an intercultural center with an international living commune attached to it. White women who insist on working closely with women of color and Jewish women have to engage in discussions on quota regulations similar to those taking place between white men and white women. The growing percentage of Turkish and other immigrant women in houses for battered women finally obliged white women to employ Turkish colleagues. The Orlanda publishing house is one of the few women's projects that consciously translated its political convictions and goals into its personnel politics: two of the four paid women are Black Germans.

To sum up: White women have focused on their own concerns for too long. The women's movement lacks any kind of infrastructure that would enable it to engage in concerted actions even if women were willing and ready for them. Since the late 1970s it has been divided up into a multitude of projects, from houses for battered women to associations for small entrepreneurs. There are hardly any regional or supra-regional networks, and the concept of leadership is largely rejected. This situation has recently motivated women in Berlin to start a group patterned after the U.S. Women's Action Coalition. The group has, however, remained fairly small—women have not adopted the direct approach as they have in the U.S.

The attitudes of many white Christian women toward women of color and Jewish women remain characterized by fear, distance, and competition. White Christian women largely engage in denial of their own power and skin privileges.

The Present Situation

Even the seriousness of the present political situation has not propelled white women to look at how they can muster their forces against reactionary and fascist developments. They legitimize their lack of resistance by claiming helplessness, without recognizing the privileges they claim by their lack of action.

By mid-1993, there have been no broad reactions of the white women's movement. Only very recently did calls for action of unions and churches move the broader German population to protest the growing racist and antisemitic violence with mass demonstrations. The limits of tolerance for racism have become higher and higher, and the population appears to have gotten used to daily reports of attacks on homes for refugees and to the desecration and destruction of Jewish memorials. People are divided into those who agree with the fascists by applauding their actions or being silent, those who believe themselves to be helpless in the face of the growing violence, and the minority who confront the fear of a rightist tide with a variety of actions and activities. It is true that the latter group is growing (from younger Leftists, who give protection to refugee homes, to big companies that announce severe reprisals for racist behavior at the workplace and engage in anti-racist publicity campaigns and grassroot citizen's initiatives in East and West such as centers for international encounters). But it is also hard to tell at this point what it will take to avoid a victory of rightist parties such as the Republican Party at the next elections (in 1994), especially in East Germany.

How can we explain these attitudes? What contributed to them? In the former GDR, the government decreed an anti-fascist attitude and international solidarity. This did not, however, mean that fascism was really dealt with. International solidarity was never practiced with people of color in the country proper. On the contrary: foreign employees, in 1990 11.2% of the East German population as compared to 8.2% in West Germany ("Informationen" 3), were hired for a specific number of years as in the early years of West Germany. They lived in closed-off quarters and had minimal contact with the population.

In West Germany, the National Socialist past has never been really confronted. In my generation, the 1930s and 1940s were not talked about. The younger generation frequently considers this period a part of history with which they have nothing to do personally. This is not surprising in view of the fact that Chancellor Kohl claimed for himself "the blessing of late birth." The government is responsible for the present move to the right in a decisive way. Chancellor Kohl and several of his ministers emphasize again and again in public: "Deutschland ist kein Einwanderungsland." Their main reaction to racist and antisemitic attacks has been to worry about the loss of the image of Germany's alleged friendliness toward foreigners. Only a minute number of politicians actually positioned themselves on the side of the victims of violence or apologized to them. Trade and industry are, in some cases, more progressive than the government, though for the wrong reasons: they are worried about losing foreign investment and realize the still-existent need for foreign labor. While government policy is oriented toward restricting access to Germany, industry is making new contracts with laborers from Eastern European countries. The federal government has continuously reacted to racist violence by using it as an argument for changing or abolishing Article 16 of the constitution, which guarantees the individual right of the status of a refugee. Again and again members of the government, including the Chancellor, claim that the violence can only be countered by curtailing the so-called flood of refugees. This way they lend legitimacy to the calls of neo-Nazis "Germany to the Germans" and give the population the impression that the problem is the flow of refugees rather than a racism and antisemitism and nationalism that would continue even if the borders were closed tightly tomorrow. Furthermore, this ideological campaign on the part of politicians distorts the fact that in 1990 only 4.4%, in 1991 6.9% of refugees were actually receiving a permit of residency ("Informationen" 3). Only very recently has the government begun to move against rightist organizations that have existed for over 20 years—mainly because of pressure from other nations.

At the same time, the perpetrators of violence are being stylized into victims. Politicians, officials, and many citizens show understanding for rightist youths and also for the applauding populace arguing with their alleged miserable economic and social conditions. However, studies have demonstrated that members of hardcore rightist organizations (between 5,000 and 6,000 in number) and their followers belong to the employed rather than the unemployed sector and that the least well-off tend to abnegate rightist views and empathize with refugees (Held et al.). Progressives argue that unemployment is no justification for violence against other people and that social programs now being installed for rightist youths should be offered to immigrant and refugee youths as well.

The newest appalling development is to employ social workers with a rightist political orientation in programs set up for neo-Nazis with the argument that this policy ensures a greater acceptance on the part of the youths.

Finally, the latest trend has been to present racist and antisemitic violence as a conflict between the Right and the Left. Usually, the comparison of present developments with the Weimar Republic and the rise of Nazism is carefully avoided. Now the head of the German FBI made the comparison, but by arguing that present developments are reminiscent of the struggles between the Right and the Left during the 1920s. He claims that in recent times leftist groups have attacked rightist groups three times more often. Chancellor Kohl followed suit by pointing out in his declaration after the destruction of the museum in the concentration camp Sachsenhausen by neo-Nazis that the government has to counter forcefully left and right terrorism—as if the Left had ignited homes for refugees and memorials against antisemitism.

In concurrence with the government's position, the police do not move forcefully against Neo-Nazis. In Rostock in 1992, they watched from side streets as rightists set fire to the refugee home, later arguing that they did not have enough men available. At the big demonstration against the violence a few days later, hundreds of police were suddenly present to prevent demonstrators from other cities from entering Rostock. In Greifswald (east Germany), the police did not stop neo-Nazis from entering a refugee center and going from door to door, dragging people out of their rooms and beating them up.

In this situation, the women's movement is largely paralyzed by its own lack of structures and by the fact that it has neglected to clarify for itself the connection between sexism, racism, antisemitism, and classism. Certainly, there are individuals and groups who have been involved in struggles against racism and antisemitism over a long period of time: women who fight for women of color receiving positions in feminist projects and in institutions like universities. (Women at the Alice Salomon School for Social Work in Berlin, where I am teaching, recently were able to get the school to vote for a quota regulation for the employment of ethnic minority members in the administration and on the faculty—this being the first institution of higher education in the country to take such a vote!). Women demonstrate, organize events, and call to life action groups, such as a group working for a change of Article 116 in the upcoming new constitution, the article that defines German citizenship as based on blood ties and cultural heritage. Women also do anti-racist work in their professional context. For instance, we initiated in the Orlanda publishing house a call to all bookstores to declare their position against racism by arranging window displays to this effect. This action contributed to a demonstration of about 2,000 people in the book trade at the recent Frankfurt International Bookfair and to the joint publication of a low-priced book against racism and antisemitism published by over 30 presses in January 1993 (*Schweigen ist Schuld*; *Silence is to Blame*).

These are beginnings that, however, will have a decisive effect only when we are able to form coalitions and alliances—coalitions among different groups of white women and among white women, women of color, and Jewish women, and even coalitions with gender-mixed groups. The Right is incomparably better organized than we are—on the national as well as on the international level. Neo-Nazi leaders in east Germany announce on television that they are only waiting for telephone lines and fax machines still not available in the East to be able to better coordinate their activities. In the United States, the number of rightist organizations and hate groups has risen dramatically during the past year. The Ku Klux Klan is training fascists in Germany and teaching them how to burn crosses, according to the *New York Times* (3 Nov. 1991). And the Right has comparatively little to fear from the population and the government:

Even though there was a demonstration recently organized by the police union to publicly declare their stance against racism, it is known that a high percentage of the police force vote for the rightist Republican Party. After three years of racist violence, during which about 30 Black, mostly African, and Asian people were killed, and countless others have been beaten up and injured, many do not even go to the police out of fear or because they feel it is useless. For too long, racist attacks have been declared robberies or assaults without political intent. While over 5,000 Nazis travel across Germany to the targets of their violent attacks, the government announces that it plans to discuss stronger political and legal measures against such attacks. Hardly any of the laws swiftly introduced at the height of leftist activities in the 1970s and 1980s have been used.

Finally, white women cannot ignore the fact that among right radicals there is a considerable number of women; a good 30% of those voting for the Republicans, who received up to 15% of the votes in some states, are women (Möller 31). And the young women among rightists have no interest in women's emancipation.

The African-American Paula Ross wrote that patriarchal society leaves perhaps 1/100 of the world to white women, and that men know they can take it from us at any time. White Christian women make up approximately 10% of the earth's population. We have no chance to change anything on this planet unless we form coalitions with the other 40% of the female population and with a part of the oppressed male population. To build coalitions we do not have to love or even like each other, although this is, of course, a much more pleasant situation. Coalitions serve first of all the purpose to survive, and to attack and dissolve power structures.

A few weeks before her death, Audre Lorde wrote a public letter together with Gloria I. Joseph during her stay in Berlin, after the violent attacks in Rostock. The letter was published by several newspapers. In it she said: "When will the moment come that the Human Rights Commission will treat the case of Germany? What do these developments say to the two of us as African-Americans? What do they say to us as members of the 7/8 percent of the world's population who are people of color?... what will we be able to tell people..., when they ask us, 'how was your last trip to Germany—what is Berlin like now?'"

The women's movement is not excluded from having to answer these questions. Aside from responding in our daily personal lives, the only way to arrive at a forceful answer seems to me to act within the context of coalitions that bridge ethnic and class differences. Building coalitions and alliances means for white women to confront their power and skin privileges and, in Audre Lorde's words, to meet women of color and Jewish women "face to face, beyond objectification and beyond guilt."

Zitierte Werke

Farbe bekennen: Afro-deutsche Frauen auf den Spuren ihrer Geschichte. Ed. Katharina Oguntoye, May Opitz, Dagmar Schultz. Berlin: Orlanda Frauenverlag, 1986. English trans.: *Showing Our Colors: Afro-German Women Speak Out*. Trans. Anne v. Adams. Amherst: U of Massachusetts P, 1992.

Feministische Studien 9.2 [Kulturelle und sexuelle Differenzen] (Nov. 1991).

Held, Josef, Hans Horn, Rudolf Leipricht, and Athanasios Marvakis. *Du mußt handeln, daß du Gewinn machst...Empirische Untersuchung und theoretische Überlegungen zu politischen Orientierungen jugendlicher Arbeitnehmer*. Tübingen: Institut für Erziehungswissenschaften, Universität Tübingen, 1991.

"Informationen zur politischen Bildung: Ausländer." *Landeszentrale für politische Bildungsarbeit Berlin* 237 (4. Quartal 1992).

Jacobi, Jessica, and Gotlinde Magiriba Mlwanga. "Was 'sie' schon immer über Antisemitismus wissen wollte, aber nie zu denken wagte." *Beiträge zur feministischen Theorie und Praxis* 13.27 (1990): 95–105.

Koppert, Claudia. "Schuld und Schuldgefühle im westlichen Nachkriegsdeutschland: Zur Wirksamkeit des Vergangenen im Gegenwärtigen." *Beiträge zur feministischen Theorie und Praxis* 14.30/31 (1991): 217–30.

Lutz, Helma. "Sind wir uns immer noch fremd? Konstruktionen von Fremdheit in der weißen Frauenbewegung." *Entfernte Verbindungen: Rassismus, Antisemitismus, Klassenunterdrückung*. Ed. Ika Hügel et al. Berlin: Orlanda Frauenverlag, 1993.

Mamozai, Martha. *Komplizinnen*. Reinbek: Rowohlt, 1990.

———. *Schwarze Frau, Weiße Herrin*. Reinbek: Rowohlt, 1989.

Mitscherlich, Margarete. *Die friedfertige Frau*. Frankfurt a.M.: Fischer, 1987.

Möller, Kurt. "Mädchen, Frauen und Rechtsextremismus." *Sozialmagazin* 16.10 (1991): 31.

Schilling, Sabine, and Sigrid Weigel. "Kulturelle und sexuelle Differenzen." Introduction to *Feministische Studien* 9.2 (Nov. 1991): 4–7.

Schultz, Dagmar, ed. *Macht und Sinnlichkeit: Ausgewählte Texte von Audre Lorde und Adrienne Rich*. Berlin: Orlanda Frauenverlag, 1991 (3rd revised ed.).

Schweigen ist Schuld: Ein Lesebuch der Verlagsinitiative gegen Gewalt und Fremdenhaß. Frankfurt a.M.: Börsenverein des Deutschen Buchhandels, 1993.

Thürmer-Rohr, Christina. *Vagabundinnen: Feministische Essays*. Berlin: Orlanda Frauenverlag, 1987. English trans.: *Vagabonding: Feminist Thinking Cut Loose*. Trans. Lise Weil. Boston: Beacon, 1991.

What's Missing in New Historicism or the "Poetics" of Feminist Literary Criticism

Sara Friedrichsmeyer and Jeanette Clausen

Judging by recent conference programs, special journal issues, and calls for papers, a great deal of critical attention is being focused on new historicism. Just what is this phenomenon, and should feminist Germanists concern themselves with it? We have chosen to address this topic because we think some demystification is needed. We would like to situate our observations in the context of the current discussion on the relationship between feminist *Germanistik* and the rest of the profession.

Touted as a way of doing literary criticism that spurns the formalism of new criticism as well as the positivism of nineteenth-century German or "old" historicism, new historicism seems poised to become one of the dominant critical positions of the 1990s. In little more than a decade it has spread from its somewhat casual coinage by Stephen Greenblatt to a variety of academic disciplines with the speed of what Adam Begley, writing in the *New York Times Magazine* last spring, likened to a "California brush fire" (32). And that despite the lack of a theory or methodology or unifying epistemology of the kind traditionally required for a "school of criticism." Greenblatt himself exhibits a postmodern disdain for systematization, stressing instead the tentativeness of the enterprise and the importance of remaining ever open to the new. Louis Montrose, another proponent of new historicism, emphasizes his refusal to call it a "school, movement, or program," opting instead for "merely...an emergent historical *orientation*" (406), by titling a recent article "New Historicisms."[1] New historicism then defies any clear definition, as little of its methodologies as of its theoretical underpinnings. Nevertheless, what Greenblatt would call a "practice" (15) threatens to become dogma. While its effect on German departments is less pervasive than on certain other disciplines, the summer 1992 issue of *Monatshefte* devoted to its discussion and even the 1993 WIG-sponsored MLA session at which another version of this essay was read reflect its encroachment.

Not that new historicism is without its detractors: throughout the country it has been the focus of a sometimes heated debate from the right and the left, both from within and outside of academia (cf. Will). The contributors to the *Monatshefte* issue do not offer unanimous praise, and feminists too are of differing persuasions. While there are certainly feminists who publish in *Representations,* the journal Greenblatt helped found at Berkeley, others have expressed their skepticism and for a variety of reasons (Lennox). We would like to add our voices to theirs, challenging new historicism's claim to uniqueness on the one hand and questioning its compatibility with the goals of feminist literary criticism on the other.

Most explicators of new historicism in fact acknowledge that it is not new and stress instead its eclectic nature. It is our contention that as part of its eclecticism, it has incorporated—not necessarily consciously—many of the underlying theoretical postulates and assumptions of feminist criticism, without, however, adopting feminism's unifying focus on gender. Thus we are skeptical of those who celebrate the new historicism—or "poetics of culture" as Greenblatt calls it—as a panacea for rejuvenating the profession (Kaes), but not because we disagree with its fundamental practices, for many of those practices are already inherent in most forms of feminist literary criticism. Rather, we believe it does not sufficiently challenge the critical practices it claims to refute.

The repudiation of new criticism did not spring newly born from the new historians, but has in fact been one of the main propellants of feminist *Germanistik* and other oppositional criticism. If we do a little history ourselves, many of us remember our own training in the methods of new criticism with its exclusive focus on the text in question and its sublime refusal to consider social, political, and historical contexts. It was partly as a reaction to that type of formalism that feminists began to develop their own interdisciplinary approaches to understanding the role of literature in society. Greenblatt may have formulated his term as a punning response to new criticism (Kaes 149), but feminist literary criticism has presented, we would argue, a more thoroughgoing challenge. Just as surely, feminist approaches to literary and cultural analysis have been a convincing disavowal of "old" historicism. Scholars of *Germanistik* in general have perhaps found it more necessary than those in other disciplines to come to terms with Ranke's 19th-century historicism and its view that writing history meant describing the past "wie es eigentlich gewesen." In this context it is important to remember that *Germanistinnen* have argued as persuasively as any others in our profession the need to overcome the purported objectivity of Ranke's thinking.

Critics seeking the intellectual roots of new historicism usually point to the cultural anthropology of Clifford Geertz, to poststructuralism and the discourse theories of Foucault, to Marxism, and less frequently to the language theories of Bakhtin. Surely it is not news to anyone that in developing methodologies for adequately examining literature and its intertwinings with history, politics, and society, that is, with culture, feminists have also been drawn to these same intellectual currents. All but those feminists who define women via their biology understand sexual difference and the hierarchical positioning of men vis-à-vis women as the products of specific historical and social conditions and use many of the methodologies now claimed by the new historians to examine those inequities. The investigation of sex differences and inequality that lies at the heart of all feminisms except those rooted in an essentialist view of the sexes cannot be and never has been separated from women's experience. And that experience can only be understood in its specific historical and sociopolitical context.

Anton Kaes concludes his *Monatshefte* piece by crediting new historicism with the "potential for energizing the writing of literary history" in "at least" three areas: 1) by radically expanding the terrain normally covered to include nonliterary as well as literary documents; 2) by dealing with representations that have a social as well as a textual dimension; and 3) by emphasizing what is nonsystematic, contradictory, and even coincidental, while avoiding totalizing claims (156). It is our argument that feminist criticism has *already* produced methodologies that could have that same effect. As articles published in this and in past volumes of the *Women in German Yearbook* demonstrate, feminism has already expanded the "terrain normally covered" by literary history to include women's diaries, letters, autobiographies, travel literature, journalistic writing, literary criticism, scientific and historical writings, films, religious writings, the "confessions" of accused witches, and much more—not to mention the *Trivialromane* by women that were widely read by their contemporaries, dramas by women that were performed but not published in their day, and feminist polemical (or other political) writing. In our view, many publications by WIG members also fulfill Kaes's second qualification in that they address not only the textual but also the social and political dimensions of, for example, women's participation in or exclusion from various spheres of activity. Further, we would like to suggest that in its very insistence on the inclusion of the discourses of not just gender, but sexuality, race, class, ethnicity, and age, for example, feminist *Germanistik* has struggled to avoid the totalizing claims that Kaes in his third point also wants to avoid.

There are, however, other notable ways in which feminist goals diverge from and are incompatible with those of new historicism: The new historians' understanding and use of history, for example, raises problems. Certainly their determination to give history a place in literary analysis is laudable; it is something feminists have long incorporated into their own work, as they have tried to understand the roots of prejudice, for example, or the formation of the canon and various kinds of inequality. But most feminists also address the issue of just exactly whose history they are dealing with. As Judith Lowder Newton, one of new historicism's earliest and most vocal critics, and others have pointed out, the task of reclaiming a historical role for women and for others outside the dominant cultures is far from completed. We believe it is important to ask what there is in new historicism to encourage such investigations. For gender, even as an issue for theoretical exploration, is frequently missing from the works of its leading practitioners, and with it a potential focus for the new historian's obsession with the dynamics of power. In addition to questioning whose history the new historians are embracing as the basis for their analyses, feminists must also ask for what purpose that history is being used. New historians are committed to the archeological uncovering of historical data in the Foucauldian sense, but not to an analysis that could somehow be transferred to life. Feminist literary critics, on the contrary, regardless of their differences, have never been afraid of showing their ideological bent; they are committed to gender equality and meaningful social change.

As Peter Uwe Hohendahl has commented in a recent article in *New German Critique,* new historians, although they see themselves as oppositional critics, remain institutionally bound. Their arguments have not transcended the university setting, and we do not sense that they are working to bring their insights, for example on power and authority, into the material world. Not unlike the works of formalism they have rejected, their studies reduce everything to the text, to its rhetorical and discursive strategies. When gender is an issue at all, the discussion typically involves textual strategies for representing women or gender inequality. As feminist critics we are hardly indifferent to textual strategies for representing gender, but we are in addition intent on understanding the historical matrix in which a given writer has worked. And although feminists searching for ways to adequately contextualize literary works recognize the importance of discourse in shaping culture and the individuals within it, they are generally concerned with going beyond analyses of those discourses. Originating in a desire for meaningful political and social change, feminism recognizes that although literature and subjectivity are constituted through discourse, the human life that is their core ultimately eludes discourse. As Sara Lennox has expressed it, new historicism can suggest ways to treat in a literary text the discursive category of "woman," but has not shown itself capable of analyzing how real "women" function within or are constituted by or even escape from discourse. To use Lennox's example, new historicism can analyze Bachmann's discourse of gender in her works, but it is not prepared to comment on or take apart the conditions of her actual life in war-time and post-war Austria, conditions that were the grounding for the understanding of gender relations that shaped her writing.

A related problem is new historicism's cultural relativism. In its insistence on contextualizing, there is a tendency to equate the various materials used, skirting the issue of influence and causality. The very existence of the sometimes arcane documents, texts, or artifacts that have been unearthed seems enough to certify their significance for a text, no matter how forced the connection. If one is interested primarily in discursive investigations, that is perhaps enough. For feminists investigating, say, the writings of a religious woman in eighteenth-century Germany, however, the dictates of the church must certainly be granted more urgency than the prescriptions flowing from other discourses. But the task of historical reconstruction the new historians are trying to enact, as Hohendahl puts it, are in the form of links, similarities, and repetitions, rather than causalities (93). Their postmodern refusal to engage in consistent investigations of influences or causes precludes them from taking positions, itself a posture at odds with the activism inherent in most forms of feminism.

Yet another hazard in new historicist practices is the tendency to neglect aesthetics. Virtually all new historians emphasize their desire to break down the barriers between works of art and other cultural texts. To a degree that is also the agenda of feminist criticism, but while feminist critics problematize the traditional criteria for aesthetic evaluation of literary works, they remain sensitive to aesthetic concerns. One result of new historians' unwillingness to distinguish between aesthetic and other forms of production is their lack of attention to the writers. Not so in feminist literary criticism, where the "death of the author" has found no echo; while remaining alert to the dangers of ahistorical readings, feminist critics are very willing to hold the author responsible for such failures of class, race, and gender, for example, as appear in the text.

In sum, we view the various practices of new historicism as either overlapping with the concerns of feminist criticism or directly opposed to them. We therefore urge great caution when approaching these practices. Clearly, we must remain open to fresh ideas; we must continue developing new ways of evaluating ourselves and literary texts within the broadest interdisciplinary contexts. But we can do so, crediting the ideas of specific new historians when appropriate, without calling what we do "feminist new historicism," as has been suggested. Granted it is a catchy phrase, but it is one we can all do without.

September 1993

Note

[1] In remaining with the singular, we are focusing on the phenomenon itself as much as on the contours of new historicist practices.

Works Cited

Begley, Adam. "The Tempest Around Stephen Greenblatt." *New York Times Magazine* 28 March 1993: 32–38.

Greenblatt, Stephen. "Towards a Poetics of Culture." *The New Historicism.* Ed. H. Aram Veeser. New York: Routledge, 1989. 1–14.

Hohendahl, Peter Uwe. "A Return to History? The New Historicism and Its Agenda." *New German Critique* 55 (Winter 1992): 87–104.

Kaes, Anton. "New Historicism: Writing Literary History in the Postmodern Era." *Monatshefte* 84.2 (Summer 1992): 148–58.

Lennox, Sara. "Feminism and New Historicism." *Monatshefte* 84.2 (Summer 1992): 159–70.

Montrose, Louis. "New Historicisms." *Redrawing the Boundaries: The Transformation of English and American Literary Studies.* Ed. Stephen Breenblatt and Giles Gunn. New York: MLA, 1992. 392–418.

Newton, Judith Lowder. "History as Usual? Feminism and the 'New Historicism.'" *The New Historicism.* Ed. H. Aram Veeser. New York: Routledge, 1989. 152–67.

Will, George. "Literary Politics." *Newsweek* 22 April 1991: 72.

ABOUT THE AUTHORS

Ann Taylor Allen, PhD in History from Columbia University, is now Professor of History at the University of Louisville, where she directed the Women's Studies Program. She is the author of *Satire and Society in Wilhelmine Germany* and *Feminism and Motherhood in Germany: 1800-1914*. She has published articles on the history of German feminist movements and on the comparative history of feminism in Germany and the United States. She received the Article Prize of the Conference Group on Central European History in 1989. She served as Program Director of the German Studies Association Annual Convention in 1991 and now serves on the Executive Committee of the Association. She held a guest professorship at the University of Bielefeld in the summer of 1991.

Kirsten Belgum is Assistant Professor of German at the University of Texas at Austin. She has published a book entitled *Interior Meaning: Design of the Bourgeois Home in the Realist Novel* and articles on topics such as women's work in the nineteenth century and feminist aesthetics. The essay in this volume is part of larger research project on the popular construction of a national identity in nineteenth-century Germany. This broader study will examine the various discourses of national identification and belonging that were popularized in mass-distributed texts.

Jeanette Clausen is Associate Professor of German at Indiana University-Purdue University Fort Wayne. She is coeditor of an anthology, *German Feminism* (1984), and has published articles on Helga Königsdorf, Christa Wolf, and other women writers. She has been coeditor of the WIG Yearbook since 1987.

Friederike Eigler received her PhD in 1987 from Washington University, St. Louis, and is Assistant Professor at Georgetown University. Her research interests include twentieth-century literature, feminist criticism, and the history and theory of autobiography. She has published a monograph on Elias Canetti and articles on Goethe, Ingeborg Bachmann, Brigitte Schwaiger, and Sarah Kirsch, among others. The article included in this volume is one of several projects that reflect her interest in recent developments in the former GDR.

About the Authors

Karin Eysel is a PhD candidate in German Literature at the University of California, Irvine. Her interests include contemporary literature, women's writing, and drama. She is currently writing her dissertation on Ludwig Tieck's early plays.

Sara Friedrichsmeyer is Professor of German at the University of Cincinnati, Raymond Walters College. Her publications include *The Androgyne in Early German Romanticism* (1983) and articles on German Romanticism and nineteenth- and twentieth-century German women writers, as well as a volume coedited with Barbara Becker-Cantarino honoring Helga Slessarev, *The Enlightenment and its Legacy* (1991). She has been coeditor of the *Women in German Yearbook* since 1990.

Christl Griesshaber-Weninger is a PhD candidate in Comparative Literature at Washington University, St. Louis. Her fields of specialization include German and French literature. She is particularly interested in the interconnectedness of education, language, literature, and art and is presently focusing on the representation and construction of gender, body, and otherness.

Ika Hügel, born in 1947, studied social work in Frankfurt a.M. She has been the media contact person for Orlanda Frauenverlag since 1990. She has a teaching appointment in Antiracist Education and Awareness at the Technical and Free Universities in Berlin and has published numerous articles on these topics. In addition she teaches self-defense and Tae Kwon Do, especially for Black women.

Sara Lennox is Associate Professor of German and Director of the Social Thought and Political Economy Program at the University of Massachusetts, Amherst. She is editor of *Auf der Suche nach den Gärten unserer Mütter* and coeditor of *Nietzsche heute: Die Rezeption seines Werkes nach 1968.* She has published articles on various twentieth-century German and Austrian authors, on women's writing in the FRG and GDR, and on feminist pedagogy, literary theory, and the feminist movement. She is currently writing a book on Ingeborg Bachmann.

Dagmar C. G. Lorenz was born in West Germany. She studied in Göttingen and completed her PhD in German and her MA in English at the University of Cincinnati in 1974–75. She teaches at The Ohio State University, where she is Professor of German and a member of the Executive Board of the Melton Center for Jewish Studies. She is the author of *Ilse Aichinger* (1981), *Franz Grillparzer—Dichter des sozialen Konflikts* (1986), *Verfolgung bis zum Massenmord: Diskurse zum Holocaust in deutscher Sprache* (1992), as well as numerous articles on

German and Austrian 19th- and 20th-century literature, particularly women and Jewish authors.

Susan Signe Morrison received her PhD in Comparative Literature at Brown University. She is Assistant Professor of English at Southwest Texas State University. She has published on Middle High German works (*Parzival, Iwein*), English literature (Shakespeare, Malory), feminist literary theory, and popular culture (political cartoons that responded to the "marriage" of the former-GDR to West Germany). She is currently co-editing a volume of essays on the pedagogical implications of reading marginalized Old English genres through the lens of contemporary literary theory.

Gertrud Bauer Pickar is Professor of German at the University of Houston. She is the author of *The Dramatic Works of Max Frisch,* editor of *Adventures of a Flounder...Grass' Der Butt,* and co-editor of *Expressionism Reconsidered* and *The Age of Goethe Today.* In addition, she has published articles on Novalis, Eichendorff, Droste-Hülshoff, M. Walser, Böll, Frisch, and Grass. She has just completed a book manuscript on Droste and is currently working on a study of narrative perspective in contemporary German fiction.

Dagmar Schultz, born in 1941, is a professor at the Fachhochschule für Sozialpädagogik in Berlin and publisher of Orlanda Frauenverlag. From 1963 to 1972 she studied and worked in the USA. From 1973 to 1986 she taught at the John F. Kennedy Institute for North American Studies at the Free University of Berlin. She was a cofounder of the Feminist Health Center for Women in Berlin where she worked until 1980. Her doctoral work was on sexism in education. She is coeditor of several books, among them *Farbe Bekennen.*

Katrin Sieg received her PhD in Drama from the University of Washington. She looks forward to the imminent publication of her book *Exiles, Eccentrics, Activists: Women in Contemporary German Theatre.* Her articles have appeared in *Theatre Studies, Theatre Journal,* and *Genders,* and are scheduled for publication in the forthcoming volumes *Euterpe's Daughters: German Women Dramatists from the 18th Century to the Present* and *Unnatural Acts: Theorizing the Performative.* She is a lecturer in the Literature Department at the University of California, San Diego.

Katharina von Ankum is Assistant Professor of German at Scripps College. She received her PhD from the University of Massachusetts at Amherst in 1990. She has worked predominantly in the area of GDR literature and culture. Her study *Die Rezeption von Christa Wolf in Ost und West* appeared with Editions Rodopi, Amsterdam in 1992. Her next book-length project explores the discourse of motherhood and the construction of woman as other in texts by women writers in the Weimar Republic.

Petra Waschescio, PhD Marburg 1991, lives in Duisburg, Germany. From 1990 to 1992 she taught recent German literature at the universities of Marburg and Duisburg and has served as the coordinator for international cultural exchange and political education of the association "Frauen der Welt e.V." since 1991. She is the author of *Vernunftkritik und Patriarchatskritik: Mythische Modelle in der deutschsprachigen Literatur der 80er Jahre,* and has published articles on Heiner Müller and Irmtraud Morgner.

NOTICE TO CONTRIBUTORS

The *Women in German Yearbook* is a refereed journal. Its publication is supported by the Coalition of Women in German.

Contributions to the *Women in German Yearbook* are welcome at any time. The editors are interested in feminist approaches to all aspects of German literary, cultural, and language studies, including teaching.

Prepare manuscripts for anonymous review. The editors prefer that manuscripts not exceed 25 pages (typed, double-spaced), including notes. Follow the third edition (1988) of the *MLA Handbook* (separate notes from works cited). Send one copy of the manuscript to each coeditor:

Sara Friedrichsmeyer	*and*	Jeanette Clausen
Foreign Languages		Modern Foreign Languages
University of Cincinnati, RWC		Indiana U.-Purdue U.
Cincinnati, OH 45236		Fort Wayne, IN 46805

For membership/subscription information, contact Jeanette Clausen.

CONTENTS OF PREVIOUS VOLUMES

Volume 8

Marjorie Gelus, Birth as Metaphor in Kleist's *Das Erdbeben in Chili*: A Comparison of Critical Methodologies; **Vanessa Van Ornam,** No Time for Mothers: Courasche's Infertility as Grimmelshausen's Criticism of War; **M.R. Sperberg-McQueen,** Whose Body Is It? Chaste Strategies and the Reinforcement of Patriarchy in Three Plays by Hrotswitha von Gandersheim; **Sara Lennox,** The Feminist Reception of Ingeborg Bachmann; **Maria-Regina Kecht,** Auflehnung gegen die Ordnung von Sprache und Vernunft: Die weibliche Wirklichkeitsgestaltung bei Waltraud Anna Mitgutsch; **Maria-Regina Kecht,** Gespräch mit Waltraud Anna Mitgutsch; **Susanne Kord,** "Und drinnen waltet die züchtige Hausfrau"? Carolina Pichler's Fictional Auto/Biographies; **Susan L. Cocalis,** "Around 1800": Reassessing the Role of German Women Writers in Literary Production of the Late Eighteenth and Early Nineteenth Centuries (Review Essay); **Konstanze Streese und Kerry Shea,** Who's Looking? Who's Laughing? Of Multicultural Mothers and Men in Percy Adlon's *Bagdad Cafe*; **Deborah Lefkowitz,** Editing from Life; **Walfriede Schmitt,** Mund-Artiges... (Gedicht); **Barbara Becker-Cantarino,** Feministische Germanistik in Deutschland: Rückblick und sechs Thesen; **Gisela Brinker-Gabler,** Alterity—Marginality—Difference: On Inventing Places for Women; **Ruth-Ellen B. Joeres,** "Language is Also a Place of Struggle": The Language of Feminism and the Language of American *Germanistik*.

Volume 7

Myra Love, "A Little Susceptible to the Supernatural?": On Christa Wolf; **Monika Shafi,** Die überforderte Generation: Mutterfiguren in Romanen von Ingeborg Drewitz; **Ute Brandes,** Baroque Women Writers and the Public Sphere; **Katherine R. Goodman,** "The Butterfly and the Kiss": A Letter from Bettina von Arnim; **Ricarda Schmidt,** Theoretische Orientierungen in feministischer Literaturwissenschaft und Sozialphilosophie (Review Essay); **Sara Lennox,** Some Proposals for Feminist Literary Criticism; **Helga Königsdorf,** Ein Pferd ohne Beine (Essay); **Angela Krauß,** Wieder in Leipzig (Erzählung); **Waldtraut Lewin,** Lange Fluchten (Erzählung); **Eva Kaufmann,** DDR-Schriftstellerinnen, die Widersprüche und die Utopie; **Irene Dölling,** Alte und neue Dilemmata: Frauen in der ehemaligen DDR; **Dinah Dodds,** "Die Mauer stand bei mir im Garten": Interview mit Helga Schütz; **Gisela E. Bahr,** Dabeigewesen: Tagebuchnotizen vom Winter 1989/90; **Dorothy J. Rosenberg,** Learning to Say "I" instead of "We": Recent Works on Women in the Former GDR (Review Essay); **Sara Friedrichsmeyer and Jeanette Clausen,** What's Feminism Got to Do with It? A Postscript from the Editors.

Volume 6

Dagmar C.G. Lorenz, "Hoffentlich werde ich taugen." Zu Situation und Kontext von Brigitte Schwaiger/Eva Deutsch *Die Galizianerin*; **Sabine Wilke,** "Rückhaltlose Subjektivität." Subjektwerdung, Gesellschafts- und Geschlechtsbewußtsein bei Christa Wolf; **Elaine Martin,** Patriarchy, Memory, and the Third Reich in the Autobiographical Novels of Eva Zeller; **Tineke Ritmeester,** Heterosexism, Misogyny, and Mother-Hatred in Rilke Scholarship: The Case of Sophie Rilke-Entz (1851–1931); **Richard W. McCormick,** Productive Tensions: Teaching Films by German Women and Feminist Film Theory; **Hildegard M. Nickel,** Women in the GDR: Will Renewal Pass Them By?; **Helen Cafferty and Jeanette Clausen,** Feministik *Germanistik* after Unification. A Postscript from the Editors.

Volume 5

Angelika Bammer, Nackte Kaiser und bärtige Frauen: Überlegungen zu Macht, Autorität, und akademischem Diskurs; **Sabine Hake,** Focusing the Gaze: The Critical Project of *Frauen und Film*; **Dorothy Rosenberg,** Rethinking Progress: Women Writers and the Environmental Dialogue in the GDR; **Susanne Kord,** Fading Out: Invisible Women in Marieluise Fleißer's Early Dramas; **Lorely French,** "Meine beiden Ichs": Confrontations with Language and Self in Letters by Early Nineteenth-Century Women; **Sarah Westphal-Wihl,** Pronoun Semantics and the Representation of Power in the Middle High German *Märe* "Die halbe Decke"; **Susanne Zantop and Jeannine Blackwell,** Select Bibliography on German Social History and Women Writers; **Helen Cafferty and Jeanette Clausen,** Who's Afraid of Feminist Theory? A Postscript from the Editors.

Volume 4

Luise F. Pusch, Totale Feminisierung: Überlegungen zum unfassenden Femininum; **Luise F. Pusch,** Die Kätzin, die Rättin, und die Feminismaus; **Luise F. Pusch,** Carl Maria, die Männe; **Luise F. Pusch,** Sind Herren herrlich und Damen dämlich?; **Ricarda Schmidt,** E.T.A. Hoffman's "Der Sandmann": An Early Example of *Écriture Féminine*? A Critique of Trends in Feminist Literary Criticism; **Renate Fischetti,** *Écriture Féminine* in the New German Cinema: Ulrike Ottinger's *Portrait of a Woman Drinker*; **Jan Mouton,** The Absent Mother Makes an Appearance in the Films of West German Women Directors; **Charlotte Armster,** Katharina Blum: Violence and the Exploitation of Sexuality; **Renny Harrigan,** Novellistic Representation of *die Berufstätige* during the Weimar Republic; **Lynda J. King,** From the Crown to the Hammer and Sickle: The Life and Works of Austrian Interwar Writer Hermynia zur Mühlen; **Linda Kraus Worley,** The "Odd" Woman as Heroine in the Fiction of Louise von François; **Helga Madland,** Three Late Eighteenth-Century Women's Journals: Their Role in Shaping Women's Lives; **Sigrid Brauner,** Hexenjagd in Gelehrtenköpfen; **Susan Wendt-Hildebrandt,** Gespräch mit Herrad Schenk; **Dorothy**

Rosenberg, GDR Women Writers: The Post-War Generation. An Updated Bibliography of Narrative Prose, June 1987.

Volume 3

Ritta Jo Horsley and Richard A. Horsley, On the Trail of the "Witches": Wise Women, Midwives and the European Witch Hunts; **Barbara Mabee,** Die Kindesmörderin in den Fesseln der bürgerlichen Moral: Wagners Evchen und Goethes Gretchen; **Judith P. Aikin,** Who Learns a Lesson? The Function of Sex Role Reversal in Lessing's *Minna von Barnhelm*; **Sara Friedrichsmeyer,** The Subversive Androgyne; **Shawn C. Jarvis,** Spare the Rod and Spoil the Child? Bettine's *Das Leben der Hochgräfin Gritta von Rattenzuhausbeiuns*; **Edith Waldstein,** Romantic Revolution and Female Collectivity: Bettine and Gisela von Arnim's *Gritta*; **Ruth-Ellen Boetcher Joeres,** "Ein Nebel schließt uns ein." Social Comment in the Novels of German Women Writers, 1850-1870; **Thomas C. Fox,** Louise von François: A Feminist Reintroduction; **Gesine Worm,** Das erste Jahr: Women in German im Goethe Haus New York.

Volume 2

Barbara Frischmuth, Am hellen Tag: Erzählung; **Barbara Frischmuth,** Eine Souveräne Posaune Gottes: Gedanken zu Hildegard von Bingen und ihrem Werk; **Dagmar C.G. Lorenz,** Ein Interview: Barbara Frischmuth; **Dagmar C.G. Lorenz,** Creativity and Imagination in the Work of Barbara Frischmuth; **Margaret E. Ward,** *Ehe* and *Entsagung*: Fanny Lewald's Early Novels and Goethe's Literary Paternity; **Regula Venske,** "Männlich im Sinne des Butt" or "Am Ende angekommen?": Images of Men in Contemporary German-Language Literature by Women; **Angelika Bammer,** Testing the Limits: Christa Reinig's Radical Vision; **H-B. Moeller,** The Films of Margarethe von Trotta: Domination, Violence, Solidarity, and Social Criticism.

Volume 1

Jeanette Clausen, The Coalition of Women in German: An Interpretive History and Celebration; **Sigrid Weigel,** Das Schreiben des Mangels als Produktion von Utopie; **Jeannine Blackwell,** Anonym, verschollen, trivial: Methodological Hindrances in Researching German Women's Literature; **Martha Wallach,** Ideal and Idealized Victims: The Lost Honor of the Marquise von O., Effi Briest and Katharina Blum in Prose and Film; **Anna Kuhn,** Margarethe von Trotta's *Sisters*: Interiority or Engagement?; **Barbara D. Wright,** The Feminist Transformation of Foreign Language Teaching; **Jeanette Clausen,** Broken but not Silent: Language as Experience in Vera Kamenko's *Unter uns war Krieg*; **Richard L. Johnson,** The New West German Peace Movement: Male Dominance or Feminist Nonviolence.